RISE OF THE

RISE OF THE DESTROYER

A Novel by James Dennis

Published by Midland Imperial Books

First Edition

November 2014

CONTENTS

EPISODE I
HUBRIS

Chapter One

The starship moved silently through the darkness, its silver hull gleaming in the faint light of the distant stars.

The void was a black canvas, dotted with a million pinpricks of light – the stars of the galaxy, spread out in every direction. Uninhibited by an atmosphere, they did not twinkle, but glared mercilessly across the infinite shadow, unwavering and constant. Two stars were brighter and larger than the others – burning eyes of yellow flame, glaring fiercely back at their countless neighbours.

The ship was a silver disc about one hundred metres in diameter, deepest at its hub and tapering out at the rim, although the edge itself was easily twenty metres deep. The ringed edge rotated around a stationary core at the hub, simulating gravity to allow the crew to function normally. On the ship's underbelly, the core protruded from the disc, opening out in a scorched and blackened aperture – the exhaust for the ship's Ion Drive, used for sub-light propulsion. On the other side, the core was covered by a dome of hardened glass, pulsating with a strange, blue light – the Terculium Reactor, the ship's power source, capable of propelling the ship at super-light speeds.

The hull was studded with shallow, grey domes – the ship's sensor arrays, delivering visual and scientific data to the crew. They allowed them to perceive the wonders in the emptiness beyond the hull. The edge of the rim was illuminated by formation lights, winking in the darkness as the rim rotated. Arc lights projected onto the ship's hull near the Terculium Reactor, revealing an inscription in a semicircle just inset from the ship's rotating rim:

PSS PROVIDENT

S-2705

Captain Psinaez Anzaeus walked into the Command Centre. He was tall, over six feet, with black hair and dark eyes. He walked steadily and deliberately, with an attitude that commanded respect from those around him. He was around fifty years old, his hair going grey at the temples and spreading upwards. His face was worn, but not haggard – his eyes glinted with determination and experience.

The Command Centre was roughly rectangular in shape, but one wall was dominated by a large, concave screen which curved upwards to cover part of the ceiling and two side walls. This huge, quarter-spheroid screen was the Flight Display, which gave a panoramic view of the space around the ship. There were no windows on the

Provident, as they would simply serve to remind the crew that they were spinning around the ship's hub in order to simulate gravity. Such windows would provide no meaningful information, and indeed, give anyone looking out of them motion sickness. Instead, where visual information was needed from outside the ship, the sensor arrays, studded all over the hull, collected the necessary information and displayed it in a usable format. The Flight Display was also showing a technical readout of a nearby planetoid, which the *Provident* was approaching.

Directly in front of this enormous display were two touch-screen computer consoles, each equipped with a steering array. The left-hand seat was the Helm, the seat of the pilot and Commanding Officer of the ship. The right-hand seat was the Primary Support, reserved for the First Officer, who acted as co-pilot and the main support for the ship's mission. In this instance, the console was configured for Science, giving control over the ship's many sensor arrays.

The other walls of the Command Centre were lined with computer consoles. Engineering was on the starboard side, with Communications on the port. The aft terminals were dedicated to Tactical.

The Command Centre was relatively small, perhaps five metres wide and eight metres long, but the huge curved Flight Display gave it the disconcerting effect of being open to space. The ceiling was low and bowed in the centre, the floor matching the ceiling's curvature. Consoles and screens flickered and glowed, and the air was filled with the sound of tapping screens and muttered orders. All the crew wore headsets with a single earpiece and mouthpiece.

'Captain on deck!' came a voice from the starboard side, and every crew member visibly stiffened their posture.

'Report, Commander,' ordered Anzaeus as he stepped up to the Helm. The First Officer, Commander Coltran, sat in the Primary Support position, nodded to his superior.

'We're approaching the outermost planetoid, sir,' he replied. 'Relative velocity currently one quarter thrusters, decelerating for orbital insertion. ETA in fifteen minutes.'

'Excellent,' said Anzaeus, and sat down at the Helm. 'Continue deceleration and prepare for high orbit. Begin detailed scans of the planetoid.'

'Aye, sir.'

Anzaeus looked ahead at the Flight Display. A detailed image of the approaching planetoid was on screen – it was nothing more than a frozen lump of rock, orbiting the two stars at the outermost fringe of the system. Very little light ever reached this death-cold world as it hurtled through the endless shadow. The preliminary scans showed that it was comprised primarily of rock and frozen methane, ammonia and carbon monoxide. Analysis of its orbit indicated that it was a planetoid, although if it had been erratic enough to take it into the heart of the star system, it could easily be classed as a comet.

Anzaeus smiled. He found the notion of this strange, dark, inhospitable rock somehow deeply romantic. It was barren and alone, and yet it held wonders that no man had ever beheld. Giant craters larger than the lakes of Szotas, mountain ranges to rival those of Vulpes, and desolate plains to match the moons of Canis. He felt his heart flutter with excitement – that driving urge, the need to explore and see the wonders of the universe. That excitement had made him join the Protectorate Starforce, and had driven him to pursue the lonely career of a starship captain. And now, his dream was finally being realised – he was Captain of the *PSS Provident*, commanding the first manned mission into the Panthera System.

The Panthera System was of great interest on Szotas, and had been ever since man had first looked up at the stars. It bore striking similarities to Szotas's own star system – it had a warm, yellow star at the centre, with a smaller, red dwarf orbiting. They now knew that the larger star was in fact two, orbiting each other in a great celestial dance. It was estimated to have gas giants, as well as smaller, terrestrial planets which could be capable of supporting life. And here, on the system's outermost edge, they had discovered its first planetoid – perhaps the outermost orbiting body.

Anzaeus turned to the Deputy Science Officer, working at one of the ancillary consoles behind Commander Coltran, who was now busy honing the *Provident's* extensive sensor arrays onto the planetoid.

'Mr. Astrus, report.'

'Telemetry is coming in thick and fast, sir,' replied Astrus, without looking up from his screen. 'Wait...' He turned around, pulling his headset off. His face creased with a frown. 'That can't be right...'

'Well, don't keep it to yourself, Lieutenant,' Anzaeus said, raising his eyebrows. 'What do you see?'

'There appears to be something in orbit of the planetoid... no...' The Lieutenant looked straight at Anzaeus, an expression of confusion on his face. 'It's moving toward us.'

Anzaeus felt a chill slide down his spine. 'I'm bringing us to a full stop,' he said as he slid his finger down his panel to drop the thruster gauge. 'Ready Stations.'

'Aye, sir,' came the reply. Coltran quickly swept his hand across his control panel, immediately pushing his scientific controls to one side and replacing them with a tactical layout. Orange strip lights immediately lit up along the walls and ceiling of the Command Centre. Coltran's voice echoed over the ship's intercom. 'All hands, this is the First Officer. Ready Stations, I repeat, Ready Stations.'

'Mr. Astrus, I want some information,' said Anzaeus, as he pulled his seatbelt on. The other members of the command crew did the same.

'Scanning, sir,' replied Astrus. The image on the Flight Display changed, shifting focus from the rocky planetoid to an object close to it.

Anzaeus noted a green light on his console as his reverse thrusters stopped firing. The ship was now stationary relative to the planetoid.

'Lieutenant!'

'Object comprised primarily of titanium, lead, and aluminium. Internal composition is mainly nitrogen, oxygen and carbon dioxide. I'm also detecting silicon, iron and explosive compounds.' Astrus turned back to face Anzaeus. 'It's a starship, Captain.'

Anzaeus's blood ran cold. There was no possibility of this being a Protectorate starship. The nearest colony was over nine light years away. Even travelling at maximum speed, it had taken the *Provident* six months to get to the outermost edge of the Panthera System.

'Captain, we have incoming!' shouted Coltran.

'Battle Stations!' ordered Anzaeus. 'All hands to Battle Stations! Mr. Coltran, deploy counter-measures.'

Anzaeus grasped hold of the steering column in front of him, taking manual control of the ship. It was structured like a double-joystick, the two handles upright and joined at the bottom by a U-bar. He twisted the right-hand stick, watching a gauge on the Flight Display light up half-way, showing his thrusters at one half of maximum. He simultaneously turned the column a quarter-turn to the right, feeling his stomach wrench as the *Provident* lurched to starboard, trying to evade the incoming missile.

At the same time, Coltran tapped his screen, shouting into the microphone on his headset. 'All hands, this is the First Officer. Battle Stations, I repeat, Battle Stations. This is not a drill. All hands to Battle Stations!' The orange strip lighting changed to red, and a harsh klaxon sounded.

'Interceptor missile ready, Captain,' shouted Coltran. 'I'm locked on.'

'Fire when ready, Commander,' ordered Anzaeus, staring impassively ahead at the Flight Display.

'Aye, sir.'

A port opened on the starboard side of the *Provident's* hull, and in a brief, silent blaze of fire, an Interceptor missile veered off into the darkness towards the planetoid, which could only be seen as a vague silhouette in the dim light from the distant stars.

'Transmit the following message on all frequencies,' ordered Anzaeus. 'This is Captain Psinaez Anzaeus of the Protectorate Starship *Provident.* We are on a mission of peaceful exploration. We intend you no harm. The missile we have launched is a defensive measure only. We are now withdrawing from this system.'

'Transmitting, sir,' replied the Communications Officer.

'Mr. Coltran, report.'

'Impact in four seconds... three... two... one...' The Flight Display lit up with a dazzling white light. 'Direct hit, sir.'

Anzaeus took a deep breath. 'Can we confirm the destruction of the target?'

Astrus's terminal beeped madly. 'Negative, sir – target remains, and is still incoming! Impact in five seconds!'

'All hands, this is the Captain – brace for impact, I repeat, brace for...'

The missile smashed into the *Provident's* hull on the port side and exploded, leaving a gaping chasm. Debris spewed outwards as the space beneath de-pressurised, and several crew members were blown out into the empty void to face an agonising death in the airless, frozen vacuum.

Anzaeus felt the world tilt crazily as the *Provident* was knocked almost full circle by the ferocity of the impact. He felt a sick, churning feeling in his stomach as the ship's rim momentarily slowed its rotation, disrupting the artificial gravity. He rose out of his chair before being pulled back down by his seatbelt and the changing gravity. Several computer terminals on the port side of the Command Centre exploded, spraying blunt chunks of shatter-proof glass and fragments of hot circuit boards across the room. The air was filled with the stench of wet tin, and sparks flew, crackling dangerously, threatening electrical fire.

'Damage report!' shouted Anzaeus, as the ship re-established its orientation and continued its withdrawal.

'Hull breach in Section Twelve,' reported Coltran. 'Emergency bulkhead seals are in place and holding. Sir, we have ten more missiles incoming!'

Anzaeus watched the Flight Display with a deepening horror. While they had been struggling with the single incoming missile, their opponent vessel had drawn in closer.

It was a giant sphere, nearly three hundred metres in diameter, making it at least three times as wide as the *Provident*. Its hull was a dull grey, pocked and scarred by a thousand battles. It was so close Anzaeus could see windows in its hull, panes of glass gleaming like a thousand watching eyes.

'May the Guardians have mercy,' Anzaeus muttered, and felt a crushing sense of doom. Here was his end – he could feel it in his bones.

The missiles hit.

The helpless *Provident* was sent wheeling through the darkness by the powerful explosions, unable to defend itself against the sphere's merciless onslaught. The hull was wrecked and torn with explosions and impacts. Different sections of the ship de-pressurised, causing the hull to buckle and in some places explode. Sometimes the ship's wounds would bleed fire for an instant, as the oxygen in the air inside ignited, but the flame was quickly extinguished.

Anzaeus felt his entire chair torn from the deck. He was flung through the air and hit the Flight Display with bone-jolting force, cracking the toughened glass screen. His teeth clicked together, and he felt a warmth spread over his chin – blood from his bitten tongue. He crashed to the floor, aware of the roaring heat from burning computers. His stomach lurched again as the gravity gave way – he felt himself momentarily floating, tied into his chair, then pulled back to the curved floor with a bruising crash. After what seemed like an age, the barrage finally ended.

Anzaeus released his seatbelt and crawled out from under his chair. He limped out from under the dome partially smashed Flight Display. The Command Centre was in tatters – the ceiling had partially collapsed, revealing exposed bulkheads. The floor was littered with broken and burnt circuit boards, shattered glass and debris. The air smelled of smoke and tin, made even worse by the heat from the some of the computers, which were now burning. The lights flickered erratically, but the Battle Stations klaxon continued to sound weakly.

Several of the command crew were injured, their chairs dislodged by the ferocity of the assault, most with cuts or abrasions to their faces and arms. Anzaeus leant his hand briefly on Lieutenant Astrus's shoulder. He didn't move or reply, and then Anzaeus noticed that he had massive burns on his face and arms, and a section of circuit board protruding from his neck. His console had exploded in the attack, and it had killed him.

Anzaeus covered his face with his hand in a moment of grief, and closed the young Lieutenant's tortured eyes with trembling fingers. 'Commander Coltran,' he said. 'Damage report.'

Coltran pulled himself to his feet from under his chair. He had a bad wound to his shoulder, and a gash across his forehead. His left arm appeared to be broken – he clenched his jaw and moaned slightly whenever it brushed against something.

'We've lost wormhole capability and the Ion Drive is functioning at fifty percent capacity. Hull breaches in Sections Four through Nine and Section Twelve. Life support is failing. Sensors are damaged, but operable, as are Communications.'

'Weapons?'

'We still have weapons capability, sir,' replied Coltran. 'For all the good it'll do us.'

'Captain, we're receiving a message from the enemy ship,' said the Communications Officer. 'They're offering a ceasefire and visual communication, to discuss the terms of our surrender.'

Silence fell across the Command Centre, and Anzaeus looked around. The room was a mess, ruined and broken. The survivors of the assault stood around the Command Centre, looking to him, waiting expectantly for an answer.

The thought of surrender was sickening – an abhorrence to everything he had ever been taught. But he had little choice. The *Provident* was heavily damaged and alone, with no chance of support. Their Wormhole Drive was destroyed, and with it, any chance of returning to the Protectorate under their own power. Although they had established a semi-permanent wormhole in order to shorten the return journey, their Wormhole Drive was still required to traverse it, otherwise the ship would be torn apart by the gravitational shear. Travelling home using the Ion Drive was impossible – its maximum speed was a hundred million kilometres per hour. The distance involved meant that it would take them nearly a hundred years to get back to the Protectorate.

'Put them through,' he said, grimly.

'But, Captain...' said Coltran, horrified.

'Put them through, Commander,' snapped Anzaeus.

'Aye, sir.'

The cracked Flight Display flickered for a moment, and the image changed. It displayed the interior of the enemy ship, presumably their own Command Centre. The screen was dominated by a tall humanoid figure, wearing a dark grey uniform. Every part of it was covered – the hands were gloved, the feet booted, and even a full helmet covered the head.

The helmet was a steel-grey, a thin strip of dark glass covering the eyes. The top was square and box-like, covering the head and coming down to the shoulders. Beneath the visor, it protruded forward into an ugly-looking snout, covered by a wide grille. It reminded Anzaeus of a pig – a metal pig, with murder on its mind.

'I am Brigadier Arcturus, of the Confederate Battleship *Iron Crown*,' the figure rasped, the voice sounding hollow and grating through the helmet's metal snout.

A murmur of astonishment echoed around the surviving command crew. *The Confederacy?*

Anzaeus gritted his teeth with barely concealed rage – a racial anger borne out of nearly a thousand years of cultural hatred. 'Captain Psinaez Anzaeus, of the Protectorate Starship *Provident*,' he retorted.

'Captain, your ship is heavily damaged and adrift. You have been punished for violating sovereign Confederate territory. You will lower your defences, disarm your weapons and prepare to receive boarding parties. You will surrender your vessel to the Confederacy. If you do this, you and your crew will not be harmed and your government will be contacted to negotiate your release. If you do not meet these conditions, you will die. You have one minute to make your decision.'

The transmission cut off.

Anzaeus exhaled slowly, his heart thumping sickly in his chest. His arms and hips throbbed with a dull ache, and he winced at the sharp pain where he had bitten his tongue. He spat out blood.

'Commander Coltran, patch me through to the crew.'

'Aye, sir.'

'All hands, this is the Captain. The enemy has offered terms for our surrender. They wish me to yield the *Provident* to them, and submit her crew to confinement.' Anzaeus took a deep breath. 'I will not visit this dishonour upon all of us. I therefore order all hands to abandon ship. I repeat, all hands, abandon ship. Launch lifeboats on my command.'

Coltran cut off transmission. 'You heard the Captain,' he ordered the rest of the command crew. 'Abandon ship. Report to your designated lifeboats.'

The few remaining officers filed out of the Command Centre, leaving Coltran and Anzaeus alone.

'You too, Commander,' ordered Anzaeus.

'Sir, is it your intention to stay behind?'

Anzaeus sighed. 'You know the law, Commander. The Captain goes down with the ship. Always has, always will. I'm ordering you to leave. Now.'

Coltran moved his broken arm slightly, gritting his teeth as he did so. 'Respectfully, Captain, I request permission to stay aboard.'

'Denied. Report to your lifeboat.'

Coltran grinned darkly. 'Then I insist. Court-martial me later.'

Anzaeus nodded. 'Take your station, Commander.'

Coltran staggered over to the aft consoles, gritting his teeth as every step jarred his injured arm. Thick blood stained his uniform where the bone had broken, part of it protruding through his skin.

Anzaeus took the Communications station on the port side. There was an automatic beep as the computer scanned his iris and recognised his authority. The screen displayed various options for him, including one labelled 'Emergency Transmission'. He pressed it.

'Captain Psinaez Anzaeus, Commanding Officer, *PSS Provident*,' he said. 'Mission: exploration of the Panthera System. On entering the system, the *Provident* was subjected to an unprovoked attack by an alien vessel. Weapons capability: significantly superior. Commander, alien vessel, identified himself as Brigadier Arcturus, Confederate Battleship *Iron Crown*. He claimed that the Panthera System is 'Confederate territory', and demanded our immediate surrender. The *Provident* is severely damaged, and is unable to return to Protectorate territory. Many crew casualties.'

He took a deep breath. 'Pursuant to Starforce Regulations, I will not turn over possession of the *Provident* to an enemy. I have ordered the crew to abandon ship. I will remain behind with my First Officer, Commander Coltran, to delay or destroy the attacking vessel by any means necessary. Request immediate dispatch of appropriate task force to recover my surviving crew, in lifeboats near these co-ordinates.'

He paused for a moment. 'Special recognition for Lieutenant Astrus, who died at his post in the face of extreme danger. Special recognition also for Commander Coltran, who has demonstrated incredible bravery and dedication to his crew, even at the expense of refusing a direct order from his Commanding Officer to abandon ship.'

He paused. 'Tell my son... that I love him.'

He sent the transmission.

'All lifeboats reporting ready for launch, Captain,' reported Coltran.

'Lock all weapons onto the enemy vessel, Commander,' replied Anzaeus as he stood at the Helm. 'I'm setting a collision course.'

'Aye, sir. Weapons locked.'

Anzaeus took a deep breath and closed his eyes. He remembered Szotas, the planet of his birth, the capital of the Protectorate. He remembered the twin lights of its stars, Kaathar and Kraegan, reflecting off the pearly white marble of Central Plaza, the great tower of the *Inominate* at its head, gleaming a stunning silver. He remembered the rich, fragrant perfume of the jungle flowers which lined Central Plaza, and the cool feel of the cold water from glistening fountains caught in the breeze.

He remembered Amaera, his wife, the mother of his son. He remembered her brown hair, her deep brown eyes. He remembered the feel of her skin, the taste of her lips. He remembered her funeral, the choking soot of her pyre, and the sting of desperate tears. He remembered his son, Jamek, only three years old, squeezing his hand tightly as he watched his mother's body burn.

He remembered Karaea. He remembered her piercing green eyes, her brown hair, her happy smile. She had been like a mother to Jamek for a time, but they had grown apart – he pursuing his career in the Starforce, and her pursuing hers in politics. Karaea was now the Protector – the High Queen of the Protectorate. She had awarded him command of the *Provident* personally. He remembered the bitter-sweet touch of her hand at the command ceremony.

He remembered his son, Jamek. Tall, slender, quiet. Hair so brown it was almost black, and dark eyes, pools of mystery. His mother's eyes.

He would never see him again.

Anzaeus opened his eyes as stinging tears welled in them. 'I love you, Jamek,' he whispered. 'I'll see your mother soon.' He turned to Coltran. 'Order the lifeboats to leave,' he said, 'and prepare to fire.'

The lifeboats detached themselves from the hull of the battered *Provident*, leaving square holes where they had been docked, their rectangular shapes catching the dim light of the distant stars. They clustered together, making for the nearby planetoid. Opposite the *Provident*, the massive spherical bulk of the *Iron Crown* rotated slowly, its windows glimmering in the starlight.

'Fire!' shouted Anzaeus.

Four missiles emerged from silos dotted over the *Provident's* hull, speeding towards the *Iron Crown.* At the same time, the *Provident* fired its manoeuvring thrusters, charging silently across the black emptiness at its aggressor.

The missiles plunged silently into the hull of the *Iron Crown* before exploding, tearing great chasms into its surface, debris blasting out into the shadow, where it froze instantly. The *Iron Crown* backed off, firing more missiles at the *Provident* which was blasted this way and that. Another four missiles emerged from the *Provident*, lit at the rear by plumes of blue flame, smashing into the *Iron Crown.* The Confederate starship, caught unawares by this sudden onslaught, was unable to accelerate away fast enough, and the smaller *Provident* bore down on it inexorably.

The Command Centre exploded around Anzaeus. He heard a brief scream from the back as Coltran's terminal exploded, tearing the man apart and splattering his remains onto the floor and wall behind him. The klaxon screamed madly, sparks flew, several computers burned, and the air filled with the stench of fried metal. The ceiling collapsed, and another bulkhead tore away from the ship's hull, smashing down onto the deck.

Anzaeus stood at the Helm, staring impassively at the Flight Display. He fired the *Provident's* Ion Drive. The ship lurched forward, picking up speed, and the ghastly glaring sphere of the *Iron Crown* filled the Flight Display. Anzaeus laughed wildly as he could see through the windows of the enemy vessel, its crew watching in stunned silence, or running in fear and panic as the deadly wheel of the *Provident* grew closer and closer.

Anzaeus fired the thrusters one last time, turning the *Provident* edge-on to the *Iron Crown*, so that its spinning outer ring would be the first thing to hit the *Iron Crown's* surface.

'For Szotas!' Anzaeus screamed, 'and the Protectorate!'

The two ships collided in a savage and crushing embrace. The spinning wheel of the *Provident* bit deep into the unprotected hull of the *Iron Crown*, hacking great chunks out of the starship. The outer ring of the *Provident* was crushed and shattered as it tore into the larger vessel, but its momentum carried it forward. By the time the ruined hull of the *Provident* had completed a full rotation, the *Iron Crown* itself had nearly been cut in half.

Finally, the *Provident's* Terculium Reactor exploded in its final death throe, and a blue-white shockwave expanded out in a deadly sphere, blasting the last broken remains of the two duelling starships into dust and rubble. The shockwave faded after about a thousand kilometres, and the superheated debris finally froze as even the terrible energy of that awesome blast dissipated in the empty, frozen silence of deep space. A shroud of darkness fell over the scene, lit only by the distant stars burning in the blackness of space, and a handful of lifeboats limping away into the void.

Chapter Two

Psinaez Jamek woke slowly, shielding his eyes against the harsh sunlight slanting in from his bedroom window. The light made the backs of his eyes throb with a dull ache. He groaned as consciousness made him aware of another pain running across the top of his head and down the back of his neck into his shoulders. His mouth was dry and felt furred, as if a coat of some vile growth covered his tongue and the insides of his cheeks.

He was hung over.

He grunted and rolled over in bed, trying to pull the blankets over his face to block out the intrusive sunlight. He felt a weird, tilting feeling in his stomach, and his mind, slowed by the alcohol he had consumed the previous night, struggled to recognise the sensation. It was only when he felt for a moment that he was flying that he realised that he had been off balance, teetering on the edge of the bed. A moment later he hit the floor, taking the brunt of the blow on his back and shoulders. Sparks of pain danced across his vision as his brain protested at this harsh treatment, and he gasped for air.

'Ouch,' he muttered, and opened his eyes a fraction.

The glorious, warm, yellow light of Kaathar flooded in, and he winced. There was nothing for it now – he was fully awake, and there was no chance of him getting back to sleep again. He sat up. His body and mind protested, his vision swimming briefly, and he rested his head against the bedstead, the black wood feeling warm against his skin. Despite the pain, his face split into a smile.

Today was Jamek's twentieth birthday, an age which held special significance on Szotas. Twenty was the age at which a child reached their majority – the age at which they became an adult. Jamek had been celebrating his coming of age the previous night.

He closed his eyes briefly, smiling at the memory. The sky had been a deep black, the stars glimmering jewels on velvet. Nights on Szotas always seemed amazing compared to the dazzling daylight from its twin stars, Kaathar and Kraegan. Central Plaza in the city Capitol had gleamed in the darkness, the lights from the towering *Inominate* reflecting off the marble flagstones which shone like pearls. Jamek remembered the sweet exotic aroma of the forest flowers growing in the ornamental beds, the cool spray of the crystal clear drinking fountains caught in the warm summer breeze, and the noise of laughter ringing out like pealing bells.

He remembered Adraea – her dark brown eyes, wells of emotion and mystery, her soft brown hair, shimmering in the light like chocolate gold. He remembered the feel of her pressed against him, her fingers interlaced with his, her smooth skin caressing the back of his hand. He remembered the scent of her, sweet and heady. He remembered the taste of her.

He opened his eyes, and lifted up his head. Adraea's eyes met his, shining in the sunlight, her hair down over one shoulder. She was lying across his bed, a sheet wrapped around her, but leaving her shoulders and neck bare. The sheet clung tightly to her figure, highlighting the delightful curvature of her body. Her breasts were small and firm, her waist curved upwards away from her hips. Her jawline was firm, almost boyish, her mouth small, but her lips were full and red.

'Good morning,' she said, smiling, and kissed Jamek on the mouth. 'Happy birthday.'

Jamek's smile fell from his face in surprise. 'I must be dreaming,' he said to himself, shaking his head.

Adraea kissed him again. 'Are you sure?' she asked, the corners of her lips turning upwards in amusement.

Jamek smiled again. 'Not quite sure,' he said, and bent forward, kissing her. 'Still not sure...'

Adraea laughed, and sat up, pulling the sheet more closely around herself. 'Psinaez Jamek,' she said, pouting. 'I believe you're trying to take advantage of me.'

'Am I succeeding?' asked Jamek, starting to climb back into the bed. Adraea squealed with laughter, and threw some of Jamek's clothes at him.

'Get dressed,' she said. 'But go outside – it's not polite to watch a girl dress.'

Jamek grinned. 'I'd rather stay!' he said.

Adraea giggled. 'On second thoughts, don't bother getting dressed,' she said. 'You need a cold shower first.'

Jamek laughed and quickly pulled some clothes on. Adraea pretended to close her eyes while he dressed, but he caught her a few times with her eyes open. She stifled another laugh. When he was fully dressed, Jamek leaned over her, stroked her hair, and kissed her on the mouth. This time, she did not push him away, but kissed back. After what seemed like an age, they finally broke away, breathless.

Jamek smiled. 'See you downstairs,' he said, and walked out of the room.

He ran along the corridor towards the kitchen, happier than he had ever been in his life. *Adraea!* His heart thudded crazily at the thought of her, and he felt dizzy at the prospect of what lay ahead of him.

Jamek had known Adraea for over ten years – they had been in the same class at school. In all this time, Jamek had dreamed desperate, frustrating adolescent dreams of her. She had been the object of his fantasies for as long as he could remember. However, at school, Adraea had been one of the social elite, a level of standing to which Jamek had never risen. He had spoken to her on sixteen occasions throughout their time at school, and he could remember each incident perfectly.

At school, Jamek had been quiet and studious, which, in a culture obsessed with warfare and military prowess, had earned him a reputation as somewhat of an outcast. Normally, this would have led to bullying, but fortunately for Jamek, he had not suffered. The bullies seemed to pass him over, preferring others that were perhaps easier prey. However, he had still been excluded from the pupil aristocracy. But somehow, at the beginning of the mad summer which was now drawing to a close, something had changed.

It was as if the world had come alive for Jamek. The feelings of freedom, frustration, terror and excitement had exploded across his life, and he felt that anything was possible. After ten years of watching from a distance, clutching at dreams that would never come to life, he had finally steeled himself and asked Adraea out to provide himself with an absolution, one way or the other. To his astonishment, she had said yes.

Of course, worshipping a girl from a distance and actually laying the foundations of a relationship are very different things. He quickly discovered that Adraea was not a perfect goddess to be placed upon a pedestal of crystal, but just another flawed human being. What surprised him about that discovery was that his feelings for her, previously nothing more than sexual fantasies, transformed into something much stronger. He could no longer imagine a life without her. He ached when he was parted from her, his spirit soared when he was with her. It was now becoming very apparent that she felt the same way. Jamek and Adraea were falling in love for the first time.

He skipped into the kitchen, and narrowly avoided a collision with someone walking in the opposite direction. Jamek slipped, and for a brief moment of panic, thought he was going to fall, but strong arms grabbed hold of him. He found himself looking into the face of Mavrak, his oldest friend.

Mavrak was over six feet tall, even taller than Jamek, but where Jamek was slender, Mavrak was muscular. His shoulders were broad and heavy-set, his face open and honest, his hair a dirty blonde. His eyes were a brilliant blue. He and Jamek had been close friends since they were small children – they had been to the same nursery and the same school, lived on the same street.

'Whoa!' exclaimed Mavrak as he put Jamek back onto his feet. 'Where are you going in such a hurry? I'm surprised you have the energy, after... you know...' he winked suggestively and poked Jamek hard in the ribs.

Jamek blushed, and punched his friend on the arm, his small fist bouncing ineffectively off Mavrak's solid bicep. 'Shut up,' he said. Mavrak howled with laughter.

'I knew it!' he said, his face split into a wide grin. 'It's about time – you've only been pining after each other for about five years. It was beginning to get on my nerves!'

'Bastard,' said Jamek, a smile spreading across his face. Mavrak was incorrigible. In some ways, that was why he was Jamek's friend – Jamek felt in awe of him, his ease of communication with others, especially women. Secretly, he had always been jealous of Mavrak's successes, but of course, he would never admit that to him.

'You want some breakfast?' asked Mavrak. He returned to the grill, where he was cooking bacon and eggs. Jamek regarded the greasy fare, and his still-sensitive stomach churned. He swallowed hard, and wiped a few beads of cold perspiration from his forehead. His head was still aching from the punishment he had inflicted on his body the night before.

'Just a coffee, I think,' he said. 'I'm still feeling a bit delicate.'

Mavrak laughed again, and poured his friend a large cup of coffee from a heated jug next to the grill. 'Wimp,' he said. 'I drank twice as much as you, no problem. You have one thimble-full of wine, and you're hung over.'

'Mavrak, you're about twice my size,' protested Jamek, laughing as he sat down at the kitchen table. 'You could drink the whole planet dry and you'd only get a tired arm from raising your glass! I don't envy your liver, though.'

'Bastard,' replied Mavrak in kind, grinning, and passed Jamek his coffee. Jamek sipped it, relishing its dark aroma and smooth, bitter taste. 'So what's the plan?' said Mavrak. 'You high-tailing it out of here before the Commodore shows up?'

Jamek spluttered, spraying coffee over the kitchen table. 'Oh, shit!'

Adraea's father, Fedrus, was a Commodore in the Protectorate Starforce – a grizzled veteran of countless expeditions against the marauding pirate bands which raided the trade routes between colonies. He was the direct superior and a close friend of Jamek's father, Anzaeus, who was away on a mission. Jamek had been staying with him during his father's absence. But regardless of how close Jamek's father was to him, Commodore Fedrus was not hugely likely to approve of Jamek taking advantage of his daughter whilst he had been guesting with them.

Mavrak roared with laughter again, obviously enjoying Jamek's social discomfort. 'What am I going to do?' said Jamek frantically, absent-mindedly grabbing a cloth to mop up the spilled coffee.

'I'd get your arse down to the Guardian Temple,' said Mavrak, teasing. 'Claim sanctuary, become an Acolyte. Maybe then Fedrus will go easy on you!'

Jamek shot him a lethal glance. 'You're a great help,' he said, and quickly drank what was left of his coffee. He winced as the hot liquid scalded the inside of his mouth. 'How the hell am I supposed to explain it to him? Thank you, Commodore, for putting me up while my father is away. By the way, I slept with your daughter last night?! I can see that going down really well!'

'Well, I wouldn't put it to him like that,' came a voice from behind him, and Jamek turned to see Adraea standing in the kitchen doorway. 'Morning, Mavrak,' she said, smiling sweetly. 'Your bacon is burning.'

'Oh, shit!' Mavrak swore and lurched over to the grill. Jamek half-smiled, but paced up and down nervously, wondering at the unusual social predicament he found himself in. Adraea calmly poured herself a coffee as

Mavrak battled with the grill, serving the sizzling bacon and eggs onto a few plates. The air was filled with the silky aroma of buttered scrambled eggs, and only slightly burnt bacon.

'It's okay,' said Mavrak, 'it's salvageable.' He wafted a tea-towel over the grill to clear away some of the smoke, before turning the heat off and bringing three plates over to the kitchen table. 'Breakfast is served,' he said, and presented the plates with a flourish.

Jamek ignored his food, chewing a fingernail in worry. Adraea smiled and took hold of his hand. 'Don't worry,' she said. 'We'll tell him together.'

'Tell me what?'

At the sound of that voice, even Adraea's calm composure evaporated. She turned to see her father standing in the kitchen doorway. He was wearing his military uniform, a gold twelve-pointed star embroidered on his epaulettes and sleeves. His jacket was a dark blue, his trousers black. A light blue shirt with a loosely-knotted tie could be seen underneath his jacket. His hair was a steel-grey, and he had a neat, trim beard which covered his throat and cheeks. His eyes were a bright blue, hard like flint.

'Dad!' said Adraea, and stood up. Jamek paled and lowered his head to the table, wishing the earth would simply open and swallow him whole to spare him the humiliation. Even Mavrak's roguish smile disappeared in the presence of the stern officer.

'Ah...' said Adraea, 'Jamek and I... we... that is... with your permission...'

Fedrus's stern face broke out into an open smile. 'Of course, you silly girl,' he said. 'It's about time! You've been pining after each other for what? Five years?' Mavrak giggled as the Commodore echoed his own earlier words.

Jamek stood up, trembling with a mixture of fear and relief. 'Thank you, sir,' he said. 'Please be assured that I mean no offence...'

Fedrus held up his hand to silence him. 'Nonsense,' he said. 'I have to admit, part of the reason of my inviting you to stay was precisely this – I didn't want Adraea seeing some brainless imbecile of the sort she has fallen for in the past. At least she's chosen wisely this time – a sensible, intelligent, honest boy like yourself will go far.' He extended his hand, and Jamek grasped it, smiling as Fedrus shook it in a powerful handshake.

Adraea stood agape. 'You planned this?!' she said, haughtily. 'I am not something to be planned around!'

Fedrus laughed at her temper. 'Relax, my girl,' he said, 'you made the choice, not me. I'm just pleased you chose correctly – it would have made the next bit all the more difficult if you hadn't!'

Mavrak roared with laughter again, and even Jamek broke down in hysterics. Fedrus grinned, and put his arm around his daughter's shoulders. Eventually, even she started to laugh.

'Congratulations to you both,' said Fedrus, and sat down at the table, pulling across Mavrak's plate. Mavrak began to protest, but Fedrus interrupted. 'Who bought the bacon? Ah, yes. Me. My bacon.' He put a forkful in his mouth, grimaced, swallowed and then handed the plate back. 'You burnt it. Remind me never to let you near my grill again.'

Fedrus stood up, Adraea and Jamek this time laughing at Mavrak, hopelessly cut down by Fedrus's scathing wit. 'I'm going to get some real food, and leave you kids to eat that,' he said, smiling. 'Just clean up after you're done, will you?' He headed out of the door.

'Oh, and Jamek?' he said. Jamek looked enquiringly at the Commodore. 'Your father was in on this too.' He shut the kitchen door behind him, grinning at the sound of uproarious laughter from all of them. *Oh, to be young*, he thought, and smiled to himself.

Chapter Three

Marshal Xoanek stalked down the wide hallway. His boots were a highly polished black, below a deep navy blue longcoat reaching halfway to his knees. A golden metal epaulette on his right shoulder was connected to his left hip by a slim golden chain which joined with a wide black leather belt. The epaulette was engraved with four twelve-pointed stars, indicating his rank as Marshal of the Protectorate Starforce. The same insignia were emblazoned on each side of his jacket's high collar.

Xoanek was about sixty years old, his hair a steel grey, his face clean-shaven. His eyes were a bright blue, his jaw square and set. Despite his age, muscles bulged under his sleeves, and he measured well over six feet in height. A giant of a man, he was possessed of a cunning intellect as well as powerful ambition, which had brought him to his position as the most senior officer in the Starforce.

The hallway ended with a grand doorway, where two men dressed entirely in black stood guard. Xoanek grimaced. These men were from the Guardian Order – warrior clerics that oversaw the functioning of the Protectorate. Since the Civil War four hundred years before, they had maintained oversight of the Protectorate's entire political system. Candidates for public offices had to be approved by the Guardian Order before they could stand for election. The Guardians themselves acted as judges and arbiters. The Guardian Conclave, the high council of the Order, presided over by their Master, was the highest Court of Appeal in the Protectorate. Although some of them served in the Starforce, the Guardians bestowed with the privilege of serving in the Protector's personal guard were specifically excluded from the military command.

Xoanek frowned. He could command every soldier in the Protectorate. He was its highest-ranking military officer, answering only to the Protector herself, and yet he could not command the Guardians. They obeyed only their Master's silent commands from his mysterious monastery on Beltrus, Szotas's sister planet.

Xoanek stopped outside the door, and one of the Guardians looked at him expectantly, his hand resting on the hilt of his *aelrak*, a terculium sword. They were deadly weapons wielded by all Guardians, and a symbol of fear and great heritage in the Protectorate.

It was precisely this weapon that the Guardians took their name from, for it was the founder of the Order, Tarsus, who forged the first *aelrak* from the terculium core of the *Inominate* itself. In the ruin and wreckage after Planetfall,

Tarsus forged *Seyotaal*, the Sword of Unity, from the starship's heart of fire. The ancient sword still rested in the Guardian Temple opposite the *Inominate*, waiting for his prophecied return.

It was said that Tarsus would be reincarnated as a Destroyer of Worlds, to reclaim *Seyotaal* and strike down the Sorceror, a deadly enemy of the Protectorate. Xoanek had little time for such nonsense, however – and he disliked the Guardians' interference and seeming omnipresence.

'Inform Protector Karaea that Marshal Xoanek requests an immediate audience with her, on a matter of national security,' he said gruffly. The Guardian's eyes widened slightly at the request. Although Xoanek's distaste for the Guardians – and even the entire democratic process – was well-known, he was rarely a man to exaggerate. The Guardian opened the door and stepped inside.

After a moment, he returned, holding the door open for the Marshal. 'The Protector will see you,' he said, and indicated for Xoanek to enter.

'Of course she will,' muttered Xoanek, and strode past the Guardian into the Office of the Protector.

The Office was a large circular room, easily twenty feet in diameter. The rear wall was dominated by a massive elliptical window, which showed a panoramic view of the city of Szotas spread out below. The Office occupied most of the top storey of the *Inominate*, the great starship on which the founders of the Protectorate had been borne to Szotas from their exile, nearly a thousand years ago.

Now, their prison had become their throne, as it housed the Senate and Government.

Golden light from Kaathar – Szotas's largest star – poured in from the huge window. It was late afternoon, and Kaathar was setting on the western horizon. Kraegan, Szotas's smaller star, could be seen high in the southern sky, glowing bright red like a watching eye in the golden sky. The city spread out below, gleaming as the sunlight from the two stars was reflected by glass and metal. Great skyscrapers towered up, bastions of steel and mirrors, some almost matching the height of the *Inominate* itself, but none matched the altitude of this tremendous viewpoint – the top of the tallest structure on the entire planet. Even though Xoanek was a practical man, who had little time for art, music or poetry, his breath felt stolen away at such an awesome sight.

In front of this window stood a large, black wooden desk, slightly curved to match the almost semicircular window. Behind the desk sat Protector Karaea. She was dressed in simple white robes, but they were edged with gold – it adorned the cuffs of the sleeves, and the hems at her ankles and down the front of the robes. A wide belt of golden fabric was cinched around her waist, and a circlet of gold rested on her head – a simple crown, but symbolic of tremendous power, for the Protector was the elected Queen. She alone had the power to make the Acts of the Senate law, or to strike them down.

Karaea was in her early forties, but looked ten years younger. Only the sternness of her green eyes betrayed her age and experience. Her skin was fair but tanned. Short, brown hair hung down only to her shoulders, when the fashion for women on Szotas was to have hair down to their waist. During her time in the Senate, her piercing gaze and caustic oratory had earned her the nickname 'the viper'.

To her right stood Laruak, the Proconsul, the chairman of the Senate, and arguably the second-most powerful person in the Protectorate. He also wore the white robes of state, but his were not trimmed with gold, and he wore no crown upon his head. Laruak was a bookish, studious man – he had arisen to the rank of Proconsul through his love of the Senate and its processes, and although he was respected by everyone, he did not inspire love. Karaea inspired love and hate in equal measure – in some circles, she was regarded as the greatest Protector to have ever served, but she was decried and despised in others.

'What can I do for you, Marshal?' she said.

Xoanek marched up to the table and saluted by placing his left fist on his right shoulder, touching the golden epaulette. 'Your Magnificence,' he said, 'I bring grave news. Less than one hour ago, the High Command received an emergency transmission from the *PSS Provident* on an exploratory mission in the Panthera System. Captain Psinaez Anzaeus reported that the ship has been attacked by a vessel identifying itself as a Confederate Battleship. Although he undertook a suicide attack on the aggressor to prevent his ship from falling into enemy hands, he has requested that a task force be dispatched to recover the surviving crew, who evacuated the ship.'

Karaea was stunned into a shocked silence, unable to fully comprehend the information that had just been given to her. Although the Starforce were regularly pitched against pirates plaguing the trade routes between the colonies, it had been centuries since a Protectorate vessel had been destroyed in battle.

'Anzaeus...' she said, her voice weaker than usual. Her heart ached at the awful news, and she could feel her hands trembling. Tears pricked into the corners of her eyes.

'Captain Anzaeus died with honour, defending his ship, crew and nation,' finished the Marshal. He paused, and then said softly, 'I understand that you were close to him, Protector, and I apologise for being the bearer of such ill news.'

Karaea nodded. Her eyes glistened moistly for a moment before she set her face in a stern expression. 'The Confederacy?' she said. 'Are you certain?' Her eyes flashed with a lurid anger.

'We cannot be certain at this time,' replied Xoanek. 'However, we have long suspected that the Panthera System is inhabited, that it may perhaps even be the location of Therqa. This unwarranted aggression towards a vessel on a purely scientific mission does suggest that we may finally have found our ancient enemy.'

The founders of the Protectorate were not native to Szotas. They had created their new nation when they emerged from the ruins of the starship *Inominate* which had crashed on Szotas nearly a thousand years ago, at the time of Planetfall. Before then, the *Inominate* had drifted in space for innumerable years, its inhabitants exiled to the dark wastes in suspended animation. They had awoken on Szotas with only vague recollections of the place they called home, the planet they called Therqa. On that planet, in the time before their exile aboard the *Inominate*, they had fought a great war with the Confederacy of Nations, a despotic alliance of powers which had overthrown the free peoples of Therqa. Ever since the founding of the Protectorate, their sworn enemy was the Confederacy. The high purpose of the Starforce was to locate their homeworld, and to avenge their exile by destroying their ancient enemy and reclaiming their lost home.

If they had truly found the Confederacy again, it was the most revolutionary discovery in the Protectorate's history. For nearly a thousand years, their entire society had been waiting for this day, straining for the goal of reclaiming their legendary homeworld of Therqa from their jailers. For the *Inominate* had been precisely that – a ship with no name, a prison in which to serve an endless exile. Contact with this ancient enemy, and the start of the sacred crusade to reclaim their conquered home, was both terrifying and exciting.

Laruak spoke up. 'Have we received any communication from the survivors?'

Xoanek shook his head in the negative. 'No, Your Grace. Only the emergency transmission from Captain Anzaeus,' he said. 'He stated that he ordered the crew to abandon ship. They are most likely in a handful of lifeboats, and will have established a temporary settlement on some space body – a nearby planetoid or such. The lifeboats can be used as emergency shelters, but they will not have enough supplies to last them for more than a few months. If they have not already been captured by the Confederacy – or whoever it was that attacked the *Provident* – they cannot survive without immediate assistance.'

Laruak leaned closer to the Protector, who was sat with her eyes closed in a silent agony. He rested his hand on her shoulder, in an intimate gesture which surprised Xoanek. 'The first course of action would surely be to recover the survivors, Protector?'

Karaea sat in silence, trying to shut out the pain of Anzaeus's death and think rationally. All her life, she had dreamed of becoming the Protector – a great Queen, an Empress of magnificence, and of leading the Protectorate into a new era. She had never expected that she would lead the nation into war.

Anzaeus, thought Karaea, and her heart ached. She had given up so much to be where she was now, and Anzaeus had been one of those things. Yet despite that, she felt like a great chasm had opened in her life at the news of his death. She closed her eyes, and a wave of grief washed over her, but one that was quickly replaced by a more primal emotion – a need for justice, and for vengeance.

She opened her eyes again. 'Mobilise the Starforce, Marshal,' she said, through gritted teeth. 'And prepare an Expeditionary Force to recover the survivors and investigate the system further. On receipt of that intelligence, I will expect battle plans to be drawn up as a contingency. If it is the Confederacy...' she paused and stood up, her eyes flashing with rage. 'Then we will take back what is rightfully ours!'

Xoanek smiled. The Great Crusade, in which he would deliver his people to their birthright, was about to begin.

Chapter Four

Fedrus sat back in his favourite armchair, a cold beer in one hand. Warm sunlight spilled through the open window overlooking the garden. The lazy drone of bees could be heard, as well as the sizzle of meat on the barbecue, and the laughter of teenagers. He smiled as he saw his daughter teasing Jamek while he attempted to cook burgers on the grill outside.

In the distance, beyond the garden, the clouded and vague shapes of the Capitol skyscrapers could be seen on the horizon. In the midst of them, the towering *Inominate* rose overhead, its sharp apex like a spear pointed at the sky. A few wispy clouds drifted overhead in an otherwise perfect sky, blue as sapphire.

It had been a few weeks since he had discovered Adraea's relationship with Jamek, and he was pleased to see that they seemed very happy together. Of course, it had been inevitable – he and Anzaeus, Jamek's father, had thought this for some time. Although they had moved in different social circles at school, they had frequently met out of school, with their fathers being such good friends. They also had a lot in common – both of their mothers had died when they were young. Fedrus felt no small affection for the lad – he thought of Anzaeus as a kind of surrogate son, and so Jamek was, in his mind, something akin to a grandchild. As he had watched Adraea and Jamek grow closer, he had thought that it might bother him, but now that it came to it, it didn't.

He watched as Adraea wrapped her arms around Jamek's waist, kissing the back of his neck, and he smiled to himself. He remembered her mother doing that to him, in years that now seemed beyond count, and watching as Jamek's mother had done it to Anzaeus.

He swigged his beer, grunting in appreciation at the cool liquid. After six months of duty with no days off, he was pleased that he had been granted two months' leave.

He had accepted promotion to Commodore nearly four years ago, and had recognised that it effectively meant the end of active duty. Although he was a Squadron Commander in the 1st Fleet, with ten starships under his command, he rarely left the Lupus System. The 1st Fleet was primarily a garrison and security detail for the trade routes between Szotas and the nearest colonies. Fedrus spent most of his time on Szotas at the High Command, planning his own squadron's positioning and escort duties. The execution of the orders was largely left to the capable Captains under his command.

He had served in the Starforce for nearly thirty years, and had been a Fleet officer aboard a starship for the first twenty-five. When the offer of promotion to a desk job had come, Fedrus had accepted immediately. He had wanted to spend more time with his daughter while he still had the chance, and although he didn't have as much free time as he would like, he still had considerably more than before.

He was hoping that Anzaeus would return from his mission to the Panthera System soon. Although it would've taken him six months just to get there, his ship, the *Provident*, had been equipped with two portable Terculium Reactors. These could be used to form a semi-permanent wormhole to shorten the return trip, and any subsequent journeys to the system. Hopefully, it should only take the *Provident* a month to return to the Protectorate. Upon his return, Fedrus was hoping to secure Anzaeus promotion to Commodore as well.

Fedrus's communicator beeped, indicating that he had received a message. Absently, he pulled it from his pocket and tapped the screen. He sat up straight when he saw who it was from – Marshal Xoanek.

Although Fedrus was based at the Starforce High Command in the Capitol, his direct superior was Admiral Kaltrek, Commanding Officer of C Group, 1st Fleet. Marshal Xoanek, the Chief of Staff, who answered only to the Protector herself, was two full ranks above Kaltrek. It was highly unusual for the Marshal to bypass the chain of command – orders were given through the Generals and Admirals who were directly answerable to him. In all of his time serving in the Starforce, Fedrus had never received a direct communication from the Marshal.

He tapped the screen again to open the message and read carefully.

PROTECTORATE STARFORCE

SECURE COMMUNICATION SYSTEM

FROM:	Marshal Xoanek, High Command
TO:	All Staff Officers
TIME:	1800, 02/05/943 (Capitol Time)

URGENT – TOP SECRET – URGENT

All Staff Officers will report to Starforce High Command for Special Orders by 1200 hours, 03/05/943 (Capitol Time).

However, for reasons of National Security, this Order is not be divulged to or discussed with anyone other than those for whom it is strictly necessary without explicit written authority.

Signed,

Marshal Xoanek

Chief of Staff, High Command

Fedrus's brow wrinkled into a frown. *This is damned peculiar*, he thought to himself. *Urgent? Top Secret? National Security?* These were not words that one often read in communications from the High Command. The fact that such a wide-ranging, mysterious communication had been sent to all Staff Officers was, to be blunt, alarming. Fedrus felt a chill settle over his heart, and wondered what it all could mean. He finished his beer and stood up.

'Adraea!' he called. His daughter kissed Jamek quickly, and ran smiling towards her father.

'I've been recalled,' he said bluntly.

Adraea's smile fell from her face. 'What? Why?'

'They didn't say,' replied Fedrus, 'but they did say it's important. Probably those damn pirates again. I've got to report tomorrow.'

'But I thought you were on leave for another month!' Adraea seemed close to tears, and Fedrus saw Jamek look over his shoulder, a puzzled frown on his face.

Fedrus sighed. 'I know, darling, and I'm sorry. But orders are orders. I'll tell you what, though – how about I give you a lift into the Capitol tonight? I'm sure this stuff will all be cleared up in a few days – you can have a few drinks, spend the day in the Capitol tomorrow, then come home. You can bring Jamek.'

Adraea's face lit up again, and she hugged her father, kissing him on the cheek. 'Can Mavrak come as well?' she asked. 'Jamek will want him there, but he'll be too scared to ask you.'

Fedrus laughed. 'Yes, I'll give him a lift as well,' he said. 'If there's two miscreants looking out for my daughter, I suppose that'll put off the ones that aren't!'

Adraea smiled and ran back to Jamek. Fedrus sighed again. Although he had told Adraea that he thought everything would be back to normal in a few days, he had a nagging feeling that it wouldn't be. In fact, he had a terrible feeling that their entire world was about to be shaken to the core.

-#-

By night, the Capitol was an impressive sight – the towering *Inominate*, gleaming white and silver in the glare of dozens of spotlights, stood out even amongst the giant skyscrapers of glass and steel that surrounded it. The ancient spacecraft pointed at the black sky, tapering outwards from its blade-like tip, forming a long, vertical column, nearly one thousand metres from the ground to the top of the tower. The main trunk of the building was nearly fifty metres in diameter. Two hundred metres from the ground, the trunk tapered out again to a diameter of about seventy metres, with six separate rockets, each over a hundred and fifty metres high, clustered around its base. The colossal spacecraft-skyscraper was taller than some mountains, and the tallest structure in the entire Protectorate.

The towering buildings that surrounded it were various shapes and sizes, all impressive in their own right. They were edifices of glass and iron, some old, some new, a living testament to the history of the Protectorate, which had been written in the square mile of the Capitol – the political, administrative, commercial and cultural hub.

The Capitol itself was enclosed by a high stone wall made of brown stone, towering some ten storeys up. This was the first major defence built by the founders of the Protectorate, nearly a thousand years ago, to protect their emergent city from the savagery of the rainforest beyond. It still stood, an honoured guardian to the beating heart of the interstellar empire which it had nurtured.

The *Inominate* stood at the hub of a semicircular lawn, divided down the middle by a wide pavement leading to the High Command building, which encircled the lawn and the *Inominate*. In front of the *Inominate* was a platform leading to a wide stairway, carved from marble. On each side of the stairway, a statue of a predatory bird stood on a pillar, each carving some eight feet tall. The marble steps, glowing in the spotlights which illuminated them, lead down to Central Plaza – the exact centre of the Capitol.

Opposite the *Inominate*, on the Plaza's southern side, stood the Guardian Temple, the oldest building on Szotas, built from brown stone, a cathedral of soaring archways, regal statues, and proud domes. Jamek shivered slightly as he regarded the Temple. One of his earliest memories was visiting it with his father when he was a boy, standing in front of the High Altar and looking up at the fabled *aelrak* of *Seyotaal* – the Sword of Unity. It was said that one day, Tarsus, the first Guardian, would return as a Destroyer of Worlds, to reclaim the sword and usher in a thousand years of peace.

Central Plaza itself was paved with marble, and four fountains stood in the centre, each in a separate square walled pool. The walls were lined with flowerbeds, filling the cool, night air with the rich, heady scent of jungle flowers, the sound of splashing water and the cool spray of the fountains.

The Plaza was filled with life – people sat laughing, drinking and joking at tables outside the bars and restaurants which lined the left and right sides of the square. Others leaned against the walled fountains and flowerbeds, smiling and talking. Occasionally, even a black-robed Guardian could be seen leaving the Temple, smiling as they breathed in the sights, sounds and smells of the culture they watched over.

Jamek sat at one of the tables outside a bar on the left side of Central Plaza, smiling as he looked across the great square. The towering height of the *Inominate* dominated the skyline. The sky was a sheet of black canvas flecked with silver stars. The night was cool, but Jamek felt comfortable in a short-sleeved shirt. He held a bottle of beer loosely in his hand, and looked up at the distant stars.

He turned as he heard laughter behind him, and his smile broadened as he saw Mavrak and Adraea approaching the table. Mavrak grinned as he sat down, and distributed three shot glasses filled with a black liquid amongst them. Jamek shook his head, laughing.

'What's this?' he asked, pointing to the glasses.

Mavrak put his finger against his lips mischievously. 'Don't ask,' he said with a grin, as Adraea sat down and handed out three taller glasses. Jamek turned to look at her, and his heart fluttered in his chest, his stomach knotting into a ball.

Her hair fell in loose curls around her shoulders, shimmering a golden brown in the starlight. Her skin was burnt a shining bronze, her eyes were wide and clear, full of passion and happiness. Jamek's eyes roved over her – she wore a close-fitting dress which accentuated every curve and contour of her body, from her delicate arms to the gentle undulation of her hips.

Adraea smiled as she noticed his gaze, and reached out to squeeze his hand, smiling happily. The touch was like electricity for Jamek, and he squeezed back, pulling her towards him before kissing her.

'What was that for?' she said, as their lips parted.

'For being so beautiful,' replied Jamek, smiling. Adraea's eyes closed partly, and she smiled.

'For goodness' sake, put her down!' said Mavrak, jokingly. 'And drink up!' He nudged their two shot glasses towards them before raising his own. 'A toast,' he said, and stood up.

Jamek laughed at his old friend, who was already well on the way to being drunk. 'What to?' he asked.

Mavrak paused, and his brow furrowed. 'To adulthood, and to the future,' he said. 'Peace, happiness, and long life!'

'I'll drink to that,' said Adraea, and tipped her head back, emptying the contents of the shot glass into her mouth and swallowing in one gulp. Mavrak watched in astonishment as she laid the glass calmly on the table. 'Your turn, boys.'

Not to be outdone, Jamek tipped his own drink down his throat. The burning liquid coursed down his gullet, hot and volatile, and he swallowed quickly, coughing and spluttering, his eyes streaming. He looked across at Mavrak, and saw his friend in a similar state. Adraea laughed – a joyous sound like tinkling bells, and Jamek collapsed in laughter himself. After Mavrak had finished his coughing fit, he also joined in.

Grinning, Jamek lifted his other drink and sipped, feeling a cold liquid pass his lips. His head swam pleasantly with the effects of the spirit he had just drank, and he sighed contentedly, feeling relaxed and happy. He smiled as he felt Adraea's hand move onto his leg under the table, stroking his thigh, and he looked across at her, seeing a familiar hunger in her eyes. *Tonight will be interesting*, he thought to himself, smiling.

He found himself gazing at the majesty of the Guardian Temple again. A Guardian Cleric stood on the stone steps, looking out across Central Plaza. Jamek wondered what he was thinking. Did he hold the scene in contempt, a bunch of drunken youths causing trouble on the steps of his Temple? Or did he look upon them as incorrigible children, to be guided and protected?

Jamek shivered slightly. The Guardian Order had always held some fascination for him. There was a point when he had seriously considered becoming an Acolyte, but Adraea had definitely changed that. He still marvelled at their dedication, though – they guarded the Protectorate, ensured peace and security, and yet still they waited for the day when their prophet Tarsus would return.

The Destroyer of Worlds.

A legend and myth to some. A religion and a prophecy to others. Jamek wondered if he would ever see the day when the Destroyer finally did rise again.

He turned and looked up at the night sky again, looking north-east across Central Plaza, at a small constellation of stars high in the sky. Six stars twinkled brightly in the darkness, four in a crooked but vertical line, pointing to the top of the sky, then two higher up, on either side, the left higher than the right, forming a crooked 'Y' shape. The second star from the bottom was noticeably brighter than the others – a yellow spark in the endless void.

Jamek caught his breath as he watched the star, as he had done countless times since his father had left. The star was Panthera – the system his father was exploring, as Captain of the *PSS Provident*, the first starship ever to venture there.

Of course, it was not one star, but three – telescopes had confirmed this some time ago. Two yellow stars, very similar to Kaathar, and one distant red star, very similar to Kraegan. Its similarities to the Lupus System, Szotas's own, had made it a source of interest since the founders of the Protectorate had first pointed a telescope to the heavens from which they had descended.

Jamek felt a pang of loneliness as he looked up into the night sky, and he thought of his father. He closed his eyes, and thought of the feel of his hand, his raucous laugh, his easy smile. Anzaeus had been Jamek's world for so long after his mother, Amaera, had died.

Adraea leaned close to Jamek, trying to discern what he was gazing at. 'Panthera?' she murmured, and Jamek nodded. He turned to her and kissed her cheek, tasting her sweet skin and smelling a hint of perfume. She smiled and kissed him back.

'He'll be back soon,' she said, smiling. 'And then you can tell him.'

Jamek nodded, happily. Yes, soon, his father would be back, and he would tell him that he planned to marry Adraea. Everything would soon be perfect.

Jamek and Adraea drank from their glasses as Mavrak snorted in feigned disgust at their affection for each other. He still smiled at them, and also gazed up at shining Panthera, which in turn gazed down on them, a panther's eye, watchful, silent... and predatory.

Chapter Five

The alien spacecraft soared soundlessly over the horizon of the blue planet, its metal hull shining in the light of the bright star. The spacecraft was unlike the disc-shaped starships of the Protectorate, or even from the spherical behemoths of the Confederate Starfleet. It was relatively small, approximately the size of a house. It was a shuttlecraft – a vessel used for transporting people to and from the surfaces of planets, not dissimilar from those used by both the Protectorate and the Confederacy. It was shaped like a fighter jet – a conical nose tapering back into a cylindrical fuselage, with swept triangular wings on either side. A dark window at the vessel's cockpit stared eyelessly at the planet below, stretching almost up to the roof of the spacecraft.

It inclined itself slowly towards the planet, its nose rising slightly as it descended. Fire flared across the hull as it entered the atmosphere. It streaked across the sky in a bolt of flame, and began to turn this way and that, decelerating steadily.

After a few minutes, it was screaming across a crystal-blue sky, slicing through the howling wind at supersonic speed. Tail fins at the back of the wings flicked up, and it began to slow even further, descending steadily.

Spread out below the ship was a great continent. Flashes of lush green forests, harsh yellow deserts and barren white glaciers could be seen through the clouds. Occasionally the sparkle of a blue river winding its way across the living earth could be glimpsed, and the dull reflection of grey, where the great cities of the ancient civilisation stood. This planet was Therqa, the capital world of the Confederacy of Nations.

The spacecraft drew closer, spiralling downwards towards the largest of the cities, before finally pushing its nose down and committing itself to a shallow, linear dive on the approach to its landing site, deep in the centre of the ancient city.

The Spaceport was in the centre of the city, amid towering skyscrapers of mirrors, like shining jagged teeth protruding from dead flesh. A blue river wound its way through the city like a vein, sparkling in the muted sunlight. The wind blew hard, blustering through busy streets as the shuttle banked round for its final approach to the runway.

Hatches in its ventral side slid back, and landing gear descended. The tyres hit the tarmac with a squeal, and the shuttle's tail fins went up full, slowing its thunderous progress along the runway. It finally coasted to a stop, and taxied slowly up to the airport terminal building.

Soldiers in dress uniform marched out onto the tarmac, and a red carpet was rolled out towards the craft. The soldiers took up position on either side of the carpet, standing to attention. A delegation of men stood at one end, waiting patiently.

A hatch in the side of the craft's fuselage opened with a hiss, and a set of retractable steps immediately deployed downwards, tapping onto the tarmac with a clink. The doorway gaped like a black chasm.

A figure stepped out onto the staircase, and the soldiers standing guard watched in awe and horror as they regarded it. The figure was at least seven feet tall and clothed in a heavy black robe, hooded and cloaked. A vague outline of a face could be seen under the shadowed hood, but no features could be determined – the hint of a nose, high aquiline cheekbones, but nothing more. The figure began making its way down the steps to the carpet, every step fluid and purposeful.

At the other end of the carpet, Chancellor Ulestran, the Confederacy's head of state, breathed deeply to calm his nerves. He had waited for this moment for years, ever since first contact had been made with the mysterious alien Empire of Feragoth. So little was known about them – they had desired very little contact with the Confederacy, let alone diplomatic exchanges or trade. But with the sudden discovery of the Protectorate and the prospect of an interstellar war, this Empire had requested permission to send an Ambassador to Therqa. And here he was. It was a fortuitous opportunity, and Ulestran planned to make the most of it.

Ulestran set off down the red carpet, accompanied by two bodyguards. He was a nondescript man in terms of appearance – he was of medium height, a little overweight, and had grey hair. His skin was flushed red from the brandy he drank. His exceptional attribute was his political prowess – he had become Chancellor through playing the system, forming and breaking alliances at the time when it was convenient for him. He was cunning, devious and lethally intelligent.

The alien paused as its feet touched the ground, and it seemed to relish the moment, before walking briskly to meet the Chancellor, his black cloak billowing behind him slightly in the snapping wind. Ulestran fixed a welcoming smile on his face as he approached this mysterious figure, although something about the way the alien moved set his teeth on edge. His palms were slick with sweat, his breath coming in shallow pants. Something about this figure was familiar to him, and he felt some kind of sickening revulsion towards it – the way prey fears its predator.

'Your Excellency,' he said, offering his hand to the cloaked figure, 'I am Ulestran, Chancellor of the Confederacy of Nations. Welcome to Therqa.'

The cloaked figure regarded the hand for a moment, before taking it in his own. Ulestran tried to hide his disgust at the sight and touch of the alien's hand. The skin was white as snow, stretched thinly over sculptured bones, each finger tipped with a black, pointed nail. It reminded him of a raven's claw. When he grasped it, Ulestran expected it to feel weak and frail, but was shocked when he found his hand in a grip of iron. He was left under no doubt that this creature could crush every bone in his hand without effort.

'Greetings from the Emperor of Feragoth,' the figure said, in a voice with a sibilant hiss, 'may he live forever.' He released Ulestran's hand quickly, as if it were loathsome to the touch. Ulestran was relieved, but almost insulted at the same time.

He smiled again, turning on his full political charm. 'How may I address Your Excellency?' he said, enquiring as to the Ambassador's name.

'Ambassador will suffice,' retorted the emissary. 'I grow weary under your sun. Let us retire to your Palace, and we may discuss my representations in private.'

Ulestran realised that it was not a request, but a command. He smiled again, trying to keep things amicable. 'As you wish, Your Excellency,' he said, and indicated for the alien to walk past him. The creature did so, and Ulestran fell into step beside him. 'I have arranged for you to stay in the State Apartments of the Chancellery Palace,' he said, 'our most prestigious accommodation.'

The alien said nothing.

'Perhaps, after you are rested, you will provide co-ordinates for the dispatch of our own Ambassador to Feragoth?' pressed Ulestran.

'The Emperor does not feel that will be necessary at this time,' replied the alien. 'My representation here on...' he paused slightly, 'Therqa... will suffice for the time being.'

'Of course,' said Ulestran, slightly crestfallen. He had been hoping to establish full diplomatic ties with the Empire as soon as possible. 'Will you be establishing a permanent embassy?'

'Perhaps,' replied the alien, 'however, your Palatial accommodation will be adequate for now.'

Ulestran nodded, and without another word, the alien swept ahead, a figure of shadow and night in the cold spring sunshine. Ulestran looked after him, and a chill went through his heart, filling him with a deep sense of foreboding, and another emotion which was almost unknown to him – fear.

-#-

Detective Superintendent Turan of the Confederate Police sat in the corridor of the Chancellery Palace, waiting. He fidgeted ceaselessly – he had been waiting for nearly three hours now. *The Chancellor's reception must be taking longer than expected*, he thought to himself wryly.

The arrival of the Feragothic Ambassador had been heavily publicised by the State-controlled media. Chancellor Ulestran had been very keen to stress to the populace that the establishment of diplomatic ties with the alien Empire of Feragoth was a magnificent accomplishment. Turan, like many others, was sceptical.

Just because the Confederate Government said a thing was good did not necessarily make it so.

Turan was a tall, slender man, about forty years old. He was clean-shaven, with a firm jawline, short, brown hair, clear blue eyes and an easy smile. His grey suit was cut perfectly, his jacket unbuttoned, showing a powder-blue silk shirt underneath, with a dark blue tie. Everything about him signalled danger – from the ease with which he carried himself, to the bulge under his right arm, indicating the presence of a concealed gun. The short butt of an expensive cigarette was clamped between his lips, a thin trail of green smoke drifting from the glowing embers, filling the air with a sickly-sweet smell. Although tobacco had long-since been banned in the Confederacy, the genetically-modified corch weed, a hybrid of various mildly narcotic plants, had swiftly grown to replace it – it had greater intoxicating effects than tobacco, but without the unpleasant health consequences.

Turan had been made a Superintendent two years previously, after a brief but astonishing career in the Confederate Police. He had joined the Force when he was eighteen, and had quickly established a name for himself as an efficient and ruthless officer. After five years, he had been transferred to the Political Branch and became a Detective Constable. Then his career had really come alight. Political investigations and protection became his speciality. He had been regarded as the official attaché to the Chancellery Palace for some time – usually contracted by some official in the Palace to do some work that needed doing quickly and quietly.

He had received the call from the Chancellor's office that morning, which had been a first. Although he had been 'assisting' the Palace for some time, he had never done any work directly for the Chancellor before – only through one of the Palace officials. '*Deal with* this troublesome rogue', or 'escort this dignified gentleman'. Kill a political activist, or make sure a political ally had a favour returned – usually guarding them on a journey, or delivering a high-class prostitute. But it was always *on behalf of* the Chancellor, never directly *for* the Chancellor.

That had changed this morning.

Turan inhaled sharply from the butt of the cigarette, before dropping it on the floor and grinding it into the polished marble floor with the heel of his expensive shoe. He smirked at the dark, ashy stain on the marble, then pulled a hip flask from his jacket pocket. He unscrewed the cap, and emptied a mouthful of whisky into his mouth, clenching his teeth as he swallowed.

Just as he put the hip flask back in his pocket, he heard footsteps clicking on the marble further down the hall. He looked to his left, and stood up as he saw a Palace official approaching him.

The official was a tall woman, with dark red hair, green eyes, white skin and full, sensuous red lips. Turan raised his eyebrows as he regarded her – she was easily one of the most beautiful women he had ever seen. Her face was attractive but hard, almost mean-looking. Even the way she walked had a predatory, aggressive quality to it. She was wearing a black business jacket, which clung to hourglass hips, her red blouse open at the top, plunging down to her cleavage. A short skirt revealed long, slender legs finished with stockings and high heels.

'Detective Superintendent Turan?' she asked. Her accent had a rolling lilt to it, indicating an expensive education.

'That's me,' replied Turan, setting aside his physical attraction to the woman. He disliked the tone of her voice – it seemed loaded with contempt. 'You are?'

'Secretary Tellanor,' answered the woman. She looked over Turan with some disdain, and did not offer to shake hands.

The Secretary of State was the most powerful political position in the Confederacy, next to the Chancellor. Although rarely seen in public, the office was involved in almost every aspect of the Confederate government.

'I've been waiting for three hours,' said Turan, irked by her snobbish attitude. He didn't care if this woman was the Secretary or not. 'Do you mind telling me what the hell I'm here for?'

'Follow me please,' said Tellanor curtly, and turned on her heel, walking back up the corridor. 'The Chancellor wants to see you immediately.'

'Fucking wonderful,' said Turan, 'but perhaps you'd like to tell me why I'm here?' He grabbed Tellanor's arm in a tight grip, not enough to hurt her, but enough to make her wince and stop walking. She turned to face Turan again, looking at his hand with an expression that could only be described as disgust.

'You are here,' she said, spitting the words at Turan, 'to act as the Feragothic Ambassador's attaché. Someone told the Chancellor that you're the best.'

'I am,' said Turan. 'But the Chancellor didn't need to tell me himself. You could have told me – or sent someone to tell me – when I arrived. That's called common... fucking... courtesy.' He emphasised each word.

Tellanor pulled her arm free and glared at Turan, who matched it with his own cool, even gaze. She dropped her eyes. 'The Chancellor did say immediately,' she muttered. 'If you'll please follow me.'

She turned on her heel again, and Turan followed her, smirking to himself, watching her hips sway from side to side as she walked.

-#-

Ulestran's car pulled up in the Palace Quadrangle, just outside the Grand Entrance. Built in an era long since past, this magnificent doorway was rarely seen, as the courtyard was enclosed on all sides by the Palace, each wing having been built on either side. The Grand Entrance was built in a classical style, a portico made of up of a triangular centre block supported on eight columns in four pairs. The triangular centre block was ornately carved with statues in a frozen tableau, their original meaning lost in the mists of time. Larger statues stood on either side, and at the point of the triangle, staring sightlessly over the courtyard.

The pillars were crossed two-thirds of the way down with a great balcony, which dropped back slightly, and ran the full length of the building to the wings on either side. Beneath the balcony, three great doorways between the four groups of pillars opened out onto a magnificent hallway.

Ulestran waited impatiently as porters ran through these doors towards the waiting cars. One of them opened his door, and he swung himself out of the car, fixing a welcoming smile on his face as he walked towards the Grand Entrance. He stopped when he reached the central doorway, and waited as the Feragothic Ambassador emerged from his own vehicle.

The dark, towering figure seemed even more alien and terrifying here in the midst of the Chancellery Palace than he had done at the Spaceport. Ulestran tried not to shudder as the creature walked almost soundlessly over the gravelled courtyard, his arms not moving by his side, the hands still and talon-like. Despite his instinctive loathing of the emissary, Ulestran continued to smile, though it felt like a rictus grin.

'Welcome, Your Excellency,' he said, gesturing with one hand towards the Grand Entrance, 'to the Chancellery Palace – the heart of the Confederate Government, and the personal residence of the Chancellor.' The alien paused to regard the statues, carved in stone high above them. Ulestran felt some emotion swell from the emissary when he regarded them, the first he had detected from him other than a mild contempt. He seemed to feel a cold, malicious rage for a moment, but then it was gone. The ambassador ducked his hooded head as he moved through the doorway into the Chancellery Palace. Ulestran, his throat dry and his heart racing, followed him.

Once inside the confines of the Palace, the alien seemed even more terrifying – he seemed taller, and even more out of place. His dark robes seemed blacker than ever, and in the lower light, the shadow under his hood seemed darker. Ulestran stepped to the alien's side and they began walking together, following a footman through the corridors of the Palace. The Chancellor could almost have sworn he saw a flicker of dull red light from the creature's eyes, obscured by the darkness of the hood.

They finally reached Ulestran's private office on the First Floor, overlooking the long boulevard that stretched out in front of the Palace, leading into the heart of the city. The road was empty, but the trees lining it were in blossom, waving gently in the spring breeze.

Turan was waiting for them there. He bowed his head as the Chancellor entered the room, and Ulestran glanced at him questioningly. Tellanor, who was standing next to Turan, immediately gave an answer.

'This is Detective Superintendent Turan, Chancellor,' she said evenly, 'you requested his presence here this morning?'

'Ah, yes,' nodded Ulestran, and smirked at Tellanor lecherously. She returned the grin with a dazzling smile, and Turan immediately surmised the situation. She was sleeping with the Chancellor, which was probably how she came to be Secretary in the first place.

Ulestran stepped into the room and the emissary followed him. Turan looked up, beholding the ambassador for the first time, and stood agape. He stared at the apparition before him in a mixture of astonishment and horror, trying to fight the instinctive revulsion which welled up inside him. Turan was naturally confident and brash, and to be suddenly confronted by something which terrified him on such a primal level was a great shock.

'Your Excellency,' said Ulestran, his attitude one of fawning appeasement, 'this is Detective Superintendent Turan of the Confederate Police, our most trusted political guardian. He is to be your Chief of Security during your stay with us. If you require anything, please address it to the Superintendent, and he will be only too happy to oblige you.'

The alien turned to face Turan, and the policeman gulped as he found himself staring into the nothingness under the dark hood. He offered his hand. 'A pleasure, Your Excellency,' he said, trying to stop himself from stuttering. He noticed Ulestran glaring at him over the creature's shoulder, making his meaning clear – failure in any way would not be tolerated.

The alien grasped Turan's hand, and Turan stifled a shudder at the touch of the alien's skin. It felt like the crawl of locusts, and the grip was firm to the point of being painful. The strength there was easily sufficient to break bones. The grasp was thankfully released quickly.

'Would you care for some refreshments, Your Excellency?' said the Chancellor, sitting down in an armchair on one side of the room.

'Actually, I am quite tired,' remarked the emissary. 'I will retire to my quarters. We will discuss my representations shortly.' He turned to Turan again. 'Show me to my room,' he ordered.

Ulestran was silent, his mouth open in astonishment at the alien's level of discourtesy. As if sensing this, the ambassador turned again to the Chancellor. 'Thank you for your welcome, Chancellor,' he said, with a hint of distaste to his voice, as if the minor thanks were an inconvenience to him. Turan looked to Ulestran, who motioned for him to proceed. Unsure of himself in this entirely new situation, Turan opened the double-doors of the Chancellor's office, opening out onto the corridor beyond.

'After you, Your Excellency,' he said, indicating with his hand, and the creature swept past him into the corridor beyond.

-#-

Turan walked down the corridor of the ancient Chancellery Palace. The late morning sun slanted in from the glass windows on his right, catching the gold-gilded wood, silver mirrors and framed paintings that decorated the opposite wall. A few lonely particles of dust floated idly in the streams of light.

He looked over his shoulder, and saw that the Feragothic Ambassador was following him. He tensed to withhold an involuntary shudder as he regarded the mysterious figure, only a vague outline of his facial features visible in the shadow beneath the hood.

Something about the ambassador, a feeling who couldn't quite put his finger on, made Turan's skin creep with dread. He felt his heart thumping madly in his throat, and the palms of his hands were damp with a cold sweat. The cold chill of terror froze his heart. He maintained his composure only by force of his will. *I need a whisky*, he thought to himself, as he fought to control a primordial instinct to flee this creature.

Turan turned right at the end of the corridor, which opened out into a wide hallway. The right hand wall was punctuated with windows and grand doorways leading out onto balconies, overlooking the quadrangle at the centre of the Palace. Through the windows, Turan could make out the Grand Entrance at the head of the courtyard. The majestic construct had always seemed more magnificent to Turan than the façade that covered it from public view.

He forced himself to walked steadily, ensuring that he did not pull too far ahead of the alien, even though every instinct in his body was screaming at him to flee. He passed the kitchen and servants' quarters on his left, before finally stopping as the hallway began to narrow into a corridor again. He turned to a double door on his left, which led to the State Apartments. The doors were painted white and trimmed with gold gilding, set inside an ornate, decorated door-frame. Out of the corner of his eye, he could see the ambassador approaching him, his steps so even, smooth and eerily silent that it seemed like the creature was gliding along the floor rather than walking on it.

Turan forced himself to take a shallow breath in an attempt to calm himself, and grasped the handle of the door. It felt cold, solid and reassuring in the menacing presence of this terrifying apparition. The emissary stopped about a metre away from Turan, towering over him, the warm morning sunlight barely highlighting the outline of his features under the black hood. Turan could make out vaguely human features, but something about them seemed disquieting and horrifying, as if some ancient racial instinct buried deep in his psyche was trying to warn him of the nature of the creature.

Turan turned the door handle and pulled the door open. He stepped back and motioned for the ambassador to enter the rooms beyond. 'After you, Your Excellency,' he said.

The creature regarded him for a moment, standing motionless, before sweeping past him. Turan almost jumped back in revulsion as its cloak brushed against his shins, then it was past him. Turan felt some semblance of relief. At least now the alien was not between him and the door. He followed the ambassador in, but left the door open.

The State Apartments were sumptuously designed and laid out. They were decorated with tapestries and fine carpets, priceless paintings adorning the walls, and hand-crafted furniture laid out optimally to make the rooms appear even larger and grander than they already were. The room was almost as wide as the grand hallway outside. The windows on the left wall provided a commanding view of the western Palace Gardens, which had been extended following the Confederate conquest of the city over a thousand years earlier. Another set of double doors at the opposite end led to the sleeping quarters.

The Feragothic Ambassador glanced around the room, his hooded head swivelling from side to side. He strode up to the doors at the opposite end and flung them open with a crash that made Turan wince. He was shocked at such obvious and callous disregard, but said nothing.

The bedroom beyond was just as lavishly decorated as the sitting room. A four-poster bed stood at the far end of the room, with a large semicircular bay window on the left hand wall providing a panoramic view of the Palace Gardens. The bed was laid with crisp white sheets, the carefully folded curtains hanging from the post-rail almost symmetrical on each side.

'The door on your right leads to the harem,' said Turan helpfully. 'The Chancellor has put several concubines at your disposal, should you require them.'

The alien did not reply, but continued his survey of the rooms. After a moment, he said, 'these will suffice. However, I will require several modifications.'

Turan was taken aback. The State Apartments were equal in stature to the Chancellor's own quarters on the opposite side of the Palace. It was considered one of the highest honours to be housed there. No one, to Turan's knowledge, had ever described them as merely sufficient, nor requested, let alone demanded modifications.

'Anything to satisfy Your Excellency,' said Turan.

'I will require these windows to be blacked out,' said the ambassador. 'My species is extremely sensitive to the harsh light of your sun.'

'Of course,' said Turan.

'I will also require the temperature in this room to run at exactly thirty-eight degrees Celsius,' continued the alien.

'I thought your homeworld was cold,' began Turan, before immediately regretting it.

The creature turned his hooded head in Turan's direction. Turan felt the alien's eyes upon him, and forced himself not to cringe at that hollow gaze. It made him feel like his soul was draining out of him. 'Are you questioning me?' asked the alien in a quiet, dangerous voice.

'No, Your Excellency,' blurted Turan immediately. 'I was merely curious. Forgive my indiscretion.'

The ambassador seemed satisfied with this, and said nothing more. He stepped into the bedroom, his gaze fixed on the wooden box at the end of the bed. He parted his robe on his left side, and Turan was astonished to see him draw a long sword from a scabbard at his waist.

The sword was nearly six feet long, the hilt made of ivory. It was riven and cracked with age, but it had obviously been well cared for. The pommel was a ruby, almost as big as a fist. Turan's jaw dropped when he laid eyes on it. *It must be worth a fortune*, he thought. The crossbar of the sword was also ivory, studded with diamonds, rubies and sapphires. The blade itself was over five feet long, double-edged and serrated near the hilt, jagged teeth shining malevolently in the morning light.

Strange, alien runes were carved on the blade, their meaning unknown, but their shape hinted at some of their nature. They were twisted, contorted figures, and Turan was certain their meaning was nothing pleasant.

What struck him most was the blade – it was not silver, but a lustrous black, gleaming like polished night. The alien moved his hand down the blade, muttering in some language which Turan could not understand, although the words were harsh and guttural. He sheathed the sword, and then unbuckled it from his waist, scabbard and all. He then lifted it up, the sheathed blade resting on his open palms, and knelt down at the same time, before placing it on the wooden trunk.

'You may leave,' said the ambassador as he rose to his feet in a fluid, effortless movement. Turan, needing no further excuse to leave the emissary's presence, merely bowed and backed out of the State Apartments. He closed the door behind him and breathing a desperate sigh of relief before mopping a brow daubed with cold sweat.

Chapter Six

The Senate Chamber bustled with activity, grey-robed Senators holding a hundred conversations and arguments as they jostled with each other for their seats. Four hundred chairs were arranged in a semicircle in the ancient, wood-panelled room. The high vaulted ceiling was painted with ornate frescos, depicting the history of the august assembly, and the carpet of the room was a rich navy blue, embroidered with gold.

Laruak sat in the Proconsul's Chair at the front of the Chamber on a three-tiered dais. In keeping with the history of the office, originally being the Protectorate's Head of State, it was more like a grand throne. It was a high-backed seat with the emblem of the Protectorate – a giant predatory bird with outstretched wings, the ancient *aelrak* of *Seyotaal* in its claws – carved into the back. In front of it stood a high lectern, and below it, on the lower tiers, were stalled seats – long benches with integrated desks, for lower officials of the Senate, including the

Clerks and Secretaries. Directly in front of the Proconsul's Chair, a central aisle divided the four hundred Senate seats, leading to the oval windows at the back.

The windows commanded a magnificent view of Central Plaza, the warm, brown stone of the towering Temple standing on the opposite side. The marble slabs of the square outside glimmered like pearl in the afternoon sun, and warm sunlight slanted in, flooding the room in glorious yellow light.

Laruak, wearing his plain white robes of state, waited patiently as the Senators continued to squabble, watching the clock on the wall opposite. When it reached two o'clock, he struck a gavel on the lectern in front of him, calling the Senate to order.

'Order!' he shouted, and the grey-robed Senators fell silent, taking their seats. 'This session of the Protectorate Senate is convened. The Senate calls Protector Karaea to the Proconsul's Chair.' The last muttering Senators fell silent as a pair of double doors at the back of the room on the right opened, and Karaea walked in. Her official robes of state flowed behind her, the golden trim and crown on her head catching the light as it streamed in from the oval windows. She walked down the aisle in front of the Proconsul's Chair, and took position on one of the lower lecterns.

She cleared her throat. 'Senators of the Protectorate,' she said, 'it is my solemn and grave duty to inform you that the Starforce High Command has received an emergency transmission from the Protectorate Starship *Provident.* The *Provident*, while on an exploratory mission in the

Panthera System, has been attacked and destroyed.' Several Senators gasped in shock at this, but Karaea pressed on. 'Captain Psinaez Anzaeus ordered the crew to abandon ship after the initial assault, before launching a suicide attack on the aggressor. He reports the aggressor as the Confederate Battleship *Iron Crown*.'

At this, the Chamber erupted. The Senators shouted madly, several rising to their feet in passion and indignation. Laruak struck the lectern with the gavel again. 'Order!' he shouted. 'The Protector is making a statement! I will have order! There will be time for debate, I can assure you.'

The Senators fell silent again, some of them clearly dumbfounded by this astonishing revelation.

'Although this report has yet to be confirmed,' continued Karaea, 'it is my belief that we have finally made contact with the Confederacy of Nations, our ancient enemy which banished our forefathers to the cold recesses of space in a forgotten age. I have ordered a full mobilisation of the Protectorate Starforce, and asked Marshal Xoanek, Chief of Staff of the High Command, to assemble an Expeditionary Force to search for and recover any survivors.

'I most humbly place the following proposal before Your Honours for consideration: that an Expeditionary Force be dispatched to the Panthera System to search for and rescue survivors of the *PSS Provident,* and to confirm the presence of the Confederacy of Nations. If it is confirmed that the Confederacy is responsible for the destruction of the *PSS Provident*, then in accordance with the most basic principle of our society, that this Senate gives legal force to the conduct of a war to avenge the destruction of the *Provident*, and to reclaim the lost homeworld of Therqa.'

The Senate Chamber echoed with shouts and screams as Senators leapt to their feet, arguing with each other and gesturing emphatically at the Chair. Laruak held up his hand, and struck the lectern again. 'Order!' he shouted, and the Senators once more fell silent, a few remaining standing, trying to catch Laruak's eye to be called to speak.

'Senator Genna,' said Laruak, and one of the grey-robed Senators nodded as the others sat down. Genna was one of the younger members of the Senate, being only thirty years old. She stood on the right hand side of the central aisle, in one of the seats close to the back of the chamber. Her hair was red, her eyes a startling green. She was known as a supporter of Karaea.

'Thank you, Proconsul,' she began. 'For the purposes of record, I would like to clarify a few points. Protector, may I ask when the High Command received this transmission, and how long ago did the attack on the *Provident* take place?'

'The High Command received the transmission yesterday,' replied Karaea. 'Marshal Xoanek advised me of it less than one hour afterwards. We estimate that the attack on the *Provident* occurred four or five days ago.'

'Have we received any communication from the Confederacy regarding the circumstances of the attack?' asked Genna.

'We have received no communication from the Confederacy of any kind,' answered Karaea. 'We do not know for sure if this *is* the Confederacy, which is why I propose, as requested by Captain Anzaeus in his transmission, that an Expeditionary Force be sent to the Panthera System. The aim should be recovering survivors and confirming whether it is the Confederacy or not.'

Genna took her seat, and a number of other Senators stood. 'Senator Draelan,' announced Laruak. Draelan was stood in the front row on the left hand side of the central aisle, close to the Chamber floor. He was nearly seven feet tall, his skin a pure white, almost albino. He had no hair, not even eyebrows. His eyes were a cold, piercing blue. He was a towering figure in the Senate, both in terms of his physical and political stature, and was an outspoken critic of Karaea and her policies. Although political parties were illegal, many Senators voted with Draelan on a range of issues, so that he was as close as the Senate could get to a leader of the opposition.

'Thank you, Proconsul,' he said. 'Senators, if this ill news is accurate, then it is perhaps the most astonishing discovery in our history. We must be very careful, for the decisions we make in this Chamber today may have consequences that are felt for years afterwards. Firstly, I must say that I appreciate the Protector bringing this matter before the Senate so quickly – it makes a refreshing change for this legislature to be consulted before executive action is taken.'

Several Senators hissed at this obvious political dig at Karaea's style of government. Karaea smiled, but ignored the quip, staring impassively at Draelan.

'Secondly, I must say that I am most alarmed by the motion the Protector has placed before us today,' he continued. 'Of course, we must ascertain if there are any survivors from the *Provident*, but I suggest that perhaps sending an invasion fleet into the Panthera System is not the most diplomatic way of proceeding. What if this nation is not the Confederacy? And even if it is, although it might offend some sensibilities, is it not a better course of action to try to establish *peaceful* contact with it? Our last war with the Confederacy did not end well. I would hate to see a new one end in the same manner.' Several Senators muttered approval at this, and Draelan fixed his gaze on Karaea as he awaited a response.

'I thank you, Senator, for your observations,' replied Karaea. 'Allow me to allay your fears. At no point have I proposed that we send an *Invasion Fleet* to Panthera – I believe the words I used were *Expeditionary Force.* Its primary mission would be to search for survivors and to establish whether or not it is the Confederacy who is responsible for the destruction of the *Provident*, not to start a war.'

'But if it is the Confederacy,' pressed Draelan, 'you propose to conduct a war against them. Your own words, Protector.'

'Indeed,' retorted Karaea, 'if it is the Confederacy, then we have every *right* to go to war – in fact, it is our most solemn duty. Has it not been the aim of this society since our ancestors crash-landed on this very spot, in this very ship, nearly a thousand years ago, to recover the homeworld from which we were exiled? Has it not been the contention that the Confederacy of Nations must be destroyed in vengeance for that despicable act? If it is not, please correct me, for I fear that the Protectorate I love is not what you would wish it to be!'

Many Senators cheered at Karaea's counter-attack, and Draelan glared at her angrily. 'Indeed, Protector,' he returned, 'I would prefer a peaceful resolution to this situation rather than open war, so that the lives of our soldiers may be spared. And I fear that your blind warmongering may lead us on a path to ruin!'

Karaea laughed, making light of Draelan's comments. 'The Senator obviously has trouble hearing me,' she said. 'I move to call Marshal Xoanek to the Proconsul's Chair – I am sure that the Senate will appreciate hearing the plans directly from our Chief of Staff.'

Laruak spoke up. 'The motion is to call Marshal Xoanek, Chief of Staff of the High Command, to the Proconsul's Chair. All those in favour?' The Senators all raised their hands. Laruak nodded. 'This Senate calls Marshal Xoanek to the Proconsul's Chair.'

The double-doors at the back of the room opened again, and Marshal Xoanek walked in. When he reached the end of the central aisle, standing directly opposite the Proconsul's Chair, he saluted, placing his fist on his shoulder, and marched down the aisle. He stopped on the Chamber floor, directly in front of the Proconsul's Chair, and made a short bow to Karaea. 'Your Magnificence,' he said, and then another bow to Laruak. 'Your Grace – may I address the Senate?'

Laruak waved his hand, and Xoanek took a lectern position next to Karaea. He looked out across the

Chamber, sweeping his gaze across the rows of assembled Senators.

'Your Honours,' he began, addressing the Senators formally, 'I am Marshal Xoanek, Chief of Staff of the Protectorate Starforce High Command.' The Senators watched and listened expectantly. Xoanek cleared his throat, and tried to hide his discomfort. He disliked politicians at the best of times, although he considered Karaea and Laruak perhaps the best two. To be now stuck in a room with over four hundred of them was distasteful to say the least.

'Her Magnificence the Protector has commanded me to formulate plans for an Expeditionary Force to enter the Panthera System, search for survivors and confirm the presence of the Confederacy,' he said. 'I propose that the Expeditionary Force be limited to two hundred ships, comprising mainly of the 3rd Fleet, which is deployed in the Vulpes System. It would be reinforced by two Groups from the 1st Fleet.'

'Our scouts indicate that the *Provident* established a semi-permanent wormhole to the outer limits of the Panthera System,' continued Xoanek. 'The journey to Panthera will therefore be a matter of weeks rather than months. I plan to enter the system, search for and rescue any survivors, and gather intelligence. We will not initiate any contact or conflict with the Confederacy; however, I will not hesitate to retaliate if we are attacked.'

Senator Draelan stood up again. 'Forgive me, Marshal, but doesn't two hundred starships sound rather a lot for a rescue mission?' Several other Senators murmured in agreement.

'Captain Anzaeus indicated that the enemy ship which attacked him had significantly superior weaponry,' answered Xoanek. 'Two hundred starships will make them think twice before attacking, and will also ensure that we are capable of retaliating if we are attacked.'

Senator Genna stood up. 'Do you plan to command this mission personally, Marshal?'

Xoanek paused. He had always proceeded on that assumption – this was the most important military mission in Protectorate history, and he was the Marshal of the Starforce. 'I do,' he admitted. 'Unless Your Honours can think of someone more qualified.'

A ripple of laughter spread throughout the Senate, and Xoanek smiled.

'I appreciate your candour, Marshal,' said Laruak. 'Are there any other questions?'

Draelan stood again. 'I have to say, I am concerned,' he said. 'Firstly, although the Protector and the Marshal speak of an Expeditionary Force, its size and make-up indicate something quite different. You are proposing to send the entire 3rd Fleet and a significant portion of the 1st Fleet into the Panthera System. If I were the Confederacy, I would read this as an obvious provocation – perhaps even an invasion.'

'Secondly, are we ready for their response? Are we in a fit state to take on this nation? We have no idea what their resources are – they could be twice the size of the

Protectorate. Dreams of conquest are foolish in the face of a potentially superior enemy. We don't even know if this is the Confederacy – this could be an alien race.'

'Thirdly, sending the entire 3rd Fleet will leave the Vulpes System under-garrisoned,' said Draelan. 'I doubt my constituents there will appreciate it, although I am sure the pirates attacking trade convoys to Szotas will. Leaving the Vulpes System so under-defended concerns me greatly.'

The Senate listened in silence to Draelan. 'I propose that the Expeditionary Force be limited to fifty starships,' he said, 'and that as well as searching for and rescuing any survivors from the *Provident*, it should be tasked with establishing peaceful, diplomatic contact with the nation that controls the Panthera System. We should not be seeking to legitimise any war against any nation.' He sat down, and several Senators applauded him, while others on the right side of the Chamber booed and cat-called.

'Order!' shouted Laruak. 'We have a counter-proposal. Correct me if I am wrong, Senator Draelan, but I interpret your full proposal as such: that an Expeditionary Force be dispatched to the Panthera System to search for and rescue survivors of the *PSS Provident,* and to establish peaceful diplomatic contact with the nation that controls the Panthera System. This Expeditionary Force should be limited in size to fifty starships.'

Draelan nodded in agreement.

'Very well,' said Laruak. 'All those in favour of Senator Draelan's proposal?' Many Senators, most on Draelan's side of the Chamber, raised their hands. Laruak glanced at two clerks on either side of the Chamber to begin counting – this was a very close vote. After about thirty seconds, they nodded to him. 'All those against?' The remaining Senators raised their hands. It was impossible to tell which argument had the majority – the numbers were too close. Again, the clerks completed their count.

The Chief Clerk at the back of the Chamber marched down to the Proconsul's Chair. 'Your Grace,' he said, addressing Laruak, 'those in favour: one hundred and ninety-two. Those against: two hundred and eight.' The Senators whistled, and Draelan shook his head in dismay. He had lost, but the vote had been very close.

'Senator Draelan's proposal is rejected,' said Laruak. 'The Protector's proposal: that an Expeditionary Force be dispatched to the Panthera System to search for and rescue survivors of the *PSS Provident,* and to confirm the presence of the Confederacy of Nations. If it is confirmed that the Confederacy is responsible for the destruction of the *PSS Provident*, then in accordance with the most basic principle of our society, that this Senate gives legal force to the conduct of a war to avenge the destruction of the *Provident*, and to reclaim the lost homeworld of Therqa.'

'All those in favour?' The same Senators that had voted against the last proposal voted for this one. 'All those against?' A few of the Senators that had supported Draelan raised their hands defiantly, including Draelan, but most simply abstained. The majority was clear. 'The proposal is adopted,' said Laruak.

Karaea smiled and turned to Xoanek. 'Marshal, I hereby award you personal command of the Expeditionary Force,' she said. 'Assemble your fleet.'

-#-

The High Command was a semicircular building six storeys high which partially encircled the *Inominate*. Though it was an impressive structure in its own right, it was dwarfed next to the impossible height of the *Inominate*, and stood always in that great starship's shadow. At either end of the semicircle, the building showed a profile which was a right-angled triangle – a vertical rear wall, with an angled front wall facing the *Inominate*, meeting together at the roof. Windows on this front wall were inset into the structure.

It was built of a grey stone, not the cool brown stone from which the Guardian Temple, on the opposite side of Central Plaza, was made, but a cold granite, imported from the borders of the city. The building cast its own odd shadow on the semicircular lawn between it and the *Inominate*, divided down the middle by a wide pavement leading from the starship to the Main Entrance of the High Command.

The Main Entrance was a huge double-doorway nearly two storeys high, inset into the angled face of the building like the many windows. It was arched at the top, in the style of the Guardian Temple. At the peak of the arch a sculpture of a giant predatory bird, clutching the ancient sword of *Seyotaal* in its claws – the symbol of the Protectorate – was carved into the façade.

Fedrus walked down the path through the Capitol Green, and looked up as he approached the Main Entrance. These hallowed halls were, perhaps, the greatest symbol of Protectorate military might, and he never ceased to feel awe and pride when he walked through them. Today, as he passed under that magnificent arch into the hallway beyond, he felt a cold chill, as if some great force was mustering its strength to test the will of the Protectorate.

He paused for a moment as he entered the Entrance Hall. It was paved with diamond-shaped blue and gold tiles, and blue curtains hung from the high domed ceiling. Statues and portraits of great military commanders lined the walls, fierce and stony gazes fixed on him. The Hall was quite busy – a dozen or so Commodores, Admirals and even the odd General could be seen milling about, most clustered around the main reception desk, which was manned by a Captain and two Commanders. Fedrus laughed to himself – that was to appease the vanity of the Staff Officers. It was normally manned by a solitary Sergeant, but many Admirals and Generals disliked addressing themselves to anyone with a rank below that of Commander. The thought of discoursing with an enlisted man was almost too much to bear.

He walked up to the desk, and one of the Commanders immediately attended to him, the Captain being engaged in a loud argument with a General about why his leave had been cancelled. 'Sir?' said the Commander.

'Commodore Fedrus, 1st Fleet, reporting as ordered,' replied Fedrus. The Commander lifted an electronic pad from the desk and began scanning down the list.

'Commodore Fedrus,' he repeated as he found the entry. 'CO, Red Squadron, Battle Group C?'

Fedrus nodded in the affirmative. The Commander tapped the pad, and blinked. 'Excuse me a moment, sir,' he said, and turned to the Captain, who was still politely arguing with the loud General.

'Commodore Fedrus is here, sir,' he said quietly. The Captain immediately broke off the argument with the General, and came over.

'Commodore,' he said, and saluted by putting his left fist on his right shoulder, touching the golden epaulette that bore his rank insignia, four eight-pointed stars. 'You are to report immediately to Marshal Xoanek.'

Fedrus was taken aback. 'What about the others?' he said, gesturing to the assembled Staff Officers, who at the mention of the Marshal who had summoned them all, were now listening intently.

'Marshal Xoanek was very clear that he wanted to see you first, sir,' replied the Captain. 'I'm afraid I don't have any more information.' He presented his pad to Fedrus for scrutiny. Fedrus glanced at it, and next to his name, it said in clear red lettering:

REPORT TO COS IMMEDIATELY

COS. Chief of Staff. Marshal Xoanek himself.

Fedrus shook his head slightly in disbelief. 'Thank you, Captain,' he said, conscious of the other Staff Officers watching this exchange intently. He walked past the desk and made for the corridor behind it, which led to the elevators.

After a brief journey through the labyrinthine High Command, Fedrus found himself standing outside the double-doors to the Marshal's office. The words were engraved on the door in golden lettering:

MARSHAL XOANEK

CHIEF OF STAFF

Fedrus, with a profound sense of apprehension, knocked on the door. It was opened after a few seconds by yet another Captain. Fedrus recognised him as Captain Shivaeus – they had served together when Fedrus was a Lieutanant, and Shivaeus an Ensign. He was about thirty-five, a little younger than Anzaeus. He had a round, pale, chubby face which Fedrus associated with wealth and soft living. Shivaeus was well-known throughout the High Command as Xoanek's adjutant. He was an amiable and competent officer, but Fedrus suspected his selection had more to do with his family background – his brother was married to Xoanek's daughter.

'Ah, Commodore,' said Shivaeus, and pulled the door open wide. 'The Marshal is expecting you.'

Fedrus nodded and entered the room beyond. It was an antechamber which acted as an office for the adjutant. Another set of double doors behind Captain Shivaeus's desk were open, and Fedrus could see Marshal Xoanek sitting at his desk in the room beyond. Shivaeus shut the outer doors, and then walked briskly across the room into the Marshal's private office.

'Commodore Fedrus is here to see you, Marshal,' Fedrus heard the Captain's voice quietly.

'Good – send him in,' answered the Marshal, and looked up from his work.

Shivaeus saluted, and returned to his own desk. He looked up at Fedrus. 'The Marshal will see you,' he said, and indicated for Fedrus to enter the room. Fedrus nodded and walked into the office of the Marshal. He marched up to the desk and saluted.

'Commodore Fedrus, Commanding Red Squadron, Group C, 1st Fleet, reporting as ordered, sir.'

Marshal Xoanek stood up, and offered his hand. Fedrus shook it. 'At ease, Commodore,' said Xoanek. 'Have a seat.' Fedrus sat down in front of the Marshal's desk, and took off his hat. 'I'll get straight to it,' said Xoanek. 'You're probably wondering why you've been summoned here, while the pompous asses who call themselves Admirals and Generals are forced to wait.'

'The thought had crossed my mind, sir,' admitted Fedrus.

'I'm afraid it's not good news,' said Xoanek. 'We received an emergency transmission from the *PSS Provident* yesterday.' He paused. 'I'm afraid Captain Anzaeus is dead.'

Fedrus sat back in shock. *Anzaeus? Dead? This is a bad dream. This isn't happening.*

'I understand you were caring for his son during his absence,' said Xoanek, as he flicked through a file on an electronic pad in front of him. 'I also understand that you were close friends, together with the Protector. I thought it best to advise you of this in private, rather than during a military briefing.'

Fedrus nodded dumbly, and cleared his throat. 'I appreciate that, sir,' he said. 'May I ask, has the Protector been informed?'

Xoanek nodded. 'Immediately after we received the transmission,' he replied. 'She was... upset.'

'As am I, sir,' admitted Fedrus. 'Anzaeus was... like a son to me in many ways. How did he die?'

'The *Provident* was heavily damaged in an unprovoked attack,' answered Xoanek, 'by a ship identifying itself as the Confederate Battleship *Iron Crown*.'

Fedrus's eyes widened in astonishment. 'The Confederacy?' he spluttered.

Xoanek nodded seriously. 'It appears so. We may have inadvertently stumbled across one of their colonies. It is typical of them to simply attack without warning. The Protector has ordered me to mobilise the entire Starforce and to prepare for war. We will shortly be forming an Expeditionary Force to enter the Panthera System to search for survivors from the *Provident*. Captain Anzaeus ordered the survivors to abandon ship before he attacked the *Iron Crown* in a suicide run.'

Fedrus closed his eyes briefly. He could imagine the Command Centre burning around Anzaeus, the floor littered with debris, the air filled with the stink of electrical fire, and the ruined hulk of the *Provident* smashing into its enemy...

'He died for his nation,' said Xoanek, sternly. 'No soldier can ask for a greater honour.'

Fedrus nodded mutely. 'Sir, I would volunteer for this Expeditionary Force, but I have a young daughter, and I know that Anzaeus appointed me to care for his son in the event of his death. Indeed, the two have recently started seeing each other.'

Xoanek looked at the old soldier with some sympathy. 'I understand,' he said. 'I was considering you for a role in the Expeditionary Force based on Admiral Kaltrek's reports on you. But if you have a family to care for, and Captain Anzaeus's son...' he paused. 'We'll miss you at the party. I'll ensure that you're retained in a garrison position on Szotas, to reassure the civilians and the like. I trust that will be acceptable?'

'Yes, sir,' said Fedrus. 'Thank you, sir.'

Xoanek nodded. 'Consider yourself back on leave,' he said. 'Once the Expeditionary Force is assembled, I'll ensure you're placed in the Szotas garrison. If I can bump you up to Admiral, I will – a better salary will help to care for the young Psinaez.'

Fedrus stood up. 'Thank you, sir.'

Xoanek saluted, and Fedrus did so in turn. 'Dismissed, Commodore,' he said, and turned back to his work.

Fedrus turned and walked out of the door, and bit his lip to stop the tears rolling down his cheeks. His stomach felt empty, his heart rent. Anzaeus, the man he had considered his best friend, and his son, was dead, the Starforce was gearing up for a war with the Protectorate's most ancient and hated enemy, and he now had the solemn duty of informing Jamek of this ill news.

-#-

Jamek lay in the garden, stripped to the waist, basking in the warm sunlight. Beads of sweat stood on his brow, and the warm touch of the sun was a contrast to the sharp cold of the iced beer in his hand. He shifted slightly, feeling the grass underneath to him stick to his back. He turned his head and found himself staring into Adraea's dark brown eyes, shining with happiness. He smiled and sighed contentedly.

'What's the matter?' asked Adraea.

'Nothing,' said Jamek, simply. 'Absolutely nothing.' He turned his head back, looking straight up at the aquamarine sky, listening to the buzz of insects in the trees and flowers, and the call of birds far above. 'I think I'm in heaven.'

'You said that earlier,' giggled Adraea.

'Oh, yes,' said Jamek, remembering with a wry grin. 'Well, that was better. But this is almost as good.'

Adraea laughed and kissed him on the cheek, before gently biting his earlobe. 'Getting better...' said Jamek, and Adraea leaned over to kiss him on the mouth. 'Even better...' he said, before kissing her again. He turned towards her, his arms encircling her waist, pulling her towards him. 'Even better...'

Adraea shrieked with laughter and swatted him gently. 'Take another cold shower, Psinaez Jamek!' she said, and stood up. She was wearing a sun-faded red bikini, which clung to her hips and bosom. Jamek felt a pang as he regarded her – every part of him ached for her. He grinned as his eyes roved over her figure, and she blushed.

'I'm getting another drink,' she said. 'You want another beer?'

Jamek smiled and shook his head, settling back. 'I'm good, thanks.' He sighed again as he watched Adraea head back towards the house, her hips swaying from side to side as she walked. 'Hmm-mmm...' he murmured to himself. 'I hate to see you go, but I love to watch you leave!'

After spending the night partying in the Capitol with Mavrak, they had all caught a taxi back to Adraea's house. Mavrak had gone home to see his parents, who he had not seen for nearly a week, and Jamek and Adraea had been enjoying a quiet day in the sunlit garden. Fedrus had said that he would be at the High Command for at least a few days, so they were looking forward to a long stretch of days ahead, which would be spent sunbathing, resting, and making love.

Jamek closed his eyes, wondering at the turn his life had taken. This summer had been the best of his life – the time when everything had changed, when dreams had been realised. He smiled to himself. In the space of a few short weeks, he had transformed from a boy into a man. He had fallen in love, and it had changed everything.

He felt a sudden sense of loss, and realised that he missed his father, the guiding influence in his life since his mother had died. He smiled to himself – his Dad would be home soon, and then he could tell him about Adraea, and his plans for the future. For he planned to marry Adraea – as soon as he could.

Yes, life was good.

Jamek was broken from his reverie by the ice-cold assault of spraying water accompanied by mischievous laughter. Jamek screamed and jumped to his feet, yelling as the freezing water splashed his warm skin, the shock making him take short, sharp breaths. He looked around and saw Adraea standing over him holding a hosepipe. His face split into a grin.

'You are for it now, young lady!' he shouted, and Adraea shrieked with laughter, running away from him, turning occasionally to spray him with the hose. Jamek caught a blast full in the face, and shook his head, wiping the water from his eyes. He was dripping wet, the light breeze chilling his skin, which prickled into gooseflesh. He leapt forward blindly and seized the hose from Adraea's hands, delighting in her girlish squeals as he sprayed her with the cold water.

She turned off the hose at the wall and mock-pouted, her hair dripping water down her skin onto her bare feet. Her bottom lip soon curved upwards into a smile, and she threw herself at Jamek, kissing him deeply on the lips. After a long pause, Jamek pulled back, breathless.

'What was that for?' he said.

'For being wonderful,' she said happily, and hugged him tightly. 'I love you.'

Jamek closed his eyes and wrapped his arms around her. 'I love you,' he murmured, and kissed her soaking wet hair. It tasted vaguely of lavender. He felt his heartbeat slow slightly, as if time itself was conspiring to preserve this perfect moment. Then his eyes opened, and he saw Fedrus standing in front on him.

'Fedrus!' he said, startled, and Adraea jumped backwards, grabbing a towel from a nearby sun-lounger and wrapping it around her. Jamek stood back from her, almost apologetically, for this moment of intimacy.

'Dad!' said Adraea, turning to face him. 'I didn't realise you'd be back so soon...' she stopped when she saw his face. His eyes were downcast, his expression grim, not with anger, but with exhaustion and worry. 'What's happened?'

'You'd better come inside,' replied her father. 'Both of you.' He turned on his heel, unbuttoning his military jacket, and loosening his tie. He sat down at the kitchen table, and waited as Jamek and Adraea, puzzled and concerned expressions on their faces, sat down opposite him.

Fedrus cleared his throat. 'Jamek,' he said, 'I'm afraid I have some bad news... about your father.'

Jamek's blood ran cold, and tears began to needle the corners of his eyes. 'Dad?' he said, quietly.

'You know he was exploring the Panthera System?' asked Fedrus, and Jamek nodded silently, his face grim. 'His ship was attacked... by the Confederacy. He's dead, Jamek. I'm so sorry.'

Adraea seized Jamek's hand as he sat bolt upright at the terrible news, squeezing it tightly. Jamek's eyes narrowed with thinly veiled anger, and for some reason, Fedrus became suddenly afraid, as if some latent power, long dormant, had suddenly manifested itself, before disappearing again.

'How?' asked Jamek, his voice choked.

'Anzaeus ordered the crew to abandon ship when a Confederate battleship attacked them and demanded their surrender,' explained Fedrus. 'He performed a suicide run on the enemy ship.'

Jamek nodded, tears streaming down his cheeks. That was his father, all right. Defiant and courageous to the last. 'The Confederacy?' he said, hoarsely.

Fedrus nodded. 'It appears so,' he said. 'The Protector has ordered the entire Starforce to mobilise. They're assembling an Expeditionary Force to search for survivors.' He reached into his pocket and pulled out his communicator. 'I took the liberty of copying Anzaeus's last transmission before I left the High Command. Do you want me to send it to you?'

'Play it now.'

Fedrus shifted uncomfortably. 'Jamek, maybe now is not the time...'

'Commodore,' Jamek's voice was level and calm, but with a hint of menace that made it impossible to disobey. It was disconcerting coming from Jamek, who was barely a man. 'Play it now.'

Fedrus nodded, and tapped the screen of his communicator. Anzaeus's garbled voice rang out.

'Captain Psinaez Anzaeus... *Provident*. Mission: exploration of... Panthera... entering the system, the *Provident* was... attack by an alien vessel. Weapons capability: significantly superior. Commander, alien vessel, identified... Confederate Battleship *Iron Crown*... Panthera System is 'Confederate territory'... demanded... surrender. The *Provident* is severely... unable to return to Protectorate territory. Many crew casualties.'

'...Starforce Regulations, I will not turn over possession of the *Provident*... the crew to abandon ship. I will remain behind with my... Commander Coltran... destroy the attacking vessel... Request... task force to recover... lifeboats...'

'...recognition for Lieutenant Astrus, who died at his post... Special... Coltran, who has demonstrated... his crew... refusing a direct order... to abandon ship.'

'Tell my son... that I love him.'

The transmission went dead.

Jamek slowly and silently lowered his head, his body shook by hitching sobs. *Dad? Dead? It can't be!* The stunning perfection of life, only a few minutes before, had boiled away in grief, to reveal the cold, hard reality. Hot, stinging tears dripped onto his bare thighs, and he was conscious only of Adraea squeezing his hand, her arm around his shoulders, as agonising grief smashed over him like a tidal wave.

'We are going to war?' he said, looking up at Fedrus with blood-shot eyes.

Fedrus nodded. 'If it is the Confederacy,' he said, 'the Protector is committed to beginning the Crusade.'

'To reclaim Therqa,' muttered Jamek. 'Yes.'

Fedrus leaned forward. 'Both of you,' he said sternly. 'I know you're grieving, but I urge you not to do anything rash. These are dangerous times now, and if it should come to war...' he paused. 'I would hate to see either of you hurt.'

Jamek looked at him, hatred burning in his eyes. 'I swear to avenge my father's death,' he muttered. 'If it takes me on the Crusade to reclaim our homeworld, then so be it!'

-#-

Jamek stood in Fedrus's garden, watching Kaathar sink below the horizon, its last red and orange glow silhouetting the ghostly form of the skyscrapers in the far distance. The shadow of the *Inominate* towered over them all, clearly visible despite the Capitol being nearly fifty miles away.

A cold wind blew across the garden, and Jamek angrily wiped away bitter tears from his cheeks. His father was dead. He was an orphan.

Jamek felt grief well up inside him, and a terrible fear and loneliness. He was barely a man himself, and now he was orphaned and alone, with no family left to turn to. His thoughts turned briefly to Karaea, the Protector, who had lived with his father for a while after his mother had died, but he dismissed them. She had left his father, caring more for her career in politics than she had for a family. Jamek angrily blinked back tears, glaring at the shadow of the distant *Inominate*, the throne of the woman who could have been a mother to him.

He turned away, the pain being too much to bear, and instinctively cast his eyes to the north-east, where he laid eyes on the Panthera constellation, and its capital star. The grief he had tried to escape came flooding back in, and he bit his lip, a single drop of blood welling there as tears streamed down his face.

'Dad,' he moaned, as his face crumpled, and a choking sob mounted in his throat. In his mind's eye, he saw his father, inn the Command Centre of the *Provident*, under fire by some unknown enemy, the ship being rocked this way and that. Computer terminals were burning, flickering shadows playing on the walls, and finally the squeal of metal on metal as the ship collided with its opponent...

'No!' screamed Jamek at the impassively staring star. 'Why him? Why my father? Why now?' Panthera gazed back, an unblinking eye regarding Jamek with indifference. Jamek's chest heaved in wrenching gasps, and he crumpled to the floor, his eyes streaming tears, bloodshot from crying, soundless, agonising sobs shaking his entire body. The pain was like a hole in his heart.

Adraea watched her boyfriend crying in the garden, and tears of sympathy welled in her own eyes. She went out to him and sat down, pulling her arms around him and kissing his neck. 'I'm sorry, Jamek,' she said, her own voice faltering in the gathering dusk. 'I'm so sorry.'

'Why?' came Jamek's unanswerable question, muffled as his buried his face into Adraea's shoulder, staining her dress with his tears. 'Why did it have to be him?'

Mavrak came outside and laid his hand on his friend's shoulder. Adraea had called him and he had come around straight away. Fedrus had gone out, trying to deal with the death of his friend in his own way, and allowing Jamek some time to deal with his more personal grief.

Jamek looked up, and Mavrak saw his red-rimmed eyes, sore with rubbing and crying, but filled with a burning rage. For a moment, Mavrak saw something in Jamek's eyes he had never seen before – a glimmer of light deep inside the black irises, like a flicker of flame, before it vanished.

'I will avenge him,' spat Jamek. 'Marshal Xoanek has already left with an Expeditionary Force, heading there.' He pointed to the yellow eye of Panthera, growing brighter in the lengthening shadow. 'I swear that I will avenge my father's death. I will destroy this Confederacy that has taken him from me, and I will reclaim Therqa, our ancient homeworld! I swear it on my life! On my very blood! Tomorrow, I will enlist in the Starforce.'

Adraea was taken aback. 'But Jamek...'

Mavrak stood up and offered his friend his hand. Jamek took it and Mavrak pulled him to his feet. 'If you mean to go,' he said, looking into Jamek's eyes, 'then I'm going with you.'

Jamek nodded, and grasped Mavrak's arm. 'I do. Thank you.'

They both turned to Adraea and her expression hardened. 'Then I will too,' she said, determinedly. Jamek kissed her and wiped the tears from his eyes.

'Thank you both,' he said, his voice breaking with emotion. 'Adraea, I love you more than anyone else in the world. Mavrak, you are my closest friend. It will be an honour to serve with you. Even if we die in the attempt, we will fight, to avenge my father's death, and to deliver our people to their homeworld!'

He looked up at Panthera again. 'May your path lead to the stars,' he murmured, in a silent prayer for his father, and for the soldiers of the Protectorate speeding towards the star, with conquest on their minds.

Chapter Seven

In the freezing cold emptiness of the Panthera System, a lonely planetoid hurtled silently through the dark, orbiting the two distant yellow stars at the centre of the system. Its surface was pocked and scarred with valleys and craters, rendered in carbon dioxide and water ice frozen as hard as steel.

In high orbit, small chunks of frozen debris from the recent battle between the ill-fated *PSS Provident* and the *CBS Iron Crown*, spun around the planetoid in eccentric ellipses. They occasionally collided silently, their orbits deteriorating slowly before smashing into the planetoid's surface.

In the far distance, beyond the shadow of the planetoid, hundreds of stars clustered together approached slowly. As they grew larger, it swiftly became apparent that they were not stars at all, but starships – great rotating discs of steel and titanium, windowless wheels of destruction, their hulls blackened with the scars of a thousand battles, their central hubs pulsing with a weird, blue light. They travelled together in a V-shaped arrangement, their outer rims rotating steadily, their formation lights winking in the darkness.

The vessel at the tip of the arrowhead formation was larger than the others, about a hundred and fifty metres in diameter and thirty metres thick. Inset from its spinning rim, letters were engraved on its hull, painted black and illuminated with an arc of light shining from the hub:

PSS VEHEMENT

S-2442

Marshal Xoanek sat in the Command Centre of the *Vehement*, staring impassively ahead at the dark planetoid. 'Signal the fleet to stand at Ready Stations,' he said. 'Scan the planetoid.'

After a brief pause, the Science Officer spoke up. 'There's a high level of debris in high orbit, Marshal,' he said. 'I'm reading iron, titanium, silicon, carbon dioxide, ice... and terculium.'

Some of the crew murmured to themselves. 'So,' said Xoanek, 'this is the site of battle. The remains of the *Provident*.'

'It appears so, sir,' replied the Science Officer. 'I'm also detecting unusual gravitational signatures in the area.'

'Unusual how?'

The Science Officer frowned as he tried to understand the readings on his screen. 'There's another gravity well nearby, but I can't seem to detect any corresponding mass!'

'Another planetoid?' asked Xoanek.

'No, sir – it must be something very small, and very dense.' The Science Officer paused for a moment, tapping the screen of his terminal. 'I have it,' he said. 'It's tiny, about a centimetre in diameter! It's orbiting the planetoid.'

'Well, what is it?'

'I think it may have been a very, very small star, which has effectively gone supernova. What's left is a tiny neutron star.' He turned to Xoanek. 'It's extremely dangerous – if we get too close, the gravitational shear could tear the ship apart.'

Xoanek swiped his own console, adjusting the ship's heading. 'Steering clear,' he said. 'I'll keep an eye on it. What could cause something like that?'

'It's possible that the Confederate ships use an artificial star in a magnetic containment field to power their ships and to generate artificial gravity,' answered the Science Officer. 'High Command conducted some research into the technology some years ago, but it was deemed too unstable for practical use. That would be consistent with the gravitational readings – the star probably collapsed when the Confederate ship was destroyed.'

Xoanek shook his head. 'What kind of people would use technology like that?' he muttered. 'Casting gravitational fallout all over the place? Savages.' He paused. 'Scan the planetoid and the surrounding area for lifeboats – I want to know if there are any survivors from the *Provident*.'

'Sir... I'm detecting starships approaching our position from the planetoid!'

Xoanek set his teeth. 'Battle Stations!' he shouted. 'Signal the fleet to deploy into attack formation! Put them on screen.'

The view on the Flight Display shifted, zooming in on a fleet of vessels emerging from the far side of the planetoid. They orbited the planet quickly, appearing as giant steel spheres, their hulls pocked and scarred.

'By the Guardians,' muttered Shivaeus, Xoanek's adjutant, and now acting as First Officer. 'There's *hundreds* of them!'

'There's hundreds of us,' spat Xoanek through gritted teeth. 'General transmission.'

'Transmitting, sir,' said the Communications Officer.

'Attention, unidentified fleet,' said Xoanek. 'This is Marshal Xoanek, Chief of Staff of the Protectorate Starforce, commanding the *PSS Vehement* of the Expeditionary Force. We are on a rescue mission to recover survivors from the *PSS Provident*, a Protectorate vessel destroyed here in an unwarranted act of aggression three months ago. Any attempt to interfere with this mission will be considered an act of war. This is your only warning.'

The Communications Officer spoke up. 'Reply coming in on the same frequency, sir.'

'Put them on.'

The view on the Flight Display changed, lighting up with the shape of a man. He wore a metal helmet completely covering his head – a visor down over the eyes, a metal snout protruding from underneath it ending in a grille.

'Protectorate Commander,' came a voice through the crew's headsets, 'I am Chevalier Rigel of the Confederate Battleship *Golden Eagle*. This system is sovereign territory of the Confederacy of Nations. I am sure that name is familiar to you.'

A hush fell over the Command Centre. The Confederacy of Nations. It was true. This ship, and the fleet that accompanied it, were from the hated empire which had banished their forefathers to the dark recesses of space in a forgotten age.

'You will immediately withdraw, or we will destroy you,' said Chevalier Rigel.

Xoanek's face twisted into an ugly snarl, baring his teeth. 'Take your best shot, *Chevalier* – I'll look for you on the field!' He slammed his fist onto his computer panel, cutting off the transmission, and restoring the display to a view of the planetoid.

'Marshal, we have incoming!' shouted Shivaeus, as the Primary Support console in front of him flashed red.

'Order the fleet to break formation and engage the enemy!' shouted Xoanek, as he quickly switched flight controls to manual, feeling his stomach churn as he threw the ship hard over to port. 'Tactical, target the *Golden Eagle*.'

The ship lurched to one side and in the darkness outside, the other ships broke away in all directions, most charging directly for the enemy fleet rounding the planetoid. The nimble *Vehement*, being a battleship and designed for manoeuvrability, easily avoided the incoming missile. When the missile veered around for another attempt to hit the *Vehement*, a blaze of flares erupted from the ship's hull, and the missile collided harmlessly with one, exploding in a silent flash of fire.

'Target locked, sir,' reported Shivaeus.

'Fire!'

The ship shuddered as four missiles were launched simultaneously, speeding across the dark sky. Several other Protectorate ships also fired, and the void was illuminated by dozens of pinpricks of light as missiles bearing their deadly payloads raced towards the Confederate fleet.

'Engage thrusters – full speed!' shouted Xoanek. 'The missiles will smash their lines and we'll be in and amongst them before they know what they're doing!'

'Aye, sir!'

Xoanek felt his stomach lurch slightly as the *Vehement* shot forward, accelerating towards the enemy fleet, chasing the missiles they had just launched. His hands clenched the arms of the Captain's chair tightly, and his heart beat madly in his chest. The bloodlust of battle was upon him.

The missiles smashed into the front line of the enemy fleet with devastating effect, exploding in silent flowers of blazing fury. The command crew cheered as they saw them smash into the hull of the *Golden Eagle*, easily distinguishable as the largest ship in the Confederate fleet. It began to lose altitude, veering down towards the surface of the planetoid.

'Starship down! Starship down!' shouted Captain Shivaeus.

'Ahead full!' screamed Xoanek. 'All ships, ahead full! For the Protectorate, and for Therqa!'

The Protectorate fleet smashed into the Confederate lines, some ships colliding in devastating balls of burning flame, quickly extinguished by the airless vacuum. The *Vehement* took fire as it manoeuvred rapidly between the giant metal spheres, most of the missiles glancing off its armoured hull. More missiles poured from its silos in silent, furious reply.

In the Command Centre, the lights blacked out for a moment, and the ship shook violently as it took heavy fire, but this was a warship, and its crew were well-prepared for combat. A console exploded at the back of the Command Centre with a particularly heavy blow.

'Damage report!' demanded Xoanek.

'Missile hit to Section Four,' reported the Chief Engineer. 'No hull breach, damage to secondary systems only. Minor casualties only.'

'Communications, signal Groups Two and Three to move to the flanks – try to encircle them. Group One is to follow our lead to the centre and try to push them out,' ordered Xoanek.

'Aye, sir!'

The ship rocked with another blast, sending it surging forward. Another terminal exploded, and the lights dipped.

'Hull breach in Section Four!' reported the Chief Engineer. 'I'm sealing it off.'

'What was that?' shouted Xoanek.

'Their flagship, sir,' reported Shivaeus. 'It appears to have regained attitude control – it's away aft.'

Xoanek grinned. 'Right,' he said. 'Tactical, target that ship. When the *Vehement* shoots down an enemy flagship, it stays down!' He swung his steering column hard over to starboard, bringing the ship about.

In the midst of the carnage, the *Vehement* swung around in a loop to face the monstrous *Golden Eagle* which approached it from behind, firing steadily. The *Vehement* inclined at a narrow aspect, presenting only the edge of the rim to the oncoming Confederate vessel, appearing as a smaller target. It accelerated again, charging directly towards the sphere.

'Wait until we're within five hundred metres,' said Xoanek, 'then fire all weapons. I'll strafe past it, and then come about for another pass.'

'Aye, sir...'

Xoanek opened the throttle and thrashed the ship forward, watching the tactical data on the Flight Display, where the distance from target counted down, and the shape of the huge glinting sphere grew larger. When it passed five hundred metres, and it seemed as if they were about to crash into the terrifying behemoth, he shouted, 'fire!'

Four missiles erupted from the cannons mounted on the *Vehement's* hull, smashing into the hull of the *Golden Eagle* with deadly fire, throwing up chunks of debris. The *Vehement* shot past the lumbering Confederate starship at breakneck speed, before looping around for another charge. Around the two duelling champions, the battle raged, both Protectorate and Confederate starships alike taking heavy fire. A Protectorate starship exploded, chunks of white-hot metal spinning out in all directions, heavily damaging several nearby vessels.

The *Golden Eagle*, bleeding fire from a dozen hull breaches, began to lose attitude again, but continued firing at the *Vehement* as it made another approach. A missile glanced off the hull of the *Vehement*, exploding behind it.

'Fire!' shouted Xoanek, and more missiles crashed into the hull of the Confederate flagship, which was unable to match the speed and manoeuvrability of its Protectorate counterpart. The *Vehement* arced past it in another strafing pass, before again coming around. The *Golden Eagle*, unable to compete with its smaller, more aggressive counterpart, was adrift.

Xoanek sat forward. 'Bring us alongside,' he said. 'Prepare boarding parties. I want that ship captured.' He stood up. 'I'll lead the assault myself,' he said, and turned to Captain Shivaeus sitting next to him. 'You have the Conn.'

'Aye, Marshal.'

Xoanek unbuckled himself from his chair and fairly ran from the Command Centre. The corridor lurched as the ship took fire, and crew members ran to and fro. Arriving at the nearest Armoury, he found several platoons of Contingent Infantry – field troops attached to a starship for precisely this type of mission – readying themselves with body armour, helmets and heavy-duty pulse rifles. They stopped as he entered the room, staring at him.

'As you were,' he said abruptly, and pulled off his epaulette and chain, casting them to one side. He strapped on a chest plate, greaves and vambraces, before finally pulling a large, visored helm over his head. This was not a full helm, like those used by the Confederacy, but was open under the transparent visor, and only came down to the ears, giving the best balance between protection and mobility. He then mounted his epaulette onto the shoulder of his chest plate, slotted a side-arm into a holster at his waist, and slung a large pulse rifle over his shoulder.

He nodded to the Ensign, commander of the Contingent Infantry, who saluted. 'Marshal,' he said.

'I'll be coming with you, Ensign,' said Xoanek. 'The Company's yours, but the mission's mine.'

'Aye, sir.' He saluted again, and then raised his voice. 'Listen up!' he said, and the troops in the Armoury fell silent. 'First Platoon is with me. Marshal Xoanek will be accompanying us. Krachaez, Tolgan – you will stay by the Marshal at all times. Do you understand?'

Two Privates nodded, and moved to stand close by the Marshal. The Ensign nodded. 'First Platoon's shuttle will be docking close to what we believe to be their Command

Centre. It is likely to be heavily guarded – expect fierce resistance. Our objective is to seize control of the Command Centre and capture the command crew – especially their CO. We're then to await confirmation that 2nd Platoon has captured the Engineering Section, but be prepared for a quick evacuation. The remaining Platoons will be distributed throughout the ship to disrupt communications and deal with the crew. Keep your eyes sharp, and your hands steady. Let's move into the shuttles quickly. For the Protectorate!'

The troops lifted their weapons and cheered, and Xoanek grinned to himself. This was what war was all about. He hefted the pulse rifle in his hands, feeling its weight, and memories of his early days in the military flooded back to him. He had spent years fighting the pirates which raided the trade routes, one day dreaming that he would take part in this Great Crusade to reclaim their lost homeworld. And now, here he was, leading his troops into battle against the Confederacy.

The troops quickly ran out into the corridor, and carried on down it until they came to their shuttle. They quickly filed in. The shuttle was about thirty metres long, single-decked, with the main cabin having fifty chairs, enough to hold a Platoon of men. The cockpit held the command crew of two men, with a wide, deep window, giving the pilot as full a view of the battlefield as possible. Both the port and starboard sides of the vessel were high and flat, with wide doors and descending ramps. This was not a shuttle for ferrying people to and from planets – this was an attack shuttle, designed to latch onto the hull of an enemy vessel, burn through it, and allow troops to board it.

Xoanek quickly sat down in one of the chairs, and fastened a double-strapped seatbelt over his shoulders. Once the shuttle detached from the hull of the *Vehement*, the artificial gravity would dissipate, so the seatbelts were needed to stop the troops inside from floating out of their seats. He slotted his rifle into a holster next to the seat, and waited, his heart thudding, his mouth dry with fear and excitement.

After a few minutes, the rest of the troops were belted into their seats, and the doors on the starboard side slid closed. There was a lurch as the shuttle disconnected from the hull of the *Vehement*, and Xoanek felt his stomach churn and the straps of the seatbelt press into his shoulders as the gravity was lost. Now for the short but slow journey across to the *Golden Eagle*, and then the fury of battle.

The shuttle rocked as nearby explosions buffeted it, the lights in the cabin fluttering occasionally. Xoanek looked around at the grim faces of the Infantry troops, their brows sweating, their expressions fixed with a mixture of fear, excitement and resolve. Time seemed to slow, and nothing moved, only the occasional rock of the shuttle, the beating of his heart, the grain of the butt of his rifle on his palm, worn smooth through use.

Six shuttles detached from the spinning outer rim of the *Vehement*, at first matching its rotation, then slowing to a halt before firing their thrusters and moving steadily towards the prostrate *Golden Eagle*. The battlefield was littered with drifting debris and the burned out hulks of destroyed starships. Missiles raced silently across the black sky, smashing into blasted and scarred metal. The silent fury of the battle raged as Protectorate ships duelled with their Confederate enemies, questing for the glory that their ancestors had aspired to for a thousand years.

A missile from a Confederate starship struck one of the attack shuttles, sending it spinning out of control down towards the planetoid's surface. The *Vehement* responded by launching a full broadside of missiles which smashed into the smaller Confederate ship's hull, before it exploded in a flash of light. A spherical shockwave expanded outwards, rocking the small group of attack shuttles as they made their perilous journey across the pitched battle.

Finally, they reached the *Golden Eagle*. The ship rattled, and there was a loud crunch as it latched onto the hull. Xoanek felt gravity take hold once more, but this time, instead of pulling him down towards the deck of the ship, it pulled him sideways to the starboard door. 'Damn,' he muttered to himself, and pulled his rifle from his holster. He unbuckled his seatbelt, and rolled out of his seat, landing heavily on the starboard wall.

'The gravity's messed up!' he shouted. 'We'll have to drop down into their ship! Get out of your chairs, now!'

The troops, upon receiving the order from the Marshal, unquestioningly obeyed him. Some on the port side grunted as they collided with other chairs on their way down to the starboard wall, and one man screamed as his leg was broken by such a collision. Xoanek and the troops gathered around the sliding doors, now trapdoors.

The air was filled with an ear-piercing, high-pitched whine as the cutting lasers around the doors began burning their way into the hull of the Confederate flagship. 'Load your weapons!' ordered the Ensign, and the Platoon Sergeant, a grey-haired man about five years younger than Xoanek, who looked as if he had spent his entire career doing just this, began barking orders.

'Come on, you dogs!' he shouted. 'Get those weapons armed, or those Confederate bastards will shoot you down faster than you cream yourselves! And be ready with your bayonets!'

Xoanek pulled a large ammunition magazine from his belt, and slotted it into a socket on the underside of his rifle. The magazine was effectively a large, powerful battery, and the rifle focused the electrical energy into a concentrated laser pulse. The weapons were efficient and deadly.

The whining stopped and the doors slid open, revealing a charred, black hull plate. Xoanek kicked it hard and it dropped out, falling nearly a full storey below onto the deck of the Confederate flagship. 'Shit,' he swore – they would have to jump down into the ship. 'Fix bayonets!' he shouted, and locked his own onto the end of his rifle before roaring and jumping down into the Confederate ship. Krachaez and Tolgan, the two Privates assigned to him, dropped down after him.

Xoanek landed on the deck of the ship heavily, and gasped as he felt the gravity bite harder. It was stronger aboard the *Golden Eagle* than the artificial gravity aboard starships, which was equivalent to that on Szotas. It made his limbs felt heavy and sluggish. He saw Confederate troops running towards him across the room he had landed in, and immediately lifted up his weapon, firing wildly at them. He hit three, sending them reeling backwards with the force of the shots. Then more Protectorate troops dropped from the ceiling. The world was filled with the heat of laser pulses, the thrum of his rifle in his hands, the hoarse screams of his troops and the wails of the wounded and dying. Xoanek's mind was filled with a deadly calm as the battle-frenzy descended, and he fired again and again, taking down target after target as more Protectorate troops dropped into the room.

Finally, after what seemed like an age, the room fell silent, and Xoanek found himself standing alongside the other troops in the Platoon, breathing heavily, his hands shaking slightly.

The Ensign pulled an electronic pad from his waist. 'The Command Centre is just up the next corridor, near the top of the sphere,' he said. 'We'll be moving into corridors, so everyone fix bayonets. It's going to get messy.' He glanced around. 'Any casualties?'

'None, sir,' replied the Platoon Sergeant.

The Ensign nodded. 'Good,' he said. 'Let's move out!'

Krachaez and Tolgan, Xoanek's escorts, immediately moved to his side, and he nodded in appreciation. Their training was excellent, and they were following it to the letter – the professionalism of the soldiers was more than he expected. He felt a swell of pride to be in command of such men.

Two troops moved to either side of a sliding door on the opposite side of the room, waiting for the rest of the Platoon to move out of the way. One hit a panel on the wall, opening the door, while the other leaped in front, checking the corridor beyond before moving out quickly, waving his arm after him. Steadily, the rest of the Platoon moved out into the corridor.

The corridor was dark and bleak, the lights fluttering weakly, the air filled with the stench of burned copper. The faint crackle of electrical fire could be heard in the distance. The floor was littered with debris from the ceiling, which had partially collapsed in places from the battle. Xoanek pushed the butt of his rifle against his shoulder, breathing deeply and steadily as he watched for movement in the gloom.

The Ensign moved off down the corridor, accompanied by a squad of men. Xoanek followed in the centre, while another squad took up the rear, acting as a rearguard as they moved steadily down the corridor. They moved along for a short while, before the air was split by the thunder of machine gun fire.

'Contact! Contact!' shouted the Platoon Sergeant, and the vanguard immediately dropped to the floor, firing their rifles down the corridor. The air immediately heated up with the power of the pulse rifles, gleaming flashes of light searing down the corridor. Xoanek looked ahead and saw several Confederate troops blasting heavy machine gun fire towards them.

'Damn,' he muttered, before dropping to the deck. One of the troops behind him was hit, falling to the floor in a gurgling scream. He had been shot in the throat. Blood gushed from the open wound, making the floor hot and slick. Xoanek grimaced at the sight, and stood, firing his rifle a few times before dropping again. Another troop fell, screaming in pain as a spray of bullets hit him across the chest, knocking him backwards with the force of their impact.

Xoanek realised at once that they were in serious trouble. If they were pinned down by gunfire, they would be butchered in the corridor. Their only chance was to charge the Confederate position, and cut them down with bayonets. His own bayonet fixed, glittering silver on the end of his rifle, Xoanek jumped over the crouched troops in front of him, and sprinted down the corridor, screaming.

'For the Protectorate!' he yelled, and charged. The other troops followed him, shouting 'Protectorate!'

The Confederate troops were taken completely by surprise by such a desperate and dangerous gamble. Xoanek ploughed into their lines, taking one of them in the belly with his bayonet, before discharging his rifle at point-blank range. The energy pulse left a gaping, charred hole in the enemy soldier's abdomen. Xoanek quickly discarded the corpse before looking around for his next target, his eyes bloodshot with fury, his teeth bared in an ugly snarl. He slashed another across the belly, spilling his intestines. Another he took in the throat, before swiping the blade out sideways, virtually decapitating the man.

He felt hot, piercing pain as a bullet took him in the shoulder, but without hesitation, stabbed another soldier in the chest. He slashed, stabbed and hacked his way through a wall of armoured flesh in the flickering darkness, conscious only of his thudding heart, the blood-frenzy beating in his head and the pushing, heaving bodies of his men behind him.

He saw the Ensign take a shot in the head, and fall backwards. He knew immediately that he was dead. Roaring in anger, he threw himself on the Ensign's killer, stabbing him in the thigh, then again in the visor of his helmet, which shattered with the force of the blow. After what seemed like an endless, bloody slaughter, it finally ended, and Xoanek found himself still screaming. He stopped, exhaling slowly, his hands shaking.

The Platoon Sergeant stood and looked over the body of the dead Ensign. He nodded and stripped the corpse of ammunition, quickly dishing it out amongst the other men. 'What now, sir?' he said, turning to the Marshal.

'Where's the Command Centre?' said Xoanek, his voice hoarse.

The Sergeant indicated to the end of the corridor, some twenty feet further down, where a pair of solid blast doors were sealed shut.

'Get me inside,' growled Xoanek.

'Aye, sir,' said the Sergeant. 'Mortar team! I want that door taken down!'

'Yes, Sergeant!' shouted two men from the lead squad, and immediately ran down the corridor. They fixed a small device to the door, and then ran back, one shouting 'take cover!'

The rest of the Platoon immediately dropped to the floor, holding their hands over their heads. There was brief and brilliant flash of white light, accompanied by a thunderous explosion. The ship rocked with the force of it, blasting the entire bottom end of the corridor away, exposing the titanium bulkheads beyond. Xoanek looked up, and saw through the flames that the blast doors were open.

'Charge!' he roared, jumped to his feet, and ran.

Inside the Command Centre, they met more resistance. Tolgan and Krachaez were at Xoanek's side when he ran in, and were met by a hail of gunfire. Tolgan took the worst of it, collapsing in a bleeding heap. Xoanek sprayed the room with pulse fire, taking out a few of the command crew. He saw his target at the front of the room – Rigel, the fleet commander, aiming at him with a machine gun. Xoanek fired, but no energy came from his rifle – his magazine was discharged. He ran at his Confederate counterpart, unfastening his bayonet and throwing it like a dagger.

The blade caught Rigel in the shoulder, and he howled in pain, dropping his machine gun. Then Xoanek was upon him. He hit the Chevalier in the stomach with his shoulder, lifting him off the floor with the force of the impact, before they both smashed back down onto the deck. Xoanek howled as Rigel pulled the bayonet from his shoulder and stabbed him in the thigh with it. He lashed out, kicking him hard in the stomach, and the

Confederate commander doubled up. Xoanek reached for his side-arm, but Rigel grabbed his arm, twisting his hand round in an attempt to break his wrist. Xoanek bared his teeth, and drove his knee into Rigel's throat.

Rigel fell back, and Xoanek, wincing, pulled the bayonet out of his thigh. Thick, hot blood flowed down his leg. He felt for his side-arm, but it was gone – cast to the other side of the room by the fight. Left with no other choice, Xoanek brandished his bayonet. Rigel pulled a vicious-looking knife from his belt, and the two commanders circled each other.

The Protectorate troops watched their Marshal in awe, the rest of the Confederate command crew dead. They did not dare to intervene, as they watched the two champions move together in a deadly dance. After the silent devastation of the space battle, and the bloody carnage of the fights in the corridors, it all came down to this – two commanders, each armed only with a knife, circling each other, weighing each other's strengths, waiting for the first strike, and the killer blow.

Rigel struck first. Xoanek parried with his bayonet, slashing across Rigel's chest, smashing the Chevalier with his shoulder and then finally, driving the bayonet into his heart. Rigel grunted, and his hands went limp, dropping his dagger. Xoanek stepped back, and breathing deeply, removed his helmet.

'Xoanek...' muttered Rigel weakly.

'The same,' said Xoanek grimly. He grasped Rigel's helmet at the neck, and pulled it off his head. Underneath was a face which looked remarkably similar to his own.

His eyes were a clear blue, his hair black, flecked with grey. His neatly shaven chin was now spoiled by blood trickling from his mouth. Rigel sank to his knees, his eyes rolled back in his head, and he finally fell backwards, dead.

'Take stations,' Xoanek ordered. 'Figure out how to fly this ship, and signal the fleet that the *Golden Eagle* has been captured.'

He threw himself down in the nearest chair and exhaled slowly. The Platoon medic immediately came over to him, and began dressing the wound in his leg. Xoanek winced as the medic pulled a bandage tightly around his thigh. He gripped the arms of the chair to stop his hands from shaking, looking down at the body of Rigel, prostrate on the deck.

'The Expeditionary Force is responding,' reported a Corporal manning what was presumably the Communications station. 'The Confederate fleet is in full retreat!'

The rest of the Platoon cheered and Xoanek smiled. 'Dispatch three Groups to pursue them,' he said. 'I want as many of their ships as possible either captured or destroyed.'

'Aye, sir,' replied the Corporal. 'What about the planetoid? There appears to be an outpost on the surface – do you want to deploy ground troops?'

'No,' answered Xoanek. 'Maintaining orbital superiority is sufficient. Hold our position here with the remaining Groups, and begin repairs of the captured ships.'

Xoanek stared ahead at the flickering screen, breathing deeply and calming his racing heart. The Great Crusade had begun.

Chapter Eight

Chancellor Ulestran stormed into his office and threw the electronic pad in his hand across the room, where it smashed against the wall in a crystalline spray of glass and hot circuits. He sat down behind his desk, turning his chair to glare out of the windows at the back of the room.

The warm sunlight slanted into the room from the high windows and Ulestran looked out over the great Chancellery Boulevard. The long, straight road was lined with ancient trees, going straight through the Palace's extensive grounds to the Grand Gatehouse, into the heart of the city. In front of the Palace, a memorial to a long-forgotten ruler stood, glistening gold in the morning sun. A slight breeze rustled the leaves in the trees, and the sunlight was distorted slightly by imperfections in the old windows.

Ulestran smiled to himself with no small hint of irony. The Palace he sat in, the other buildings of government, the entire city, had once been the seat of power of the Kingdom, the last nation on the planet to oppose the Confederacy's supremacy. Now, over a thousand years later, the city was a mausoleum to that nation, and the Confederacy's living heart resided there. Yet now, the heirs to that forgotten Kingdom had returned, like spectres from the past. They held the guise of a new nation which they had forged on some unknown planet in the dark recesses of space to which they were banished.

Ulestran's face twisted into a mask of rage and disgust. It was out there – the Protectorate – somewhere in the black shadows and frozen dark. It had been for centuries, growing like a cancer in the abyss, and now, it had finally come back into contact with the great nation which had sent it hence. This was the greatest threat to the Confederacy since its formation – the return of its oldest adversary.

He turned back to his desk, feeling the warm sunlight on the back of his neck, and his mind began to grapple with the problem that faced him. He ran his hand along the desk, his fingers feeling the irregular grain of the dark, stained wood, worn smooth with age. There was a knock at the door, breaking his train of thought.

'Enter!' he shouted irritably, and one of the large double-doors directly in front of him opened, its heavy-set black bulk swinging inwards into the room. Ulestran smiled as he saw Tellanor, the Secretary, standing in the doorway.

Her red hair cascaded around her shoulders, her green eyes wide and mysterious. Her full, red lips were slightly parted, revealing the hint of perfect white teeth. A thin, white blouse clung to her shapely figure, as did the narrow, hip-hugging black skirt she wore. Her long legs were on display in black stockings, their shape accentuated by her high-heeled shoes. She held another electronic pad in one hand, and bowed briefly, revealing the shadow of her cleavage for a tantalising moment.

'Chancellor,' she said, and stepped into the room, closing the door behind her, smiling as she noticed the effect her presence had on the leader of the Confederacy. That smile disappeared as she noticed the smashed electronic pad on the floor next to the door, and she looked at the Chancellor, a puzzled and questioning expression on her face.

'Secretary,' said Ulestran, and motioned for her to approach the desk. 'I'm afraid I have received some bad news from the Alpha Centauri System. It appears that the Protectorate have invaded.'

Tellanor raised her eyebrows in alarm. 'What's the situation?'

'A Protectorate 'Expeditionary Force' under the command of a Marshal Xoanek entered the system two days ago,' replied Ulestran. 'We were expecting such an attempt, but not one of such proportion. The Alpha Centauri garrison fleet intercepted them in orbit of Ureus. They lost the battle, their flagship was captured, and the Chevalier was killed. The Protectorate fleet is now conducting strikes throughout the system.'

Tellanor sat down, placing the electronic pad she was carrying on the Chancellor's desk. Never one to allow any situation to affect the way she could manipulate men, she crossed her legs and arched back in the chair. Ulestran, despite the gravity of the situation, felt an unbearable urge at the sight of the woman, who was over twenty years younger than him.

'What do you plan to do?' asked Tellanor.

'I plan to strike back!' retorted Ulestran. 'I cannot allow the people to think that the Confederacy is weak – that would invite disaster from within, as well as without. The problem is money. Government borrowing is already very high, and raising taxes is bound to be unpopular, regardless of the cause. The Confederacy is going to need help.'

Tellanor smiled. 'The Feragoths,' she said.

Ulestran returned the smile. 'Precisely,' he said. 'Although I am still unsure as to what they want. The Ambassador is... not exactly forthcoming.' The Chancellor suppressed an involuntary shudder at the thought of the tall, dark-robed alien. 'Still, circumstances now demand it,' he said. 'Send for Detective Turan – he can deliver the message to the Ambassador.'

-#-

Turan half-ran through the corridors of the Chancellery Palace, hurriedly sucking in the smoke from his corch cigarette. His palms were sweating with fear, his hands shaking, and his heart was beating furiously in his chest. His heels clicked on the marble floor of the corridor, the echo bouncing back from the gilded walls. He brushed his hair back against the side of his head with a shaking hand.

He had been acting as the Feragothic Ambassador's Chief of Security for nearly two months now, but found that his services were seldom required. The emissary had remained secluded in the State Apartments of the Palace for almost the entire time. On the one occasion when Turan had contacted him to see if he required any assistance, the alien's response barely hid the contempt in his voice.

Turan finished his cigarette, taking a last drag and feeling his head clear as the narcotic suffused into his bloodstream. He absently flicked the butt out of an open double-doored window, where it flew out into the Quadrangle, dropping onto the gravel courtyard a floor below. He reached for his hip flask and swallowed a mouthful of whisky, clenching his teeth as he did so. The alcohol stung the back of his throat and gave a warm, spreading feeling in his stomach.

Given that it seemed to be only nominal, the job was an easy one, but Turan still hated it. He didn't understand why, but something about the Feragoth fundamentally terrified him. Whenever he was in his presence, the only thing that he wanted to do was to get as far away from the creature as he possibly could. He found himself drinking and smoking more, to create some refuge from the horrors that haunted his thoughts. And now, at the order of the Chancellor, he was to face the emissary once more – his second official duty as the Ambassador's attaché.

Turan stopped outside the gold-laid double doors to the State Apartments, his breath coming in shallow, rapid gasps. He wiped his forehead, daubing away the cold sweat from his brow. His throat felt dry, his loins and bowels too loose. He tightened his pelvic muscles in a desperate attempt to avoid defecating himself.

'He's just an ambassador,' he muttered to himself, trying to drive the irrational terror from his mind, but the words seemed hollow. His thoughts were dominated by the visceral image of the dark, cloaked figure, his clawed hands, white skin stretched over thin bones, like the hand of a corpse.

Turan shuddered, and finally brought composure to himself with a last heroic effort. He raised his hand and knocked firmly on the door.

'Enter!' came a voice from within, loaded with anger at the disturbance. Turan physically cringed at the sound of it, clamping his eyes shut. He forced them to open again, and pulled one of the doors wide.

The darkness inside was almost total, but with a vague hint of a dark red light coming from some unknown source. The door yawned at him like the gaping maw of some awful creature. A wave of heat washed out of the room, like devil's breath. For a moment, Turan was assaulted by a smell, something terrifyingly familiar, but one which he could not place. The scent echoed back to his childhood, and to a primitive instinct buried deep in the oldest recesses of his mind. Steeling himself, he stepped into the room.

'My apologies for the interruption, Ambassador,' he said, trying to pick out the figure of the alien in the gloom. His cold sweat grew warm with the heat of the room, sweltering like a hot summer's day. 'The Chancellor requests your presence as a matter of urgency.'

'Does he?' came a voice from the darkness, dripping with sarcasm. Turan forcibly stopped himself from flinching as he saw a movement in the shadows. Suddenly the alien was standing before him, cloaked, his face obscured by the shadow of his heavy hood. 'Then I will attend to the Chancellor to deliver the representations of the Emperor,' he said.

Turan gulped, staring up at the towering figure, easily seven feet tall. 'If you'll follow me, Your Excellency,' he said, and turned, heading down the corridor. The alien walked beside him, keeping step, and Turan shuddered in fear as he heard his own footsteps echoing down the corridor, but no one else's.

-#-

Turan pushed open the doors to the Chancellor's Office, and bowed briefly before he entered. The Ambassador followed him into the room without paying the same courtesy to the Confederacy's head of state, but it did nothing to wipe the fixed smile from Ulestran's face. His smile was conciliatory, welcome, and completely false. Turan couldn't help but admire the Chancellor's resolve – he surely must be as fundamentally terrified of the alien as Turan, but he was truly a master at hiding his emotions.

Out of the corner of his eye, Turan noticed Tellanor, the Secretary, seated at a side desk on the right hand side of the room, leaning forward just enough to display the shadow of her cleavage down her loosely buttoned blouse. Turan's eyes locked with hers for a moment, and she smiled archly, knowing full well what he was looking at. Turan, pleased to find himself back in familiar territory, simply smiled back, knowing that she had intended to arouse a blush from him.

'Ambassador,' said Ulestran, still smiling and spreading his arms wide. 'Please accept my apologies for disturbing you from your meditations. Unfortunately, circumstances have now changed, requiring expediency in relations between the Empire and the Confederacy.'

'That is quite all right, Chancellor,' replied the Ambassador, and Turan raised his eyebrows in surprise. Given the normal way that the Feragoth interacted with humans, he had expected a blunt retort, but his tone was almost friendly. 'I am now prepared to deliver the Emperor's representations to you.'

Ulestran's smile broadened. 'I am pleased,' he said. 'Won't you take a seat, Your Excellency?' The Chancellor motioned to a chair in front of his desk, and the emissary sat down, his body language difficult to read. 'You have already met Secretary Tellanor?' the Chancellor said, motioning to the red-haired young woman, who gave the alien a bewitching smile. Turan felt his most base desires erupt at the sight of her, juxtaposed with a dislike of her personality. She was harsh, aggressive, manipulative, and ruthless, none of which were qualities he found attractive in a woman, and yet he was attracted to her, simply by virtue of her beauty. It was an unusual contradiction.

The emissary nodded in return, and the Chancellor nodded for Turan to leave. 'I would prefer it if the Superintendent could stay,' remarked the alien. 'His services may need to be provided, and his opinion sought, on my representations.'

Turan stopped in surprise. The alien had made no use of his services since his arrival – he had made it patently clear how irrelevant he considered Turan to be. And yet now, in what appeared to be a complete change of heart, he was asking a mere policeman to be involved in high level diplomatic negotiations.

Ulestran was taken aback, but recovered quickly. 'Of course,' he said, and glared at Turan, making it very clear that if he did anything that would weaken the Confederacy's hand in the negotiations, it would go very badly for him. Turan nodded, and took a seat on the opposite side of the room, where he could continue to keep an appreciable eye on Tellanor. He smirked to himself. Despite his fear of the creature – which was now abating considerably, largely attributable to his sudden change of attitude – he could still build in time for flirtation.

'Let me be direct, Chancellor,' said the emissary. 'The Empire is aware of the outbreak of hostilities between the Confederacy and the Protectorate. We have been watching them for some time, but they are of little interest to us.'

Ulestran sat agape, astonished at the alien's knowledge.

'Our interests lie with the Confederacy,' continued the Ambassador, 'but we are aware that this war with the Protectorate may present problems for you.'

'What problems do you refer to?' asked Ulestran, cautiously, not wanting to reveal his own hand.

'The Confederacy is weak,' replied the alien, abruptly. 'Your economy is faltering, your people restive. Your military is ill-equipped and under-funded. The Protectorate, meanwhile, is armed and ready for war. They have been preparing for this conflict for centuries, and they intend to win.'

Ulestran sighed, realising that there was no way he could bluff the alien. That is what he had been doing for the past two months – watching, waiting and learning. He could not have failed to notice the news reports. This, coupled with his own ample intelligence of both the Confederacy and the Protectorate, put him in a unique position.

'What is it that the Empire offers?' he asked.

The Ambassador settled back in his chair, putting his hands together and arching his fingers. Turan shivered at the sight of the long, white, black-tipped skeletal talons flexing against each other, arched like a cathedral, a living shrine to some deathly god.

'I am authorised to offer you payment of thirty trillion Confederate Credits,' answered the Ambassador. Turan's eyes widened in shock and surprise. Even Tellanor gasped in astonishment at the size of the sum. 'I understand that this represents about half of your government's annual budget deficit,' continued the alien. 'With an appropriate measure of spending reductions and tax rises, you should be able to balance your economy within a matter of months. You will find it much easier to manage the campaign against the Protectorate then.'

Ulestran nodded and wiped his brow. 'How would this payment be guaranteed?' he asked.

'A portfolio of natural resources,' replied the creature. 'Gold, silver, platinum, copper, iron, titanium, diamonds, silicon, lithium... I can provide a complete list, but suffice it to say that they are resources that are essential to your economy, and difficult to obtain.'

'And what does the Empire want in return?' asked Ulestran.

'Our homeworld, *Hqen'Tulaa*, is not our planet of origin,' said the alien. 'My nation, my culture, pre-dates our arrival on that world. Our true homeworld is lost in the mists of time. However, your world bears a close resemblance to the stories told of our ancestral home. That, and the many parallels between humans and Feragoths, are suggestive that we may have a shared heritage. My Emperor wishes to send an archaeological team to this planet, in order to better investigate your history to see if we do share a common ancestry.'

Turan's eyes narrowed slightly. There was something about the alien's change in demeanour which bothered him. Like Ulestran's, it was utterly false. *I may not know much about these aliens*, thought Turan to himself, *but I know a liar when I see one*. There was no doubt in his mind that the emissary had an ulterior motive, one which he was keeping from Ulestran.

'That's all?' said Ulestran, scarcely believing what he was hearing, for it sounded too good to be true. 'You want to pay us thirty trillion credits simply to... study broken stones?' The ambassador nodded slowly. Ulestran's face broke into a delighted smile. 'Done!' he declared, and stood up, walking around the desk, offering his hand to the emissary. The dark-robed creature stood, and took Ulestran's hand.

'I am pleased that you agree to this arrangement, Chancellor,' he said, 'as my Emperor will be.' He released the Chancellor's hand. 'If you will excuse me, I will make the necessary arrangements for the delivery of your materials.' Without waiting for Ulestran to give his permission, he turned and stalked off. His entire demeanour had changed once more, the warm and peaceable stance evaporated and replaced with a cold, hard intent.

Turan stood and dashed over to the large double-doors, opening them for the Ambassador before he strode through them without even a nod of acknowledgement. Turan looked back and saw Ulestran engaged in an animated conversation with Tellanor as they plotted the restoration of the Confederacy and the downfall of the Protectorate. He closed the doors, and almost had to run to keep step with the silent, dark figure.

Whatever it is that he really wants, thought Turan to himself, as he grimly followed the terrifying apparition through the corridors of the Palace, *he's just got it. And everything else was just an act, dispensed with as soon as he achieved his aim*. Turan couldn't help but marvel at the efficiency, the coldly calculated shrewdness and the sheer ruthlessness of the alien. He truly was a force to be feared. Turan couldn't help but feel that whatever the alien had just secured, it would not be to the benefit of the Confederacy at all.

-#-

The Governors' Council Chamber was a huge hall above the Grand Entrance to the Chancellery Palace. At the eastern end, a huge semi-cylindrical bay window dominated the hall, flooding it with the pale morning sunshine. The western end of the room was dominated by a huge wall of glass – a giant window giving a view of the Quadrangle below. A large glass double door was set into the window opening out onto the balcony just above the Grand Entrance.

A high vaulted ceiling stretched upwards, a full two storeys up, decorated with exquisite patterns, gilded in gold and silver. The floor was laid with mahogany and teak, glowing with lustre in the sunlight. Everything about the room expressed opulence and power, for this was the heart of the Confederacy – the nation's primary legislature, as well as its highest court.

In front of the eastern bay window, an ornate oaken throne, upholstered in purple velvet and inlaid with silver and gold, stood on a raised dais, casting a shadow into the main hall in front of it. This was the Chancellor's Throne, the presiding chair of the Governors' Council.

Along the side walls of the hall, smaller thrones stood alongside each other, facing across the centre of the room. These were the chairs of the Confederate Governors – the legislators and judges of the Confederacy, and the enforcers of Confederate law in their own territories.

Slowly, the room began to fill with people as the fifty Governors of the Confederate territories filed in from doors on either side. They chattered with each other, milling about in the centre of the hall, as they waited for the Chancellor to arrive.

Secretary Tellanor entered the hall from the left side, striding across the hall, her stiletto heels clicking loudly on the parquet floor. Her red hair bounced around her shoulders, and her sexuality and confidence immediately changed the atmosphere in the room. The chatter of the Governors fell quieter as she made her way across the hall to the Chancellor's throne. Tellanor was the second-most powerful person in the Confederacy, next to Ulestran. Although she did not hold a particularly high public profile, they were all very familiar with the manner in which she conducted her office.

As she took position standing next to the Chancellor's throne, the Governors began to take their seats, the Secretary's presence a sign that the Chancellor was on his way. At last, silence fell over the Chamber, and the door on the left side opened again.

Ulestran entered the Chamber, walking to the centre of the hall, before turning and walking up towards the throne at the eastern end. Unlike the politicians of the Protectorate, who wore formal robes to signify their rank, the rulers of the Confederacy wore simple business suits. Ulestran's was grey, tailored to his portly figure, and obviously expensive. He smiled at Tellanor as he sat on the throne, and she returned the gesture with a smile of stunning radiance.

'I declare this session of the Council of Governors open,' he stated, his voice echoing slightly in the cavernous Chamber. 'Esteemed Governors, I have called you here today to update the Council on the recent developments in the Confederacy's relations with the Empire of Feragoth.'

Any residual chatter immediately fell silent at the mention of the alien nation, and every Governor looked expectantly at Ulestran, who sat back in his throne, smiling insufferably to himself. 'I am pleased to announce that I have received the representations of the Emperor of Feragoth, via his most excellent Ambassador, currently residing with us as our guest at the Chancellery Palace.'

'His Excellency the Ambassador,' intoned Ulestran, revelling in the high language, 'has requested to land a small team to engage in archaeological research, examining the possibility that we and the Feragothic race may have a shared heritage. In exchange for this, the Empire has offered the Confederacy payment of thirty trillion Confederate Credits, guaranteed as a portfolio of natural resources. I am placing a full list in the Council Library, but suffice it to say that these resources are invaluable to our war effort, and crucial to our current economic circumstances. Needless to say, I have accepted this offer. The Ambassador has assured me that payment will arrive within a matter of weeks.'

The Governors murmured in astonishment. The sudden attack from the Protectorate had caught the Confederacy off-guard, and in the midst of an economic crisis. Their response had not yet been decided, but with this huge diplomatic coup pulled off by the Chancellor, it completely changed their attitudes.

One of the Governors stood up to be heard – Governor Voltar, Ulestran's primary supporter in the Council. He was a short man in his mid-forties, with greying hair and an insidious, cruel look – a product of the Confederacy's political system, tipped to succeed Ulestran as Chancellor when Ulestran retired.

'May I be first to welcome the Chancellor's statement to the Council on this matter,' he said, his voice oily with ingratiation. 'Will the Chancellor confirm how the Feragothic payment is to be used by the Government?'

Ulestran sat back in his seat, smiling. 'I have instructed the Treasurer to bring forward a new budget within the next few weeks,' he said. 'Suffice it to say that this payment, combined with a package of budgetary adjustments, will be sufficient to end the current problems with the public finances.'

Several Governors supporting Ulestran cheered at this. The ongoing issues with the Confederate budget had been a political problem of Ulestran's for some time. He now appeared to have resolved it.

Voltar stood up again. 'And if the Chancellor would in particular make a statement regarding the invasion of the Alpha Centauri System?'

The chamber fell silent again, and Ulestran's smile disappeared, not angry with Voltar for asking the question but merely a pretence appropriate to the seriousness of the situation.

'As this Council knows,' said Ulestran, gravely, 'the Alpha Centauri System has been invaded by an enemy nation identifying itself as the Protectorate. They claim to be the descendants of those exiled from this world one thousand years ago – the last remnants of the Kingdom, in whose Palaces and Halls we now conduct our government.'

He took a deep breath. 'Their stated aim,' he continued, 'is to reignite a centuries-old conflict which killed hundreds of millions of people, to invade and subjugate our citizens, and to overthrow the Confederacy, which has kept the peace for a thousand years.'

'Already, their 'Expeditionary Force' has begun conducting strikes throughout the Alpha Centauri System, using Ureus as a base. This unwarranted aggression on our sovereignty must not be tolerated!'

The Governors murmured in approval.

'I therefore propose to send a Task Force of two hundred starships to reinforce the Alpha Centauri System,' said

Ulestran, 'and to help drive these invaders from our territory.'

The Governors again cheered and stamped their feet, and Ulestran held up his hand for silence. 'Furthermore,' he said, 'I can report to the Council that Confederate Intelligence has intercepted transmissions from the Protectorate fleet, and identified several star systems under their control. One is of especial significance – the Epsilon Indi System.'

'Epsilon Indi,' continued Ulestran, 'appears to be of extreme strategic importance – it is less than ten light years away from Alpha Centauri, and thus appears to be the primary staging ground for their invasion. They seem to have established a wormhole – similar to our own Interstellar Corridors – between the two systems. However, our intelligence sources indicate that the Protectorate also appear to have colonised both the Delta Pavonis and Gliese 783 Systems – both of which appear to be connected to Epsilon Indi.' He paused. 'Occupying Epsilon Indi puts us within striking distance of their entire territory.'

'But the most useful piece of information to this puzzle,' continued Ulestran, 'is that Epsilon Indi is less than twelve light years away from Therqa. The Commissioner for Infrastructure has advised me that it is possible for us to build a new Corridor to the Epsilon Indi System and attack it directly.'

The Governors began to talk amongst themselves, the chatter rising in volume excitedly. Ulestran raised his hand again. 'I therefore propose to the Council,' he said, 'that a fleet of two hundred starships is dispatched to the Alpha Centauri System, that immediate work begins on constructing a Corridor to the Epsilon Indi System, and that a further three hundred ships be dispatched there as soon as possible.'

The chatter rose to a cheer, and Ulestran sat back in his chair, satisfied. The majority he held in the Council ensured that his policies were generally well-received, but the two announcements he had just made would surely be enough to silence the few members of the opposition.

Amidst the howls of applause and stamping of feet, one of the Governors rose to their feet, and Ulestran's smile disappeared. He looked across at Tellanor, and she rolled her eyes at him, her mouth fixed in a grimace of distaste. The Chancellor held up his hand for silence, and the other Governors returned to their seats, leaving only one standing.

Governor Allanor was Leader of the Opposition, and had the support of fifteen other Governors. She was an outspoken critic of Ulestran's government, and had a reputation for calm, incisive questioning that often revealed his political weaknesses. She was something of a maverick in Confederate politics, advocating reform of the electoral system, which was rife with fraud and often subservient to vested interests. She was a woman in a political system dominated by men. But what made her especially controversial amongst the ruling classes was that she was Secretary Tellanor's identical twin sister.

Allanor stood on the right side of the chamber, her seat close to the floor, indicating her superiority as Leader of the Opposition. Hoots and heckles from the government benches sounded loudly, and Ulestran had to stifle a smirk from spreading across his own lips. Allanor ignored the sounds, waiting expectantly for the chamber to fall silent. Her hair was red, like her sister's, but tied back in a ponytail. Her face was just as beautiful, her eyes the same deep green, but her features lacked the cruelty that was so evident in Tellanor's, giving her a softer, gentler and more noble appearance. She wore a smart business suit, which clung to her figure, but revealed little, a sharp contrast to Tellanor's blatant sexualisation. Allanor was certainly not without beauty, but rather than flaunting it as a butcher would his wares, she was reserved, and that added to her beauty, rather than detracted from it.

'I join with the whole Council in thanking the Chancellor for this statement,' she said, as the chamber fell silent. 'I must say it is a welcome change for him to consult the Council *before* taking action on one issue, but a sorry reminder of his contempt for the legislature in terms of his foreign policy with the Empire of Feragoth.'

The calm statement was met with cheers from the opposition side, and howls of derision from Ulestran's supporters. The Chancellor himself seemed irked by it, but said nothing.

'Can the Chancellor inform the Council where the Feragothic research team plans to excavate, or whether he has just given them *carte blanche* to conduct any research they please? Will the results of their research into our 'common ancestry' be shared with us – surely, it concerns us just as much as it does them? And why does he consider that such a generous offer would be made from an alien Empire that we have only just met? Can we be certain that they have no ulterior motives?'

'And as regards the Protectorate invasion of the Alpha Centauri System,' she continued, 'what this Council seems to forget is that the *CBS Iron Crown* destroyed a Protectorate vessel in the Alpha Centauri System three months ago, in an *unprovoked attack*. The *Iron Crown* was also lost with all hands during the skirmish. The determination of the Protectorate seems clear, as does their resolve to defend themselves. Would it not be more appropriate to pursue a course of peaceful negotiation, before we commit the Confederacy to a war which the Protectorate may well fight to the bitter end? And if we are to proceed with this ill-conceived invasion, perhaps it would also be prudent to wait until the budget has been settled, one way or the other, before making defence commitments which may prove unsustainable? I am eager for the Chancellor's answers.'

Allanor sat down, her expression serious, but her own supporters cheering at her forensic demolition of the Chancellor's statement, whilst those on the Government benches continued their tribal howls of derision. The Chancellor stood up, his face fixed in an expression of anger. Tellanor regarded her own sister with outright scorn and hatred.

'I am happy to respond to the Governor's points,' he said. 'As regard to the location of the Feragothic research, I haven't asked, and given the offer they have made to us, which will solve our financial problems and allow us to defend the Confederacy, I think it is a rather churlish point to make! I am sure that such research will be shared with us, but if it isn't, again, it doesn't really matter, given the gravity of our economic condition and defence problems. The Governor could perhaps benefit from the application of perspective!'

Cheers rose up from Ulestran's supporters, and Tellanor smiled sarcastically at her sister. Allanor ignored her, listening carefully to what Ulestran had to say.

'As to her insinuations of ulterior motives,' snarled Ulestran, 'she may do well to remember that it is common courtesy not to insult someone who offers to pay you thirty trillion credits. Of course, given that she knows little of familial ties, I can't expect her to know much about courtesy.'

The opposition benches booed at Ulestran's reference to the well-known disagreement between Allanor and her sister, which was often painted as a betrayal on Allanor's part by her political enemies.

'And on the subject of the Protectorate,' continued Ulestran, 'the Governor proposes peace! Peace with a nation that started the most costly war in our history! Peace with a nation that aggressively invades our own territory, that destroys our starships, and whose stated aim is the conquest of our homeworld! I will be happy to come to the negotiating table with the Protectorate – once we are in possession of the Epsilon Indi System, and our troops are at their gates! You bring your enemies to their knees before you negotiate – then you're in a far better position to dictate terms!'

Ulestran sat down again, and Allanor immediately rose to her feet, her eyes flashing with anger. 'Once more the Chancellor has to revert to personal insults when his policies can bear no scrutiny,' she said, her voice carrying over the howls of her opponents. 'It is clear that this government has nothing but contempt for democratic scrutiny. I urge the Governors opposite to consider this, and rise above petty tribalism.'

Ulestran laughed at Allanor, who once more resumed her seat. 'Thank you, Governor, for your contribution,' he said sarcastically. 'All those in favour of my proposal?' The Governors on Ulestran's side of the chamber all raised their hands, in a clear majority. 'The motion is carried,' he said. 'The Council is dismissed!'

Allanor and the rest of her supporters stood and immediately filed out of the chamber, paying no attention to Ulestran and his supporters heckling them as they left. Tellanor smiled in satisfaction at what appeared to her to be Allanor's humiliation, but Allanor continued to ignore her, leaving the corrupt government to its celebrations.

Chapter Nine

'You did *what?*'

Fedrus was aghast. He stood in his office in the High Command, the view from the window one of the back of the *Inominate* and the Protectorate Lawn which surrounded it. The milk-white marble of Central Plaza could just be seen beyond it.

Adraea and Jamek stood in front of him, fidgeting nervously. He had seen them just leaving the High Command building, after signing up to join the Starforce.

'I told you *both...*' he said angrily, 'not to do anything foolish. Do you understand the situation we are in? The Protectorate is going to war! This is not a game!'

'I understand that, Fedrus,' said Jamek, 'but my father has been killed! What would you have me do – stand idly by and let others avenge his death? You have said yourself that you want to serve in the war!'

'Jamek,' said Fedrus sternly, 'Anzaeus appointed me to be your custodian in the event of his death. I realise that now you have come of age, I cannot stop you from making your own choices, but I would have thought that you would at least heed my advice!'

'I did consider it,' said Jamek, 'but as you say, I am an adult now, Fedrus. And I have made this choice as an adult.'

'You have made it as an angry young man set on vengeance,' retorted Fedrus. 'I grieve for Anzaeus as well, Jamek – but this is war. The Starforce is used to dealing with pirates in forty-year-old ships, not a well-equipped and battle-hardened enemy. We have not had to fight a war in over a thousand years, and we lost the last one.'

'Are you saying we shouldn't fight the Confederacy?' Jamek's eyes flashed with anger.

'I am saying we should not assume that it will be easy to beat them,' snapped Fedrus. 'And that is what I sense here – from the politicians, from the Staff here at High Command... and from you.'

Jamek fell silent, unsure of what to say.

Fedrus turned on his daughter. 'And Adraea!' he almost shouted. 'By all the Guardians... despite my misgivings, I understand Jamek's motivations... but you?! What did you think you were doing?!'

'Dad...'

'I taught you to have more sense than this!' raged Fedrus. He sat down heavily, loosening his tie and drumming his fingers on his desk. 'You are aware that I have deliberately transferred *off* combat duties in order to care for you both? If I had known you were going to do this, I would have gone for a combat role myself, to ensure that you were both serving on my flagship! I suppose Mavrak has engaged in this lunacy as well?'

Jamek nodded, feeling embarrassed. He wasn't quite sure why Fedrus had transferred off combat duties, and the revelation of the reasoning behind it shamed him. 'It wouldn't have made any difference,' he said quietly. 'We've volunteered for the Infantry.'

Fedrus shook his head, putting his hands to his face. 'This lunacy knows no bounds,' he muttered. 'The Infantry?! Both of you are intelligent – so is Mavrak! You could have *walked* into a Fleet unit!'

The Protectorate Starforce was broadly divided into two sections – the Infantry and the Fleet. Fleet soldiers served on starships and starbases, whereas the Infantry were the ground troops and heavy combat units. By joining the Infantry, Jamek, Mavrak and Adraea had made the likelihood of combat significantly higher.

Adraea shifted from one foot to the other uncomfortably.

Fedrus sighed. 'Well, there is nothing for it,' he muttered. 'I suppose you have already taken the oath?'

They nodded.

'Then it's done,' he said. 'Have you received your orders yet?'

'We're assigned to the 103rd Infantry,' said Adraea. 'Under Lieutenant Milus.'

'Don't know him,' said Fedrus shortly. '103rd? That's a new Battalion – brand new. I'll find out who your Regimental CO is. When do you report?'

'Tomorrow.'

'Tarsus have mercy,' he muttered. 'You've volunteered to become bloody *grunts,'* – he spat out the colloquial word for Infantry – 'in a totally new Battalion that's unlikely to have any experienced officers, and you report for duty tomorrow. Utterly superb.'

'I wish you'd spoken to me,' he said. 'Even if I couldn't sway you from joining, you could have gone into the Fleet, and served on the *Combatant* with me. But with the way you've done it, I can't do anything.'

He stood up and walked round the front of his desk to stand in front of Jamek and Adraea. 'You'd better get going,' he said gruffly. 'You'll need to pack. I'll see if I can get your officers to keep an eye on you, but I don't know how much influence I'll be able to exert.'

He turned to his daughter. 'Message me when you arrive at your posting,' he said. 'I want to know where you're stationed. Can you do that for me, at least?'

Adraea nodded, dumbfounded. Fedrus was rarely angry and it always surprised her. She was almost ashamed as she felt the spike of childhood fear in her belly at the sound of her father's voice.

He embraced his daughter. 'Good luck,' he said, hugging her tight. 'And stay safe.'

'I'll try,' she said, her voice breaking slightly. Fedrus pulled back and grasped her shoulders.

'None of that,' he said sternly. 'You're a soldier now.'

She nodded and scrubbed her eyes sharply.

Fedrus turned to Jamek, looking into his eyes and at the strange light that seemed to flicker deep within them. A cold chill ran up Fedrus's spine as he looked into the young man's eyes, and he wondered what his destiny would be. He suspected that he would be no ordinary soldier.

'Good luck, Jamek,' he said and offered his arm. Jamek grasped it by the elbow, and Fedrus did the same. 'Look after my daughter. You understand?'

'I will.'

Fedrus stood back and saluted, placing his fist on his shoulder. His daughter and ward did the same.

'Soldiers of the Protectorate,' he said. 'May the Guardians protect you.'

Chapter Ten

Three starships moved slowly through the darkness, heading towards the light of the distant star. Each ship was shaped like a flattened ovoid, moving forward along the direction of its major axis. The back of each ship opened out in a blackened orifice – the vent aperture for the Ion Drive, propelling the ship forward at sub-light speeds. The hull itself was lined with windows, making the ship design highly unusual – it indicated the presence of decks within the hull. No Protectorate or Confederate ship had more than one deck, due to the methods by which they simulated gravity.

These were ships of the Imperial Feragothic Starfleet, a small convoy recently arrived from their distant, frozen homeworld of *Hqen'Tulaa*.

As they made their silent approach, their hulls reflected starlight and moonlight. They were oddly iridescent, sketching weird patterns on the curved metal. Above them, Therqa's moon shone down, part of the planet's surface barely illuminated by its comparatively dim light. They slowed steadily on their final approach to Therqa, matching speed and velocity with the planet's rotation to enter a geostationary orbit above its North-Eastern continent.

As they did so, giant bay doors on the underbellies of the three ships opened, and half a dozen smaller shuttlecraft emerged, delta-winged and designed for atmospheric flight. They immediately began a descent to the surface of the planet.

-#-

Ulestran's communicator beeped loudly, awaking him. He sat up in his darkened quarters, swearing quietly, pushing a concubine's arm to one side from across his fat, pale chest. The girl – no more than sixteen years old – moaned gently in her sleep, but settled down again. Ulestran grabbed his communicator and tapped the screen.

'Yes, what is it?'

'Chancellor, this is Chevalier Colarian,' came a voice through the communicator's speaker, and Ulestran stood up, pulling on a dressing gown as he did so. The lights in the room immediately lit up, revealing another two young women lying in his bed. One of them scrunched up her eyes at the bright light, and rolled over, burying her head in one of the silk-covered cushions.

Ulestran walked out of his bedroom into the lounge area of the Chancellor's Apartments. The lights went out automatically in the bedroom, and came on in the lounge, as he pushed through the heavy, gold-inlaid double doors, a grim expression on his face.

Colarian was the Commandant of the Confederate Starfleet, the highest ranking officer in the military. If he was waking the Chancellor in the middle of the night, then something was wrong.

'Go ahead, Chevalier,' said Ulestran, tapping the communicator's screen and turning on a video feed.

'Chancellor,' said Colarian, his face clean-shaven, with grey hair and piercing blue eyes. 'We've detected three unidentified vessels entering orbit. They've just dispatched six shuttlecraft to the surface. Their power signatures indicate they are Feragothic in origin.'

Ulestran paused. The Feragothic exploration party. The Ambassador had said they would be arriving soon, but he hadn't expected them for at least another month.

'Have they requested permission to land?'

'No, sir. When we hailed them, they simply told us that they had permission from you to conduct 'archaeological research', and to contact you to confirm.'

'Do not interfere, Chevalier,' ordered Ulestran. 'They are indeed Feragothic ships, and they do have permission to conduct their research. However, I wasn't expecting them to arrive so soon.' He paused. 'Track them, and see where they land. Keep me informed of their movements.'

'Yes, sir.'

The screen went dead. Ulestran tapped the screen again to contact Tellanor, swearing quietly to himself. The Council of Governors would need to be informed, but if it were declared in open Council, Allanor would have a field day. He hoped that Tellanor would be prepared to break the news to her sister privately.

-#-

The Secretary's Palace Office was located on the first floor, just down the corridor from the Chancellor's office, in the corner of the building. The view from the window was very similar, the great, tree-lined avenue leading into the heart of the city to the left, rather than centred. The morning sun seemed cold, the wind moving the leaves in the trees gently. Grey clouds streamed overhead amidst the blue sky.

Tellanor stood behind the desk, looking out of the window. Her dark red hair hung in loose curls around her shoulders, framing her face, where her wide, green eyes sparkled. Her high-heeled shoes clicked on the parquet floor as she tapped her feet impatiently.

It was moments like this in her career which she despised – having to run errands for the Chancellor, because he was too cowardly to do them himself. She shuddered involuntarily as she thought of his clammy hands running over her body. Still, he served his purpose. Without his affections, she would not hold the position she currently did. The inconvenience of duty was simply part of the price of position.

There was a knock at the door. 'Come in,' she said, turning to face the entrance. The gold-gilded double-doors opened, and Tellanor had to physically restrain a grimace as she saw Allanor, her twin sister, standing there.

Allanor was dressed in her typical way – a smart, conservative business suit, her hair pulled back into a simple ponytail. Her eyes glimmered with intelligence, but an open and honest intelligence, without a hint of cunning or cruelty. She stepped into the room, glancing around briefly.

'You asked to see me, Secretary?' she said, addressing her twin sister formally.

Tellanor nodded, and waited as the door closed. The two sisters stood alone in the room, almost diametric opposites of each other. Both exuded sexuality and confidence, but whereas Tellanor came across as aggressive and adversarial, Allanor was calm and rational.

'The Chancellor has asked me to advise you of a development in our relations with the Empire of Feragoth,' said Tellanor, indicating for her sister to sit down. Allanor did so, waiting patiently for Tellanor to continue. The silence visibly irked the Secretary.

'Three Feragothic ships were detected entering orbit of Therqa in the early hours of this morning,' continued Tellanor. 'They launched six shuttlecraft which entered the atmosphere shortly afterwards.'

Allanor sat forward. 'I take it that this is the 'archaeological research team' that the Chancellor was expecting?'

'Yes.'

'They arrived quickly – we weren't expecting them for another month or so, if I understood the Chancellor's most recent statement to the Council,' said Allanor. Tellanor remained silent. 'And the fact that you're informing me about this now means that you didn't know about it until last night, either.'

Again, Tellanor remained silent.

So, either the Feragothic Ambassador is lying about the Empire's technological capabilities in being able to get ships here and well into the Therqan System without being detected,' said Allanor, 'or he brought the ships with him, and he's been planning this little expedition before he even arrived here. Either way, we're being played for fools.'

'It's immaterial,' retorted Tellanor. 'We need their economic support, especially in light of the war against the Protectorate.'

'We wouldn't require their support if we negotiated with the Protectorate,' said Allanor, calmly. 'But I'm not going to be pulled into that particular debate now. I take it the Chancellor wanted this broken to me in private in order to avoid me making a scene in the Council Chamber?'

Tellanor laughed sarcastically. 'He thought that, as Leader of the Opposition, you had a right to know.'

'Spare me,' snapped back Allanor. 'His contempt for the democratic process, or what passes for it in the Confederacy, is well known. So, are we actually aware of where the Feragoths have elected to conduct their research, now that we've let them in without so much as a murmur?'

Tellanor gritted her teeth, trying to keep her patience with her sister. 'They've landed in Dacia,' she said. 'They appear to have settled on a site in the mountains there – it's desolate, and uninteresting. No threat to national security, if that's what you're concerned about.'

'Don't you think it's odd that their exploration team is ready and standing by, and starts landing before the ink on the treaty is even dry?' asked Allanor. 'And that they don't bother with a planetary survey, or a passing glance at our history, but just head straight for one particular site? It's almost as if they know exactly what they're looking for, and where it is.'

'You're paranoid,' snapped Tellanor. 'I'm only informing you as a courtesy.'

Allanor sighed. 'Tellanor, can you put aside your ambition for once and look at this objectively? I have genuine concerns about the Empire. We don't know anything about them or their real intentions. Can we not at least question the Ambassador a little more thoroughly?'

'Out of the question.'

'What about this Detective that's been assigned to him? He seems to have the alien's favour.'

Tellanor laughed sarcastically again. 'You mean Turan? He's a thug – an assassin that Ulestran has assigned to the Ambassador because he's under the illusion that the man is competent. The imbecile is terrified of the Ambassador – it's all he can do to keep from pissing himself whenever he's near him.'

Allanor rolled her eyes at her sister. 'Not your type, sis?'

Tellanor scoffed. 'Don't take your moralising tone with me,' she snapped. 'I'm a realist. I've managed to get where I am today because I've made the best use of what I have. I don't waste my gifts, hiding behind my emotional inadequacies.'

Allanor shrugged her shoulders. 'We can sit here all day and argue about how much we hate each other,' she said, 'but it won't really accomplish much. If you won't let me talk to the Ambassador, am I permitted to talk to this Turan?'

'If you want, although I'm not sure what you good you think it'll do,' said Tellanor. 'I'll tell him to expect your call.'

Allanor stood up. 'If that's everything?'

Tellanor nodded, stood up, and turned her back on her sister, looking out of the window again. Allanor sighed at the gesture. 'I wish things were different between us, Tellanor,' she said.

'No, you don't,' retorted Tellanor. 'You like it just the way it is, so you can continue to take some fictitious moral high ground. But your scruples get you nothing, Allanor – you'll be condemned to lead the Opposition forever.

That's what your so-called principles buy you – failure. And that's just the way you like it.'

Allanor shook her head in dismay, and left her sister alone. She never saw Tellanor's single tear, nor the anger with which she scrubbed it off her cheek.

EPISODE II

REALISATION

Chapter Eleven

Jamek sat in the shuttle, harnessed into his seat with heavy shoulder straps, looking out of the small, porthole-like window. He was wearing his new Starforce uniform – plain green trousers and tunic with a golden metal epaulette on his shoulder, affixed to his belt by a golden chain crossing his chest. The epaulette was blank, indicating his rank of Private.

Outside the window, the shuttle was passing a gas giant to starboard – a huge, mustard yellow ball of swirling ammonia and sulphur clouds, raging storms and lightning bolts the size of Szotas itself. The planet was Vulpes IV, and its inner moon was the home of one of the largest Fleetyards in the Protectorate. It was to this moon that Jamek was now heading – his first posting as a soldier of the Starforce.

Jamek looked across the shuttle, and caught a glimpse of the bright Vulpes star through a window on the port side.

The main shuttle fuselage – a large, boxlike structure – was filled with rows of seats on either side, three men abreast, and a narrow gangway between them. Jamek was sat on the starboard side, Adraea in the middle seat, and Mavrak in the aisle seat. Neon strip lighting behind metal grilles punctuated the ceiling along the central aisle.

After enlisting in the Starforce, all three of them had been subjected to over two gruelling months of physical training on Szotas. That was twenty days ago, when they had departed the planet of their birth for the first time on the three-week trip to Vulpes.

Jamek sighed. The last three months had been hard. He had been thrown into a difficult training regime and fitting into a command structure. Having to deal with grief over his father's death and his burgeoning feelings towards Adraea at the same time had made it even harder.

The Protectorate had already gone to war against the Confederacy, with the Expeditionary Force having won their first victory. Jamek felt worry settle in his stomach at the thought of it – he had not joined the Starforce only to watch the Crusade from the sidelines. He was concerned that the war would be won before he even got to the front lines. And yet, the front lines were closer than ever – the Expeditionary Force had made the wormhole between Vulpes and Panthera permanent, meaning that the front lines were only three weeks away.

Jamek clenched his fists as the rage and grief at his father's death continued to burn inside him. *I will go to Panthera*, he thought to himself, *and avenge my father's death. And then I will go to Therqa, and make them suffer for a thousand years of exile.*

Adraea, sitting in the seat next to Jamek, leaned across and kissed him briefly on the cheek. 'Hey, you,' she said, smiling.

Jamek awoke from his reverie. 'Just thinking about Dad,' he said, trying to smile, but his face remained creased in a frown. Adraea rested her hand on his.

'He'd be proud of you,' she said. 'And he's watching you now.' Her expression clouded at the memory of her last conversation with her own father. Fedrus had been angry, but had grudgingly accepted their decision. Adraea felt that he was trying to force her to choose between him and Jamek.

Jamek smiled in return. 'Call him when we get to the Fleetyard,' he said. 'He'll be happy to hear from you.'

Adraea pulled a face. 'I'll see,' she said.

'He cares about you, and he wants what's best for you,' said Jamek. 'And he's not necessarily convinced that running off on some damn-fool Crusade with me is the best course of action.'

'I know,' sighed Adraea. 'But I still wouldn't be anywhere else.'

The shuttle jolted slightly as it accelerated out of the gravity well of Vulpes IV, rounding the planet and leaving it behind them. Jamek grimaced as he felt his gut churn. The shuttles did not have artificial gravity, and so the contents of his stomach were floating around. It was a disconcerting sensation. He turned to look out of the window again, the thick, tempered glass scratched and worn on the outside, set into the metal hull of the vessel. His chin itched as it rubbed against the thick, heavy shoulder-straps holding him into his seat. His hands brushed against the raised, worn stitching of the shuttle's name embroidered onto the shoulder-straps: the *Diligent.*

The planet outside began to grow smaller and fall back as the shuttle moved away from it at high speed, using its gravity as a slingshot to give it more momentum and conserve fuel. It now sped forward, away from the planet, and towards the moon on its far side.

An intercom speaker above Jamek's head crackled, and they heard the shuttle pilot's voice. 'We have now begun our final approach to Vulpes Fleetyard,' came the voice. 'We should reach the Fleetyard in approximately fifteen minutes.'

There was a murmur of approval from the new recruits. This was their first journey in space, and it had not been a particularly enjoyable trip. Cramped quarters, boredom and having to cope with the occasional zero-gravity environment when not aboard a starship had been testing for them all.

Mavrak cheered. 'Thank the Guardians!' he whooped. 'Let me out of this tin can, already.'

'Shut your mouth, Private,' came a gruff voice from behind them, and Jamek grinned as he recognised the voice of their Company's First Sergeant, Orsus. A seasoned veteran, he had very little patience with new recruits at the best of times, but he was liked and respected by all of them. 'If I have to get out of this damn chair and float over to you, I'm going to be upset. Clear?'

'Yes, sir,' replied Mavrak, cheerily.

'Don't call me sir. I'm not an officer – I work for a living,' growled Orsus. Many of the new recruits laughed, Jamek and Adraea included.

'Yes, Sergeant.' Mavrak smiled to himself. Jamek laughed quietly, and the shuttle hurtled through space, starting to decelerate on its final approach to the Fleetyard.

A few minutes later, Jamek could see the small, rocky moon out of his window. Its surface was a light brown, pocked with overlapping craters from ancient asteroid impacts, and twisted and rent by the gravitational forces from its giant mother planet. He watched it drop down the window as the shuttle oriented itself in line with the moon's horizon, preparing for orbital insertion and landing.

The shuttle's thrusters fired as it decelerated further, and assumed high orbit of the moon. It began to slowly cycle down in altitude, reaching low orbit, before beginning its final positioning for landing. Jamek watched out of the window as the moon's cratered surface gradually drew closer and closer, and he felt its gravity take hold of the shuttle as it slowed down even more.

At the edge of the view, Jamek caught his first glimpse of the Vulpes Fleetyard. It was a massive complex of wide domes built on the surface of the moon, glinting in the pale light from the distant star. Between them, enclosed in great circular arrays, starships in various states of construction rested on the moon's surface.

Up close, it became apparent that the domes were built on stilts, not directly onto the moon's surface, and connected by criss-crossing tunnel bridges. This was part of the reason that the Fleetyard was built here. The moon's proximity to Vulpes IV meant that it was constantly being stretched and pulled by the relentless gravity. This created friction deep below its surface, which gave rise to geothermal energy. With this limitless energy supply, it provided a perfect environment for the high-powered requirements of a military fleetyard. However, it did mean that the moon suffered from frequent earthquakes. The buildings of the Fleetyard were mounted on stilts fitted with special dampers, and each had buffers and counterweights inside to absorb the shock of sudden tremors without damaging the buildings.

The shuttle approached one of the drydocks where the ships were moored, and touched down on a landing pad extended from the superstructure of the building. The shuttle jolted slightly as it set down, and then again as it eased back into the docking port. The moon had no atmosphere, so any ships had to be physically connected to the buildings when docking. Finally, the shuttle's engines powered down, and the pilot's voice came over the speakers again.

'We have now docked with the Vulpes IV Fleetyard,' he said. 'You may now release your shoulder harnesses. The Fleetyard is a low-gravity environment – please activate your magnetic boots and wristbands immediately.'

Jamek unclipped his shoulder restraint and loosened the heavy straps, sighing in relief as he massaged his shoulders. He could immediately feel the low-gravity of the moon, noticeable compared to the weightlessness they had encountered on the shuttle whilst in flight. It was still only slight compared to the gravity of a planet, or that simulated by a starship, however. He tapped buttons on the two metal wristbands on his arms. The powerful electromagnets inside immediately activated, pulling his arms downwards towards the floor and simulating the pull of gravity. He did the same for the heavy, cumbersome boots he wore, and felt more slightly more comfortable as the quasi-graviational effect took hold.

He, Adraea and Mavrak waited patiently as the other new recruits filed off the shuttle through the rear of the ship, where a large, square door had opened out onto a corridor of the Fleetyard facility. Mavrak, impatient at waiting, jostled into the queue of soldiers and held them back, allowing Adraea and Jamek to step in front of him. After a few uncertain steps in their magnetic boots, they stood in the corridor.

Their grizzled First Sergeant shouted down the corridor at the milling troops. 'Line up, you mother-lovers!' he shouted. 'What do you think this is – some high society *soirée*? Get in ranks, and stand at attention – you're in the Starforce now! And clear that airlock – you think the Ensign wants to smell you when he gets off? Move out of the way!'

The troops jumped to attention, forming ranks quickly and marching about twenty feet down the corridor in perfect step. Jamek fell into ranks at the back, just next to First Sergeant Orsus on the outside.

'Platoon, halt!' Orsus roared, and the fifty or so soldiers stopped in unison. He nodded in satisfaction and marched back to the airlock. Jamek risked a sideways glance, and smiled as he saw the Sergeant stand to attention and salute as the Ensign stepped out of the airlock. Ensign Kaelkar was a fresh-faced young man, about five years older than Jamek, but he had received his training at the Starforce Academy. As such, despite his youth, he was a commissioned officer, not an enlisted man. Their Sergeant commanded their Platoon, and also acted as second-in-command of their entire Company, second only to Kaelkar.

Kaelkar returned Sergeant Orsus's salute. 'Report, Sergeant,' he said evenly.

'1st Platoon stands ready, sir,' said Orsus impassively. 'Awaiting your inspection.'

Kaelkar smiled faintly. 'Do they meet with your approval, Sergeant?'

'Barely, sir. I just managed to drag them kicking and screaming into line before you disembarked, sir.'

Kaelkar laughed. 'High praise indeed,' he said, and glanced down the corridor. 'Ah,' he said. 'We have company.' He nodded down the corridor past the assembled troops. Jamek snapped his head round to see a stern-looking man dressed in blue with four eight-pointed stars engraved on his epaulette. A Captain – presumably the Fleetyard Commandant.

Kaelkar and Orsus marched down the corridor to meet him in front of the troops. Kaelkar saluted.

'Ensign Kaelkar, commanding Bravo Company, 103rd Infantry. Permission to come aboard, sir?' he said.

The Captain returned the salute. 'Captain Terrus, Vulpes Fleetyard,' he said. 'Permission granted. You have orders?'

'Aye, sir.' Kaelkar pulled an electronic pad from his pocket and handed it to the Captain, who scanned it briefly.

'The rest of the Battalion is on the way?' he asked.

'Aye, sir,' replied Kaelkar. 'This is my 1st Platoon – my others will be arriving shortly.'

The Captain nodded, and handed Kaelkar back his orders. 'Who commands the Battalion?'

'Lieutenant Milus, sir.'

'I take it he is with Alpha Company?'

'Aye, sir.'

'And that you are his First Officer?'

'Aye, sir.'

'Very well, Ensign. Fall your men out. Report to Commander Tyrus in the Command Centre – he will assign you quarters. Have Lieutenant Milus report to me on his arrival.'

'Aye, sir,' replied Kaelkar again, and saluted. Captain Terrus returned the salute and walked off back down the corridor. Jamek half-smiled as he saw Kaelkar and Orsus physically relax once the Captain had left. Even Jamek's own commanders were not immune to the effects of rank.

'Attention!' barked Orsus, noticing Jamek's smile. Jamek immediately stood to attention, his expression serious once more. Orsus stepped up close to him, his scarred face only inches from Jamek's own. 'You find something amusing, Private?'

'No, Sergeant!' answered Jamek firmly, remembering not to address Orsus as 'sir'. That would probably have earned him a punishment.

'Good,' snapped the First Sergeant, pleased at Jamek's definite and confident response. 'Private Psinaez, isn't it?'

'Yes, Sergeant!' Again, Orsus looked pleased, or as pleased as it was possible for the old soldier to look. It was customary to only say 'Aye' to an officer.

Orsus glanced briefly at Kaelkar, who nodded in assent to some silent exchange which passed between them. Orsus stepped back and addressed the whole Platoon.

'You may notice something about this Platoon,' he said. 'We have no Corporals. This is because this is a new Battalion, formed entirely from new recruits, because all our best soldiers are with the Expeditionary Force, kicking the Confederacy's guts out of its arsehole!'

The soldiers shouted a single grunting syllable in appreciation, and Orsus nodded. 'So, Ensign Kaelkar has decided to go for try-outs,' he said. 'We need three Corporals, no more and no less. Each of you will be assessed. If you happen to meet the Ensign's exacting standards, you will be promoted. If none of you meet those standards, I will personally kick every single one of your lazy arses back to Szotas. Do I make myself clear?'

'Yes, Sergeant!' shouted the Platoon in response.

'The Ensign and I are to report to the Command Centre, to get you pitiful excuses of soldiers beds for the night,' sneered Orsus. 'Although the Captain may yet decide to let you sleep in the corridors. Private Psinaez!'

Jamek nearly jumped out of his skin as Orsus turned to him and screamed in his face. 'Yes, Sergeant!' he roared back.

'You will assume command of the Platoon, retrieve all Platoon gear from the shuttle and transport it all to Assembly Hall C,' shouted Orsus. 'The Ensign and I will meet you there in exactly one hour for inspection. If it is inadequate, I will hold you personally responsible. Is that clear?'

'Yes, Sergeant!' said Jamek, his eyes widening with astonishment at the responsibility. He had commanded fire-teams and the occasional Squad in training exercises, but he had never commanded more than fifteen troops at a time, and never on actual duty.

'Carry on, Acting Corporal.'

Jamek snapped off a salute, and stepped forward out of rank. In response to Jamek stepping out of ranks, the other troops immediately re-organised themselves to present as a seamless and uniform block. Orsus and Kaelkar stepped back, watching.

'You heard the Sergeant!' shouted Jamek. 'Private Mavrak, bring me the Platoon inventory. Private Fedrus, locate Assembly Hall C. The rest of you, break into your squads. First squad, inside the shuttle, breaking seals and opening hatches. Second squad, shuttle door, passing gear out. Third squad, with me, inventory and ready to carry – heaviest loads first. Let's get to it!'

Orsus smiled briefly, the expression misplaced on his gritty features. Kaelkar nodded in satisfaction and turned, his Sergeant next to him as they headed towards Command Centre, leaving Jamek barking orders and falling into the natural step of command.

Chapter Twelve

Xoanek strode through the corridors of the *Vehement*, heading towards the Command Centre. The warning klaxon sounded, its atonal pulse echoing loudly in the corridor. Over every doorway, red warning lights flashed, indicating that the ship was at Battle Stations.

Crewmen ran up and down the corridor, rushing to their positions. The air was not filled with panic, but rather a cool, urgent professionalism, and Xoanek nodded to himself in satisfaction. The crew of the *Vehement* had conducted themselves excellently thus far, as had the crew of every ship in the Expeditionary Force.

Since the first action in the Battle of Panthera six weeks ago, around the planetoid which had been dubbed Panthera III, the Expeditionary Force had pressed deeper into the Panthera System, engaging sporadic Confederate defences. With the fleet now *en route* to their next target, they were the subject of harrying attacks by Confederate forces, probably in an attempt to slow them down.

Abruptly, the Battle Stations sirens fell silent, and Xoanek heard his First Officer's voice over the intercom. 'Normal Stations,' he reported. 'Stand down from Battle Stations.' Xoanek smiled to himself, but kept on heading towards the Command Centre, in the knowledge that the fleet would now resume its course deeper into the system.

Panthera was a tertiary system, containing three separate stars. The two main stars were bright and yellow, much like Kaathar, and orbited each other at the centre of the system. The third star was a red dwarf, a small, cold, dark star, orbiting the central stars at a distance of over a fifth of a light year. It was almost far enough away to be considered out of the Panthera System proper – its orbit was so slow it was almost unnoticeable.

The Protectorate fleet's efforts had been based around the central stars. The red dwarf was too cold and dark to really sustain life, and therefore was of little strategic importance. The other stars were a different matter entirely. Two major planets orbited the larger, hotter star – one a gas giant, smaller than Astralas, the largest planet in the Lupus System, but still impressive. This had been named Panthera II. The other was the Expeditionary Force's primary target – the only inhabited planet in the system, Panthera I. However, in order to achieve the objective of occupying the planet and thus annexing the system, Xoanek needed to secure high orbit of Panthera II, to prevent it being used as a staging ground for a counter-attack.

Panthera IV was a scorched ball of blasted rock in a tight orbit around the second central star. Although Xoanek thought that it may be of some scientific interest, it held no strategic value, being too hot to colonise, and with no significant resources to warrant occupation.

Xoanek walked into the Command Centre, limping slightly as he favoured his left leg. He frowned to himself and ignored the pain. The wound had healed well, but it still ached from time to time. The ship's surgeon told him that the pain was only in his mind, so Xoanek tried to disregard it. It wasn't always easy.

The command crew stiffened to attention. 'Marshal on deck!' shouted one, and Captain Shivaeus, Xoanek's First Officer, turned and saluted. Xoanek nodded in return.

'Report,' he said.

'Another routine attack,' replied Shivaeus. 'A Confederate squadron made a strafing run across the fleet's ventral aspect, trying to break through to the centre to scatter us. I issued orders to let them through, and close the gap behind them. Total enemy losses, no damage, no casualties.'

'Good,' said Xoanek. 'Carry on, Captain. I'll be in my quarters.'

'Aye, sir,' replied Shivaeus, and saluted again as Xoanek left the Command Centre.

These sporadic attacks had been persisting for the last few days as the Expeditionary Force made its way across the interplanetary gulf, heading for the gas giant of Panthera II. Apart from slowing progress in order to conduct minor repairs, they had had little effect on the fleet. The Expeditionary Force had settled into a tactic of deliberately opening their lines, absorbing the attack and then destroying the intruding vessels as they became trapped in the steel shoal of ships travelling through the emptiness.

The planetoid Panthera III, the site of the first action, and of the attack on the ill-fated *Provident,* had been occupied by a small holding force. A few dozen survivors from the *Provident* crew had been found in crashed lifeboats on the far side of the planetoid. The rest of the crew had either been killed on the *Provident*, had their lifeboats destroyed in the subsequent explosion, or died after the crash onto the planet.

Xoanek was keen to get to Panthera II as soon as possible. He wanted to demonstrate the power of the Protectorate Starforce, both to galvanise support for the Crusade at home, and to drive fear into the hearts of his Confederate opponents. He smiled to himself wryly. His personal battle on the Command Centre of the *Golden Eagle* had served well – his men now looked on him with a sense of adoration, of utter loyalty and devotion. They would follow him into the mouth of Hell.

Yet, despite all of his plans and machinations, doubt still lingered at the back of Xoanek's mind. He couldn't help but feel that there was something he had missed, but he couldn't, for the life of him, conclude what it was. He shrugged it off as he returned to his quarters, and sat down in an armchair, picking up the electronic pad he had been reading and sighing contentedly.

After a short while, the Marshal began to doze, and the electronic pad slipped from his hand, sliding gently to the floor. Xoanek slept, dreaming of conquest.

-#-

The ship rocked with the sudden impact, flinging Xoanek from his chair and awaking him with a bone-jolting blow as he crashed onto the floor. He grunted and pulled himself to his feet as the Battle Stations klaxon began to sound again.

'Damn it,' he muttered, as the ship was hit again. He ran from his quarters, down the corridors where the sirens blared and the warning lights flashed. He sprinted into the Command Centre, and met a scene of confusion, almost panic. The crew were dashing from post to post, madly relaying orders. Some were trying to keep fires under control, others were busy obeying the frantic orders of the First Officer.

'Marshal!' he said, relieved as Xoanek sat in his chair.

'Report, Captain,' said Xoanek smoothly.

'We're under attack,' replied Shivaeus, urgently. 'They came out of nowhere...'

'How many ships?'

'At least a hundred and fifty, sir,' answered the Sensors Officer behind him. 'They're in a crescent formation, trying to encircle us.'

Xoanek swore. This was a different tactic to the ones the Confederates had been using thus far, one that threatened the position of the Expeditionary Force significantly. 'Signal the fleet to break formation,' he ordered. 'Our Group is to lead a charge straight into their centre. Signal Group Two to follow us. They must not encircle us – I want their lines broken!'

'Aye, sir!'

In the darkness of space, the Expeditionary Force was a glinting shoal of silver fish swimming in the black tide. It was encircled by a crescent fleet of giant spheres, silently lashing the ovoid formation with deadly fire. The horns of the crescent gradually widened as the Confederate fleet tried to surround the Protectorate formation.

The *Vehement*, larger than most of the other ships in the fleet, suddenly burst out of the fleet, blazing fire from its missile apertures, and another sixty or so ships followed it. The fleet broke formation, dividing this way and that as it sought to defy the attempted encirclement by the Confederate starships.

The *Vehement* plunged into the Confederate lines, turning this way and that amongst the wreckage and burning hulks of starships that lay in its path. Missiles flared and exploded, blasting searing-hot shockwaves across the night sky. The *Vehement* took a heavy blow on its port side, sending it spinning away to starboard.

Xoanek felt his stomach lurch as the ship careened out of control. 'Get us back!' he shouted, fighting the controls at the Helm, trying to stop the ship pitching madly. It finally righted itself and continued its smashing charge through the Confederate lines. It dipped and weaved, dodging fire, dealing out death and destruction as it went.

Xoanek bit his lip, his heart racing. His palms felt cold and clammy as they held scant grip on the steering column. The Flight Display showed complete carnage – Protectorate ships colliding head-on with their Confederate counterparts in deathly embraces, silent explosions and the glint of the system's two yellow stars, cold and distant, on metal hulls. The *Vehement* took another hit, and a computer behind Xoanek exploded, spraying out hot circuits and broken glass. The air was filled with the familiar stench of burning metal, and Xoanek screwed up his nose, fighting the gag reflex in his throat.

'Tactical, fire at will,' he said grimly. 'Stop for nothing. Get us through their lines.'

'Groups Three and Four reporting that the Confederate fleet is separating in the centre!' shouted the Communications Officer.

Xoanek grinned. 'We've broken their lines,' he said. 'I'm bringing us about...' Xoanek stopped as the Flight Display cleared, the last ships of the Confederate fleet pulling apart. His blood ran cold. Ahead of them was *another fleet.*

'May the Guardians have mercy,' he muttered. The crescent formation had been a feint. They had deliberately goaded him into charging their centre, then pulled back to reveal another fleet behind. Now, the Expeditionary Force was trapped between two fleets – one behind, and one in front. Completely surrounded.

'Dive!' screamed Xoanek, as he pushed his steering column forward. 'Signal all ships to drop pitch ninety degrees!'

The Protectorate ships immediately nose-dived, scrambling to get away from the two converging Confederate fleets before they were completely trapped. Four out of the five Groups managed to drop out of the way before the Confederate fleets met in the centre, but the rearguard of the Expeditionary Force, nearly thirty ships, was trapped.

'Switch to aft view,' ordered Xoanek, and the view on the screen shifted to give a display of the rear perspective, looking behind the *Vehement.* The command crew watched in horror as the Protectorate ships were blasted to pieces by the converging Confederate fleet. They were outnumbered nearly ten to one against their enemies, and unable to use their manoeuvrability to secure an advantage. The disc-shaped ships exploded in bursts of deathly flame, burning briefly before being extinguished in the freezing, airless vacuum, the ruins of their broken hulls drifting slowly apart as they finally died.

Xoanek cursed himself. *Thirty ships, destroyed.* The Confederate response had been masterful. Attacking consistently and continuously, using apparently obvious tactics, to lull him into a false sense of security. They had been planning this since the Expeditionary Force left Panthera III.

'Signal the fleet to drop pitch another ninety degrees,' he ordered, gritting his teeth, 'and full Ion Drive. Set a course to Panthera III.'

'Sir?' Shivaeus looked at him in astonishment.

'You heard me!' Xoanek barked at his First Officer. 'We need to fall back and re-group. The Expeditionary Force cannot win the Battle of Panthera alone. The Confederacy has more teeth than we imagined. I will not blunt ours fighting uselessly.'

Xoanek sat back, exhaling deeply and slowly. He had underestimated his enemy. He would not make the same mistake twice. He only hoped that his mistake had not cost him more than he yet realised.

-#-

After a few hours, Panthera III came back into view, the planetoid which they had left only a day or so earlier. Of course, with every ship in the fleet rocketing towards it at full speed, it didn't take long to reach it.

Xoanek's blood ran cold. Orbiting the planetoid was not a Group of thirty Protectorate starships, but a fleet of nearly one hundred Confederate starships.

'Panthera IV,' he muttered to himself. 'They came from Panthera IV. They were hiding there, betting that we would attack Panthera II first. They've been leading me along since we first entered the system.' He realised for the first time since entering the Panthera System, the true measure of his enemy – far beyond anything he had ever fought before. Their grasp of strategy was supreme, their resourcing excellent. Their steely resolve in being able to sacrifice men and ships for a greater strategic aim was almost unbelievable, and their ability to assess his own tendencies uncanny. Disastrous though it was for him, and ultimately the Protectorate, he couldn't help but marvel at their brilliantly ruthless efficiency.

'Battle Stations,' he said. 'All hands to Battle Stations! Signal the fleet to strafe past the planetoid, and set course for the Vulpes wormhole.'

'Aye, sir,' said the Communications Officer, and the Protectorate fleet, with three Confederate ones converging on it, began to take fire.

Xoanek closed his eyes and muttered a silent prayer as the *Vehement* took heavy fire, blasting the ship this way and that, its escorts exploding in fiery plumes. His hopes of conquest were gone, evaporated in the heat of battle, burned in the crucible of defeat. His only real hope now was to get back to the Protectorate with as many of his men alive as possible, and prepare for the attack that would inevitably follow such an audacious and stunning strategic victory.

Chapter Thirteen

Jamek led his Squad of fifteen troops, running in circuits around the edge of the gymnasium in full body armour, complete with packs, weapons and ammunition. The room was filled with the sound of their heavy magnetic boots slamming onto the steel floor, and the pants and gasps of the troops as they ran.

Jamek glared ahead through the tinted visor of his helmet, designed as a shield against shrapnel and the bright sunlight of the planets which the Starforce Infantry found itself deployed to. He exhaled sharply, briefly fogging up the toughened glass. His chest was burning with the effort, his arms and legs were leaden with the magnetic boots and vambraces on his forearms. His back ached with the weight of his pack, and he could feel hot sweat running in thin rivulets between his shoulder-blades.

With the Vulpes Fleetyard being a low-gravity environment, First Sergeant Orsus had set the entire

Company a gruelling training schedule to prevent their muscles from wasting. Jamek was leading his Squad in a two-hour run in full gear in the gymnasium. After an hour's break, during which they would eat one of their five daily meals, was weight training.

Orsus stood in the centre of the gymnasium, in black shorts and a white T-shirt, his grey hair cut short, his arms and chest thick with solid muscle. He glanced at his watch, strapped just below the magnetic vambrace on his forearm.

'Five minutes left, Corporal!' he shouted. 'Quicken the pace!'

'Yes, Sergeant!' barked Jamek. 'Squad, with me!' He began to run faster, and some of the soldiers behind him groaned.

'Silence!' shouted Jamek, and forged ahead, his chest burning, his eyes streaming. His troops matched his pace, assured by their commander's willingness to lead them from the front.

Orsus nodded approvingly, letting the Squad run. He glanced at his watch – at twenty seconds out, he issued another order.

'Form ranks!' he shouted suddenly. 'Form ranks now!'

Jamek raised his open right hand, and immediately the running huddle behind him reformed into a running square of troops, each matching pace perfectly with the others. Jamek ran at the front, glancing behind him and noting his Squad's change in formation.

'Charge!' roared Orsus. 'Charge!'

For the last fifteen seconds, the Squad broke out into a full sprint, their footsteps like thunder as they clanged in the empty gymnasium. A loud, guttural roar echoed round the room as the Squad changed course, running down the centre of the room, passing Orsus at a distance of a few feet, screaming at the tops of their voices. Six feet from the opposite wall, Jamek raised his right fist, signalling an immediate halt, and in perfect time, the Squad stopped, slamming their feet into the steel deck. Jamek dropped his fist, and they immediately stood to attention, turning to the right.

Jamek swivelled on his foot to face right, then marched out four steps, then turned right again, marching until he was in front of his troops. He then turned left, to stand directly in front of them, facing the same direction, and stood at attention.

Orsus nodded and walked up to Jamek, his metal boots ringing on the deck. He looked up absently at the ceiling, crossed with bulkheads which also ran down the walls. Strip lighting cast a pale glow on the floor, which reflected dully.

Orsus stood in front of Jamek. 'Good job, Acting Corporal,' he said. 'You may stand at ease.'

'Yes, Sergeant,' said Jamek, slowing his breathing down, visibly relaxing. The other troops behind him did the same.

Orsus grinned savagely. 'Ensign Kaelkar wants to make sure that our Company is the best in the Battalion,' he said. 'And I'm going to make sure that our Platoon is the best in the Company.'

'Then my Squad will be the best in your Platoon, Sergeant,' said Jamek.

Orsus laughed gruffly. 'We'll see,' he said. 'I want a longer sprint tomorrow. You are in the Infantry, Acting Corporal – and the emphasis is on mobility. A Protectorate Infantryman is expected to be able to run twenty miles in a day, then charge across two hundred metres of broken ground to meet the enemy at full sprint and still have enough energy to fight and defeat them. Do I make myself clear?'

'Yes, Sergeant.'

'Good.' Orsus nodded. 'Fall your men out, and go to mess. Report back to me in one hour for weight-training. Don't over-eat – any man who's sick in my gymnasium gets to eat it cold for breakfast.' He took a step back.

Jamek nodded, and turned to face his men, stamping his feet together. 'Squad!' he shouted, 'Attention!'

The troops each stamped their left foot down hard next to their right, standing up straight. Jamek smiled slightly as Adraea risked a brief smile to him from the second rank. Even in the most serious of moments, she could always be relied upon to lighten the mood.

'Good work today,' said Jamek, 'but you heard the First Sergeant, and you heard me – we will be the best Squad, in the best Platoon, in the best Company in the Starforce, and I won't settle for anything less! Do you hear me?'

'Yes, Corporal!'

'Lunch is served in the mess hall,' continued Jamek, 'and you will report back here in one hour for weight-training. Squad, right turn!'

The soldiers turned to the right.

'Squad, fall out!'

The squad marched forward three steps as one, before breaking ranks, and sighing in relief at the end of the ordeal. Jamek pulled off his helmet, blinking at the bright lights in the gymnasium, and wiped the sweat from his brow.

'Acting Corporal!' said Orsus, and Jamek looked up. 'Can I have a word?'

Jamek walked over to the First Sergeant, an enquiring expression on his face. 'Yes, Sergeant?'

'Ensign Kaelkar has concluded his try-outs for Corporals,' he said. 'You're being awarded permanent command of this Squad.' He held up a gold, five-pointed star, and handed it to Jamek. 'Congratulations,' he said brusquely. 'Don't let me down.'

Jamek smiled. 'I won't, Sergeant. Thank you.'

Orsus waved his hand in dismissal, and Jamek closed his fist around the new rank insignia. He turned, looking for Adraea, a smile on his face.

-#-

Jamek sat back on his bunk, crossing his hands behind his head. He smiled to himself, turning his head to look at his dress uniform hanging on the chair next to his bed, with the gold star embroidered on the sleeves and collar.

'Corporal Psinaez Jamek,' he murmured to himself, relishing the sound of it. Not bad for his first assignment. Adraea, curled up on the bunk next to him, laughed quietly.

'Are you still on about it?' she laughed playfully, digging her fingers into Jamek's ribs. 'Yes, yes, well done. Everyone's very impressed.'

'Everyone's very impressed... Corporal,' corrected Jamek, grinning.

Adraea pouted and smacked Jamek lightly on the arm. 'Don't you pull rank with me,' she said, kissing him on the cheek. 'Not when we're off duty, anyway.'

Jamek's brow furrowed. 'Have you spoken to your father yet?'

Adraea fell silent. 'I sent him a message the other day,' she said. 'It'll reach him in about a week, I guess.'

'Good,' said Jamek. 'What did you say?'

'Just trying to explain why I joined up,' she said, looking awkward. 'I don't know whether he'll understand.'

'Do you feel better for it?'

'A bit, I guess. You were right.'

Jamek nodded. 'Believe me, if I had the chance to talk to my Dad...' his voice trailed off. 'When's Mavrak back?' he said, changing the subject.

Mavrak had been assigned to a patrol ship – the *PSS Constant* – temporarily, while it conducted a routine patrol of the trade routes in the Vulpes System. The routes were plagued by pirates, and the Starforce's presence was constantly required to police the interplanetary shipping lanes. He had been on patrol for about a week, and so had not yet heard the news about Jamek's promotion.

'Another week,' said Adraea, swinging her legs off the bunk as Jamek stood up. Her magnetic boots hit the floor with a clang. Jamek stretched his arms. Despite the low gravity of the base, his chest and arms were now thick-set with muscle, a result of the gruelling training schedule.

'It'll be good to see him again,' said Jamek, looking around the empty bunk room. He shared the room with the rest of his Squad, but they were currently out at lunch, giving him a few scant moments alone with Adraea.

'Do you miss him?' asked Adraea. Jamek snapped his head round, looking for signs of teasing in her face, but saw none.

'Yes,' he said. 'He's my best friend. I...'

Suddenly, the base rocked with a violent impact, and the strip lights dipped briefly. The shock threw Jamek to the floor, but he quickly leapt up. 'What the...?' he muttered, but was interrupted by another jolt, this one accompanied by the sound of a distant explosion.

The base's intercom crackled. 'Battle Stations – all hands to Battle Stations!' came a voice over the speakers. 'The Fleetyard is under attack! Repeat, Battle Stations – all hands to Battle Stations!'

The emergency klaxon immediately began to sound, red alarm lights flashing madly. 'By the Guardians,' muttered Jamek, a spike of panic jabbing his heart. He and Adraea immediately ran over to the far side of the bunk room, pulling open several cupboards which contained their combat uniforms.

The rest of the Squad quickly filled the room, shouting as they strapped on chest-plates and pulled on helmets. Jamek's mind flashed – he had to contact Sergeant Orsus and find out exactly what was going on, but he also needed to get his Squad armed, and quickly.

'Red Squad!' he shouted, and the room fell silent, fifteen pairs of eyes turning to look at him. 'Report to the Armoury on the double! I want you fully armed in one minute! Let's move, move, move!'

They ran out into the corridor, falling seamlessly into formation as they jogged easily in their heavy combat gear. It felt light and mobile compared to what they had trained in. Jamek tapped a communicator mounted on his forearm. 'Sergeant Orsus, this is Corporal Psinaez, Red Squad,' he said urgently.

'Go ahead, Corporal,' came the First Sergeant's voice.

'We're *en route* to the Armoury, Sergeant – we'll be armed in one minute, and in position in two,' continued Jamek.

'Belay that, Corporal – once you're armed, report to the Command Centre,' said Orsus. 'The enemy are launching attack shuttles – looks like they intend to board the base. I want our best men protecting the commandant – and that's you.'

'Yes, Sergeant,' said Jamek, feeling a private thrill at Orsus's praise. 'Who's the enemy?'

'It's a Confederate fleet,' came the answer. 'They've invaded in a surprise attack.'

Jamek's blood ran cold for a moment, and then his world was filled with a raging hatred. He felt more alive than he had ever done before, as if some flame was burning inside of him. 'Understood, Sergeant,' he said. As he turned into the Armoury, he shouted to his troops.

'Take as much ammunition as you can carry!' he shouted. 'The Confederacy have invaded the Protectorate, and look set to board the base! We have been assigned to defend the Command Centre. Fix bayonets, and let's teach these Confederate scum a lesson! For the Protectorate!'

His troops roared in anger and determination, ready to meet their ancient enemy in battle for the first time.

-#-

Within minutes, Jamek and his Squad were setting up a heavy blockade in one the corridors outside the Command Centre. Jamek watched as Adraea directed the effort to install bulletproof shields at staggered points along the corridor. The base's commandant, Captain Terrus, stood next to him, watching.

'I told Kaelkar I wanted the Command Centre defending heavily!' he muttered. 'He sends one Squad? Is that all?'

'Ensign Kaelkar will be defending the other exit, and Sergeant Orsus's Squad will be here momentarily,' replied Jamek, evenly. 'I assure you, sir, the deck will be well-defended.'

'I can't spare officers to help you with a firefight in the corridors,' said Terrus, leaning against the wall as the base rocked with another impact. 'Return fire!' he shouted at the Tactical Officer.

'I don't expect you to, sir,' answered Jamek. 'Indeed, I think it would be a good idea if you close the blast doors on both sides of the Command Centre.'

Terrus looked at Jamek, amazed. 'But you'll be cut off,' he said. 'If they hammer you, you'll have nowhere to retreat to.'

Jamek's soldiers stopped their work temporarily, as they heard this. Jamek grinned at Terrus. 'We're soldiers of the Protectorate, Captain,' he said. 'We don't retreat. We'll cut them to pieces, or die trying.'

'Corporal!' came Adraea's voice, 'Sergeant Orsus is here!'

Jamek nodded. 'If you'll excuse me, Captain,' he said, and turned to meet Orsus, who had arrived with his Squad.

'Report,' he snapped at Jamek.

'I've set up staggered defences along the length of the corridor,' said Jamek, indicating. 'Ensign Kaelkar is defending the other entrance to the Command Centre with two Squads. I've requested that Captain Terrus seal the blast doors to better protect the command crew.'

Orsus nodded. 'Good,' he said. 'My Squad will take the forward four positions.'

Terrus watched Jamek and Orsus calmly deal with the prospect of being shut out in the corridor against a well-armed and determined enemy, with no possibility of retreat. Just then, another shattering impact shook the base, and the Chief Engineer shouted. 'Hull breach, Captain! Confederate troops have entered the base!'

Orsus turned to the Captain. 'Better go, sir,' he growled. 'Lock yourself in. We'll handle them, but fight off those bloody ships!'

'We'll do our best,' said Terrus, stepping inside the Command Centre. He pressed a button next to the doors, and the blast doors – two feet thick and made of solid steel – began closing on either side. 'Good luck, gentlemen.' The doors sealed with a clang, leaving the two Squads alone in the corridor.

Jamek took his position, next to Adraea, and Orsus patted him on the shoulder as he walked down towards the front of the fortifications. Jamek's face was grim.

'They've sealed us out?' asked Adraea.

Jamek nodded. 'No falling back.' Adraea looked at him, and could have sworn for a moment that she saw something in his eyes – a flicker of yellow flame in the darkness. She shook herself and held out her hand to him.

'For the Protectorate,' she said.

Jamek took her hand. 'For my father, Psinaez Anzaeus,' he said. 'And revenge.'

-#-

They came only a few minutes later.

At first, there were only a few shadows moving at the end of the corridor, barely visible. But then came two heavy smoke grenades, billowing out a thick fog. 'Masks on!' shouted Orsus as a precaution, just in case it was some form of poison gas. Jamek clipped his respirator across his face, where it fitted snugly under his yellow visor.

Then they heard the roars, and the thundering footsteps. 'Fire on my command!' ordered Orsus, kneeling behind one of the forward defences. They were staggered in height to give maximum coverage, allowing those behind to shoot without fear of hitting their own troops in front.

Jamek's heart pounded, his mouth dry. He felt sick. His hands were sweaty under his armoured gloves. His neck and ears burned with heat. That awful moment, staring ahead at the broiling fog, seemed to never end.

Finally, the Confederate troops burst through. They were armoured, wielding heavy machine guns, and their heads covered by thick, heavy helmets, a protruding metal snout under a thin, black visor. They looked completely alien to Jamek – it was hard to imagine that under the armour was a being just like him.

'Fire!' bellowed Orsus, and the world was filled with the hum of electricity.

The first hail of laser pulses took out four Confederate soldiers, sending them collapsing in shrieking heaps of burnt flesh. One of them threw a grenade as he fell to the floor, but it bounced off one of the makeshift fortifications. It exploded on the Confederate side of the barricade, scorching the corridor walls, but doing little damage.

They kept coming. Jamek felt his rifle thrum in his hands as he fired pulse after pulse, each scorching blast hitting a Confederate troop and bringing him to the floor. All he knew was a world of death, his terrible focus solely on killing as many of the enemy as he could. The pigs that had stolen his homeworld. The bastards that had murdered his father.

One of the Confederate troops threw a grenade, which arced high into the air, before dropping down over the first fortification and exploding. The shrapnel tore into the two troops there, shredding them into chunks of ragged flesh. Immediately, two Confederate troops took up position behind it, using it as a base to lay fire on the barricade staggered behind it, on the opposite side of the corridor.

'Damn it,' muttered Jamek, and pulled one of his own grenades. He took aim, throwing it high, and it landed just on the opposite side of the barricade, where it detonated, incinerating the two Confederate soldiers there. He smiled and continued firing.

A hail of grenades came through the fog, exploding like thunder in the air. A few troops at the front were hit, wailing in agony. Jamek saw Orsus stand up, clearing his view, and unload a wide spread of rounds, taking down six charging Confederate soldiers. To his horror, he saw the big Sergeant hit by Confederate fire and fall to the floor.

Jamek yelled out and charged down the corridor to Orsus. He waved for his own Squad to move further down to man the barricades. He found Orsus lying between two fortifications, clutching a bullet wound in his stomach. Jamek pulled him back up the corridor to the blast doors and propped him up against the wall.

Orsus groaned, and pulled his helmet off, spitting blood on the floor. 'The bastards got me,' he said. 'Thirty years I've served the Protectorate – never been hit. And some Confederate *fuck* manages it.'

Jamek moved quickly, cutting the straps that held Orsus's armour on and trying to bandage the wound as best as he could.

'You're going to be fine, Sergeant,' he said. 'We'll get you out of here, just as soon as we've finished off these bastards.'

Orsus grabbed Jamek's arm. 'Leave it,' he said, and looked into Jamek's eyes. 'I've been fighting for thirty years, son – I know a fatal wound when I see one.' He coughed up blood, wheezing as he struggled for breath, his skin pale, his eyes beginning to glaze.

He pulled Jamek close. 'You're in command now, Corporal,' he said, weakly. Don't...' he fell silent and slumped to the floor, his eyes still open.

He was dead.

Jamek closed his eyes in silent grief, then picked up his rifle again. 'For the Protectorate!' he screamed, and charged back down the corridor, firing wildly.

The Confederates had managed to secure the first three barricades and were pressing the Protectorate troops further back. Jamek laid as much fire on as he could, but there were simply too many of them. They were outnumbered over ten to one. He watched as his men were cut down one by one, until there were only ten left, and he realised that there was no escape.

He turned to Adraea, who was sitting next to him, and squeezed her hand one last time. She squeezed back and fixed her bayonet to her rifle. Jamek did the same. 'I'm sorry,' he said, as a single tear rolled down his cheek. He scrubbed it away angrily.

'Don't be,' she said, and hugged him, her helmet clashing against his. 'No one could foresee this.'

'I guess we'll be seeing my Dad sooner than we thought,' said Jamek bitterly. 'Squad!' he shouted. 'Charge!'

They charged the Confederate line in one final act of desperation. Jamek jabbed his bayonet into the neck of one enemy soldier, bringing him down, before impaling another in the gut. He watched as his soldiers were mowed down by Confederate bullets, the air filled with the stench of electricity and gunpowder, the floor slick with blood. He screamed as he saw Adraea fall, shoulder-charged by a Confederate soldier who threw her into the air like a rag doll. But then he was hit himself, knocked to the floor, and darkness, sudden and complete, overtook him.

-#-

Mavrak sat in the Command Centre of the *PSS Constant*, studying the console screen in front of him intently. He had been aboard for just over a week now, on a temporary rotational assignment to give him some experience of shipboard duties. Today was his first duty shift in the Command Centre, manning the Engineering position.

The Command Centre itself was laid out very similarly to that of the *Provident* – both ships were *Adamant*-class frigates, which formed the backbone of the Protectorate Starforce. They were used routinely for patrols, light convoy escorts and could also be configured for scientific expeditions.

'Watch your ion intermix levels,' murmured Petty Officer Sorris, sat next to Mavrak. Mavrak nodded, tapped the screen of his terminal, and Sorris nodded approvingly.

Sorris was the Ion Drive Foreman, one of the Engineering Staff. Although only a Corporal, he had earned himself the non-commissioned officer rank of Petty Officer, and was treated as equal to an Ensign. He was only a few years older than Mavrak, perhaps twenty-five, with dark hair and eyes, and a thin, wiry frame. His blue uniform had a gold, five-pointed star and a black, eight-pointed star on his rank epaulette.

Mavrak sighed. He had considered his basic Infantry training difficult, but shipboard duties were considerably more challenging. The Protectorate expected all of its military staff, even Infantrymen, to be at least familiar with shipboard operations, and all the complexity that it entailed. Over the last week, Mavrak had been working with the Engineering team, learning how to regulate the *Constant's* Terculium Reactor and Ion Drive, monitoring its power systems, life support and engines. It was a far cry from push-ups, tactical fire-teams, and running in heavy armour. Nevertheless, he enjoyed it – it was a welcome change of pace.

The ship's commanding officer, Captain Tecris, sat at the Helm, in front of the huge, curved Flight Display. He was a native of the Canis System, which was evident from his dark skin, which gleamed in the light from the massive screen. He had dark eyes and startlingly white teeth, his head and face smooth and hairless.

The Canis System had a single star which was over six times brighter than Kaathar. Out of the three inhabited planets in the system, Tecris was from Shivor, the colony closest to the star. Although much of Shivor's surface – particularly in the equatorial regions – was uninhabitable, the poles were densely populated. The colonists there generally had dark skin, an adaptation to the Canis sun's blistering heat.

Although Tecris was nearly fifty, he had an ageless quality which Mavrak envied. *I hope I look that good when I'm that age*, he thought to himself, but somehow doubted it.

'We are on approach to Vulpes III – ETA in three hours at this speed,' said Tecris. 'Sensors, any suspected pirate activity?'

'None, sir – all quiet.'

Tecris nodded. Their job was to patrol the system's trade routes for pirates, and to engage and destroy them if they found any. Tecris knew from long experience that they tended to congregate around the poles of Vulpes III – the large gas giant was unusual in that it had no moons, and was therefore generally deserted, but high orbit was a fuel-conserving oasis in the desolation of space. It was even rumoured that the pirates had established a permanent base in the high reaches of the planet's atmosphere.

'Continue scans,' said Tecris. 'Communications, monitor all frequencies – I want to know if anyone's talking out there.'

'Aye, sir.'

Sorris chuckled to himself. 'Same shit, different day,' he murmured quietly, nudging Mavrak in the ribs.

'I don't follow,' said Mavrak.

'It's the same every time we go on patrol,' explained Sorris. 'We go out pirate-hunting, scanning for activity and monitoring radio frequencies, but we very rarely find anything. It's almost as if the pirates turn tail and hide when the Big Bad Starforce comes looking for them... I mean, if you're a thief just trying to earn a dishonest living in your forty-year-old *Reliant*-class spacebound wheelbarrow, and then a whopping great frigate turns up that's three times the size of your ship, what would you do?'

Mavrak smiled. 'I guess I wouldn't just pop up and say hello,' he said.

'No, you'd shut the hell up and stay still,' grinned Sorris. 'And pray to the Guardians that said frigate doesn't find you and blow you to bits. And surprise, surprise – there's nobody here but us.'

'Petty Officer,' said Tecris, turning his head to face Sorris, who was sat behind him and to the left, 'you have a suggestion?'

'Only that the Starforce could perhaps give us one or two transports to act as bait so we could catch some pirates, sir,' answered the engineer, smiling. 'Because without temptation, they sure as hell aren't going to come out and say hello to us!'

Tecris smiled faintly. 'You may be right, there,' he said. 'I'll be sure to bring it up with the Commodore when I talk to him.'

The other officers laughed quietly.

The Sensors Officer interrupted. 'Sir, I have something!'

'Yes?'

'Reading several ships approaching from the planet – on an intercept course, sir!'

'Ready Stations,' ordered Tecris. 'You were saying, Petty Officer Sorris?'

Sorris gulped. 'I guess I spoke too soon, sir.'

'They'll scatter as soon as they see what they're up against,' muttered Tecris. 'They must be bloody fools to think they can take on a frigate.'

'Uh, Captain?' said the Sensors Officer, a hint of fear in his voice. 'These ships aren't pirate sloops. They're... much bigger, sir.'

'What? Tactical view.'

The Flight Display flashed, displaying a tactical outline of the sensor readings. It showed several ships, approaching the *Constant's* position, not the disc-shaped ships of the Protectorate, but spherical spacecraft.

'By the Guardians...' breathed Tecris. 'Battle Stations!' He turned the ship around, opening up the throttle for the Ion Drive at the same time. The ship lurched as the gravity was momentarily disrupted by the sudden maneouvre.

Mavrak felt panic rise in him, and he swiped his console, transferring the control to Sorris. He was happy to deal with it when on a training mission, but in a combat situation he was out of his depth. Sorris took control, tapping the screen.

'What the...?' Sorris muttered. Mavrak looked at the Flight Display and realised where he had seen those ship schematics before... these were Confederate battlecruisers.

'Oh, shit,' said Mavrak.

The Battle Stations klaxon sounded loudly. Tecris turned to the Communications Officer. 'Contact the Vulpes

Fleetyard,' he said. 'Tell them to get reinforcements here as soon as possible – we're not going to be able to outrun them.'

'Sir, the Fleetyard isn't answering!'

'How can that be?' said Mavrak. 'We only had contact from them a few hours ago! Unless...' A cold chill settled over his heart.

'They've already been attacked,' finished the Captain. His expression was severe. 'I'm setting a new course for the Tarsus colonies. Sensors, how long until those ships reach us?'

'At full speed, they'll be within weapons range in about an hour, sir.'

Tecris nodded, accepting it with calm. 'And we won't reach the Tarsus colonies before then.' It was a statement, not a question. 'All hands, this is the Captain. We are being pursued by Confederate battleships. Prepare to engage the enemy!'

-#-

The *Constant* weaved through the slow Confederate battleships, dodging missiles that flared past its hull. Occasionally, it would take some fire, a missile exploding as it impacted the armoured hull, knocking it this way and that.

The ship used its speed and manoeuvrability to good effect as it whipped madly between the cumbersome

Confederate ships. It darted between two, causing them to crash into each other in pursuit, exploding in silent spherical plumes of violent flame.

Inside, Tecris issued more orders as he deftly piloted the ship, steering it hard to port. 'Sensors, any indication of weaknesses yet?'

'Still working on it, sir!'

'Work quickly – I want targets to shoot at!' snapped the Captain. 'I'm not going to be able to dodge and weave forever!'

The ship rocked with an impact, knocking Mavrak to the floor. He was now wearing his heavy infantry armour, wielding his pulse rifle, along with a few other infantrymen assigned to protect the Command Centre. He exhaled sharply as the breath was knocked out of him, but leapt to his feet without complaint.

'Hull armour is buckling, Captain!' shouted the Tactical Officer. 'We can't take another hit like that!'

Tecris cursed, and pulled his steering column backwards, pitching the ship ninety degrees. Mavrak's stomach lurched as the ship rocketed upwards.

'I have a target, sir!' shouted the Sensors Officer. 'Their Command Centres appear to be on their polar regions!'

'Any armour?'

'Likely to take a few missiles to get through, sir.'

'We haven't got many!' shouted Tecris. 'It'll have to do. Tactical, you heard the man – lock target and fire when ready.'

'Aye, sir.'

The *Constant* bore down on one the Confederate ships, and its gun ports blazed silently. Four missiles blasted out, smashing into the hull of the enormous ship and exploding as the *Constant* pulled up, almost grazing the hull of the Confederate vessel as it wheeled and dived away.

'Direct hit!' shouted the Tactical Officer, and the command crew cheered as the Confederate ship began to drift listlessly. For a giddy moment, Mavrak thought they could do it – *if we can just keep moving, we'll be able to outwit these slow, dull-witted Confederate ships...*

Two workstations nearby exploded, showering him with broken glass. The ship spun full circle with the impact, and Mavrak felt the world tilt crazily as the ship lost gravity, flinging him up to the ceiling and down to the floor again. One of the other troops landed on his head, and Mavrak winced in horror as he heard the sickening crack as the soldier's vertebrae shattered, breaking his neck. Part of the ceiling caved in, exposing the bulkhead above, and Mavrak tasted blood in his mouth as he bit his tongue.

For a moment, he lay on the floor, gasping for air as he struggled to draw it in to his protesting body. It finally came in a thin, ragged gasp. He heaved himself to his feet, clutching his rifle. He looked around – the Command Centre was a scene of total carnage. The ship had obviously been hit badly. The lights flickered, the computer panels crackled with static. He saw that Captain

Tecris was lying on the deck, his dark eyes open, staring sightlessly upwards. He was dead.

Mavrak looked around. 'All the officers are dead,' he muttered. He leaned against the Tactical station. 'Sorris, are you there?'

'I'm here,' came a croaking voice. Sorris sat up. He had a nasty-looking cut on the flesh of his neck – close to the artery. It was bleeding heavily. He tore a strip off his uniform, binding it tightly across the wound.

'The officers are dead,' said Mavrak. 'What are your orders?'

'Oh, I don't know!' said Sorris, the panic evident in his voice. 'I'm a bloody engineer, Mavrak! I don't know the first thing about this kind of shit! I've never even been in a battle.'

'Neither have I,' said Mavrak. 'Can you drive this thing?'

'A bit.'

'Take the Helm. I'll handle Tactical.'

Sorris nodded, and stepped over his Captain's lifeless body to take his place. Mavrak slid into the chair next to him.

Mavrak tapped the Tactical console, trying to get a picture of the ship's status. It was bad. The hull armour was compromised in several places, leaving them vulnerable to further fire and boarding parties. 'Get us moving!' he shouted.

Sorris tapped his console, and the ship began moving forward again. 'I don't know what to do!' wailed Sorris. 'I'm not supposed to be here!'

'Corporal!' shouted Mavrak, grabbing hold of Sorris's collar. 'Get a hold of yourself! You are a soldier of the Protectorate! Act like one, or I'll fucking shoot you! Is that clear?'

Sorris turned and found himself staring down the muzzle of Mavrak's pulse rifle. The cold reality of it seemed to calm him somewhat. 'Aye, sir,' he said, leaving Mavrak almost dumbfounded, as he realised that he was in command.

'We've got three attack shuttles aft,' he said. 'Can you bring us about?'

'Turning a hundred and eighty degrees to starboard,' said Sorris, and Mavrak felt the ship swing around. The Flight Display settled on three shuttles heading towards them, containing boarding parties.

'Oh, no, you don't,' he muttered between clenched teeth, and fired. One of the shuttles exploded, hit by a missile. Another exploded a moment later. Mavrak targeted the last ship, but realised that the *Constant* had ran out of missiles.

'Jamek,' he murmured. 'Adraea.' If the Fleetyard had been attacked, he had no way of knowing if they were alive or dead. He somehow doubted he'd ever see them again.

It seemed ridiculous. He'd volunteered to help conquer the Confederacy, and here he was to meet his end. Not even a year into his military career, barely out of training, and dying on a starship in the cold depths of space, defending the Protectorate from invasion.

The last attack shuttle latched onto the hull, and there was a clanging noise from behind the Flight Display as it did so.

'They're coming through the fucking screen,' spat Mavrak. 'Prepare for boarding parties!' He and the other surviving infantryman cocked their rifles. Sorris jumped out of the Helm seat, running over to Mavrak and pulling his own sidearm, pointing it at the viewer. Mavrak nodded, as the Corporal had now regained his composure.

The air was filled with a deafening screech as the attack shuttle's saws cut through the hull. Sparks flew from the Flight Display, which shattered and crumbled to the floor, exposing the now white-hot deckplates behind. 'Steady!' shouted Mavrak over the noise. 'Fire only on my command!' He flicked down his yellow visor, staring at the dancing sparks in the gloom. His heart beat steadily, and all the world seemed to slow.

Suddenly, the howl of the saws stopped and the hull plates behind the shattered Flight Display collapsed. A thick piece of the hull came crashing into the room, painted white and bearing a large letter 'T' from the ship's nameplate. Then four Confederate troops ran screaming into the room, and the air was filled with the deafening ratchet of machine gun fire.

'Fire!' shouted Mavrak, and his rifle hummed as laser pulses blasted two of the enemy soldiers. Sorris took a bullet in the head, collapsing to the deck. Mavrak glanced at him briefly, and noticed a bleeding, star-shaped hole in his forehead. He was dead.

More troops ran onto the Command Centre from the yawning breach in the hull. Mavrak roared in anger, firing wildly at them, gunning them down. He noted their faceless helmets and their heavy armour, but they did nothing to stop his laser pulses.

The other Protectorate soldier fired in conjunction with him, giving an even spread of fire, as they had been trained. Maximum kills using minimum ammunition. A pile of corpses lay on the fallen deck plate, and still more Confederate soldiers came.

After what seemed like age, but must have only been minutes, Mavrak's magazine was depleted. He pulled his sidearm and continued firing. Finally, another Confederate troop managed to return fire. A spray of bullets took the other Protectorate soldier in the neck and chest, knocking him to the floor in a mangled heap of blood and bone. Mavrak screamed as he felt one take him in the shoulder, biting through his armour, and he collapsed with the pain.

'Cease fire!' he heard someone shout, and through the fog of agony, he saw a masked face looking down at him. The figure raised a gun, and Mavrak stared into the muzzle, wondering what it would be like in Heaven.

'You are under arrest,' came the voice again, raspy through the helmet, 'and are now a prisoner of the Confederacy of Nations.'

That was the last thing Mavrak remembered before he blacked out.

Chapter Fourteen

Xoanek sat at the Helm of the *Vehement*, staring ahead at the Flight Display. The stars wheeled around, arced lines of blurred light spinning in crazy circles. The ship was now in a wormhole, travelling through warped space-time at a speed faster than light, streaming across interstellar space – the vast, empty gulf between the stars. They were travelling through the wormhole established by the *Provident* on its fateful mission to the Panthera System. Since then, Xoanek had ordered it upgraded to a permanent one. As such, the journey back to Vulpes would not take much longer.

The journey had been horrendous. Their flight out of the Panthera System to the entrance to the wormhole had taken nearly a week at sub-light speed, and they had been harried by the Confederacy every single step of the way. Only fifty-seven of the two hundred ships that comprised the Expeditionary Force had survived.

The *Vehement*, like the other surviving ships, was in poor condition. Xoanek looked around the Command Centre. Consoles were still broken and smashed, and the light still flickered. Although the ship's engineers had been working round the clock since they entered the wormhole to repair the ship, the damage was so severe that there was limits to what they could do. And yet, the *Vehement* had managed to return home.

Xoanek closed his eyes in silent grief at the memory of the final battle at the vortex to the wormhole. The wormhole throat was not wide enough for all of the starships to enter at once. They had only be able to go through two at a time, and the journey back was limited to those ships who still had Wormhole Drive capability. Some ships had voluntarily stayed behind, to fight off the Confederate attacks while the others escaped.

Xoanek cursed himself silently. He had gone to Panthera with the aim of conquest, of glory, of reclaiming their lost homeworld and avenging his people against the Confederacy. And now, because of his own arrogance, his fleet was in tatters, his soldiers dead or defeated, his campaign ruined, the survivors fleeing back across space with their tails tucked between their legs. He would probably lose his position as Marshal as a result of this. He'd be expected to retire, although others in the General Staff would privately advocate his suicide.

The old man shook himself angrily. Now was not the time for such thoughts. Now was the time to develop plans for the defence of Vulpes, for the Confederacy would surely attack it. And Vulpes, having been stripped of its garrison to form the Expeditionary Force, was not currently in a position to defend itself. It would take some considerable effort to fight off the Confederate forces if they did invade.

'Marshal,' the Captain Shivaeus, the First Officer, spoke up, shaking Xoanek from his reverie. 'We're approaching the exit vortex of the wormhole.'

Xoanek sat up straighter, his eyes regaining a little of their lustre. He scratched the days-old grey stubble that covered his chin, and coughed to clear his throat. 'Prepare to deactivate the Wormhole Drive as soon as we've cleared the vortex,' he said.

'Aye, sir. We're leaving the wormhole throat... now.'

The view on the Flight Display began to change. The wheeling stars and patterns of light slowed and finally stopped, arranging themselves in familiar constellations, yet the view became tinged with a silver, metallic glow. They were in the wormhole vortex – the doorway to the tunnel in the Vulpes System. Xoanek sighed with relief. They had made it.

'Hull pressure decreasing,' said Shivaeus, managing the controls. 'I'm letting our momentum carry us to the interface edge.'

The *Vehement* cruised forward steadily in the ghostly silver light, until finally it burst forth from the vortex and into open space. The vortex itself was a giant, translucent silver sphere of viscous, metallic liquid, the size of a small moon, glowing with a weird, ethereal light. The throat of the wormhole was at the sphere's core, and now, the *Vehement* had journeyed from its materialisation at the core through to the liquid ball's outer edge, and burst through the surface into the darkness of space.

'We're out,' said Shivaeus, smiling in relief. 'Wormhole Drive disengaged. Ready for sub-luminal flight, sir.'

'Assume high orbit of the vortex,' ordered Xoanek. 'I want to make sure everyone who's coming got back in one piece.' He turned to the Communications Officer. 'Contact the Vulpes IV Fleetyard,' he said. 'Let them know our condition. Tell them we are in urgent need of repair.'

'Aye, sir.'

'Several other ships are already in high orbit of the vortex, sir,' said the Sensors Officer. 'More of the fleet is coming through now.'

'Good,' said Xoanek.

'Sir, the Vulpes IV Fleetyard isn't responding,' said the Communications Officer. 'I'm just reading radio silence.'

Xoanek's brow furrowed. 'That's odd,' he said. 'Try the Vulpes II colonies.'

'I have them, sir. Audio only.'

'On speakers,' ordered Xoanek. 'Vulpes II, this is Marshal Xoanek of the Protectorate Starforce, Commander of the Expeditionary Force. Do you copy?'

'Marshal Xoanek...' came a voice, crackling over the speakers. 'Thank the Guardians you're here! We're under attack... Confederate forces... Felis System... shipyards on Vulpes IV... destroyed... landed ground troops. Please come as quickly as you can! Wait... no... wait...'

The transmission cut off.

Xoanek felt his blood run cold. He turned to the Sensors Officer. 'I want a full sweep of this system!' he ordered. 'I want that transmission confirmed!'

The Sensors Officer nodded, his face pale. 'Confirmed, sir,' he said. 'I've detected close to three hundred Confederate ships in the system. Most of them are in orbit of the Vulpes II colonies, but there's also around fifty in orbit of Vulpes III and IV.'

Xoanek collapsed back into his chair, his heart cold as stone. He had fled back to the Protectorate, only to find it in the midst of a Confederate invasion, with them already in possession of most of the Vulpes System. If Vulpes were to fall, there would be nothing to stand between the Confederacy and the Lupus System – Szotas itself.

'May the Guardians have mercy,' he muttered to himself. He felt exhausted. The terrible retreat from Panthera had taken its toll on all of them. The handful of ships he had left under his command were in poor condition, their crews despondent and depressed by the agony of defeat. They were in no condition to take on a well-equipped, battle-hardened Confederate fleet, and yet Protectorate territory was now compromised. Honour demanded that they intervene.

Xoanek took a deep breath. 'Have all ships cleared the vortex?' he asked.

'Aye, sir,' replied the Sensors Officer.

Xoanek turned to the Communications Officer. 'Put me through to the entire fleet,' he said.

'Attention, Expeditionary Force,' began Xoanek, speaking aloud. 'This is Marshal Xoanek. I have just received word, confirmed by our sensor reports, that the Confederacy have invaded the Vulpes System. The Protectorate is under attack.'

He took a deep breath. 'I know you are all tired, and I know that our ships are badly in need of repair and re-supply. I know we have seen friends and comrades die. I know we have tasted the bitter pill of defeat. But now we must put that to one side. The Great Crusade is a noble cause, but now it must wait, for our homeland is under attack. So I ask you to lift your hearts, to rise up, to shake the fatigue from tired limbs and minds. The Protectorate needs us all, and I, for one, am prepared to fulfil my oath as a soldier, and to give my life in defence of her. We fly to Vulpes II, and we will strike at these Confederate oppressors that dare attack us! Long live the Protectorate! And long live Szotas!'

-#-

Although Vulpes was technically a tertiary system, the other two stars were so small and dim and orbiting the larger, yellow star at such a distance that it was effectively a single star system. Vulpes II was a large, ringed gas giant planet in a close orbit of the main Vulpes star, its atmosphere rent by powerful storms, ribbons of cloud, and violent aurorae that burned permanently on its poles. Its rings were a grey-blue, pulled close to the planet by its immense gravitational field. Although the planet itself was completely uninhabitable, its moons made it an ideal colony location.

Vulpes II – nicknamed Tarsus, after the Guardian who forged *Seyotaal* and built the Guardian Temple on Szotas – possessed two large moons, which were large enough to be planets in their own right. At the distance from the star, only one of them – Telsor – was warm enough to host liquid water on its surface, and the polar ice caps dominated sixty percent of its surface. Yet the equatorial regions had a moderate temperature, and so it could support life. Because of this, it had grown into one of the Protectorate's key colonies.

The other moon, Alvor, which moved around its parent planet in a closer orbit, was locked in permafrost, yet an ocean of water existed just beneath the thick crust of ice, one teeming with life. It was this ocean, this rich source of food, which made it an ideal colony, despite the harshness of its conditions.

Now, both moons, each home to millions of people, were besieged. The great, glinting spherical hulks of Confederate starships orbited them, spread out uniformly around each moon, stars of iron. Every now and again, one would fire at the surface, delivering lethal ordnance in support of their troops on the ground. Others would launch small troop transports to their Command Centreheads on the surface, reinforcing and re-supplying.

Xoanek watched the scene unfolding on the Flight Display, his heart burning with desperate rage. The Fleetyard in orbit of Vulpes IV had indeed been destroyed. It wasn't known whether there were any survivors, and with a Confederate fleet still occupying high orbit, Xoanek had ordered the remnants of the Expeditionary Force to head straight to Tarsus to relieve the colonies. And this was the sight that awaited them.

'We'll make them pay,' Xoanek snarled through gritted teeth. 'Have they detected us yet?'

'If they have, they're showing no sign of it,' reported the Sensors Officer. 'But the gravitational disruption should hide us effectively. Unless they have a telescope trained out of a window, we're effectively invisible.'

The Expeditionary Force was maintaining position over the gas giant's North Pole, very close to the ring of the burning aurora, as particles of solar wind were funnelled down its gravitational field onto the atmosphere. This made them very difficult to see, and gave them at the least the possibility of a surprise attack.

'We'll go for Telsor,' said Xoanek. 'Signal the fleet to assume attack formation and punch straight through their mesh. They're not expecting an attack from above. Once we're in amongst them, stay together – do not break formation. Pick them off one by one. With any luck, with concentrated firepower, we'll have taken out a handful of them before they even realise what's happened. They'll panic and break orbit.'

'Aye, sir,' replied the pilot and Communications Officer, who relayed the commands to the rest of Xoanek's fleet.

Xoanek slowly clipped his seatbelt, looking around the Command Centre at his crew. He took a deep breath, and felt the blood rush in his temples, the familiar deathly calm before the fury of battle. 'Battle Stations,' he said.

-#-

The *Vehement* weaved to and fro between the burning hulks of Confederate vessels, the remnants of the Expeditionary Force in tight formation around it. Its gun ports blazed fire, silent missiles streaking across the curved, white horizon of the colonised moon. One of the neighbouring Protectorate ships exploded in a brief shower of flame, before the fire quickly extinguished in the frozen, airless vacuum of space. Another ship came to the fore to take its place, and the fleet swung to port in complete synchrony, like a flock of steel birds in flight, before diving down on another Confederate ship, missiles blasting towards it.

The *Vehement* rocked as it took fire from its new target, and the Command Centre deck shook beneath Xoanek's feet. 'Hold course!' he shouted, glaring ahead at the Flight Display. 'Tactical, target their Command Centre and life support. I don't want their core to breach this close to a Protectorate colony. Fire to disable only.'

'Aye, sir.'

'Fire!'

The deck plates thrummed as the *Vehement's* missiles were launched, slamming into the spherical hull of the Confederate starship, which began to drift out of orbit. The lights shining from windows in its outer hull flickered before disappearing completely.

'The ship's beginning to lose attitude control, sir,' reported the Sensors Officer. 'She'll fall out of orbit in about four hours.'

'We'll worry about her later,' said Xoanek, grimly, as he brought the ship about. 'Note her position. Communications, any idea of which one is her flagship?'

'Not yet, sir – their transmissions are a bit frenetic. They weren't expecting us to attack.'

'I want to identify their flagship as soon as possible!' shouted Xoanek over another powerful blast which rattled the ship. Another missile hit which knocked the ship in a loop, and Xoanek felt his stomach lurch. Instinctively, his hands gripped the the steering as the ship's gravity was momentarily disturbed, his seatbelt keeping him from being thrown from his chair.

'Hull breach!' shouted the Chief Engineer. 'Hull breach in Section Fourteen! Sealing emergency bulkheads.'

'Tell the fleet to maintain formation,' said Xoanek. 'We'll only get out of this if we can concentrate our firepower. Target the ship that just fired at us, and signal all ships to do the same.'

'Aye, sir.'

The Protectorate fleet swung about again, this time charging straight upwards, away from the planet to the Confederate ships above them. Some of the Confederate vessels were still in a loose grid formation to provide maximum coverage over the planet's surface for orbital bombardment. The Expeditionary Force, in an arrowhead formation, tore upwards and smashed through the

Confederate lines, several ships being blasted apart by the concentrated fire. Once the fleet was above the lines, it re-grouped before diving down again, thundering past the slower Confederate ships at breakneck speed.

'I've found their flagship, sir!' shouted the Communications Officer. 'All their primary fleet communications are directed there. I'm sending the co-ordinates to you now.'

Xoanek smiled. 'Setting a course. Signal the fleet to lock on target.'

'Aye, sir.'

The enemy flagship quickly came into view on the screen, hovering above the wintry horizon. The ship was noticeably larger than many of the others in the Confederate fleet, its hull scarred and seared from weapons fire. Xoanek grinned tightly as he saw the ship, and he felt his heartbeat quicken as he regarded his enemy. He need only destroy this ship, and the rest of the fleet would become disoriented, and likely withdraw.

The ship began firing.

The first blast destroyed three ships next to the *Vehement*, incinerating them with a powerful explosion. More ships immediately drove forward to fill the gap, and the fleet, still in arrowhead formation, accelerated towards the Confederate flagship.

'Hold your fire until we're within two hundred metres,' ordered Xoanek. 'We'll strafe past them on the starboard side, firing as we go. Indiscriminate targeting – fire at will.'

'Aye, sir.'

The flagship began firing again, its powerful weapons blasting the Protectorate ships apart, causing heavy damage. Still the Expeditionary Force bore on.

'Steady!' shouted Xoanek, as the *Vehement* rocked with the force from a nearby explosion. The Confederate flagship now loomed large on the Flight Display, a massive sphere of steel and mirrors, glinting malevolently in the light of the Vulpes star.

'Fire!'

The Protectorate fleet fired as one, a huge volley of missiles slamming into the surface of the Confederate vessel as the Protectorate fleet strafed past, before turning behind it, ready to make another run. However, another attack was not necessary. The Confederate vessel, almost cleaved in two by the massive synchronised attack, exploded, a spherical shockwave blasting outwards and incinerating the desolate, drifting hulks of nearby starships. The shockwave hit the *Vehement*, knocking it backwards and severely damaging several other Protectorate ships, but as soon as it had dissipated, the fleet quickly reformed into its arrowhead formation.

Xoanek clenched his fist and snarled at the destruction of his enemy. Now leaderless, the Confederate fleet would be somewhat easier to deal with.

'Marshal!' shouted the Sensors Officer. 'They're pulling back! They're retreating!'

The command crew broke out in cheers of celebration, and Xoanek watched as the rest of the Confederate ships broke their grid formation and left orbit of the colony, heading out to the gas giant Tarsus, no doubt to regroup with their other forces besieging the other moon, Alvor. The battle was over, but the war had yet to be won.

Xoanek slumped in his chair, breathing deeply, allowing himself a rare moment of peace. Relief washed over him in a wave as he closed his eyes. 'Thank the Guardians,' he murmured to himself, listening to the cheers of the command crew. The enemy had been driven back – he had redeemed himself, at least partially. But now, he had to finish the job – to drive the Confederacy from Protectorate territory completely.

He unbuckled his seatbelt, stood and held up his hand for silence as he watched the Confederate ships break orbit on the Flight Display. 'Signal the fleet not to pursue,' he said. 'Assume high orbit and deploy in a defensive formation.'

'Aye, sir.'

'Damage report,' he said, looking at the Chief Engineer.

'We've sustained hull breaches in several sections, but emergency bulkheads are sealed and holding,' the Chief Engineer replied. 'Communications systems have taken a bit of a hammering, as has life support. Propulsion systems are workable – but don't expect anything spectacular.'

Xoanek nodded. Not bad, considering the beating the *Vehement* had taken over the last few weeks. He turned to the Communications Officer. 'Number of ships reporting in?'

'Only thirty-six,' he replied, 'and twelve report heavy damage to life support, weapons and propulsion.'

Xoanek felt a sinking feeling in his stomach, and his gut churned. 'Thirty-six?' he murmured quietly. They had won the battle, but twenty-one ships had been destroyed, with a further twelve so heavily damaged that they were useless in combat. 'Begin scanning the area for lifeboats,' he ordered the Sensors Officer. 'I want as many crewmen rescued as possible.'

'Aye, sir.'

'And send an emergency transmission to Szotas. We require immediate reinforcements if this system is to hold. We're in the fight of our lives now, gentlemen, make no mistake about that.'

Chapter Fifteen

Jamek awoke.

He was freezing – the cold bit his skin like freezing knives, and his teeth chattered uncontrollably. His entire body throbbed with agony, but his head was the worst – the back of his skull felt thick and heavy, as if some tumour was growing there. He sat up and immediately regretted it. A wave of nausea washed over him and he collapsed on all fours. The world tilted crazily and he vomited, the hot liquid burning his mouth and splattering his hands. He fell over again, writhing in pain, the agony like a thousand needles pressing into his skull.

After what seemed like an eternity, the pain subsided slightly, and Jamek wiped the vomit from his mouth, spitting to rid himself of the vile taste. He gingerly touched the back of his head, wincing as his fingers probed a huge bruise from where the rifle butt had hit him. *I'm lucky not to have a fractured skull*, he thought.

He was surprised to feel rough stubble on the back of his head, and ran his hands forward. His head had been shaved.

He looked down at his clothes and saw that his military uniform was gone. He was wearing a simple sleeveless shift made of rough sackcloth which covered his chest, coming down to just above his knees. It made his skin itch and offered little warmth from the freezing cold. He rubbed his arms in an attempt to drive off the icy chill.

Jamek looked around and found himself in a small, dark cell, the walls and floor a flat, grey concrete. Shallow puddles of water rested on the uneven floor, glittering in the scant light. The gloom was illuminated by a miserable dark red half-light. It streamed in from a small grate high up in one wall, close to the ceiling. He could hear a cruel wind howling outside, and every now and again, a clump of snow blew into the room from the grate, before melting.

The cell was rectangular, three walls rendered in concrete, the other being steel bars with a locked doorway, leading to a narrow corridor. Peering into the gloom, Jamek could see other cells lining the opposite side of the corridor. He was in prison.

He thought back to the last thing he could remember. The base in the Vulpes System had been attacked – Confederate troops had come in attack shuttles, heavily armoured and masked. Their machine guns had echoed loudly, deafening in close quarters. The Protectorate forces were completely unprepared for the attack, and it threw them into total disarray. He had been defending a corridor outside the Command Centre against the Confederate advance, but there were too many of them. He remembered Orsus being shot, then he and Adraea had charged the Confederate lines...

Adraea!

A stab of panic hit him and he quickly turned this way and that, searching for her in the dark grimy light of the cell. He screwed up his eyes as a desperate, burning rage came unbidden, forcing himself to be calm, and opened them again. Peering into the dark, waiting as his eyes adjusted to the light, he saw another figure lying on an old mattress on the other side of the cell. He crawled over carefully, trying not to aggravate his injuries, and saw that it was her.

Her long brown hair was gone, shaven close to her skull. Her lips were swollen, her face cut and bruised. One eye was blackened. She slept, although like Jamek's slumber, it could not properly be described as sleep – it was the oblivion brought on by exhaustion.

Jamek's face contorted in anguish as he beheld her – her delicate beauty had been brutalised, yet she seemed all the more beautiful for it. She was like a princess in an ancient tragedy. His heart felt rent, and tears flowed freely down his cheeks. 'Oh, Adraea,' he whispered to the darkness, 'what have they done to you?' A trembling finger stroked her bloodstained cheek.

She stirred as he touched her. 'Jamek,' she murmured.

'I'm here,' he replied, smiling through the tears.

'Where are we?'

'In some sort of prison,' said Jamek. 'We've been captured by the Confederacy.'

Adraea sat up slowly, wincing as she pulled herself upright. She was wearing the same type of hessian shift as Jamek. He noticed that a four-digit number had been stamped onto the front of the garment, and saw the same on his. Adraea looked around, taking in the cold, grey cell, barely visible in the gloom.

'They attacked Vulpes,' murmured Adraea. 'They've invaded the Protectorate.' She paused for a moment, then said, 'Jamek, I'm scared.'

Jamek hugged her fiercely. 'I'm here for you,' he said. 'And I'll look after you. And we'll both get out of here.'

Although he wanted to believe his own words, a dark foreboding fell upon his heart.

-#-

They didn't see anyone else for the rest of that day, or the day after that. Neither of them could keep track of the time in that sunless dungeon – they slept when they could no longer stay awake, and awoke when they could no longer stay asleep. Occasionally, Jamek noticed that the pale red light that shone through the grate high in the ceiling was slightly brighter, but that was the only indication of the environment beyond the prison walls changing at all.

Once, when they awoke, they found food in the cell – a single wooden bowl of bitter, cold gruel, most of it spilt on the floor from where it had been thrown. They had shared it eagerly, even mopping the freezing bile off the floor with their fingers and eating it, such was their hunger.

Occasionally, they could hear vague moaning in the darkness beyond their cell. Jamek presumed it was other prisoners, in a similar or worse state to him and Adraea – they must be in some sort of hospital wing, such as it was.

Their toilet was a hole in the concrete floor in one corner of the cell. The stench emanating from it was almost unbearable – the bitter, rancid stink of urine and excrement.

On the third day, a guard came to their cell. He was dressed like the Confederate troops which had stormed the base. 'Come here,' he said, his voice rasping through his metal helmet, tapping the steel bars with a long truncheon.

Jamek stood up and helped Adraea to her feet. They moved towards the wall of bars until they were about six inches away from it.'Turn around,' he said, and they obeyed.

Jamek felt gloved hands take hold of his wrists. For no apparent reason, a sudden fury exploded inside him, and his face set in a hard, expressionless mask of rage. With savage accuracy, he kicked backwards through the bars. He felt a satisfying crack underneath his foot as the guard's leg was snapped like a brittle twig. The man fell, screaming in pain.

Immediately, two more guards rushed down the corridor, one tending to their injured comrade. The other attacked Jamek, smashing a long truncheon through the bars into the base of Jamek's skull, where his wound was still sensitive. He writhed in agony as a white hot, searing pain flashed across his vision, and fell to the floor, shuddering with nausea. Just as suddenly as the red haze of rage had descended upon Jamek was it removed, thrown off by the paroxysm of pain now slashing across the top of his neck like forked lightning.

While Jamek lay prostrate on the floor, the soldiers quickly handcuffed Adraea, who looked on helplessly. The moans of the injured guard echoed in the cavernous concrete jail. There was a clank as the other soldiers unlocked the door to the cell. One grabbed Adraea's bound wrists before dragging her out. The other lifted Jamek up and threw him against the bars face first. Jamek grunted as his head smashed against one of the bars, before his hands were cuffed behind his back.

Both of them were frog-marched out of the cell with their wrists level with their shoulders, in a kind of walking *strappado*. The pain was unbelievable – it felt like their arms were being twisted out of their sockets. Adraea whimpered in pain, but Jamek, still stunned by the savagery of the guards' assault, could only gasp in breathless agony.

They turned right down the corridor, marching through the shadowy prison for what seemed like an age, knowing only the excruciating pain in their shoulders, and the occasional muscle-aching, bone-cracking smash from a guard's truncheon. Finally, after a dozen twists and turns through the labyrinthine maze of cells and corridors, they reached a great hall, constructed out of red bricks and mortar, unlike the cold, hard concrete of the cells.

The hall was brightly lit, making both Jamek and Adraea blink in the harsh light. It was cavernous, wide and high compared to the narrow, low-ceilinged corridors they had just traversed. A metal walkway crossed the room about halfway to the high vaulted ceiling, connecting balconies on either side. As Jamek and Adraea were pushed forward, many more prisoners emerged from other corridors opening out onto the hall. They were all bleary-eyed and sack-clothed with shaven heads. At the far end of the hall, two barred double-doors could be seen, either side of what looked like a giant chimney-breast.

Jamek gripped Adraea's hand, holding it tightly as close to a hundred prisoners were shepherded into the room, crammed together, jostling for space. He didn't want to lose her in this unknown place, and he had no idea what fate awaited them. Nightmarish tales of ancient wars on Therqa awoke in his darkest memories – of the terrors of massacres and genocide, rumours of the predilections of the Confederacy. Jamek breathed deeply, trying to calm himself, trying to resist the urge to fight, though it raged almost uncontrollably inside him.

The balconies on either side, as well as the metal walkway that joined them, were manned by masked Confederate troops armed with machine guns. In the centre of the walkway, one Confederate soldier stood with two chevrons and two horizontal lines below them embroidered on his armoured sleeves. He nodded to one of the guards next to him, who slammed the butt of his rifle onto the railing of the walkway. The sound echoed around the hall, and the gathered prisoners below fell silent.

'Welcome to the Proxima Penal Colony,' said the unarmed Confederate soldier. 'I am Cavalier Caltrian. There are simple rules here – perform the work assigned to you. If you do not, you will die. Obey the guards at all times. If you do not, you will die. You cannot escape. If you attempt to, you will die. Even if you succeed, you will die. Beyond the prison walls, there is nothing but the frozen, desolate wastes of this planet.'

'You are now to be introduced to the general prison population,' said Caltrian. 'You will not be assigned cells – find them yourselves. I suggest you co-operate with the other prisoners – there is no possibility of release, or parole. You will be here for the rest of your miserable lives, and your labour and efforts will be for the sole benefit of the Confederacy. If you want whatever days you have left in this world to pass without unbelievable agony, you would do well not to make enemies.'

Without another word, the Cavalier stalked off the walkway, and the two sets of doors on either side of the front wall grated back, opening slowly. The armed guards on the balconies and the walkway shouted, and pointed with their guns, indicating the doorways. Steadily, the crowd of prisoners moved through into the chamber beyond.

It was another large hall, with metal walkways criss-crossing the ceiling, and balconies around the walls, where troops patrolled, wielding their heavy guns. The heat was stifling. A roaring furnace bellowed its heat from between the two metal gates from which the crowd of new prisoners entered the hall, behind a large grating so that no prisoner could get too close to it. Jamek felt sweat bead on his brow as he passed it, the baking heat a pleasant change from the biting cold that he had known over the last few days.

Jamek, his heart pounding, held tightly onto Adraea's hand as they made their way past the open fire and onto the main floor of the hall. Jamek recognised the faces of some of the other prisoners – they were, or had been, Protectorate soldiers. They nodded to him, and instinctively stayed close to each other.

A large group of men huddled near the open fire, talking amongst themselves. They turned and smirked evilly as the new prisoners arrived, some of them laughing and mocking them. One of them, a giant of a man, nearly seven feet tall, with dark, short hair and bulging arms, moved over to Jamek and Adraea.

'Hello, my pretty,' he said, a lewd expression crossing his scarred face. 'Why don't you come over here and sit with me?' He grabbed Adraea's arm in a vice-like grip. Adraea responded by slapping him hard across the face, enough to rock him back on his heels. He didn't loosen his grip, but simply smiled, wiping a thin trail of blood from his chin. 'I like one who fights back!' he said, to cheers from the men near the fire, who were watching with interest. He began pulling her away from Jamek and towards the fireplace.

Jamek's vision blackened with a deadly rage, and he was about to launch himself at the big man, when all of a sudden, another tall, muscular figure leapt on the scarred man, wrenching his hand from Adraea's wrist.

'Back off, Felador,' snarled a familiar voice. 'Leave her alone.'

Jamek was astonished to see Mavrak standing in front of him, his hands holding the other prisoner's wrists in grips of iron. He could see the veins on Mavrak's arms standing out with the effort required, yet it didn't show on his face. He was overjoyed and dismayed to see his lifelong friend – overjoyed to see him alive, dismayed to see him in prison.

'This is none of your business, *Mavrak*,' Felador spat the name out with contempt, but did not hit him. 'Stay out of it. She's mine.'

'Wrong,' snarled Jamek, stepping forward, his knees bent, his right foot dropped behind his left, his fists raised in a fighting stance. Mavrak grinned appreciatively at his friend as Adraea shrank into the shadow of the two men. Sensing trouble, a few other Protectorate soldiers gathered round, supporting Jamek and Mavrak.

Swiftly realising that he was outnumbered, Felador relaxed, and Mavrak released his grip on his forearms. 'This time, Protectorate,' he muttered, and backed off, returning to the group by the fire.

Mavrak turned to Jamek. 'By all the Guardians,' he breathed, 'it's good to see you. The both of you.' He embraced Jamek in a fierce hug. 'When I heard about the Fleetyard, I thought both of you were...' He left the final word unspoken. Adraea smiled and hugged Mavrak as well.

'Thank you, Mavrak,' she said. 'I think I owe you one.'

'Just stepping into the breach before Jamek killed him,' said Mavrak, kissing her lightly on the cheek. His blonde hair was also cropped short, his face cut and scarred. He was dressed in the same rough garb as both Jamek and Adraea, but despite his appearance, he was still the same man they both loved. 'And he was ready to.' He slapped Jamek on the back, and Jamek exhaled slowly, forcing himself to unclench his fists. He put his hands behind his back, but Mavrak saw the cuts on his palms where his fingernails had bit into the skin.

'Rule One of survival in this hellhole,' said Mavrak, putting one hand into the small of Jamek's and Adraea's backs, pushing them away from the fireplace to the opposite end of the hall. It was blocked off by a barred wall running across the width of the room. 'Stay away from the fireplace. That's where the Confederate prisoners gather. We're over here.'

In the right hand corner, next to the barred wall, about two dozen prisoners were sat on short wooden boxes, or leaning against the wall. Some were smoking some type of cigarette, others were drinking from hip flasks. Beyond the barred wall, Jamek could see a few guards playing a game of cards around a wooden table.

'This is our corner,' said Mavrak, with a hint of pride in his voice. 'The Confederates won't come over here – we've agreed something of a ceasefire with them. It took some intense negotiations.' He brandished his heavy fists, and Adraea giggled despite the circumstances.

'Rule Two,' said Mavrak, 'try not to piss off Felador. He's big, he's nasty, and he'll start a fight at the drop of a hat.'

'I'll bear that in mind,' muttered Jamek, glaring back at the fireplace.

'Rule Three,' said Mavrak, 'and this applies especially to you, Adraea.' He offered her a wooden box, and she sat down thankfully. 'Don't go anywhere... and I mean *anywhere*, without either me or Jamek. Not to the toilet, not to the shower, nowhere alone. Do you understand?' Adraea nodded, a look of horror on her face. Jamek's expression darkened.

'Rape,' said Mavrak bluntly, 'is a fact of life in here. And intellectual concepts like male and female only apply insofar as the girls tend to be easier targets.' Mavrak offered a hip flask to Adraea, who took it and drank deeply before handing it back. Mavrak offered it to Jamek.

'Survival is the name of the game,' he said. 'We don't antagonise them, we don't make ourselves easy targets, and they'll leave us alone. Agreed?'

Jamek took the offered flask and drank deeply, the strong, alcoholic liquid burning his throat on the way down. 'Agreed,' he lied.

-#-

Karaea stalked into her office, her white robes fluttering behind her, her face stern and grim. Laruak followed in close step behind her. As she entered the room, Fedrus stood up and saluted. She waved away the formality, and indicated for the Guardians outside in the corridor to shut the doors.

Fedrus sat down, immediately on edge. He had known Karaea for a long time, since she and Anzaeus had been seeing each other, in what seemed like a different time. She had always been ambitious and temperamental, but there was something about her demeanour today which he did not care for. There was anger, there was frustration, but there was also fear – and that concerned him greatly.

'The Confederacy,' she almost spat the word out, 'has invaded Vulpes!'

'What?' Fedrus leapt to his feet in shock, and then watched with horror as Karaea's face crumpled. The Protector slumped forward onto her desk in grief and rage, and the crown of office fell from her head, clanging on the desk, before settling upturned.

'What have I done?' she wept. 'What have I done, Fedrus?'

The reality of the situation sunk in to Fedrus. *Vulpes. Jamek, Mavrak and Adraea were all stationed there.* His heart was chilled to the core as he suddenly realised that they were in grave danger. They were barely adults, and now they were on the front line in a war zone.

'What has happened?' he asked, trying to remain calm and quell the mad panic that surged within him at the thought of his daughter.

Karaea looked up at him, her eyes red with crying. Fedrus was shocked at the sight of it – this was a devastating contrast to the usually invulnerable Karaea that he knew. Here was a woman who was unsure of herself, who was lacking in confidence, and driven to despair with regret and guilt. This was no time for the Protector to have a crisis of confidence. He pushed those thoughts to one side.

'Karaea,' he said, dropping formality, 'what has happened?'

'The Expeditionary Force was ambushed in the Panthera System,' she said dully, her eyes blank and glassy. 'They retreated to Vulpes, only to find that the Confederacy had already invaded, and were waiting for them. We received word from Xoanek less than an hour ago.'

'The Expeditionary Force is still intact?'

'Xoanek has suffered heavy losses,' interjected Laruak, 'but he is rallying his forces to prepare for a counter-attack.'

'Protector,' said Fedrus, standing up, 'I request permission to rally reinforcements and go the Vulpes System. Xoanek cannot drive the Confederacy out without support. You must mobilise the entire Starforce. Vulpes must not be allowed to fall.'

Karaea sat in stunned silence for a moment. 'This news cannot get out,' she muttered. 'It would cause mass panic.'

She turned to Laruak. 'I am forbidding you to speak to the Senate about this matter.'

'Protector!' said Laruak, aghast. 'The Senate must be informed...'

'If the Senate are told, then the people will know,' interrupted Karaea harshly. 'That could lead to anarchy. The last thing we need now is such chaos. You are not to speak to the Senate about this until I decree otherwise. That is a direct order from the Protector. Do you understand?'

'I understand,' answered Laruak, 'but this is under duress, Protector. I will obey, but I most certainly do not agree!'

'Your objection is noted,' said Karaea, curtly. She turned to Fedrus. 'Take fifty starships,' she said. 'Go to Vulpes and help Xoanek.'

'With respect, Protector, fifty starships may not be enough!' retorted Fedrus. 'The Protectorate has been invaded! We need to mobilise the entire Starforce in order to drive them out!'

'A mass mobilisation would trigger the kind of panic I am trying to avoid,' snapped Karaea. 'You may take fifty starships.'

Fedrus tightened his lips, feeling anger surge up in him. He knew exactly what she was doing. She had made a mistake in allowing Xoanek to command the mission – the man was arrogant and hubristic, and it had led to a dangerous underestimation of their enemy. For her to admit that would be political suicide. So she was now risking the security of the Protectorate simply to prolong her political career.

He opened his mouth to speak, but then thought the better of it, and snapped it shut. 'I will take fifty starships,' he said, 'and I hope that it will be enough. I also hope to return with my daughter, and Psinaez Jamek, Anzaeus's son, who are both stationed in Vulpes.'

At the mention of Anzaeus, her one-time lover, and Jamek, his son, Karaea's eyes filled with tears again. She looked into Fedrus's eyes, knowing that he had the measure of her. For the first time since she was a child, she felt ashamed, and had to drop her gaze.

Fedrus saluted and strode out of the room. Once he was outside, he broke into a sprint. There was not a moment to lose.

Chapter Sixteen

The black emptiness of space, normally only illuminated by the merciless but faint glint of starlight, was lit by an awesome power – the glare of the Vulpes sun, a mere twenty-five million miles away. Although the sun only had half the power of Kaathar, up close, it was nevertheless an incredible sight.

Ribbons of high energy plasma rippled across its surface, which was pocked with blackened sunspots like lesions. Solar flares rose up – great columns of flame hundreds of times bigger than Szotas itself.

Next to this mighty giant, this god of the heavens, a fleet of starships, tiny by comparison, made their way across the great expanse of space, with nothing between them and the naked star. There were fifty in total, moving silently through the void – disc-shaped, their outer hulls rotating steadily as they travelled in an ovoid formation.

Their destination was what appeared to be a large, bright star on the far side of the glowering sun. It was actually a planet – the gas giant Tarsus, or Vulpes II, where a war was being fought.

In the midst of this cloud of starships was one that was bigger than the rest, its outer ring rotating slightly faster. At the edge of the rotating rim, with arc lights projecting forward from the glowing blue Terculium Reactor housing, were inscribed the words:

PSS COMBATANT

S-2367

Fedrus stood in the Command Centre of the *Combatant*, looking ahead at the Flight Display. It was showing a darkened version of the reality outside. It was incapable of showing the full luminosity of the Vulpes star, and even if it could, the sheer intensity of it would strip flesh from bone at this close distance.

'We're now in tight orbit of the Vulpes star,' reported the First Officer, sitting at Primary Support. 'We should clear the star in approximately two hours.'

Fedrus nodded. 'Once we're clear, realign our heading for Tarsus,' he said. 'The fleet has assembled in orbit of Telsor.'

'Aye, sir.'

Fedrus sat down at the Helm and breathed deeply, calming himself. It was easy to immerse himself in duty and forget about the worries he had. However, in the quiet moments like this, when duty was attended to and he was left alone with his thoughts, the spike of panic returned.

Vulpes was now a battleground.

The information coming out of the system was sketchy at best, due to the Confederate forces trying to jam all communications. Fedrus had managed to assemble a fleet of fifty starships, but no General or Admiral was prepared to lead such a paltry force into battle, his own Fleet Commander included. He had been happy to sign over command of the small fleet to a Commodore, even though Fedrus normally only commanded ten starships, including his own.

The task did not daunt Fedrus. He considered it his duty and his honour to fight for the Protectorate, like any other soldier. Far from considering it a hopeless cause, he hoped that his force could be used as a stop-gap until more reinforcements arrived.

His fleet had cleared the vortex to the Lupus-Vulpes Tunnel a week earlier, and had made straight for the heart of the system on full Ion Drive. They had avoided the major planets, which sensor reports indicated had high numbers of Confederate ships in orbit. As such, they had thus far managed to elude enemy forces. However, Fedrus considered it unlikely that they had gone undetected – they had merely delayed the inevitable confrontation. This close to the Vulpes star was dangerous. He half-expected an attack from a small harrying force, possibly hiding on the surface of Vulpes I. The closest planet to the star was nothing more than a blasted ball of scorched rock, but an excellent hiding place for a small squadron.

His mind returned to thoughts of his daughter, Adraea.

She had been stationed on the Vulpes IV Fleetyard, together with Jamek and Mavrak. Vulpes IV was currently on the opposite side of the star, so their sensor readings were somewhat chaotic. However, Fedrus found the ominous silence from the Fleetyard chilling, and couldn't shake the desperate feeling of dread from his heart. He knew that if he were leading the Confederate force, the Fleetyard would have been his first target – it deprived the enemy of a base of operations and any supplies could be appropriated.

A spike of fear slid into his heart, and he murmured a silent prayer to the ancient Guardians, calling on them to protect his daughter. This war had already claimed his best friend. He could not bear to lose Adraea as well, nor Jamek, who he had sworn to Anzaeus to protect.

'I never should've let them go,' he muttered to himself, and his heart ached with a terrible sense of failure. And yet, despite that, he knew that if he had stopped them, they would not have forgiven him. Forces far greater than him were now at work – the forces of Fate and Destiny. How could one man stand against them?

-#-

Despite Fedrus's concerns, they cleared their tight orbit of the Vulpes star without incident, and proceeded on course to Tarsus. Within twelve hours, they were close enough to determine the great planet's rings, and Fedrus was cheered by the sight of it. Whilst not as majestic as Astralas, the ringed planet in Szotas's Lupus System, what Tarsus lacked in grandeur it made up for in sheer size. If the planet had been any bigger, it surely would have been a star. Its moons, Telsor and Alvor, were big enough to be planets in their own right.

'Contact the Expeditionary Force,' he said.

'I have them, sir,' replied the Communications Officer.

'On screen.'

The Flight Display changed from its current view of the planet to show Marshal Xoanek's face. Fedrus was taken aback by his appearance. The last time he had seen the Marshal was on Szotas at the High Command, when Xoanek had to break the news of Anzaeus's death to him, and he had opted out of joining the ill-fated Expeditionary Force. Now the Marshal seemed a shadow of his former self – his face was gaunt and haggard. His eyes bore the haunted look of those who have seen too much death and destruction. His cheeks and throat were covered with days-old grey stubble.

'Commodore Fedrus,' said the Marshal. 'I'm surprised to see you here.'

'Marshal Xoanek,' said Fedrus, and saluted by placing his fist on his shoulder. 'Events have conspired to bring me to the war after all. I bring reinforcements from Szotas.'

'Excellent,' said Xoanek, the relief visible on his tired face. 'How many ships?'

'Fifty, sir.'

Fifty?! Is that all?'

'I'm afraid so, sir,' replied Fedrus evenly. 'The Protector considers it best to keep the ill news of the Confederate invasion from the public, and so wished to avoid a general mobilisation. I brought what ships I could.'

'Hence a Commodore commanding over a full Group of ships,' said Xoanek, contemptuously. 'Not to demean you, Fedrus, or your rank. But I bet you couldn't find one of those cowardly Admirals or Generals to command this mission.'

'Unfortunately not, sir,' answered Fedrus. 'They were happy to assign the command to me, however.'

'Of course. You're braver than the lot of them put together.' Xoanek sighed. 'Fifty ships is less than a quarter of what I'd hoped for. But still, some reinforcements are better than none, and you have just over doubled the size of my command. Assume high orbit of Telsor, Commodore – and you've just become the second ranking officer in this outfit. Congratulations. Once your ships are deployed, please join me aboard the *Vehement.* We have a lot to discuss.'

'Aye, sir.'

The screen returned to its view of the planet. Fedrus sat back. 'You heard the Marshal,' he said. 'Set course for Telsor. Co-ordinate with the other fleet, integrate and deploy. I will go aboard the *Vehement* and decide upon the organisation of the fleet with Marshal Xoanek, but it can be safely decided that the *Combatant* is a Group Flagship. Signal the fleet to await new orders.'

-#-

Fedrus stepped aboard the *Vehement* from his shuttle, and drew a sharp intake of breath as he looked up and down the corridor. The ship had looked a mess from the outside, but it hadn't quite prepared him for the sight he saw.

To his right, one end of the corridor was sealed off by an emergency bulkhead door – closing off a decompressed compartment from the rest of the ship. In front of the solid steel door was a pile of detritus – cables, steel girders and scorched metal panelling. The floor was also strewn with debris, data and power cabling exposed under the floor where some panels had been torn up. More cables dangled from the ceiling, one at the end of the corridor sparking alarmingly.

'She's not a pretty sight,' said Xoanek, standing in front of him, 'but she's been through a lot.'

Fedrus nodded. 'It certainly seems that way,' he said. 'I have brought extra engineering teams along. We can get them deployed to all vessels that need them.'

Xoanek nodded, scratching the stubbled beginnings of a beard on his throat. 'Welcome aboard, Commodore,' he said, and turned on his heel, walking quickly down the corridor. Fedrus fell into step alongside him, eager to ascertain the tactical situation as soon as possible, but acutely aware that the full details could not be discussed in such a public place.

After a few minutes of walking through the ruined ship, they finally reached the *Vehement's* Briefing Room. Xoanek stepped in, kicking aside a broken computer console that blocked the doorway.

The Briefing Room was a common feature on Protectorate starships – it adjoined both the Captain's Quarters and the Command Centre, serving as a conference room for the senior staff, as well as a private office for the Captain. Xoanek's Briefing Room was about twelve feet square, with three doors, one leading to the corridor from which they entered, the other leading onto the Command Centre, and the other onto Xoanek's quarters. The wall opposite the corridor entrance was decorated with portraits of the other ships to bear the name *Vehement* throughout the Protectorate's history. They illustrated a grand lineage – from the earliest ships that sailed on the lakes of Szotas, to the first rockets that explored the Lupus System, to the current holder of the name. Most of the frames were broken, having been smashed in one of the *Vehement's* numerous encounters. Fedrus shivered slightly at the omen, but shook it off.

On the left side of the room, a wide desk stood in front of the door leading to the Captain's Quarters. The rest of the room was dominated by a large metallic table, capable of seating eight people – the senior staff of the ship. Xoanek swore as he saw that the table was covered with debris from the ceiling, which had partially collapsed. He swept most of it onto the floor, and offered Fedrus a seat.

'I won't lie to you, Commodore,' he said as Fedrus sat down, 'we're in a very dangerous situation here. You've turned up just in time, and even your force may not be enough.'

'What's the tactical situation?'

'The Vulpes IV Fleetyards have been destroyed,' said Xoanek. 'Any chance we have of re-supplying is pretty much gone with it. Confederate forces are using the moons as a staging ground.'

Fedrus's heart sank into his stomach, and he felt sick. He had half-expected such news, but to hear it confirmed was a different matter entirely. 'Are there any survivors?' he muttered.

'We arrived too late to rescue any,' answered Xoanek. 'Some lifeboats managed to make it to Telsor, but only a handful.'

'My daughter... and Anzaeus's son... were stationed there,' said Fedrus, trying to maintain his composure, fighting the awful panic that was close to consuming him.

Xoanek fell silent. 'I thought you were caring for them?' he asked.

'They signed up when they heard about Anzaeus's death,' replied Fedrus. 'Now I wish I'd stopped them.' He lifted his head. 'What else?'

'They've also secured high orbit of Vulpes III,' replied Xoanek. 'Again, depriving us of a decent staging area. So far, Vulpes V seems to be clear – but it's too small and out of the way to be of any strategic significance.'

'When we arrived, they were besieging both Telsor and Alvor,' continued Xoanek. 'We managed to break their siege of Telsor, but the bulk of their forces retreated to Alvor. They're still entrenched in high orbit there – they've landed ground troops. Unless we help Alvor immediately, it will fall. But the worst news is that they have established a temporary wormhole to the Felis System. We suspect that it's their home system. Reinforcements are arriving every day.'

Fedrus swore. It was a mess. Without control of any major planets, they couldn't assemble sizeable fleets in orbit. With the Confederacy receiving such strong reinforcements, it was difficult to see how they could hold out against the enemy, let alone re-capture the planets they had taken.

'What do you plan to do, sir?'

Xoanek looked at Fedrus in something akin to astonishment. 'I intend to drive them from this system,' he said, as if it were obvious. 'Tomorrow, we will assemble our forces and attack their positions orbiting Alvor, relieving the siege there.'

Fedrus shook his head. 'Pardon me, sir, but I don't think that would be prudent,' he said. 'We don't have enough ships to mount an attack. We should reinforce our position on Telsor, and send immediate word to Szotas, requesting the re-deployment of the garrisons from Canis. With the forces we have, we can hold a defensive position for a few weeks. By that time, reinforcements from Canis should be with us, and then we can look to relieve Alvor.'

'That is unacceptable,' said Xoanek, flatly. 'Alvor is ready to fall. If we do not go to their aid, they will be conquered.'

'With respect, sir,' argued Fedrus, 'there's nothing we can do about Alvor. Not yet. If we break our defensive orbit now, we may lose the entire system.'

'I will not simply sit here waiting for reinforcements that may never come!' shouted Xoanek, and he slammed his fist down on the table. 'We must relieve Alvor immediately! And when we have done that, we will attack their wormhole vortex and destroy it, cutting off their supply chain. It will then be *months* before they can reinforce.'

'Marshal, you must realise that their wormhole vortex will be heavily defended?' said Fedrus. 'As will be Alvor! Mounting such attacks, with such limited numbers at our disposal, is suicide!'

'It is our duty to defend the Protectorate!' roared Xoanek, standing up. Fedrus was appalled by the anger in the old man. His face was flushed a violent red, the veins in his neck standing out like thick cords. 'We attack in the morning!' He breathed deeply, and his eyes narrowed. 'If you cannot follow these orders, then I will find someone else who can,' he said. 'I understand the personal losses you have suffered in this war to date, Commodore, but I need you to put those aside. You are, after all, a soldier.'

Fedrus stood up, and looked the Marshal directly in the eye. 'You are my commanding officer,' he said, 'and I will obey your orders to the letter. But I must insist that you note my protest in your log, sir. I think that to attack now is a bad idea. And this is regardless of the personal losses I have suffered.'

Xoanek's gaze wavered slightly under Fedrus's stare. 'I will note it,' he said. 'Now, *Vehement* will continue to serve as the flagship.' He handed Fedrus an electronic pad. 'Here is my signed authority to re-order the fleet,' he said. 'Organise it into three Battle Groups. I will command Group A, you will command Group B. Find a competent Captain to command Group C. Split my ships evenly among yours, and assign additional engineering teams and crew to those ships that need them. Understood?'

Fedrus took the electronic pad and saluted. 'Yes, sir,' he said. Xoanek nodded and walked out of the room, leaving Fedrus alone.

He heaved himself back into his chair, and stared at the pad in his hands. Xoanek was clearly mad. He had failed in his attempted conquest of the Confederacy, and now sought to redeem himself by attempting to drive them out of Vulpes. He was trying to save his own career, when he should be trying to save the Protectorate.

Fedrus knew he had the option of disobeying the Marshal, but it was not an option to be taken lightly. He wasn't just any other superior officer – he was the Chief of the General Staff. Xoanek could have him executed for doing so, and where would that leave the rest of his men? Helpless under the command of a zealot hell-bent on a suicide mission. No, he would not take the coward's way out. If he betrayed Xoanek, he would surely be executed.

If he participated in this psychotic attack, he may just survive, and a few men and ships with him.

Fedrus sighed. 'Adraea,' he murmured. 'Jamek. By all the Guardians, I hope you're safe.' He stood up and walked out of the Briefing Room, to ready his men and his fleet for war.

-#-

Fedrus sat in the Command Centre of the *Combatant*, looking ahead at the Flight Display. It displayed a tactical overview of the neighbouring ice moon of Alvor. It showed a gridded outline of the moon with nearly two hundred yellow marks orbiting it, overlaid in a triple grid pattern – an extremely defensive formation. The Confederate fleet was ready for battle.

Fedrus sighed. He had managed to persuade Xoanek to delay his attack for twenty-four hours, in order to better ready the fleet for battle, but there was still scant time to prepare. Out of the eighty-six starships they had, Fedrus grouped eighty-two of them into Battle Groups. The other four, arising from Xoanek's original Expeditionary Force, were so badly damaged as to be practically useless. Fedrus had ordered them stripped of resources and crew to repair and reinforce the other ships in the fleet, and had then scuttled them.

Although the ships that Fedrus had brought with him were in good condition, the remnants of Xoanek's fleet were in need of repair. Fedrus had bolstered their crew complements and dispatched engineering teams to conduct repairs. Astonishingly, almost all of them had reported as battle-ready. Now, the fleet was ready, or as ready as it could be, to launch its assault on the Confederate forces besieging Alvor.

Despite the incredible efforts of his soldiers over the last day to prepare the fleet for battle, Fedrus still had deep misgivings about the planned attack. The Confederate fleet orbiting Alvor numbered close to two hundred – they were outnumbered nearly two to one. On top of that, the enemy had assumed a very defensive formation – they did not intend to break high orbit of Alvor without a fight.

On top of these immediate military issues, there was also the awful silence coming from Vulpes IV. No more lifeboats had been detected, and Jamek, Adraea and Mavrak were not among the survivors that had made it to Telsor. There was simply the wretched absence, a great hole torn out of his life by the disappearance of his daughter. Fedrus felt his throat tightening at the thought of losing her squeezing viciously at his heart, fear's cold fingers showing no mercy.

'Adraea,' he whispered to himself, and prayed that she was alive, somewhere in the barren emptiness of space. He thought of Jamek, of his promise to Anzaeus to care for him, and felt that somehow, he had failed his old friend. 'I will find him, Anzaeus,' he whispered. 'I will find them all.'

'Sir,' said the Communications Officer, bringing Fedrus from his reverie. 'The flagship is signalling.'

'On screen,' said Fedrus, and drew himself to his full height. Marshal Xoanek's face appeared on the Flight Display.

'Commodore Fedrus,' he said, his blue eyes shining brightly under his iron-grey hair. He had found time to shave in the last few hours, but his face still bore the haunted look which worried Fedrus so – a slightly maniacal, obsessive expression.

'Marshal,' said Fedrus, saluting. 'Group B stands ready.'

'Excellent,' replied Xoanek. 'I will take the port flank, you take the starboard. Group C will form in the centre. Break orbit, and assemble in attack formation. Set your course for Alvor.'

'Aye, sir,' said Fedrus, and the screen went blank. He sighed and looked round at the command crew. 'The Protectorate is under attack,' he said. 'We are a few against many, but it is our duty to resist these invaders, lest they fall upon Szotas itself. We will strike at the enemy with all the force that we can muster. Stay at your posts, even to the last. And let's show these Confederate bastards what damage we can do!' The command crew cheered, and Fedrus bared his teeth in a vicious grin as the thoughts and worries of the campaign slid from his mind. He was left only with the simplest of instincts – the instinct to fight, and to survive.

-#-

The Protectorate fleet moved out of orbit of Telsor, a band of ocean across its equator glinting in the light of the nearby Vulpes star, its poles dominated by huge sheets of ice which covered more than half the planet.

In the distance, the massive globe of Tarsus could be seen, its atmosphere punctuated by stripes of blue, grey and green clouds, swirling in endless storms hundreds of times the size of its moons. Aurorae burned in fiery rings around its poles as the powerful solar wind from the nearby star smashed down onto its polar regions along its enormous magnetic field. Its tight orbital rings glowed in the light of the Vulpes star, casting light even on the darkened side of the planet, bathing it in an ethereal, blue-green light.

The countless, unblinking stars stared out across the darkness of space, the awesome and silent backdrop to the scene of majesty and splendour. Emerging from the far side of Tarsus, a shining sphere of light could be seen, glimmering as the light of Vulpes reflected off its ice-covered surface – the giant planet's other major moon of Alvor.

The Protectorate fleet began moving steadily across the gulf between these two moons, the giant planet of Tarsus on their starboard side. The fleet was structured into three arrowhead formations – one slightly smaller in the centre, and the other two on either side. These arrowheads were not simply the flat, two-dimensional formations used by the aircraft of long ago, however – these were tapered vertically as well as horizontally, a cavalry charge of spacecraft, perfectly suited to fighting in three dimensions.

On the left side, at the centre of its Group, the *Vehement* could be seen, its hull now pocked and scarred by a thousand wounds from countless battles. Some sections of its rotating outer rim were blackened and collapsed, twisted pylons and bulkheads punctuating the silver-white disc like charred bones protruding from a corpse. A few other ships in similar condition could be seen dotted amongst the three formations – the last remnants of the Expeditionary Force.

Fedrus sat at the Helm of the *Combatant*, watching the Flight Display. His fists were clenched, his breath coming in short, shallow gasps. His heart was racing, and a cold sweat beaded on his brow. His throat felt dry.

'Sensors?' he barked.

'Reading one hundred and ninety Confederate vessels, sir,' replied the Sensors Officer. 'They're maintaining their tight triple grid formation.'

'Of course,' said Fedrus, through gritted teeth. 'Xoanek cut them to pieces on a single grid around Telsor. They're going to maintain a tight formation to limit our manoeuvrability, and a deep formation so that we can't punch straight through and undercut them.'

'Message coming in from the flagship, Commodore,' said the Communications Officer.

'Let's hear it,' said Fedrus.

'Text only. Group B, attack southern hemisphere, focus efforts on polar region to mask your numbers. Advance immediately.'

Fedrus nodded. The order was given. 'Signal the rest of our Group,' he said. 'We attack the south pole. Signal our ships to maintain formation, full thrusters. We're going in.'

The *Combatant's* Battle Group peeled off from the main fleet, rolling to starboard and dropping down towards the approaching moon's southern hemisphere. The *Vehement's* Group, under Xoanek's direct command, headed for the northern hemisphere, leaving the central Group to plough straight into the moon's equator. Up close, Alvor was a ragged, white sphere of ice, great scars torn into its surface by the powerful gravitational field of the nearby planet. The ice moved on a mantle of water, great tectonic plates of ice several miles thick, under the constant tortuous pull from gigantic Tarsus. Around the moon, the glistening spheres of Confederate starships could now clearly be seen, orbiting steadily at uniform distance from each other in an overlaying, criss-crossing grid pattern.

The dark sky was suddenly filled with blazes of fire as the Confederate ships around the southern hemisphere began firing. Missiles trailing plumes of flame sped towards the spearhead of Fedrus's fleet. The fleet banked and rolled, dodging some of the missiles, but others collided with some Protectorate ships. They glanced off their hulls, still causing some damage.

'Inform squadron leaders to select targets,' snapped Fedrus. 'Co-ordinate their firepower. Fire at their discretion.' His fingers tightened on the steering column as the *Combatant* shook with the force of a nearby explosion. He closed his eyes briefly, the Battle Stations lights still shining through his eyelids, the alert klaxon sounding in his ears.

'Targets selected, Commodore.'

'Fire!'

The gun ports of the Protectorate ships blazed, and deadly missiles carrying lethal payloads rocketed into the dark silence of space. They hammered down onto the Confederate fleet below them, a foretaste of the carnage to come. Several Confederate vessels exploded, spheres of fire and force blasting their neighbours from their positions, only for them to quickly reform. Then, a moment after the missiles hit, the Protectorate fleet plunged into the Confederate line.

Several ships collided, blowing each other apart in violent and deathly embraces. The Protectorate fleet drove down yet deeper into the Confederate formation, but rather than try to resist the sudden and deep strike, the Confederate ships parted, almost letting them through.

Fedrus eased the throttle back, slowing the ship down. 'What are they doing?' he said, as he watched the Confederate fleet opening up in front of him. A gnawing dread took hold of him, which morphed quickly into a sudden panic.

'Switch to aft view!' he said, turning to snap at the Sensors Officer. The view on the Flight Display changed, to show what was happening behind the *Combatant*. Fedrus watched in horror as he saw the enemy fleet closing their position behind them, in an even tighter formation.

'They're trying to trap us in low orbit!' he shouted. 'Signal the fleet – about turn! Push up towards them – they'll pulverise us!'

As if on cue, the *Combatant* rocked with a heavy blow, and Fedrus was nearly knocked out of his chair, held in place by his seatbelt. Grimacing as the straps bit into his shoulders, he pulled himself back. 'Damage report!' he shouted.

'Direct hit to Section Three!' reported the Chief Engineer. 'Hull breach. Emergency bulkheads are in place and holding.'

Fedrus swore. He turned to the Communications Officer. 'Monitor their communications,' he said. 'I want to know which is their flagship!'

'Sir, they have no communications!' said the officer, a hint of panic in his voice. 'They're operating on total radio silence!'

'So, this is the battle you have led us into, Marshal,' he muttered to himself. 'Against an entrenched, prepared and experienced enemy, with an inadequate force. May the Guardians have mercy on us.' He turned to the First Officer. 'Select targets based on their potential threat,' he said. 'Communications, inform the Group to follow our lead of targets. Do as much damage as you can!'

-#-

Xoanek's chair was torn from its moorings as the *Vehement* took a heavy blow. His chest tightened painfully as the wind was knocked from him, but he pulled open his seatbelt and dragged himself to his feet, forcing his lungs to open. The lights guttered weakly and the Command Centre was littered with broken glass, shards of circuitry and debris. Smoke hung in the air, catching the back of his throat. Several consoles at the back of the Command Centre burned in crackling electrical fires.

'Maintain formation!' he roared. 'Fire at will!' He felt the deck plates hum as more missiles were launched, and watched on the Flight Display as they slammed into two nearby Confederate vessels, which bled fire for a moment before the columns of flame were extinguished. The great hulking spheres merely gazed back eyelessly and returned fire, as if the efforts of the *Vehement* were simply an annoyance.

'Sir! Commodore Fedrus is signalling!'

'On screen!' The Flight Display lit up with Fedrus's face.

'Marshal, we are badly outnumbered and taking heavy losses,' said Fedrus, urgently. 'Requesting permission to withdraw!'

'No!' shrieked Xoanek, hysteria in his voice. 'You are ordered to fight, Fedrus! Fight to the bitter end! Suicide charges, if you have to!' He signalled to the Communications Officer to end the transmission, and heaved his chair upright again.

'Sir, the Confederate fleet has us trapped in low orbit!' shouted the Sensors Officer.

'I'm setting course for the equator,' spat Xoanek. 'We'll re-group with Group C, and punch through there!'

The *Vehement* and the rest of its Group swung low, close to the glistening white horizon of Alvor. They sped along under the mesh of Confederate warships, who pounded down death and fury on them, as they sought some refuge from the deadly weapons above.

-#-

Fedrus swore as another missile hit the *Combatant*, knocking it in a full circle before it regained its attitude control. He gripped his steering column and felt his feet rise off the floor as the ship's gravity was momentarily disrupted.

'Return fire!' he snapped. 'Group status?'

'Eleven ships destroyed, sir!' answered the Communications Officer.

Fedrus's head turned round in shock. Nearly half of his ships had been destroyed in a little over fifteen minutes. He turned back to the Flight Display. They were being hammered by the Confederate ships – their fleet formation restricted their ability to manoeuvre rapidly. 'Signal the Group to break formation!' he shouted. 'Break up into Squadrons, and harry individual ships. Make for the equator – we need to rendezvous with the rest of the fleet!'

-#-

Protectorate ships exploded all around the *Vehement* as Xoanek's Group tried to battle its way south to Alvor's equator, all the while under the constant guns of the merciless Confederate fleet above, pounding down on them. Xoanek was knocked from his chair again, this time the force of the blow sending his head smashing into his own console. The screen shattered and he screamed as a shard of glass slid into his left eye, blackening his view. He felt warm liquid flow down his cheek, and knew immediately that his eyeball had been slashed.

Fighting off the instinctive panic that came with partial blindness, he pushed himself upright. He spat blood. 'Damage report!' he shouted.

'Ion Drive is non-operable!' shouted the Chief Engineer. 'We're down to thrusters!'

Xoanek stared ahead at the Flight Display with his one good eye, glaring up at the Confederate starships that dealt out death and destruction from above. Finally, at the utter end, he realised he was defeated. There was no way that he could match this enemy – they were cunning, lethal and deadly. They had out-thought and out-fought him at every turn.

He gritted his teeth as he finally accepted his fate. 'Signal the crew to evacuate the ship,' he said, and stood up. Captain Shivaeus hesitated for a moment, but Xoanek rested his hand on his shoulder. 'Get out of here, lad,' he said. 'This old soldier has got one last thing to do.'

Shivaeus stood up and ran from the Command Centre, a look of thankfulness and fear on his face. Xoanek calmly slid into the Primary Support seat.

'Right, you bastards,' he muttered. 'It's just me and you now.'

He set course for the nearest Confederate ship.

-#-

Fedrus sat in horror as the final site of battle came into view. The horizon was littered with the blackened hulks of Protectorate starships floating in space and Confederate vessels continued to deal their hellish fire from above. A few other Protectorate ships were trying to rally, but constantly dodging this way and that to avoid the deathly rain from above. In the far distance, the gas giant Tarsus rose above the horizon, its impassive gaze seeming hollow and empty over the carnage of the battle.

Fedrus exhaled slowly. 'May the Guardians have mercy,' he murmured. 'Where's the flagship? Where's the *Vehement*?'

'There, sir!' The Sensors Officer tapped his console, and shifted the view on the Flight Display to zoom in on a particular area of the battlefield ahead. The *Vehement*, its outer ring no longer rotating, heavily damaged, its Terculium Reactor flickering faintly, was limping across the void towards a Confederate ship.

'Signal it,' ordered Fedrus.

'No response, sir,' answered the Communications Officer.

'Sir...' said the Sensors Officer, 'she's on a suicide run.'

Fedrus watched in helpless horror as the *Vehement*, flagship of the Expeditionary Force, hobbled onwards towards her final enemy.

-#-

Xoanek sat in the broken Command Centre, strapped into the Primary Support chair. The ship was no longer rotating, so the artificial gravity was gone. The blood on the left side of his face was dry, a sunken hollow where his eye used to be. The Flight Display flickered madly, the lights crackled.

'For the Protectorate,' he muttered, as the doomed ship edged ever closer to the Confederate vessel.

-#-

The Confederate warship turned, as if finally noticing the *Vehement* bearing down on her, and fired three missiles at it. At such close range, they smashed into the ship's defenceless hull, one piercing the eye of the Terculium Reactor. The ship exploded in a brief burst of flame, leaving only broken wreckage and a dispersing miasma of gas and dust, drifting apart in the emptiness of space.

Marshal Xoanek, Chief of Staff of the Protectorate Starforce, was dead.

-#-

Fedrus watched in disbelief as the *Vehement* finally died, its savaged hull broken apart by the force of the Confederate weapons. He looked ahead and saw yet more Protectorate ships pummelled by the Confederate fleet, trapped in low orbit, desperately trying to escape. Still they stayed in formation, clinging to the dogmatic strategy that had doomed them from the very beginning.

'Enough of this,' he muttered, and turned to the Communications Officer. 'Broad signal to all Protectorate ships,' he said. The Communications Officer nodded.

'This is Commodore Fedrus, commanding the *PSS Combatant*,' he said, addressing any Protectorate ship within range. 'The *Vehement* has been destroyed. Marshal Xoanek is dead. I am assuming command of the fleet. All ships, break formation. Assume squadron positions. Set your course for the Lupus-Vulpes Tunnel, full Ion Drive. Abort attack, and fall back. Repeat, abort attack and fall back. Do not engage in suicide runs.'

The command crew fell silent as Fedrus issued the devastating orders. 'Sir,' said the First Officer, 'shouldn't we retreat to Telsor and re-establish our defensive orbit there?'

'With a handful of broken and ruined ships?' retorted Fedrus. 'We wouldn't last a week. We are hopelessly outnumbered, outgunned, and currently, outwitted. I intend to get as many men and ships out of this system as I possibly can, for in the weeks and months ahead we will need every ounce of strength we have.'

'But what shall we tell the colonists on Alvor and Telsor?' demanded the First Officer. 'We can't just abandon them!'

'We have no choice!' roared Fedrus, turning on his officer in anger. 'You want to be a hero? Jump in a lifeboat, launch yourself at the enemy. You saw what good it did Xoanek. Dying like a hero will not save the Protectorate!' He looked around at the command crew, who stared back at him in horror. Every core of their being, everything they had been taught as children, meant fighting the Confederacy to the bitter end. To retreat... was anathema to them. It was like asking them to cut off a limb. They could hardly bring themselves to do it.

'If we die here today,' said Fedrus grimly, 'then our knowledge and experience of the enemy dies with us, and our countrymen are doomed to repeat our mistakes.' He turned to the Communications Officer. 'Tell the colonies on Telsor and Alvor to look to their own defences,' he said. 'The Starforce can no longer protect them. Tell them that conquest must be endured. Tell them that we will return – if we can.'

'The Battle of Vulpes is over. I fear that the Battle of Szotas is about to begin.'

Chapter Seventeen

Karaea sat with her head in her hands, the sunlight from Kaathar shining into the Office of the Protector offering no comfort to the desperate situation. Tears stained her cheeks, and her eyes were flushed red from crying.

Marshal Xoanek was dead and the Vulpes System had fallen to the Confederacy. In the space of a few months, the fortunes of the Great Crusade had turned savagely against the Protectorate. Karaea now found herself faced with the prospect of ordering the Starforce to regroup to defend Szotas itself against invasion by the Protectorate's oldest enemy. The possibility of a second conquest at the hands of the Confederacy of Nations was now very real.

She had received an emergency transmission from Commodore Fedrus less than an hour ago. He had assumed command of the remaining Protectorate forces in the Vulpes System following Xoanek's death. They were *en route* back to Szotas, hoping to regroup with freshly marshalled forces to defend what was left of the Protectorate. At this time, it was hard to envisage re-capturing the Vulpes System in the near future.

And to make matters worse, it seemed that Jamek, Anzaeus's son, was missing, presumed dead, along with Adraea, Fedrus's daughter. Every family on Szotas would know someone or have a member that had been killed, wounded or declared missing in this war. The sudden and devastating loss of Vulpes could barely be contemplated. This war now threatened to obliterate everything they held dear.

Karaea thought about Jamek – her strongest memory of him was when he was six years old, only a few years after his mother's death. He had been a serious child, his dark eyes resting beneath a permanent frown, and yet, she had been able to make him smile. She had loved him, and he her. That was the most painful part of the separation from Anzaeus – losing Jamek as well.

'How did it come to this?' she murmured to herself. 'How could it go so wrong?'

She was disturbed from her thoughts by a knock on the door. She looked up, staring ahead at the double doors opposite her. After a moment, another knock sounded. 'Come in,' she said, and a Guardian, robed in black, entered the room.

'Proconsul Laruak is here to see you, Protector,' said the Guardian impassively.

Karaea nodded. 'Send him in.'

The Guardian opened the doors wide, and Laruak stepped into the Office, his hands held behind his back, his face solemn. His white robes hung loosely about him, his eyes, normally calm, betraying a hint of sadness.

'Protector,' he said, as the door closed behind him, 'the Senate has requested your presence at an emergency session.' He paused. 'The news regarding Vulpes has been leaked to the press. Everyone knows.'

Karaea sighed. 'I had hoped to make a statement to the Senate,' she said. 'I suppose it is too late now.' She stood, and lifted the golden crown from her desk, the symbol of her authority. She placed it on her head, and Laruak's heart ached as he saw her – her regal pose, like a doomed queen, proud and defiant, in the knowledge of her imminent fall. 'Now?' she asked.

Laruak nodded.

'Very well,' said Karaea, resignedly. 'Let's get it over with.'

-#-

The Senators were in a sombre mood as they filed silently into the Senate Chamber, devoid of the usual chatter and banter which marked their gatherings. Laruak watched from the Proconsul's Chair as they assembled in their seats without a word, before finally calling the session to order.

'This session of the Protectorate Senate is convened,' he said, almost dolefully, in the knowledge of what was coming. 'The Senate calls Protector Karaea to the Proconsul's Chair.'

Karaea walked into the Chamber, resplendent in her white robes trimmed with gold, the golden crown on her head flashing in the sunlight. Despite the solemn occasion, she was defiant, determined to face her fate with some dignity. She walked down the central aisle, nodded to Laruak, and took up a lectern position on the dais.

Several Senators stood, requesting the Proconsul's permission to speak. Seeing no reason to delay the inevitable, Laruak said, 'Senator Draelan.'

The other Senators sat down, leaving only Draelan standing. The expression on his face was solemn, but it was obvious from his body language that he was enjoying the proceeding. He was about to destroy his primary political opponent, and he was relishing the moment. The fact that the opportunity to do so had only been presented to him by a war which threatened his entire way of life was irrelevant.

'Protector,' he said, 'there have been headlines in the press this morning regarding the progress of the war. It appears that devastation has been visited upon us. Rumours abound that the Expeditionary Force has suffered massive failure, that Marshal Xoanek, the Chief of Staff of the High Command, is dead, and that the Confederacy have annexed the Vulpes System. Is this true?'

The Chamber was deathly silent. 'It is,' said Karaea, and the silence was broken by a moan of grief and shock from the assembled Senators. 'The Expeditionary Force's position in the Panthera System was attacked. The battle went ill, and Marshal Xoanek deemed it necessary to conduct a retreat to the Vulpes System to re-group and re-arm. Unfortunately, the Confederacy had already invaded Vulpes, cutting off the Expeditionary Force.' She paused and took a deep breath. 'Marshal Xoanek mustered what reinforcements he could at short notice, and attempted to relieve the attack on Vulpes. I regret to say that he lost his life defending Protectorate territory, and that Vulpes has indeed been conquered by the Confederacy.'

Draelan pointed at her. 'And this is despite my warnings,' he said, accusingly. 'I warned you, Protector, that sending such a large force into the Panthera System could provoke the Confederacy. I warned you that stripping the garrisons of Vulpes would leave it badly defended in case of attack. And now, look what your arrogance, your... *hubris*, has brought to our people! Our enemies stand on our doorstep – a mere three weeks' journey from Szotas itself! And in addition to this, you insult the primacy of this Senate by deliberately keeping this a secret from us!'

Karaea began to interject, but Draelan cut her off ruthlessly. 'Come now, Protector,' he said, chastising her, 'I find it difficult to believe that you were not notified of the attack in the Panthera System some time ago. You should have informed us immediately, not covered up a military defeat to save your own political career!'

'My own constituency...' he paused in his address for dramatic effect, 'has been subjugated by the Confederacy. And Szotas may be next.'

'I propose a vote of confidence in Protector Karaea's leadership.'

Karaea closed her eyes, her expression held in anguish as a murmur drifted across the Senate. She remained silent, unable to offer any defence for what had passed. The Protectorate was on the brink of ruin. In that moment, however, her political enmity of Draelan transformed into a personal hatred. He was using the dire circumstances to plunge the Protectorate into a period of political strife when it least needed it, and all for the sake of destroying a political opponent. *He truly is a wretched and opportunistic weasel*, she thought to herself.

'Order!' called Laruak, as the murmur crescendoed to shouts of anger and opposition as Draelan took his seat, smiling to himself. 'The proposal is that this Senate does remove Protector Karaea from office, and calls an election of the people to determine her successor. All those in favour?' Many Senators raised their hands. 'All those against?' A few Senators, loyal to Karaea raised theirs, but the majority was clear. 'So be it,' muttered Laruak, and descended the steps to the Chamber floor.

'Protector Karaea,' he said, standing before her on the Chamber floor, 'attend to me.' Karaea obediently stepped off the dais, and took a few steps towards Laruak, before dropping down on one knee before him, bowing her head. 'You are hereby removed from the office of Protector,' he said, and lifted the crown from her head. 'I, as Proconsul, assume the powers of the Protectorship until an election can be held.' He placed it on his own brow, his face filled with regret.

'Do you intend to stand for re-election?' he asked. Karaea looked at him and stood up. 'I do,' she said.

'Then I confer upon you the office of Praetor,' he said. 'Are there any here who will stand against Praetor Karaea?'

'I will,' said Draelan, and a great roar from his supporters went up. Karaea regarded him with new-found contempt. Not only was he seeking to remove her, he was seeking the Protectorship for himself. Laruak tried to hide his personal disgust. 'Then I confer upon you the office of Praetor,' he said. 'I shall seek approval from the Guardian Conclave for these appointments. Upon receiving them, I shall call an election. Until then, this Senate is dissolved!'

-#-

Laruak closed the door to the Office of the Protector and stood in front of the large wooden desk, gazing across it at the empty chair. The room felt bereft, as if its very soul had been torn out. Laruak's brow creased with emotion, and he took the crown of the Protector, the symbol of the highest power in the Protectorate, off his brow. He tossed it onto the desk, where it landed with a clatter, echoing in the silent room.

Tears welled in the corners of his eyes. 'Damn it,' he muttered to himself, and sat down at the chair in front of the desk normally used by guests. 'Oh, Karaea,' he said. 'I'm sorry. What have I done?'

He fought the rising tide of emotions within him, trying to put them down and replace them with his usual calm professionalism. He tried to deny the truth which had been evident to him for some time. He was in love with Karaea. He had been for nearly a year, and now, his role as Proconsul had forced him to remove her from office and take her crown.

He laughed at the bitter irony of it. He had fallen in love with a woman who was completely inaccessible – by virtue of her being the Protector, and he the Proconsul, a relationship between them would be politically impossible. The Senate's job was to hold the Protector and her Cabinet to account, and as chairman of the Senate, that was the Proconsul's primary duty. For him to become romantically involved with the Protector would give his opponents in the Senate a means to attack his judgement and professionalism. Removing her from office had overcome that obstacle, but she, in Laruak's mind, was even less likely to pursue a relationship with him because of that. She had sacrificed a lot to become Protector – even her relationship with Anzaeus, whom he knew she still cared for. Her grief at his death was swiftly hidden, but Laruak knew the signs. All he longed for in life was to kiss her and embrace her, to comfort her – to love her.

He looked up again at the empty chair on the other side of the desk – the throne of the Protector, from which countless rulers had looked out upon the world of Szotas and the dominions beyond it. A thousand years of history went with the chair, and the discarded crown which lay on the desk before it. And now, albeit only for a short time, it was his – and at the darkest time in the Protectorate's history.

Laruak looked out at the Guardian Temple standing on the opposite side of Central Plaza. The prophecy of the Destroyer – a memory from his childhood – suddenly popped into his head and he smiled bitterly. *If only.*

It was easy to put faith in the half-mad promises of a dying Guardian. Tarsus had been a great man, but Laruak found it difficult to place stock in the prophecy of his reincarnation as the Destroyer of Worlds.

The Protectorate needed a miracle, but it was unlikely to get one.

Laruak's face set in a stern mask. Normal convention during a Protectorship election was for the Proconsul to act as a caretaker pending the outcome of the election – not to present any new legislation or to pursue their own agenda. But these were desperate times, and the Protectorate could not afford to blindly follow political convention. He would not allow Draelan to damage an already dangerous situation by allowing the political chaos to leave the Starforce rudderless at such a crucial moment in the war.

He turned the computer console on the desk around to face him and tapped the screen, connecting him to the Protector's secretary. 'This is Proconsul Laruak,' he said. 'Please summon the Acting Chief of Staff.'

-#-

General Daedra stood to attention in front of the Protector's desk, and saluted. Daedra was one of the few women in the High Command, and was a powerful presence. At fifty years old, she was one of the youngest Staff Officers. She had often been an outspoken critic of Marshal Xoanek, but despite this, he had seen fit to appoint her as Deputy Chief of Staff. Following the Marshal's death, she was now Acting Chief, commander of the Protectorate Starforce.

Her hair was a light brown, streaked with grey. She looked to be ten years younger than she actually was, with only her eyes, shining with hard experience, and a few wrinkles in the corners of her mouth, betraying her age. The golden epaulette on her shoulder was engraved with three twelve-pointed stars, indicating her rank as General.

Fedrus stood next to her. His eyes were sunken, his cheeks grey, his previously bulky frame now thinner and sleeker from having lost weight. He looked tired, grief-stricken and downtrodden, but a keen fury still burned in his eyes. He saluted Laruak.

'General,' said Laruak, nodding to Daedra. He offered her a seat, but did not sit down himself – it felt wrong for him to sit in Karaea's chair. For the same reason, he left the Protector's crown resting on the desk in front of him. Fedrus also sat down.

'Proconsul,' said Daedra, 'I believe you have already met Commodore Fedrus – he assumed command of the

Expeditionary Force after Marshal Xoanek's death, and has only arrived on Szotas in the last few hours. I have requested his presence here.'

Laruak nodded. 'What is the current military situation?'

'The Confederacy has completely annexed the Vulpes System,' replied Fedrus. 'They have secured high orbit of every major planet and colony, and have landed ground troops. We cannot get reinforcements to the colonies without first breaking their orbital control. Furthermore, they have captured the wormhole vortex to the Lupus System, which gives them the capability of invading Szotas itself.'

'The Expeditionary Force has been largely destroyed,' continued Daedra. 'Commodore Fedrus returned to Szotas with twelve starships out of the two hundred which formed the Expeditionary Force, and the additional fifty which were deployed to reinforce Vulpes when it was attacked. The 3rd Fleet has been completely destroyed, and the 1st Fleet has only sixty-seven percent capacity. The twelve ships that have returned are in dire need of repair or replacement.'

Laruak nodded. 'General Daedra,' he said, 'I am hereby promoting you to the rank of Marshal, and appointing you as Chief of Staff of the High Command. Congratulations. I wish it were under better circumstances.' He handed her an electronic pad confirming the orders.

Daedra looked confused. 'I thought only a Protector...'

'I am well within my constitutional remit to appoint new officers,' interrupted Laruak. 'It is only a political convention that Proconsuls do not take an active role in Government. Given the circumstances, I have chosen to dispense with that convention.'

Daedra nodded. 'Understood, Your Grace.'

Laruak turned to Fedrus. 'Commodore, do you think it is likely that the Confederacy will move against Szotas?'

'I think it virtually certain, Your Grace,' he replied. 'They intend to crush us as quickly as possible.'

'I agree,' said Laruak. 'Marshal, I want you to re-deploy the 2nd Fleet to garrison the Lupus System, and prepare battle plans for the system's defence. If they move to attack Szotas, I want to be ready for them. Furthermore, as of this moment, the Starforce budget is tripled. I want the two hundred and fifty starships we have lost to be rebuilt by this time next year. Is that clear?'

Daedra blinked in astonishment. 'Forgive me, Your Grace,' she said, 'but I don't think that's possible. Our shipyards take some time to progress to maximum capacity...'

'Marshal,' interrupted Laruak, 'I appreciate your honesty, but we are at war. We are in very real danger of being defeated by the Confederacy. Our very way of life depends on the outcome of this war. We cannot be beaten – we *must not* be beaten. Do whatever it takes.'

Daedra nodded. 'I will see to it personally, Proconsul,' she said. 'But, if I may say so, sir, General Tarius of the 2nd Fleet has no real battle experience – certainly nothing like confronting the Confederacy. May I suggest that he be transferred to command the 1st Fleet, to assist in the rebuilding efforts?'

Laruak nodded. 'Whatever you feel is appropriate, Marshal,' he said. 'Get me the orders, and I'll sign them. Who do you plan to serve as his replacement? The 2nd Fleet is about to go on the front lines – we need someone with proven experience.'

'I recommend Commodore Fedrus, Your Grace.'

Fedrus's mouth dropped open in astonishment. He turned to Daedra. 'I'm honoured, ma'am,' he said, 'but surely there are...'

'Nonsense,' said Daedra curtly. 'Your valour and conduct have been exemplary, Commodore. I cannot think of any other Staff Officer who would have brought back battle-hardened crews which will be invaluable in training other soldiers rather than simply charge in a suicidal quest for glory. You made the strategic choice. It may well yet save us all.'

Laruak smiled. 'Commodore Fedrus,' he said, 'I hereby promote you to the rank of General, and award you command of the 2nd Fleet. Deploy your ships to defend Szotas.'

Chapter Eighteen

Adraea awoke in the freezing cell, rubbing her aching arms, trying to rid herself of the bitter cold. She shivered uncontrollably and her breath clouded as she exhaled. For a moment, she panicked, wondering where she was, but then the flood of memories rolled over her, and the realities of the prison hit home.

They had been there for a few weeks now. It was a forced labour camp – for twelve hours a day, the inhabitants worked in a factory, manufacturing weapons and ammunition for the Confederate Starfleet. The work was especially heartbreaking for the Protectorate prisoners, as they knew that their labours would be to the detriment of their own people.

Adraea looked down at her hands, which were cut and worn from the work. She had spent the day making bullets for the machine guns carried by Confederate troops, clipping the excess metal from the moulded projectiles, which was then recycled to make even more bullets. The metal shavings bit into her fingers and palms.

She lifted her head from the old mattress on which she was lying, her face creasing into an expression of disgust. It smelt vaguely of excrement and old urine. The guards hosed the cells down with water and disinfectant every few days to stop disease from spreading, but they rarely replaced the bedding.

She ran her fingers along her head, feeling the alien stubble which clung to her skull. Tears pricked in her eyes at the thought of her long hair being shorn, but she blinked them angrily back. Survival was the order of the day. All they had to do was live, and hope that the Protectorate would somehow turn the tide of the war.

She could feel Jamek lying next to her, his breathing heavy and regular, his chest rising and falling against her back. A small smile crept onto her face – at least, despite all the horrors that they had endured over the last few weeks, they were still together. The knowledge that Mavrak was nearby was also a great comfort – he seemed to act as a calming influence on Jamek, who had not taken well to captivity.

Adraea shuddered involuntarily. Jamek had changed since his father's death, but it had become even more apparent upon entering the prison. He was still loving, and he still cared for her, but he seemed to be increasingly embroiled in a battle with some inner demon. His sleep was often disturbed. And when he was angered... Adraea could have sworn she had seen something in his eyes akin to flame.

She listened carefully, trying to estimate roughly what time it was by gauging the activity in the prison. It seemed deathly silent, suggesting that it was the middle of the night. *Good*, she thought to herself, and stood up slowly, disentangling herself from Jamek. She tested the cell door – it was unlocked. She was not surprised – many prisoners that behaved well were granted a greater degree of liberty, and despite Jamek's growing frustration, neither of them had caused any trouble. As such, they had been granted that privilege. Other prisoners that were known troublemakers were locked into their cells at night.

Still shivering with the biting cold, her teeth chattering madly, Adraea slowly opened the door. One of the hinges squealed loudly, and Jamek stirred, but did not wake. Adraea slipped out of the cell and started off down the corridor, heading towards the main prisoner hall. She knew that, during the night, many Protectorate prisoners gathered there in an attempt to stay warm. As she crept down the corridor in the darkness, she remembered Mavrak's warning not to go alone.

'I'm not alone,' she muttered to herself. 'It's less than a hundred yards to the main hall.'

The flickering orange light at the end of the corridor grew brighter as she approached. She could hear the crackle of the fire and felt some of its heat drifting down to her, caressing her skin with delicious warmth. 'Only ten minutes,' she murmured to herself. 'Just to warm myself up. And then I'll go back.'

She stepped out of the corridor into the main hall, and her smile froze on her face.

There was a small group of men huddled around the fire. None of the faces belonged to Protectorate prisoners. One of them immediately caught sight of her, and his face split into an evil grin. Adraea's heart ran cold as she recognised him – it was Felador, the one who had tried to grab her on her first day in the prison. His scarred face, massive height and bulging arms were easily recognisable. 'Oh, shit,' she muttered, and immediately turned to run back down the corridor. To her horror, she found it already blocked by two of Felador's associates, both smiling darkly.

She screamed but they both grabbed her, one clapping a thick, calloused hand over her mouth, the other seizing her arms and twisting them up behind her back so far that it brought tears to her eyes. They manhandled her over to the fireplace, her fists and kicks landing ineffectually on them.

Felador came over, smirking. 'You were expecting to see your friends here?' he asked rhetorically, his face split with a vile grin. 'They cleared off when we arrived. How unfortunate for you.' He reached out and squeezed her left breast hard. Adraea gasped, both at the unrestrained and casual nature of the assault, and from the pain itself. Her heart beat wildly with fear, and her eyes opened wide in terror, her voice a muffled scream.

Felador's other hand moved to her thigh, stroking her gently. 'She's still smooth,' he crooned, and Adraea retched, the combination of the excruciating pain and the perversion of sexual contact simultaneously terrifying and revolting her. 'Of course, that'll change,' said Felador, and the others laughed maliciously. Adraea saw a dangerous, deadly, *hungry* expression on their faces, and beat madly against her attackers, trying desperately to break free, her panic growing with every second. However hard she tried, it was futile. There were too many of them, and they were too strong. Felador's face filled her vision as he bent close to her, and she shut her eyes, trying to block out the horror...

Suddenly, the world exploded in a blaze of sound, an enraged, animal roar, and her eyes flicked open to see Felador thrown back onto the floor. He hit the concrete with a bone-jarring jolt, the breath knocked out of him, and suddenly, Jamek was there, his face twisted in a snarl of uncontrollable rage. He leapt on the big Confederate prisoner, his hands hooked like clawed talons. She felt the hands on her loosen slightly, and pulled her head free, biting down hard on the hand over her face. She tasted hot blood and heard her attacker wail in pain. Other hands let go, and she tore her head away, taking a chunk of flesh from the man's hand with her. She spat it out in disgust, and bolted for the corridor, screaming, 'Mavrak!'

Mavrak emerged from the corridor, running at a full sprint, and narrowly avoided colliding with her. He immediately apprised the situation with one glance at Adraea, his face locked in a terrible mask of rage. He seized her arm, and dragged her into the Protectorate corner, where some Protectorate prisoners were already starting to gather. 'Stay here,' he hissed, and ran towards the fireplace.

By now, the prisoner hall was abuzz with activity. Metal clanked as the heavy footsteps of the guards echoed on the walkways overhead. Shouting prisoners poured into the hall from all directions, both Protectorate and Confederate alike. Adraea, her breath coming in painful wheezes, her hands shaking with the awful ordeal, looked across at the fireplace, and gasped in astonishment.

Jamek was in the middle of a vicious fist fight with Felador and the two other men who had attacked her. One of them punched him hard in the face, rocking him back on his heels with the force of the blow, and mashing his lips. 'Jamek!' wailed Adraea, only to see him spit blood, before his hands dug into the face of his attacker. Adraea screwed up her eyes as Jamek's hooked fingers slid into the man's mouth, and with a swift sideways movement, tore his cheek from his skull, exposing his bloodied molar teeth. The Confederate prisoner ran off, howling in agony at this sudden and savage mutilation.

By this time, Mavrak had reached the site of the battle, and ran full-tilt into the other attacker, smashing his powerful shoulder directly into his opponent's stomach. The force of the impact took both him and Mavrak flying nearly eight feet across the hall, where they landed in a shattering impact. Mavrak drove his heavy fists into his opponent, hammering his stomach and groin in a pulverising assault.

Jamek and Felador circled each other, Jamek's eyes narrowed, his lips drawn tightly across his bared teeth. His eyes glimmered with some dark light, and Adraea felt a cold chill as she watched her boyfriend. Something in him was completely different, a primal force of nature which this situation had awoken. A demon inside him had emerged, and it was not the man she loved that stood there.

'She is mine,' snarled Felador. 'Back off, or I'll kill you, boy.'

Jamek attacked.

Adraea had never seen anyone move with such speed. He dropped to the floor, sliding between Felador's legs and sweeping them from under him. The big man crashed to the ground in a heap, and Jamek drove his fist into Felador's throat. The big man choked, his eyes bulging in surprise, and collapsed in a writhing heap, gasping for air. Jamek leapt on him, wrapping his hands around the bigger prisoner's throat, pressing his thumbs hard into the gulley between Felador's collarbones. Felador's arms flailed helplessly against this murderous onslaught, and Adraea turned away, her hand to her mouth in desperate horror.

After dispatching his opponent, Mavrak ran over to Jamek and seized him by the arms. With a colossal effort, he wrenched Jamek's hands away from Felador's throat and pulled him off the bigger man, kicking and screaming in a savage, murderous rage.

'I'll kill him!' roared Jamek, his face contorted in a mask of savagery. 'Get off me, Mavrak – I'm going to strangle that *fucking pig!*'

Mavrak forced Jamek's arms down by his sides, his muscles straining with the effort. He gasped as he fought his best friend's strength – forcing his arms was like trying to bend iron bars. He had never known such strength – not even Felador's strength could match his own, but Jamek could. Finally, he locked Jamek in a hard bearhug, holding his arms by his sides. Jamek fought like a wild thing.

'Let me go, you *fuck!*' he bellowed. 'I'm going to rip his fucking *eyes* out! I'll tear out his fucking *gullet*!'

Felador choked, his lips turning blue, and there was an awful moment filled with a deadly silence as nearly a hundred prisoners watched the big man fighting for air. Mavrak thought that it was too late, that they were going to watch him suffocate, but after what seemed like an age, Felador finally drew a whistling, wheezing breath. He spluttered and coughed, a hacking, horrible sound as his throat fought to expand that thin stream of air. Finally, his chest opened and he breathed deeply, heaving in the air in great gasps. He pulled himself to his feet, still looking at the enraged Jamek, his teeth bared in a terrible snarl, fighting his own friend for the privilege of murdering the Confederate prisoner. Felador knew when he couldn't win a battle. He ran, stumbling out of the prisoner hall, and into one of the darkened corridors on the far side, spitting blood.

-#-

'What did you think you were doing?' shouted Mavrak, pacing up and down in the Protectorate corner. Adraea sat mutely on a wooden crate in front of him. 'I warned you, Adraea – don't go *anywhere* alone. What part of *anywhere* did you not understand?'

'Fuck you, Mavrak,' she said, her voice trembling. 'Those bastards just tried to *rape* me – the last thing I need is a lecture from you! I know I made a mistake. It won't happen again! Now leave me alone!' She burst into tears, her body shaking with the terror of the ordeal.

Mavrak stopped and sighed. 'Oh, Adraea,' he said, and knelt down next to her, putting his arm around her shoulders. 'I'm sorry,' he said. 'I'm sorry. I don't mean to... it's just that... you could've been killed!'

Adraea pushed him away angrily. 'And you think I don't know that?' she spat. 'I know, Mavrak.'

'I'm sorry,' repeated Mavrak, holding his hands up in a gesture of *mea culpa*. 'Please, Adraea.'

Adraea's face screwed up again, and more tears came. Mavrak hugged her again, and this time, she hugged back. 'I really do think you should say something to Jamek, though,' he whispered.

Jamek was stood leaning against the wall, staring off into space. Adraea looked at him and almost shook her head. What he had done, what he had become, scared her almost as much as Felador did. He was like a man possessed. She had never seen such ferocity, such wanton, savage aggression. Mavrak put his hand in the small of her back and pushed her towards Jamek.

She stood before him, looking into his eyes. After what seemed like an age, he smiled, coming out of his reverie. 'Adraea,' he said, and caressed her cheek.

Adraea's heart lifted and she threw her arms around him. 'I'm sorry, Jamek,' she said, stifling another sob. 'I'm so sorry. I just wanted to spend a few minutes by the fire...'

'It's okay,' said Jamek, kissing her. 'It's okay, Adraea. It's not your fault. But from now on, Mavrak is right. Nowhere alone. Okay?' Adraea nodded dumbly. 'I just need to have a quick word with Mavrak. You stay here, with the other guys.' He indicated the other Protectorate prisoners in the corner. 'I won't be long.' He kissed her again, and then headed into one of the nearby corridors. Mavrak followed him into the dark.

Once they were about fifty yards in, Jamek turned and slapped Mavrak hard across the face. The blow nearly knocked him over, but he stood back up in shock and amazement, ready to argue back, but fell silent when he saw Jamek's eyes. Something glimmered deep in the dark pools, like fire dancing on the surface of oil. He said nothing.

'If you try to stop me again,' said Jamek, his voice dark and level, 'I'll really hurt you, Mavrak. You should have let me kill him.'

'Kill him?' said Mavrak, aghast. 'If you'd have killed him, we'd have a full scale riot on our hands. The Confederate lot would've gone mad, and in case you haven't noticed, Jamek, there's a lot more of them than us! On top of that, I was trying to make sure that the guards didn't have an excuse to kill you. So think on that before you go slapping me about! I mean, what the hell were you thinking, diving in like that?'

Jamek grabbed Mavrak by his rough tunic, and to the bigger man's astonishment, lifted him clean off the ground. The strange, orange flicker in his eyes flared briefly, before dying down again, and Jamek whispered through gritted teeth, 'he was trying to rape her. Did you not see that? Are you blind?'

'Jamek,' said Mavrak, quietly, 'put me down.'

Jamek was silent for a moment, then lowered Mavrak back to the floor. Mavrak sighed with something akin to relief. 'I know,' he said. 'And I understand your reaction. All I'm saying is, it could've been handled better. Tearing that guy's face off and nearly choking Felador to death was not exactly what I'd call a proportionate response under the circumstances. They'll have it in for you now. And the guards will certainly have noticed you.'

Jamek laughed, a cruel, horrible sound which made Mavrak's skin crawl. 'If they try again,' he said, 'I'll kill them all. Do you understand, Mavrak? Every single one.'

He pushed past Mavrak, and then his step slowed. When he turned, Mavrak could no longer see that dangerous glimmer in his eyes, and realised that he was looking at a different person. 'Mavrak,' he said, 'thanks for helping. You're a good friend.'

He turned and walked back out into the prisoner hall, leaving Mavrak standing alone in the dark. Mavrak thought to himself. *What is going on? What is happening to Jamek? Why is my best friend going mad?*

Chapter Nineteen

Ulestran stalked into the Council Chamber, feeling a secret thrill as the assembled Governors fell silent. He took his seat on the Chancellor's throne, smiling archly at Tellanor, who was sitting next to him. She returned the smile – an expression that made the pit of his stomach ache with desire. He smirked to himself as he remembered the previous night, when she had shared his bed – running his fingers over her soft, perfect skin, enjoying the taste of her on his lips...

He allowed himself a momentary daydream, before coming out of it and focusing sharply on this moment. As much as his liaisons with Tellanor delighted him, he wouldn't miss this moment for the world, and wanted to savour every single part of it.

'I declare this session of the Council of Governors open,' he said, fixing his gaze momentarily on Allanor, who sat on the right side of the Chamber, watching quietly. She did not match his gaze, ignoring him. Slightly irked, Ulestran continued.

'Esteemed Governors, I have called you here today to update the Council on the military conflict with the Protectorate.'

The last mutterings and whispers of Governors on both sides of the Chamber immediately fell silent. Ulestran's smile disappeared, assuming a statesmanlike pose and expression that was as convincing as it was utterly false. He was a consummate politician – a master of poise and language, but with a fundamental dishonesty that ran deep.

'I am pleased to announce,' said Ulestran, 'that following our successful rout of the Protectorate invasion force in Alpha Centauri, the Task Force there has now used the Protectorate-constructed wormhole to travel to the Epsilon Indi system.'

'This morning, I received a communication from the Chevalier commanding the fleet. He has advised me that, despite continued attacks from Protectorate forces, they have now driven their Starfleet from the system, and the colonies there have surrendered. The Epsilon Indi system is now under Confederate control!'

The Governors on Ulestran's right cheered loudly, overjoyed. Allanor and her Opposition supporters sat quietly, waiting for the hubbub to die down, watching Ulestran intently as he allowed the cheers to continue for a few moments. He eventually stood, signalling for silence, and the noise disappeared.

'Needless to say,' he continued, 'this audacious victory leaves us with a massive tactical advantage. Possession of the Epsilon Indi System not only protects both the Alpha Centauri and Therqan Systems from further aggression, but also puts us within striking distance of Gliese 783 – the Protectorate's home system.'

'Our resolute action to attack the Protectorate with the economic support of the Empire of Feragoth has resulted in a swift victory. Our troops are fortifying positions in Epsilon Indi – it is highly unlikely that the Protectorate will be able to retake the system. They will either have to press for terms and accept our control of the new territories, or we will mount an invasion of Gliese 783 and crush them utterly.'

He sneered at the Opposition benches. 'It turns out that the concerns of the Opposition were unjustified after all,' he said, to much laughter from his own supporters. He sat down and Voltar, the leader of Ulestran's supporters, stood up.

'I thank the Chancellor for his statement to the Council,' he said, his wheedling voice echoing in the Chamber. 'If I might enquire as to the Chancellor's plans for the invasion of Gliese 783?'

Loud murmurs of approval echoed from Voltar's allies, and Ulestran stood up again. 'The Starfleet is currently establishing garrison positions in Epsilon Indi, so that if the Protectorate do chance an immediate counter-attack, we will not be caught off-guard. However, all the indications are that they do not have the capacity to do so. It is estimated that we have destroyed a full third of their

Starfleet. I expect to begin the invasion of Gliese 783 within a few months.'

Allanor stood up and Ulestran's smile faded slightly. Still, nothing much could dampen this moment. Despite anything Allanor had to say, she had been proven wrong. The Protectorate had proven an easy foe to beat, and her caution and calls for negotiation had been wrong. He nodded to her, granting her permission to speak.

'Once again, I find myself criticising the Chancellor for not keeping this Council up-to-date,' she said. 'The last time we received an update on the progress of the war was over four months ago! And now, we are told that not only have we invaded another nation, but we have conquered some of their territory as well!'

Boos and jeers echoed from the opposite side of the Chamber, but Allanor continued, undeterred. 'Our military victory has done nothing to ease my concerns,' she said, 'in fact, they are compounded. The Empire's payment has gone some way to alleviating the budget deficit for this year, but the governmental finances are still in an abject state. The military is drastically underfunded, and yet the Chancellor has elected to put us on a war footing. And now, we have an entire new territory to maintain, which will no doubt be filled with citizens hostile to Confederate rule! We have over-stretched ourselves.'

'The Chancellor makes grand talk of establishing garrisons in Epsilon Indi, and being able to launch an invasion of Gliese 783 within months,' she said, 'but these are not borne out by the figures we have available. Five hundred starships were needed to capture Epsilon Indi – the Chancellor says that we have destroyed a third of the Protectorate's Starfleet, but it has taken nearly half of ours to accomplish it!'

'The population of the Epsilon Indi system is approximately four billion people. The same report which the Chancellor quotes from – which I have managed to obtain a copy of, despite him censoring it from the Opposition – recommends an occupational force of *six hundred* starships and *forty million* troops. In other words, the advice of our military commanders is to commit over half of the manpower of the Confederate Military to the occupation of one system. What, precisely, does the Chancellor propose to continue the invasion with?'

'And there is the continued matter of the Empire of Feragoth,' said Allanor. 'The camp they have established in Dacia is highly secret. They have now engaged some type of disruption field in the area to prevent our satellites from monitoring it. There are reports of Feragoths intimidating citizens in the area, causing them to leave. This type of behaviour – from a nation which purports to be our ally – is completely unacceptable, and yet my requests to question the Feragothic Ambassador are routinely denied.'

'This government allows a foreign nation to establish its own private enclave within our territory, and allows it to intimidate our citizens. It then invades another foreign nation, conquering its territory in an ill-considered campaign. It is now in no position to properly defend the Confederacy's borders due to a poorly-equipped and overstretched military. And of course, it continues to flagrantly demonstrate contempt for democracy by refusing to submit even its most basic actions to legislative scrutiny. In short, this government has been, and continues to be, a disgrace to this great nation. I, myself, am no longer prepared to tolerate this charade, and so I will no longer enter this Chamber until the government is prepared to submit itself to the authority of the Council.'

She turned and walked out of the Chamber, followed by her supporters, who ignored the baleful howls and mocking laughter of Ulestran's supporters. Even Ulestran found himself laughing, but deep in his heart, he began to feel the creep of dread, and he knew that he was witnessing history taking place. As he watched the Opposition benches empty, he knew that something was starting. In the years to come, men would study the history of the Confederacy, put their finger on this event, and say, 'this was the day it began to change.'

-#-

Ulestran walked into his office, throwing open the double-doors and pacing up and down in front of his desk. Although he and his supporters had made a joke of Allanor's walk-out, it had shaken him. To have so many Governors abandon the Chamber like that... it was very disconcerting. Allanor's promise not to return also echoed in his ears. Was it just empty posturing, or did she mean something by it?

Tellanor followed him into the room and closed the doors behind her. She watched him for a moment, pacing up and down, before she cleared her throat to get his attention. Ulestran stopped and glanced at the Secretary of State.

'That went well,' she said, a slight smile in the corners of her mouth.

Ulestran scoffed. 'It depends on how you define 'well',' he said. 'I don't like her grandstanding. And she's popular, for an Opposition leader. Don't get me wrong, it's rare that someone in that position ever attains high office, but her agitations don't go entirely unnoticed.'

'She's an irrelevance,' replied Tellanor, bluntly.

'How did she get hold of that report?' snapped Ulestran. 'Find out, and deal with it.'

Tellanor nodded. 'I'll deal with it,' she said. 'I might need the assistance of that policeman...'

'Turan?' Ulestran waved dismissively. 'Talk to him. It's not like the Ambassador requires him on a day-to-day basis.' He continued his pacing again. Tellanor walked over to him and laid her hands on Ulestran's shoulders. He calmed down somewhat, relaxing as he felt her cool, soft skin caress his neck.

'Don't worry about Allanor,' she murmured, her lips brushing his ear. 'You are the Chancellor, and her dramatics don't change that fact. You have led the Confederacy to another victory over the Kingdom. You will be the Chancellor to unify our sundered race.'

Ulestran turned to face her, regarding her with a hungry look on his face. 'And you, Tellanor? What will you become?'

'You won't want to be Chancellor forever,' she said, coyly.

Ulestran smiled in understanding. 'You want me to endorse you when I step down? What about Voltar?'

Tellanor took a step forward, pressing her breasts against Ulestran's portly frame, and sliding her hand between his legs. 'I have... abilities... that Voltar lacks,' she said, her voice dark and husky.

'That you do,' muttered Ulestran, his eyes shining with lust, his mouth dry with wanting. He kissed Tellanor hungrily, pawing at her buttocks, grasping greedily. Tellanor laughed, but gently pushed him back.

'You need to talk to the Ambassador,' she said. 'Allanor was right about one thing – they *are* being secretive about their little research project. We can use that to our advantage. Ask for more money, in exchange for continuing their elevated secrecy.'

Ulestran nodded, his desire beginning to abate. 'Yes,' he said. 'Good idea. Send for the Ambassador, and Turan. Immediately.'

-#-

Turan was woken by his communicator ringing. He groaned, his head thumping from too much whisky the night before, his tongue and throat dry and hot from too many corch cigarettes. He blinked blearily, reaching for the communicator.

'Hello?' he muttered.

'Superintendent Turan?' came a familiar voice. 'This is Secretary Tellanor. The Chancellor requires your immediate presence at the Palace.'

Turan snapped awake, suddenly alert. The requirement for his presence meant one thing: the requirement for the *Ambassador's* presence. The cold chill of fear suddenly spiked his heart.

'I'm on my way,' he replied, and hung up. He reached for an almost-empty bottle of whisky by his bed, and emptied it into his mouth. The liquid burned as it went down, and Turan coughed and spluttered.

He pulled himself out of bed wearily, throwing the empty whisky bottle into the corner, where it smashed. He went into the bathroom, exclaiming as he jumped into a cold shower to wake himself, scrubbing his teeth to get the taste of day-old whisky and corch weed out of his mouth.

Ever since he had taken the assignment at the Palace, he had been plagued by terrible dreams – evil nightmares of that cowled figure that haunted the centre of government. He hated and feared the Ambassador in equal measure – there was something terrible and malevolent about him that chilled Turan's soul. He could barely maintain his composure in the creature's presence, and the harbinger plagued his thoughts and dreams. Turan found himself increasingly indulging in corch and alcohol to try and blot out the nightmares, where he awoke drenched in cold sweat and screaming, barely able to remember the dreams. At least the drugs knocked him out.

His haggard reflection stared back at him – dark, sunken eyes, two-day-old stubble, and unkempt hair, dripping wet from the cold shower. He dried himself, and as he shaved, he found his hands still shivering, but not with the cold.

-#-

An hour later, Turan stood in the Chancellor's office, dressed in a crisp business suit, his hair slicked back, his face clean-shaven. He exhibited no symptoms of stress, except his tendency to stiffen when the dark-cloaked Ambassador standing next him moved. That was a reflex exercise to stop himself physically cringing away from the alien.

He forced his mind to concentrate on other things, and fixed his eyes on anything except the emissary – a patch of light reflecting on Ulestran's desk, the curve of Tellanor's thigh, the reassuring weight of his gun in his inside jacket holster.

The Ambassador, cloaked in black, towering over the others in the room, stood silent, exuding arrogance and contempt.

Ulestran stood behind his desk, the usual welcoming smile on his face, as if trying to set the apparition at ease. Turan had to stop himself laughing hysterically at the irony of it.

'Thank you, Your Excellency, for attending at such short notice,' said Ulestran. 'I wish to discuss the archaeological expedition the Empire is currently undertaking in Dacia.'

'What about it?' The alien's voice made Turan's ears want to crawl inside his head.

Ulestran faltered for a moment, unsure of how to proceed. 'It has been noted that your colleagues have established some sort of disruption field around the site,' he said. 'It is preventing our satellites from scanning the area. I must enquire as to why.'

'I fail to see why that is any of your concern,' snapped the Ambassador. 'The treaty made it clear that we were to have exclusive rights to the site we chose.'

'I am not questioning the treaty,' continued Ulestran smoothly, 'but the Confederacy does retain sovereignty, and we have the right to monitor our own territory. There is also an understanding that you will share the results of your research with us.'

The emissary made a noise which Turan could only interpret as a sigh of exasperation – a hissing, angry exhalation. 'The dampening field is a protective measure,' he said. 'It is simply to protect our scientists from the effects of your sunlight. They are not as... acclimatised to your world as I.'

Ulestran frowned, knowing instinctively that this was a lie. 'I see,' he said. 'Well, the Council of Governors has raised concerns about it – they require reassurance that the Empire is not seeking to establish a permanent enclave on Therqa.'

'Reassure them, then,' retorted the alien, bluntly. 'I have nothing further to discuss with you, Chancellor.' He turned on his heel to leave.

'I was wondering if the Emperor would consider another token payment,' said Ulestran quickly, 'in order to appease the Governors.'

The emissary stopped and turned slowly back to face the Chancellor.

'What?' he said, his voice low and menacing.

Ulestran suddenly felt a terrible chill as he gazed into the terrible shadow under the hood. 'Or perhaps simply greater co-operation between our people in the aspect of research,' he muttered weakly.

Turan felt some form of relief at the sight of Ulestran's discomfort, suddenly knowing that he was not the only one terrified by this awful creature. Even Tellanor was silent and cast her eyes at the floor.

'Chancellor,' the alien spat the word, loading it with contempt, 'you have agreed to give us free licence on a site of our choosing, in exchange for an extremely generous package of natural resources. This unwarranted interference is not appreciated. However, in the interests of maintaining good relations between our nations, I am prepared to forget this incident. If another occurs, I will be forced to report to the Emperor. And that could *seriously* damage relations. Do we understand each other?'

Ulestran nodded, sweat beading on his brow. 'Good day, Ambassador. Thank you for your time.'

Without another word, the alien swept from the room, and Turan followed him in silence, nodding to the Chancellor as he left. As he walked the Ambassador back to his apartments, Turan knew that he had to pay a visit to this research site in Dacia. He had always suspected that the Empire had an ulterior motive, and the emissary's exchange with Ulestran had confirmed it. He intended to find out exactly what they were up to.

-#-

Turan pulled the heavy coat around him, stamping his feet to keep his toes warm. It was autumn in the Capital, but on the rugged mountain plateau, the weather was already bitterly cold. Turan looked around him in the gloom, rubbing his gloved hands together and blowing hot breath onto his fingers.

The mountains reared up against the twilight sky, ugly heads of craggy rock and jagged spires, pointing accusingly at the sky, and frowning down on the battered land below. The sky was a deep, dark blue, almost black, the mountains behind him in the west casting long shadows in front of the setting sun. The stars were coming out in the east ahead, a great ribbon of them creeping across the dome of the sky as it slowly darkened.

The mountainside was littered with scree close to the high peaks, loose grey stones that gave way underfoot. A forest of coniferous trees covered the lower slopes, washing up the alpine walls of the mountains in waves of green.

Turan cursed silently to himself as he trudged steadily up the slope, his ankles twisting occasionally on the loose ground. He paused for a moment, catching his breath, which burned in his lungs. Steam blew out of his mouth and nostrils in white columns.

Suddenly, he heard voices, easily detectable on the silent mountainside, carried on the light wind. A spike of panic slid into his heart, and he dropped to the floor as silently as he could, before crawling behind a large boulder. Ahead and above him, the ridged peaks of the mountains glared down with unseeing eyes.

The voices grew louder, until they seemed to be only a few feet away. Turan's heart hammered in his chest, yet he knew that they must be further away – their voices were simply being carried on the wind. He slid his gloved hand into his coat, pulling a semi-automatic handgun from his pocket, the silencer twisted into the barrel making it feel heavy and bulky. Reassured by the feel of cold steel through his gloves, he edged his head around the boulder, trying to glimpse the owners of the voices.

He saw them walking across the mountainside, parallel to the ridge, about fifty feet above him. They were at least seven feet tall, cloaked entirely in black from head to foot, their faces obscured by the dark shadows of their heavy hoods. They hardly seemed to walk across the loose scree, and no stones were sent tumbling down by their passage. It was almost as if they were gliding over the stones, like shadows or spectres from ancient legends.

Turan forced himself to breathe slowly as he watched them cross the mountainside above him, murmuring to themselves in their alien tongue. Occasionally, their heads turned out towards the valley, black searchlights roving across the battered and twisted landscape. For a moment, one seemed to gaze directly at Turan, before moving on.

Feragoths.

Aliens.

Turan narrowed his eyes as the cloaked figures moved back up the mountainside, before finally disappearing over the ridge, every instinct in his body telling him not to go on, to fall back away from these creatures.

His mouth felt parched, his heart thudded dully in his chest, and his palms were cold and clammy under his leather gloves. He shook his head, steeling his nerve, conscious now that he must be as silent as possible in order to avoid detection.

He waited for about half an hour, watching the ridge-line of the high peaks ahead of him for further movement in the gathering dusk. He suspected that the darkness would provide little cover for him – the Feragothic homeworld was rumoured to be shrouded in permanent twilight, and the aliens could see without light. Finally, when he was sure that no further patrols were on their way, he crept out from behind the boulder and continued his tortuous climb up the scree-covered slopes to the peak.

When he reached the top, the view nearly caused him to gasp out loud.

A great circular valley lay before him, the ridge of mountains on which he stood stretching away to the north, grey peaks glimmering in the ethereal starlight.

Across the valley, ten miles away on the eastern side, the vague, dark shapes of another mountain range could be seen, curving towards the ridge on which he stood, meeting in a maw of stone at the southern end of the valley. The northern pass also had a narrow throat, guarded by an ancient castle and a town that surrounded it. The northern end of the valley opened out onto a vast plain that stretched into the far distance. It was a spectacular landscape, stark and beautiful, the untouched, unclaimed wilderness of a forgotten world.

But it was the valley itself which held Turan's attention. The valley floor was illuminated with a dark red light, giving it a brooding feel. The strange, unearthly lights cast alien shadows on the lower slopes of the mountains. Entire foothills were being quarried away, great machines tearing out chunks of earth in a sick parody of creation, a rape of the earth. Black-cloaked figures could be seen crawling like locusts over the hills as they were demolished by tractors, diggers and trucks, great piles of black earth being moved to the northern opening of the valley. The faint rumble of machinery echoed in the valley below, but was swept away and diluted by the wind.

The activity of the Feragoths filled a great circle some eight miles across, radiating out from the centre of the valley. Turan watched in amazement as he saw the tops of buildings – ancient, ruined buildings – protruding from the muddy ground like dragon's teeth, shining blood-red in that deadly light.

'It's a city,' he muttered to himself. 'Buried in the earth.'

The Feragoths approached their work with a fervour and urgency that astonished Turan, painstakingly cleaning and excavating the terrible ruins. The architecture being uncovered was totally alien to him. Absent were the classical colonnades and pillars of antiquity, or the great domes and minarets of the old eastern religions. Great black towers of stone rose up from the ground, angry, ugly and malevolent, all the more terrifying for their ruinous state. Some of them had flat-topped roofs, with shattered, broken sails of stone rising up like sharks' fins from the sides of the towers.

The towers were totally foreign – Turan had never seen anything like them before. As he laid eyes on them, he was reminded, terrifyingly, of the Feragothic Ambassador's sword, with its twisted bone-hilt and serrated blade. In that moment, he knew without doubt that these buildings, and this ancient city buried deep in the earth, were Feragothic.

'Fucking hell,' he murmured. 'They've been here before.'

Turan pulled a holographic camera from his coat pocket. He quickly scanned across the valley, capturing a three-dimensional image, before crawling backwards away from the terrible and mysterious scene. He was suddenly filled with the desire to be as far away from that awful city as he possibly could. His heart filled with a primal fear, the air heavy with the unknown crimes that had been perpetrated there, in a forgotten age.

His throat clenched shut, Turan fairly ran full-tilt down the scree slope in his desperation to get away from that deathly place, that cemetery, that tomb of a lost empire.

He was filled with a dread sense of foreboding, his mind bringing back stories of terror from his childhood, of demons and impalers that had lived in these mountains in ages past. His mind spoke of an unnamed horror, deep in his racial memory, that chilled his blood.

Chapter Twenty

Turan swiped his palm across the scanner next to his apartment door, which beeped as it unlocked. He staggered into his rooms, squinting as the lights inside turned on automatically, and slammed the door shut behind him.

He slumped into a battered armchair, breathing heavily, his heavy-lidded eyes almost closed. He hadn't slept in nearly two days. The journey to Dacia and the immediate return to the Capital was a round trip of nearly four thousand miles. He was bone-tired, exhausted, and terrified by what he had seen.

He rubbed his eyes, trying to think. His brief investigation of the Feragothic camp had raised more questions than it had answered. The reason they had headed straight for that sight was now obvious – it was the site of some ancient Feragothic settlement. However, there was no mention of this in any history Turan had read, and he was sure that an alien colony would have been worth a mention.

The behaviour of the Feragoths was also unusual. They were excavating the ruins carefully, but with a significant portion of the city uncovered, Turan had seen no sign of research or study. They were just digging, down deeper into the earth.

They're looking for something, he thought to himself. *Something they want to keep secret from us*. It was the only explanation – and it fitted with the distortion field they had established to screen the site from satellite surveillance. And it was something they wanted very badly – something they were prepared to pay the Confederacy thirty trillion credits to secure.

Turan shuddered, blinking away thoughts of the black-cloaked figures swarming over those hideous ruins. *What on earth could be buried there, in those cold and silent mountains? Left there centuries before by the aliens' forefathers? What were they looking for?*

Given their level of secrecy, duplicity and desperation, Turan was convinced it was nothing that would serve the Confederacy's interests. However, what could he do about it? Ulestran and Tellanor were clearly not sufficiently interested in it. If they found out, they'd only use it as leverage to tease further payments out of the Empire so they could continue the war.

Turan sat forward, his head in his hands. He was trapped, with dangerous evidence of a conspiracy against an incompetent government, which could very well jeopardise the lives of everyone in the Confederacy. Only he had any idea of what was happening, but exactly what the Feragoths were looking for was still a mystery. He needed help, but he had no allies, no one he could rely upon.

He was utterly alone.

His communicator beeped and he pulled it from his pocket, blinking blearily. He glanced at the time – it was 14:00. He checked the communicator, and noticed a new message. Idly, he tapped the screen to open it.

CONFEDERACY OF NATIONS

GOVERNMENTAL COMMUNICATION

FROM: Governor Rosar, Council of Governors

TO: Superintendent Turan, Confederate Police

TIME: 14:00, 25/10/1342 (CMT)

Superintendent Turan,

I have been granted approval by the Secretary of State to question you regarding the Confederacy's foreign relations with the Empire of Feragoth. Please find a copy of this authority attached. Unfortunately, my colleagues and I are currently boycotting the Council of Governors due to the Chancellery Government's refusal to keep the legislature informed. As such, I am unable to conduct this interview within the Palace.

I therefore request that you attend my Embassy Office. It would be greatly appreciated if you could contact me as soon as possible in order to arrange a mutually convenient appointment.

Yours sincerely,

Allanor Rosar

Governor, Principality of Cerberus

Leader of the Opposition

Enc:

Turan read in amazement, and then prayed thanks to whatever god was listening. Here was his chance!

Since his assignment to the Ambassador, he had not been keeping tabs on political developments as closely as usual. However, he had read news reports announcing that the Opposition had walked out of the Council of Governors in protest against the Chancellor. And here, those same political adversaries wanted to question *him* on the state of relations with the Feragoths!

He heaved himself to his feet, walking over to a landscape painting hanging on the wall. He pulled it to one side, revealing a safe behind it. With another swipe of his hand, and a bright blue flash which scanned his iris, the safe clicked, the small, heavy door opening outwards. Turan dug the holographic camera out of his pocket and put it on the bottom shelf, together with the flight details and fake passport he had used to get out of the Capital undetected. He closed the safe and finally collapsed onto his bed, fully clothed.

For the first time since he had laid his eyes on that shadowy apparition that haunted the corridors of the Chancellery Palace, Turan felt a faint hope rise in him, and fell asleep without the need for whisky or corch. His sleep was dreamless.

-#-

The next morning, Turan walked through the Capital, breathing in the cool morning air. He loved the city in autumn – the auburn and yellow leaves drifting in the wind reminded him of country holidays in his childhood. He strode across Confederate Square, the main plaza in the city, passing between the two ruined fountains and the ancient, stone column.

He felt a slight chill as he did so – this, like many features of the city, had been built over a thousand years ago, in an age before the Confederacy. These were the remnants of the Kingdom – the Square, it was rumoured, had once been a memorial to a war hero of the Kingdom, in a forgotten time.

Turan paused for a moment, looking up at the column of stone in the centre of the Square, and at the statue that stood on top of it. Who was this man? What great act had he done for his country to honour him so? No one would ever know.

Turan shook himself, and carried on walking across the Square. Behind him, he could now see the Grand Gatehouse, which marked the entrance to Chancellery Boulevard, the long, tree-lined road which led to the heart of government, the Chancellery Palace itself. The familiar terror settled over his heart as he thought of what now resided there.

Determined, he kept walking across the Square until he finally reached his destination on the far side – a seven-storey building with a rounded corner facing out onto the Square, angling back in a triangle along the two roads of the junction on which it sat. Archways yawned at street level, glinting with the glass doors mounted in them. This was the Cerberusian Embassy, the office of the Leader of the Opposition.

Turan smiled to himself as he pushed open one of the glass doors and walked into the shadow of the building beyond. The moment he crossed the threshold, he had left directly-administered Confederate territory, and had stepped into an enclave of the Principality of Cerberus, one of the constituent nations of the Confederacy.

Turan walked into the lobby. He looked around, slightly unsure of himself in the new surroundings. The lobby was paved in expensive marble, with ornate tapestries hanging from the walls and in front of the windows. This was in typical Cerberusian style – Cerberus itself was in the Sirius System, whose main star was over twenty-two times brighter than Therqa's. The Cerberusians spent very little time outdoors, and while their buildings generally had windows, they were typically kept darkened with curtains and tapestries to filter the harsh sunlight. However, on Therqa, the effect darkened the room in a gentle twilight.

Turan walked up to the reception desk, which was staffed by a young man in his early twenties, looking bored. 'Can I help you?' he drawled in a Cerberusian accent.

'My name is Detective Superintendent Turan, Confederate Police, Political Branch,' said Turan, and held out his warrant card to the surprised receptionist. 'I'm here to see Governor Allanor, on the approval of the Secretary of State.'

That got the young man's attention. He sat up, an astonished expression on his face. 'I see...' he said. 'Erm... do you... do you have an appointment?'

'No,' answered Turan, 'but the Governor asked me to contact her as soon as possible. I understand that her duties in the Council of Governors are... lighter than usual, so I thought I'd drop by.'

'I see,' echoed the stunned receptionist again. 'I see...'

'I tell you what,' said Turan, 'I'll have a seat, and you ring round to find the Governor. See if she's available to see me immediately. If not, I'll book an appointment when she's free and come back later. How does that strike you?'

The receptionist looked almost relieved to have the burden of decision taken away from him. It wasn't very often that a Detective Superintendent walked into the Embassy, asking to see the Governor, much less one of the Confederate Police, rather than the provincial Constabularies. He nodded silently, picked up his communicator, and tapped the screen a few times.

Turan sat down, listening to the one-sided conversation.

'Yes, this is Reception... I have a Detective Superintendent Turan here, of the Confederate Police...'

'Political Branch,' interjected Turan, his voice carrying authority, but his face wearing a helpful smile.

'Political Branch,' repeated the receptionist hurriedly, nodding and smiling at Turan. 'Yes, he says that Governor Allanor wants to see him, and he has the approval of the Secretary of State...? Now? Yes, I'll send him straight through.'

He hung up on the communicator as Turan stood up. 'The Governor will see you now,' he said, and handed back Turan's warrant card. 'Corridor on the left, third door on the right. The Governor will join you shortly.'

'Thank you,' said Turan, and headed off down the corridor.

The third door on the right led into a small interview room, well-lit, comfortably warm and with soft chairs. A drinks cabinet stood in one corner. Turan withheld the urge to pour himself a whisky. His heartbeat rattled nervously – he had absolutely no idea what to expect. Although his job in the Political Branch had involved him in politics to a certain degree, he had never spent much time talking to the politicians. He was employed to either kill them or escort them. With the Confederacy effective being a one-party state, he knew next-to-nothing of the Opposition movement, or its leader. Most of his dealings had been within Ulestran's own supporters.

One wall was dominated by a large, glass mirror. Turan knew immediately that it wasn't a mirror at all, but a one-way window into a separate observation room. *So, for all its comfortable decor and furnishings, this is an interrogation chamber,* he thought. Perhaps not as forthright as the rooms Turan was used to using, but its purpose was the same, just couched in a comfortable, easy euphemism.

His train of thought was broken as the door opened, and a familiar figure walked into the room. Turan's heart jumped into his throat as he recognised her immediately. She was wearing her hair differently, and her clothes weren't as provocative as usual, but it was still her – Tellanor, the Secretary of State.

'What are you doing here?' he asked, bluntly.

'I beg your pardon?' she asked.

'You heard me,' snapped Turan. 'This is a national Embassy – the Confederacy does not have any direct jurisdiction here.'

'I...'

'Spare me,' fumed Turan. 'Have you been following me? You can't bear to have anyone talking to Ulestran apart from you? Afraid I might tell the Chancellor something about the Feragoths you'd prefer was kept hidden? I bet you arranged all this, didn't you – the message from the Governor. A damned honey-trap – I should have known better.'

'I am a Superintendent of the Confederate Police,' he snapped, 'and I do not have to justify what I do or where I go to *you* – only to the Chancellor. That might only be a small difference, but an important one. I have not broken any treaty or law, so you have no right to hold me, or try to entrap me like this...'

'Will you be quiet a moment?' she almost shouted, before regaining her calm. 'I can honestly assure you, Superintendent, that I haven't got the faintest idea what you are talking about, so if you would *please* calm down, perhaps we can start again. I am Allanor Rosar, Governor of Cerberus.' She held out her hand, and Turan gazed at it, dumbfounded.

'What?!' he said, incredulously. 'You don't expect me to fall for that? You're Tellanor, Secretary of State. Don't be so bloody ridiculous!'

Allanor sighed in frustration, but finally with some sense of realisation. 'I see,' she said. 'You will no doubt be pleased to be corrected, Superintendent. I *am* Governor Allanor. Secretary Tellanor is my twin sister. She shares my appearance and my parentage, but nothing further, I assure you.'

Turan's mouth fell open in astonishment. 'What?'

'Secretary Tellanor – with whom you appear to be familiar – is my twin sister,' repeated Allanor. 'For a policeman in the Political Branch, you don't appear to be very aware of politics, if I may say so.'

'I don't deal with the Opposition,' muttered Turan, and sat down. 'You're Tellanor's *sister*?'

'Twin sister,' said Allanor, closing the door. 'And Leader of the Opposition. You didn't know?'

Turan shook his head. It wasn't hugely surprising – the Opposition movement was treated as a lunatic fringe group by the State-controlled media, barely given any serious coverage at all. He was vaguely aware that Tellanor had a sister involved in politics, but he had no idea that she was a twin, nor that she was Leader of the Opposition.

'This is insane,' he murmured. 'Prove it,' he said. 'I'm not going to say a word more until I have proof.'

Allanor sighed again. 'You have a communicator on you?'

Turan nodded.

'Try watching any of the major news channels, live,' she said. 'Tellanor is at this moment addressing the Council of Governors. You'll notice the Chamber is half-empty.'

Turan pulled his communicator out of his pocket, flicking it over to a news channel. He watched Tellanor's face closely on the screen. 'This could have been pre-recorded,' he said.

'On every channel?'

He flicked over to another channel, broadcasting the same thing. As he watched, he could see some subtle differences between the woman on the screen and the woman sat in front of him, besides the hair and mode of dress. Tellanor's face was harsher, crueller – a cold, savage beauty. Allanor had none of that hardness or aggression. Instead, her face held a look of quiet determination. They were two entirely different women.

'You're not Tellanor.'

'No,' replied Allanor.

'Oh, bloody hell,' muttered Turan. 'I've just spent five minutes bollocking you, and...'

'I'm not Tellanor,' finished Allanor. 'That's all right, Superintendent – an easy mistake to make. Tellanor did tell me that she would warn you of my contacting you, and I assumed that would also involve a warning of our physical similarities. Presumably, that didn't happen?'

Turan shook his head.

'Yes, well,' said Allanor, trying unsuccessfully to disguise her distaste. Turan warmed to her slightly at this. 'My original intention was to question you on the Confederacy's current state of relations with the Empire of Feragoth,' she said. 'I have to say, from your earlier... comments, it appears that you are far more involved than I originally thought.'

Turan sat up, his eyes narrowed. 'What do you mean?'

'You referred to the Secretary hiding things about the Feragoths from the Chancellor?' said Allanor. 'And that you had not broken any treaty or law? I take it that you mean the treaty the Chancellor has just signed with the Empire?'

'Listen, Governor,' said Turan, 'just what are you trying to accomplish here? I mean, you're suspicious of the Empire, that's obvious enough. So am I, and believe me, I have far more reason to be concerned than you.'

'Superintendent,' said Allanor, 'I am a politician. I am trying to hold this government to account in any way I can, to scrutinise their work. I am concerned that the Chancellor has signed a treaty with a foreign power without giving the Council of Governors so much as a by-your-leave. It used to be conventional for legislatures to *ratify* treaties *before* they took effect. I am trying to ascertain its impact on the Confederacy.'

'So if I were to tell you that this treaty with the Empire of Feragoth has been made on false pretences?' said Turan. 'That the Empire has an unknown – but almost certainly malevolent – motive, what would you do about it?'

Allanor fell silent as she looked at the man sat in front of her. She had not been expecting this. She had expected a quiet conversation about how polite the Feragothic Ambassador was, not an assertion that the Empire was potentially hostile. All of a sudden, things seemed a lot more serious.

'I would bring it to the attention of the public,' she said, quietly.

'Break the law?'

'If need be.'

'Overthrow the Chancellor?'

A sudden thought spiked into her mind. Turan had accused her of being a honey-trap, but what if this was the trap? A trap laid by her sister, to put her on a charge of sedition? She looked into Turan's piercing blue eyes, but found no hint of deception. She noticed the dark shadows under his eyes, his thin and gaunt frame. The vague hint of corch and whisky around him. This was a man that had seen something terrible. He bore a burden more awful than she could imagine, and even though he was mentally strong, it was almost breaking him.

'Yes,' she murmured softly. 'I would.'

Turan smiled. 'So would I,' he answered, and in that moment, they both knew they had found an ally.

'The Feragothic Ambassador is a very dangerous individual,' said Turan. 'There is something about him...' he shuddered. 'I can't put my finger on it, or really explain why, but he is terrifying. And I don't mean in the 'not-a-very-nice-person' sense, I mean in the literal sense. Skin-crawlingly, struggling-not-to-piss-yourself, desperate-to-get-away-from-him-at-any-cost terrifying. It might sound like weird ghost tales and nightmare stories to you, but believe me, from someone who has to see him on a regular basis, he is *evil*.'

Turan had finally articulated what he had been wanting to say since he first laid eyes on the creature. There was no other word for his casual disregard, his barely-concealed contempt. The Ambassador was *evil*. He detested them all – every single human on the planet. He hated them with an intensity that Turan could barely comprehend.

Allanor sat in silence.

'He wears only black,' muttered Turan. 'A thick, heavy cloak, to shield himself from the sun. I've never seen his face, but his hands...'

'They're white. White as a corpse – taut skin stretched over bones. And he's strong – when he shakes your hand, you *know* he's holding back, that he could crush every bone in your body if he wanted to. And he does want to.'

'Their homeworld is supposed to be cold,' continued Turan, the words coming out in a flurry, 'and yet he relishes the heat. Not too hot, mind you, but he's certainly no fan of the cold. And he has a sword...' he shuddered at the thought of it. 'Like nothing I've ever seen. It's made of some kind of black metal. It's old – maybe thousands of years old.'

'It's so hard to explain,' he muttered, putting his hands to his temples. Allanor took one of them in hers.

'Don't worry,' she said. 'I'm listening.'

Turan smiled at her, taking some comfort from the human contact. It had been so long. The last few months had been like some surreal nightmare, but he finally felt that he was coming out of it, and waking up.

'The Chancellor is shit-scared of him,' he said. 'I don't blame him. I am too. But he exerts a big influence over Ulestran now. The Chancellor tried to stand up to him a few days ago over this little camp they've established in Dacia – I doubt he will again.'

'You think that the Feragothic Ambassador holds some sway over the Chancellery?' asked Allanor.

Turan nodded. 'Oh, yes,' he said. 'And his grip will tighten. There's no doubt in my mind about that.'

'You said the treaty was made under false pretences?'

Turan laughed, a short bark. 'Almost certainly,' he said. 'You know the Feragoths never bothered to scan Therqa? They just landed straightaway on that site in Dacia, and started digging. They paid us thirty trillion credits, and landed on one particular site. *And I know why.*'

He leaned close to Allanor, whispering in her ear. '*They knew where they were going. They've been here before.*'

'What?' Allanor reeled at the revelation.

'I went to the camp,' said Turan, urgent and quiet. 'Two nights ago, in secret. It's swarming with them. An entire valley in the mountains, flooded with awful, red light, and they're excavating an *entire city. Their* city. I don't know how or why, but there's a ruined city buried in the mountains. It's thousands of years old – predating the Confederacy, predating the Kingdom, even – and it was built by them. Thousands of years ago. That's why they went for that site. They've been here before. And now they've come back.'

'You think it's a prelude to an invasion?' gasped Allanor, shaken by this seismic turn of events.

Turan shook his head. 'No,' he said. 'There's a lot of them there, but they're not soldiers. They're not conquering... they're *searching*. They're looking for something, buried in that fucking place.'

'What?'

'I don't know,' said Turan. 'But whatever it is, they want to keep it secret from the Confederacy, and they were prepared to pay thirty trillion credits to get at it. And if the rest of them are like the Ambassador...' he fell silent for a moment.

'I think we should be very, *very* afraid.'

EPISODE III

TRANSFORMATION

Chapter Twenty-One

Jamek's fists were raised, his left close to his face, his right pulled back, near his chest. His knuckles were cut and bruised, the skin broken. A thin trickle of blood edged its way down to his upper lip. Scratches and grazes were clearly visible on his shaven head, the stubble of his hair starting to regrow. His right eye was blackened and swollen, his left narrow and piercing. Bloodstains streaked his grey prison uniform, and his lips drew back in concentration, the bottom one thick and red with blood.

He and a Confederate guard sidestepped slowly in opposite directions, the other guards standing around them, shouting and swapping money as they placed bets. The guard had removed his helmet, his head seeming shrunken out of proportion with his heavily armoured body. His lips were bloodied, one eye swollen shut, his mouth twisted in a sneer of anger.

Behind them was the wide, arched entrance to the main prisoner hall, blocked by a wall of iron bars stretching from the archway to the floor. In the centre of the archway, the wall of bars was punctuated by a double-doored cage – one door opening into the main prisoner hall, the other opening into the Guard Barracks. Dozens of prisoners in the main hall cheered, pressed against the gates like a wall of grey flesh, their outstretched arms reaching through. The noise was raucous.

In the throng pressed against the black bars, only two figures remained still, standing next to each other close to the cage. Mavrak, his face stern as he watched the match proceedings with a mild disgust, stood next to Adraea, who held the bars with both hands, pressing her face between the gap. Her eyes were wide with fear and concern as she watched the man she loved duelling with the Confederate guard.

The guard jabbed at Jamek, the fist connecting with his face and knocking his head back. Jamek barely felt the blow – a mad, determined rage burned slowly inside him, waiting to explode, waiting for the right moment to strike. Another jab hit Jamek, the guard keeping him back. Jamek slowed his movements slightly, to give the impression of fatigue. His dropped his fists half an inch to support the deception, and allowed another jab to connect.

The guard, sensing victory, aimed an arcing right fist at the side of Jamek's head. Jamek saw it coming almost in slow motion. He easily ducked the blow, and hammered his right fist into the guard's ribs, before sweeping his left fist up in a powerful upper cut. Jamek's fist struck heavily on the bottom of the guard's jaw, the force of the blow lifting him off the ground and knocking him to the floor.

Once his opponent was down, Jamek wasted no time in pressing his advantage. He leapt on the guard, pinning his arms to the floor with his knees. His face twisted into a snarl, his teeth, stained with blood, bared in an ugly display. He held the guard captive like a raptor pinning its prey, then after a moment's silence proved that he was in no danger from his opponent, Jamek attacked.

His fists pounded the guard mercilessly. He aimed particularly for the most vulnerable areas, that would cause the most damage – the eyes, the neck, the temples, the nose. The guard howled and choked as Jamek's fists thudded into his skull and throat. After only a few seconds, dark, thick blood stained Jamek's knuckles, and the other helmeted guards dragged him off his prone victim.

Jamek immediately turned on them, bringing his feet and knees into play to complement his fists. He attacked the other guards with equal fury, felling several of them before four managed to grab hold of him, one by each limb. Another opened the double-doored cage, and they threw him inside before slamming the door shut. The door on the other side of the cage opened, releasing him back into the main hall.

The rest of the prisoners cheered at the return of their champion, and Jamek smiled, raising his bloodstained fists to the crowd. Hands and arms clapped him on the back as he eased his way through the throng. Adraea darted towards him through the crowd, and not a moment too soon – Felador and his thugs had appeared in the main hall, and were pushing their way to the front. Mavrak followed Adraea, keeping a watchful eye on Felador.

Jamek grinned as her saw Adraea, and grabbed hold of her, kissing her passionately. She remained frozen, standing stiffly next to him, her eyes darting furtively from side to side. She spotted Felador at the back of the crowd, pushing his way through. Her blood ran cold at the sight of him.

Adraea was a soldier, and was generally capable of looking after herself. Despite her beauty, she was not one of the women in the prison who was actively targeted for rape, because she fought back. However, Felador had determined to obtain her, as a possession, and she could not defend herself against him. She was rightly terrified of him, and Jamek was the only force capable of protecting her.

Jamek's smile faded as he noticed Felador pushing his way to the front. The crowd backed away from Jamek, forming a circle around him, and the cheers gradually fell silent. Felador and four of his stooges pushed their way into the ring, fanning out towards Jamek as they did so. Adraea cowered behind him.

'The little one's been fighting with the guards again,' said Felador, his face bearing a sarcastic, predatory grin. His thugs laughed on cue. Jamek said nothing, his good eye narrowing, his right foot edging back slightly as he dropped into a fighting stance.

'You shouldn't fight with the guards,' said Felador, taking a step closer. 'It makes you weak. And you need all your strength in here.'

Again, Jamek said nothing. Adraea stood back to back with him, her eyes shut tightly, trying to screen out the horror. The silence was thick and heavy, the atmosphere electric. A brawl was minutes, perhaps only seconds away, and the faces of the crowd looked on hypnotically, waiting for the inevitable blows. The guards would let it last maybe a few minutes before they intervened, but those few minutes could count for a lot in the balance of power between Jamek and Felador. Who would emerge the least injured?

Suddenly, the atmosphere was broken as Mavrak burst his way into the circle, accompanied by three other Protectorate prisoners. 'Felador!' he shouted, and ran to Jamek's side. Jamek nodded to Mavrak in appreciation, but never took his attention off Felador.

'I've warned you,' snarled Mavrak. 'You fight Jamek, you fight all of us.' He put his hand behind his back, feeling the hilt of a hand-made knife he kept tucked into his belt under his shirt. One of the Protectorate soldiers deliberately turned to the side, and a flash of silver shone in his hand. They were armed.

Felador's smile faded somewhat as the subtle message made its way across. Five against one were odds he found acceptable. Mavrak and his associates had balanced the terms somewhat, but with knives... he was not prepared to fight under those circumstances.

Felador laughed and shook off the tension. 'Just giving some friendly advice, *Mavrak*,' he said, spitting out the name, which sounded alien on his tongue. 'I wouldn't want to see your little friend get hurt.' He turned to his gang. 'Come on, let's get out of here,' he said, and pushed his way out of the crowd, knocking a few prisoners to the side as he did so.

Adraea turned and looked over Jamek's shoulder, seeing Felador and his friends retreating. She breathed a sigh of relief, and put her hand on Jamek's shoulder, feeling the tense muscles relax. He turned to her, a strange look in his eyes, a flicker of glowering flame. Adraea exhaled sharply as she saw it, but then it was gone, and Jamek, the man she loved, was there again, his face filled with tenderness and concern. She threw her arms around him and buried her face into his neck.

Mavrak nodded to the Protectorate prisoners and they began disbanding the crowd. The guards took no interest in the entire proceedings, instead joking with each other as they exchanged money, and roughly tended to the injuries of the guard whom Jamek had beaten. Mavrak turned to Jamek.

'He is right, you know,' he said. 'You've got to stop this fighting with the guards. We need you in here to act as a deterrent against Felador. And we need to curry favour with them – if it does turn nasty, we want the guards to intercede on our behalf. We're not going to earn their support if you're beating them to a pulp one at a time!'

Jamek laughed, brushing the comment aside. 'I can handle Felador,' he said. 'And as for the guards... that's just a bit of fun.'

'Fun? How, in the name of all the Guardians, is that fun?' demanded Mavrak. 'Listen, Jamek. Things are more difficult now than they've ever been. Felador has set his sights on Adraea, and he means to have her. The only way that we can convince him to leave her – and by extension, us – alone is if we *stick together*. And that means no moving around alone, no deliberate provocation of him or his thugs, and no fighting with the guards. If we do that, he'll get bored, and move on to an easier target. But as long as you act like a wild thing, he'll see that as an opportunity.'

Jamek's easy smile disappeared. 'We'll discuss this later,' he said, his voice level and his face stern. He took Adraea's arm and pulled her along, heading further down the prisoner hall, towards one of the side corridors. Mavrak stared after them as Adraea turned to glance back at him, her eyes lit with fear and resignation, torn between the man that she loved, and the monster he was becoming.

-#-

Adraea crouched in the corner of the cell she shared with Jamek, her knees tucked under her chin and her arms wrapped around her legs. The rough cloth of her prison uniform made her back itch as she leaned against the cold, concrete wall. The cell was almost identical to the one she and Jamek had first found themselves in when they awoke in the prison. It was rendered in concrete, thin puddles forming in the uneven floor, and half-lit by a dull, red light coming from a grate near the ceiling.

The main prisoner hall and the Guard Barracks were part of an ancient building, perhaps hundreds of years old. They were built from red bricks and mortar. The prisoner cells, organised into four wings expanding from the corridors which led from the main hall, seemed to have been built later. They were not made of the same brick, but from concrete, like pillboxes. The walls were very thick – two feet, at the least. It was only late in the day when the sun was low enough in the sky to shine through the grates which passed as windows.

The sun. Such as it was. A pale red light that offered no warmth, a far cry from the golden, yellow light of Kaathar. This was a dirty, cold light, from a dim, dying star. It reminded Adraea of Kraegan, the sister of Kaathar, which orbited Szotas's parent star at a great distance. In the summer months, it appeared in the sky during the day, a faint red dot compared to Kaathar's power. In the winter months, it would appear in the night sky as a large red star, cold, distant and remote. This star was like Kraegan, or how Kraegan would appear close up – small, dark and miserable.

She looked across to the other side of the cell, where Jamek lay sleeping. Her heart ached for him as she studied the lines of his face – the coarse bristle of a few days' beard growth, pocked by scratches and bruises inflicted during his fight with the guard, his solid jawline, and high cheekbones. His hair, only weeks before being nothing but a dark stubble, was gradually beginning to regrow.

Tears rolled down her face unbidden as she looked across at the man she loved. He looked calm and peaceful – sleep was the only time that he lived in some semblance of peace, and it was by no means total. Dreams haunted him, where unknown tormentors battled with him in the darkness, and fear and brutality pursued him when he was awake. Part of her knew that his constant fighting – with the other prisoners, with the guards – was a show of strength, an attempt to let the predators know that he, and by extension, Adraea, were to be avoided. In a strange sort of way, it was his defence of her. But the fighting went beyond that.

Adraea had seen it in his eyes when he awoke screaming from the terrible nightmares that plagued him. She saw it in his eyes when he fought the guards, and the Confederate prisoners like Felador. She even saw it in his eyes when he had been warned by Mavrak earlier. A burning, scorching rage – unlike anything that she had ever seen before in anyone, barely kept in check. His eyes took on a strange aspect, as if something inside his soul was... *burning*.

Adraea wept silently. Her breath came in gasping, ragged sobs, her chest hitching with each one. Her eyes stung with the salt of cold and lonely tears. *He is still Jamek*, she thought to herself, her voice sounding desperate and hollow inside her head. *He is still the man you love!* Every part of her ached for him, longed for him to gather her in his arms and take her away from all this. She prayed that the awful madness festering within him would evaporate, and she would see his eyes – those beautiful, dark eyes – full of happiness and mystery, not burning with an unknown hatred.

But she knew that he was changing – transforming into something else. She didn't know what it was, or why it was happening, only that it terrified her, more than anything she had ever known, and on a level so primitive, so animal, she could not fully explain it. She was doomed – trapped between the man she loved with all her heart, and the creature she feared with every fibre of her being.

Jamek's face screwed into a frown and he began moaning fearfully in his sleep, bringing Adraea out of her reverie. Wiping away the sting of her bitter tears, she pulled herself upright and padded across the freezing cell, barely heeding the ice-cold water that soaked her rag-covered feet. She knelt down next to Jamek, one hand on his brow, the other laid on his chest, and tried to ease the terror of his unknown dream.

-#-

Jamek was suspended in darkness, the black emptiness stretching away in all directions. The shadow was so complete, so utter, that Jamek couldn't see his hand even when it was raised to his face. He knew that he was totally alone, and had never known such complete desolation. He screamed and there was no sound, he thrashed his arms and passed through nothing but emptiness. Not even a breath of air resisted him.

His heart pounded in his chest at the empty, thudding terror, the horror of oblivion. His hands scratched madly at his face in a desperate attempt to bring some sensation into the void, tearing at his eyes and cheeks as the insanity of loneliness beyond measure poured out of him.

Finally, when he ceased his struggling with sheer exhaustion, consigning himself to exist in this timeless, meaningless pit for all eternity, he saw something in the far distance, a tiny glint in the dark, flickering redly. The sight of it did not fill Jamek with hope, but rather with fear and hatred, and a rage beyond anything he had felt before. He wanted nothing more than to reach out for that red light and crush it into the blackness.

He approached it, or it approached him – it was impossible to tell in the void. It grew larger, not just from the approach, but also from its own growth – it seemed to feed on the darkness around it. It was a filthy red, a soiled red, like dark clay from the bowels of the earth. Then Jamek noticed the smell.

It crept upon him slowly, but it was soon intolerable – a vile stench, like wet tin. It reminded Jamek of thunderstorms, and crackling electricity. His entire being was suffused by it, and he retched with the power of it. The sound, too – a high-pitched, whining shriek. It was quiet at first, but as the red thing approached, it filled his ears with its painful assault, cutting into him like a scalpel. He clapped his hands to his ears, but the apparition seemed to sound its awful cry in his head. Jamek was convinced that were he a deaf man, he would still hear that dreadful sound, like a million voices screaming in terror.

Then the taste – filling his mouth like a cloying wine, thick and heavy, tasting of iron. Jamek spat in panic, trying to rid himself of the foulness rushing up to embrace him. He recognised the taste with horror – a flashback to his childhood, pricking his finger on a thornbush, crying and putting his finger in his mouth.

Blood.

The creature grew closer, a malevolent, pulsing red orb, assaulting his senses. Jamek sensed intelligence from it – a vast intelligence, powerful, knowledgeable and cruel, a cruelty beyond anything he had known, a callous disregard for all life. It filled almost his entire field of vision, its dull, violent light illuminating him in the dark and casting weird shadows in every direction. It dissolved into mist, reaching ever closer to him. And then it touched him.

Jamek wailed at its touch – it was like the crawl of locusts, the kiss from dead lips, the dry, lifeless touch of cold, unyielding rock in an empty desert. This creature, full of malevolence, of cruelty, of power and of despair, laughed at him. It grasped him with unseen hands, reaching out from the filthy red mist, meaning to take him and crush the life out of him, not just from his body, but from his very soul. To make him at one with this demon from the abyss, and then he would know nothing but the torture of its existence for all eternity...

Then, suddenly, a rush of wind appeared from nowhere, and the air was filled with a terrible roar, like a gathering storm. The wind was hot, and on it were carried the embers of Hell. The choking, deadly smell of soot rose up, blocking out the suffusing stench of blood. All the void seemed to shrink around Jamek, concentrating into him, into his body, into his soul. He became as a black cloud, broiling around the red demon like a noisome fume. Jamek tasted ash in his mouth, yet despite this new horror emerging from the abyss around him, he was no longer afraid. This new entity was the abyss itself, rising up to extinguish this malevolent intruder, as Jamek had longed to do.

Jamek felt himself filled with a deep and deadly rage, a hatred of this red malevolence. He felt an uncontrollable desire not just to drive it back into the emptiness, but to reach out and crush it utterly, just as it had intended to do to him. The rage overwhelmed him and exploded outwards, igniting the black cloud that rose around him, searing his skin with both agony and ecstasy. A baking, scorching heat radiated out in all directions. The very air was consumed by this awesome furnace, burning brighter than the light of a thousand stars, and all the universe was aflame...

-#-

Jamek awoke and sat up screaming, his prison uniform soaked in cold sweat, his hands hooked into claws that scratched and slashed wildly at nothing. His heart pounded in violent terror and powerful rage, and for a moment, a brief moment, the cell was illuminated by a terrible light, and a sudden and awesome heat. Then, just as soon as it had arrived, it was gone.

Jamek looked around, his eyes wide with terror, and he felt his hands, his arms, his face. Finally, he saw Adraea, sitting next to him, her eyes wide with concern and a mute horror. He exhaled slowly, trying to catch his breath and slow his hammering heart. His hands shook as he reached out to hold her.

'The dreams,' he explained weakly, and fell back onto the floor, emotionally exhausted. 'The nightmares,' he murmured again, not wanting to return to sleep, to the darkness, and to the demons that waited for him there.

Adraea lay down next to him, and without making a sound, kissed him on the mouth. Her kiss was urgent and hungry, and Jamek found himself kissing back, all thought of his nightmares and their current dire situation banished and forgotten. He felt a great swell of emotion rise in him, and he was filled with the simple desire to hold Adraea close, to protect her and shield her from the pain of the world.

His hands moved over her shoulder, pulling her crude prison uniform down off one arm. She moaned gently as his rough hands caressed her soft skin, her eyes closed, her lips parted slightly. His hand found her breast, and he pulled her towards him with his other hand, kissing her deeply.

She pulled him between her legs, pulled his thighs in towards her. Their fingers entwined, and she opened her eyes, staring straight into his. Wordlessly and slowly, they moved as one. He kissed her, pressing down onto her lips, drinking in the taste of her, and she him.

The cruelty and malice of the world faded away, and for that time, there was only each other, holding each other, kissing, caressing, and making love, silently, gently and tenderly. Adraea reached up and put her fingers round Jamek's head, moving them slowly across the lengthening stubble and tracing patterns on the back of his neck. His hands were on her, and he kissed her neck and shoulder.

All the world seemed to shrink, and was filled with a delicious silence, as they finally reached their climax. Soundlessly, they froze for a moment, only a moment, locked in a tableau of ecstasy, and then it was over. Jamek smiled, and Adraea felt nothing but pure joy, for she saw nothing of the monster, but only the happy smile of the man she loved. She fell asleep, cradled in his arms, and knew nothing but bliss.

-#-

Jamek lay awake in the freezing cell, staring up at the blank, grey ceiling. Adraea's head rested on his shoulder as she slept peacefully. Jamek listened to her breathing, slow and regular, and watched her sleeping face. He stroked her cheek gently, and a small frown furrowed her brow. She brushed away the tickling finger sleepily.

Jamek smiled. *I love you, Adraea*, he thought. *I'd do anything for you. Which is why we have to get out of here.*

He was angry at himself, for giving in to the shadow that had been growing on his mind since they entered this prison. It was as if he thrived on conflict – with the other prisoners, particularly the Confederate ones, and with the guards. His brawling made some of the prisoners give him a wide berth, but it attracted others to him. Others like Felador.

Jamek frowned at the thought of the big man. He seemed determined to break Jamek and claim Adraea as his own. If it continued, Jamek knew he would have to kill him. But that presented its own dangers. If he killed another prisoner, especially a Confederate, the guards would at the very least confine him to solitary for several months. Perhaps longer. They might even execute him. Either way, Adraea would suffer.

It would have to be done quietly. And it would be the last one. After that, there would be no more fights, no more brawls. He would just keep his head down and try to avoid making any more enemies, at least until the prison was either liberated by Protectorate forces, or until he could find a way to escape.

Jamek cursed himself quietly for creating this situation. If he hadn't have been so cocky with Felador in the first place, if he hadn't humiliated him by beating him in front of the other prisoners in the main hall, then perhaps this grudge would not have persisted. Now, there only appeared to be one way out of it.

He looked down at Adraea again and kissed her gently on the forehead. Tomorrow, he would worry about Felador and deal with him once and for all. Ambush him while he was sleeping, perhaps, or in the toilet, where there would be no witnesses. And then, peace, and eventually, escape.

Jamek closed his eyes and began to drift off to sleep himself, dreaming of freedom and liberty, and a world free of the torment he currently endured.

The blow to his head sent him reeling, lightning screaming down his spine, making the flesh of his testicles creep, his eyes thudding in their sockets with his heartbeat.

He shook his head, trying to co-ordinate himself again, and stood, only to receive another boot to the groin. He doubled up with the pain, the same lightning pain slashing up his thighs to his skull, bringing hot vomit and blood spilling out of his mouth.

Another stunning blow landed on the back of his skull, and he collapsed onto the floor, his nose breaking as his face smashed into the freezing concrete. The world seemed to become mute. The only sound he could hear was a faint humming.

He felt his face being lifted up, and a bright light was shone in his eyes. He saw a dark object moving towards him, almost a blur...

The fist struck and sent him reeling backwards. He did not really feel any more pain. He felt himself being dragged to his feet, and found himself looking into Felador's face.

'Did you miss me, little one?' he hissed, before delivering another powerful punch. Jamek fell to the floor and felt many arms grab him, lifting him up again. He shook his head and saw Felador. He heard screaming and recognised Adraea's voice, calling for him to help her.

The sound sliced through the fog of pain like a light in darkness, and Jamek dragged himself into reality.

'No!' he bellowed, and pulled, dragging three men along the floor with him as he moved for Felador, burning rage and anger rising up inside him. He heard a small high-pitched squeal as Felador punched Adraea in the face, shattering her cheek.

Jamek roared in fury, and struggled to fight the big man, but another man grabbed him, holding him back with the other three. He struggled viciously and powerfully. It took all four men to hold him back. Felador noticed his efforts and turned to face him. He laughed and delivered another punch to Jamek's face, dislocating his jawbone.

'Not this time, little one,' he said. 'This time, she's mine.' He looked up at the men holding Jamek. 'Hold him,' he ordered, 'and keep his eyes open. I want him to see.'

Jamek felt rough hands move over his skull and pull his eyelids up. A finger slipped into his eye socket, and he screamed in pain. His vision became blurred and fuzzy, but he could still see Felador with clarity.

'Does it hurt, little one?' Felador grinned. He backed off, and Jamek saw Adraea's cowering figure in the corner, nursing her broken face. Felador moved over to her and lifted her up. She struggled, screaming, but he overpowered her easily. He tore off her prison uniform, exposing her naked form – beautiful, and yet horrific in what it suggested.

Jamek shouted again, a mixture of rage and helplessness, but Felador simply smiled grotesquely. He threw Adraea onto the mattress and pulled down his trousers. His face once more split into a lewd grin. He grabbed Adraea, and pushed her head down, forcing her into a kneeling position. 'I hope you're ready, girl,' he said, and entered her.

She screamed in pain and horror as he raped her, and Jamek struggled in agony, tears streaming down his face from his stinging eyes as he was forced to watch. He struggled madly, but to no avail. There were simply too many men holding him.

With each thrust, Felador beat Adraea's skull with his hard fist, faster and faster, until he finally grunted in satisfaction and stopped. Adraea fell to the floor, whimpering. Jamek thought it had ended, but he was wrong. Felador stood and wiped his penis on Adraea's hair. He quickly pulled up his trousers, and looking at one of the men holding Jamek, he said, 'your turn.'

She was raped seven times in all, and when they had finally finished, they kicked and battered her while Jamek remained helpless, before turning on him. After what seemed like an eternity, they finally left, disappearing into the darkness from which they came.

Jamek crawled over the freezing cold floor to Adraea's broken body. His eyes were swollen almost shut, his mouth leaking blood. His face was lined with cuts, slashes of rough crimson, and welted with bruises, black flowers of agony. His nose was shattered, squashed against his face, and seeping thick blood. Lightning strikes of pain shot into his brain from every part of his body – his eyes, his nose, his fingers, his broken ribs.

'Adraea...' he moaned. His body was a dead weight, and he dragged himself along the floor slowly. He was vaguely aware of the skin on his knees scraping on the concrete floor, puddles of freezing water in the uneven floor biting his skin. His hands shook with the pain of the beating he had endured, his nails broken and blackened. His head was filled with a vague whine, but through the cloud of pain, he could hear his attackers, Adraea's rapists, laughing in the distance as they made their way back to the main prisoner hall.

'Jamek.' Her voice was quiet, and had a finality to it that chilled Jamek's soul. After several agonising minutes, he finally reached her.

'Oh, no,' he cried as he saw her. Stinging tears of grief streamed from his swollen eyes.

Her legs and arms were broken. Her eyes were blackened haemorrhages, her nose and mouth were trickling blood. Her hips were shattered, and she bled from between her legs. Her blood was everywhere. Black and hot, it spread steadily across the floor, mixing with the dirty water in the shallow puddles.

Jamek's face twisted into a mask of anguish. There could be no recovery from her injuries. His hands shook as a desperate, quiet moan of horror slipped from his lips, and he tried to wipe the blood from her face.

'Jamek,' she said. 'I'm dying.'

'No,' muttered Jamek, through the sobs which racked his body. 'No, you're going to be fine. We're going to get out of here, and you'll be all right.'

'Jamek,' she whispered through broken lips. 'Promise me something.'

'Anything,' he said, tears welling up in his eyes, and his heart in his throat.

'Get out of here, Jamek. Get out of this place, and become what you are destined to be.'

'We'll both get out of here,' he lied through tears and blood.

She shook her head. 'No,' she said. She coughed, thick dark blood staining her lips. 'Jamek,' she whispered. 'Will you remember me?'

'What are you talking about?' he snivelled, his voice breaking with the grief. 'You're going to be fine, Adraea, just fine.'

'Jamek,' she said, losing her energy, her breathing becoming shallow. 'Say that you'll remember me.'

'I will always remember you, Adraea.' She smiled, her eyes open. Her last breath came out, gently, delicately, and she fell limp and silent. Jamek shook her. 'Adraea,' he whispered softly. 'Adraea,' he said, alarmed. His face contorted, and he wailed, a desperate, howling scream of unrestrained misery and grief which echoed through the faceless grey corridors of the prison.

He fell back, and closed her eyes gently with his fingers. 'Goodbye, my love,' he stuttered through breaking sobs. She was dead.

Jamek's eyes narrowed, and an awful and terrible rage consumed him. He stood from Adraea's ruined body, and then opened his eyes wide. The cell was filled with a terrible orange light, not from any fire but emanating from Jamek's *eyes*, burning like coals in his head. A deadly and ancient power seethed through his body, mending his injuries and investing him with a force that would render him unstoppable, giving him new life and new strength.

Jamek roared, not a wail of grief this time, but the deadly and defiant roar of a predator. He lunged at the bars of the cell, and tore them from their moorings as if they were held in by paper. The metal squealed as the bars were wrenched away, and Jamek cast them aside like broken twigs.

The unholy light was now joined by a blistering heat, a searing, baking inferno burning deep inside Jamek's body. He screamed again, stretching his arms wide, and was lifted off the floor by the force of his own emotions. The floor beneath him cracked and shattered, following the curve of a sphere, as if some great weight had been placed upon it. The walls around him crumbled in the same way, as this invisible orb manifested itself around him.

His rage throbbed through his entire body, radiating out of him in a crushing, pulverising force, a demonic light and an awful heat. Jamek moved down the corridor, levitating two feet above the floor, and the concrete of the walls and floor shattered and crushed into sand and dust as the invisible ball rolled down the corridor. The building creaked and groaned as it was torn apart from the inside by the awesome force of Jamek's power.

He swept into the prisoners' hall. Alerted to the disturbance, Confederate guards on the walkways that criss-crossed above the hall floor fired machine guns at him. The bullets atomised in mid-air as they crossed the barrier of Jamek's invisible forcefield. The prisoners, panicked by the sound of gunfire, and terrified at the sight of the monstrous apparition appearing from the corridor, fled, shrieking in terror.

Felador and his friends tried to escape down one of the passages on the other side of the hall, but Jamek was too fast for them. He swept across the room with awesome speed, his movements a blur, and blocked their path. Felador screamed in terror as he looked upon Jamek's face, for the terrible light that burned in Jamek's eyes was flame, not reflected light from the hall fireplace, but fire burning from *within Jamek's own body.*

Jamek's fist shot out and buried itself into Felador's chest, tearing skin and smashing bone. Jamek lifted the big man up with one hand, staring into his eyes. Felador gasped in agony as Jamek's hand closed about his heart, and the last thing he saw was that terrible fire burning in the demon's eyes. He could feel the heat *inside him*, radiating through Jamek's very skin, and when Jamek pulled back his lips in a sneer of satisfaction, he could see tongues of flame licking between Jamek's teeth.

Jamek wrenched his hand back out of Felador's chest, tearing his heart out. Thick, dark blood splattered his skin, boiling instantly. He held out Felador's heart, which blackened in his hand, roasting in the awesome heat. He crushed it to ash in his fist, and roared again, throwing his arms wide, and then bringing them together in a thunderous clap.

The rest of Felador's friends squealed in agony, the screams cut off almost instantly. There was a sickening crunching sound accompanied by a splatter of blood as their bodies were crushed together into a single ball of bleeding flesh and splintered bone – Jamek didn't even have to touch them to kill them.

Jamek moved straight up, levitating to the walkways above. More machine gun fire peppered him, the ratcheting noise almost deafening in the cavernous hall, drowning out the sound of the shouts below. Jamek waved his hands, his face locked in a violent snarl, and the guards shrieked as their helmets were crushed by Jamek's telekinetic powers. Their bodies dropped to the walkways, some toppling over the railings and landing in the hall below.

The walkway that Jamek was floating above gave way, dropping down to the hall below, but it stopped before it hit the floor. Jamek closed his eyes, and the walkway tore free from its moorings totally, hanging in mid-air, as if suspended by some invisible thread. Slowly, it began to move back upwards, angled in the air, one end pointing at the hall's eaves, the other at the floor, near the main gates. Suddenly, the walkway flew downwards, smashing into the main gates and bursting them wide open. The prison was broken.

Jamek lowered down to the floor of the hall slowly, watching as many Protectorate prisoners rushed to the main gates, scrambling over the twisted wreckage of the walkway to their freedom. Jamek lunged forward again, blasting through the wreckage and through the gates. Once through, he stopped and turned to look at the fireplace at the other end of the hall. He raised his hand, and the fire exploded outwards, raging furiously as it ignited the very air.

The Confederate guards, faced with such a deadly foe, threw down their weapons and ran. The prison was taken, the Protectorate soldiers freed. And the ancient building, locked in the freezing ice of that bitter planet, burned like a dying star, a funeral pyre for a lost love, and a foreboding of what was to come.

The Destroyer had Risen.

Chapter Twenty-Two

Andrei Negutesco stood on the porch of his house, pulling his coat about him against the wind. It was autumn in Dacia, but the biting winds of winter had come quickly, and the weather was not above sending a brief, violent snow flurry.

Andrei was a tall, thin man in his mid-thirties, with jet-black hair and pale skin. He had a small, neatly-kept moustache on his upper lip, and dark eyes. He shivered in the cold night air, his dark eyes darting nervously to and fro.

It was twilight in the mountains. The sun had already set behind the high peaks in the west, and the stars were coming out. But there would be no moon tonight, Andrei knew. Like last night. And the night before. Only the unquenchable, empty blackness.

He looked out over the wooden rail of his porch, picking out the outline of the high mountain range in the south east, its shadow fading in the gathering dark. In the foreground, the town castle could be seen on a nearby foothill, its high walls rearing up from an outcrop of rock. He shivered as he tried to keep his gaze from drifting to the south – to the mountain pass which the castle guarded.

He took a deep drag on the corch cigarette clamped between his lips, feeling the warm smoke suffuse his lungs. He exhaled, the green smoke quickly carried away on the wind, and extinguished the stub of the cigarette regretfully. They were good cigarettes, from the Capital. It was unlikely he'd be able to get another pack any time soon. In a way, he was lucky that the policeman had dropped by.

The policeman.

Andrei closed his eyes, remembering back a few days. It was easy to think that the policeman had been the start of their troubles, but he hadn't – they'd started before he arrived. Andrei couldn't help but wonder, *what had he seen in the mountains? What had he seen when he walked into the east, searching for a way to climb the high peaks and look down into the southern valley?*

Andrei didn't think he would ever be able to forget the expression on the policeman's face when he had come back to the town, hurried along by the gathering night. *His eyes*, he thought. *Like he'd seen death... or Hell itself.*

He found his gaze had drifted to the south, staring up at the mountain pass which led to the valley. And like every night for months, the sky was filled with a blood-red light – a pernicious, filthy light, a deep scarlet, a poison crimson. He hated and feared it. For a reason he could not quantify, it terrified him beyond any measure.

For a moment, he couldn't tear his gaze away from that awful light, glowering in the high mountains, a vile cancer brooding in the dark. Every night it hung low in the sky, like a fume of death. His heart beat furiously, his palms were sweating, his knuckles were white from gripping the wooden rail. His breath coming in short, shallow gasps, he finally tore his eyes away and focused on the castle, focusing on anything but the dead light, a pall in the sky.

He had lived in these mountains all of his life. The local superstitions were well-known to him, but like many, he had dismissed them as nothing more than fairy tales, horror stories to titillate the tourists, and to encourage children to behave. Life paid little heed to myths and legends, even when they dwelt in the shadow of the physical reminders of those stories of long ago – the castle guarding the mouth to the pass, and the mountains themselves. Yet still, there was always a subconscious avoidance of certain places, and little rituals that everyone followed silently, as an homage to those myths, and the spark of truth that was buried deep within them.

That had changed about two months ago, when the Feragoths had arrived, and that glowering red pall had illuminated the southern sky.

They had landed in a handful of their alien craft, touching down in the pass, and immediately setting to work. The townsfolk had protested to the mayor, to no avail. They had taken it before the local Commissar, even up to the

Governors to present their complaints to the Chancellor himself, but the silence had been deafening. There was a war on, and the Feragoths were paying for it. As far as the Chancellor was concerned, they could dig wherever they pleased.

The first week was simply quiet, remembered Andrei. The townsfolk had fallen mute, talking in hushed whispers during the day, not daring to go outside at night. They lived their lives in silence, as if some ancient instinct had taken over – an instinct to avoid these creatures which now inhabited the mountains with them.

Then the sightings had started.

They came at night, drifting silently through the darkness, faceless, shapeless shadows, hooded and cloaked, apparitions of nightmares. Drawn by their senses, their desires, their *hunger...*

After that night, some of the townsfolk began hanging wreaths of hawthorn from their front doors.

No one mocked them for it. No one laughed. No one said a word.

Andrei heard the creak of wood behind him, and he jumped, his heart suddenly racing, turning to see his wife, Ileana, standing behind him. She was wearing her nightgown and slippers, but had pulled a winter coat on over the top. The hem of her gown could be seen beneath the coat. Her green eyes were wide in anxiety.

'Come inside, Andrei,' she said, holding out her hand, and shuddering as her eyes passed over the red light in the south. 'It's not a good night.'

'I'll come,' he said, absently, turning to stare back out at the mysterious vista of the mountains. 'Soon.'

He felt his wife's arms around his waist, and her lips touch the back of his neck. 'I love you,' she said, and he squeezed her hand. He felt her holding something, and took a step back, puzzled, lifting up her arm.

She was holding a garland of red roses... and another white flower that he knew all too well. Its pungent odour was immediately recognisable. The garland was wound with a silver chain – one he had given her for her birthday.

His wife looked at him, but cast her eyes down, ashamed to be indulging in such old superstitions.

He pulled her close and kissed her. 'Put it in Stefan's window,' he said, 'if it will make you feel better.'

She nodded and a single tear rolled down her cheek as she choked back sobs.

'Hey,' he murmured, smudging the tear away. 'It'll be all right.' Ileana nodded again, and went back inside.

Andrei's hand instinctively went to his pocket as he felt a gust of wind chill him, closing around the shaft of ash wood there.

His wife was not the only member of the family to resort to superstition.

Suddenly, the quiet night air was pierced by a terrible scream. Andrei turned round in shock, his heart hammering madly. *It was coming from inside his house.*

He darted forward to the door, and met his wife running out. Her face was wrenched into a howl of misery and terror, and she was screaming, screaming...

'Stefan!' she wailed in awful horror that sent a freezing spike of deathly cold into Andrei's very soul. 'They've taken Stefan! *They've taken our son!'*

Andrei span around, his eyes widening in terror, his world collapsing about him, and his eyes fixed on the mountain pass, which led to the Feragothic camp.

There.

Barely visible in the gathering gloom, a shadow, hooded and cloaked, gliding silently through the empty, silent night, a small, pale figure in its arms.

Andrei roared in rage and fury. '*Give me back my son, you filth!*' he bellowed, the words echoing round the valley, and he leapt over the rail of his porch, sprinting after the hooded demon.

At the roar, other townspeople came out of their houses, watching Andrei sprint down the road, his breath burning in his chest. '*Stefan!*' he roared, '*Stefan! They've taken Stefan!*'

His feet kicked up dust as he pelted down the road, his lungs burning, his eyes streaming tears of fury and panic. He became vaguely aware of others running with him, yelling and shouting, and felt a swell of pride as his neighbours joined him.

The figure seemed oblivious to the noise, its hooded head bent over the prostrate child clutched in its arms. When he was within six feet, Andrei pulled his weapon from his pocket, launching himself at the demon and hitting it in the back with his shoulder.

He gasped as the air was knocked from him – the impact was like running full-tilt into a wall. The creature didn't even flinch, and Andrei fell to the ground, hearing a sickening crack and a sudden spike of pain. His ribs were broken.

He stood, wielding his weapon, and finally the creature turned to face him. It dropped the child in its arms – so very pale – and Andrei beheld the apparition fully for the first time.

It stood nearly seven feet tall, its black cloak trailing on the floor, stained with dust. The shadow under its hood was utterly dark – a black chasm of despair, aside from two gleaming red orbs, pulsing dully. The creature's arm stretched out to Andrei, and he watched the clawed hand extend in dread horror. The Feragoth hissed at him, an open-mouthed, rasping growl that sent an ancestral terror through Andrei's body.

Bearing his teeth in a vicious display, and once more brandishing his weapon, he launched himself at the alien.

The Feragoth swept him to one side with a simple blow of its arm. To Andrei, it felt like being hit with an iron bar. He landed roughly on the ground, biting his tongue, and feeling the blood flow over his chin. Then the demon was surrounded by his neighbours. Andrei pulled himself to his feet, and they attacked.

The monster cast its attackers aside like a child discarding rag-dolls. Andrei finally managed to smash the stump of wood onto the creature's back, but it shattered into splinters, and the creature tossed him into the air. He landed heavily again, groaning in agony.

The horror scratched with its black talons, raking faces and eyes, and all the time, the air was filled with that awful, open-mouthed, breathing hiss. The people shouted and roared, but their will to fight quickly left when they realised they could not hope to defeat this demon. Andrei crawled along the ground as the Feragoth moved further up the road, heading into the mountains. He dragged himself to the body of his son, lying very still on the ground.

He finally reached him. He looked into his son's eyes, glazed and lifeless, he saw his pale, clammy skin, and saw no movement from his chest. 'Stefan?' he cried, through stinging tears, but no answer came. He took his child's hand, and recoiled in horror, for the flesh was stone cold.

The Feragoth finally disappeared around a bend in the road, gliding silently up into the mountains, and the air was filled with a high-pitched mocking laughter. Andrei took his dead son's body in his arms, and wailed in unquenchable grief at the silent night, and that awful, dead light, staining the sky above them like blood on velvet.

Chapter Twenty-Three

The Feragothic Ambassador slammed open the double-doors to the Chancellor's office, nearly smashing off their hinges. Turan looked up, alarmed, and he felt his skin shudder into gooseflesh in awful horror as he saw the creature which haunted his dreams stride into the room. Even Ulestran and Tellanor, both being consummate politicians capable of masking their feelings, almost cringed away from the hooded, towering figure as he strode up to the desk.

'Ulestran!' the creature roared, 'your contemptible *peasants* in Dacia *attacked* one of my countrymen last night! This is an utter disgrace! We are supposed to be your allies!'

Ulestran physically flinched at the alien's bellowing, his face pale. Despite his own fear, it brought Turan some comfort to know that other people did share his revulsion of the emissary as well.

'Your Excellency...' began Ulestran, but the alien interrupted.

'He was set upon by a *mob*, Ulestran – a filthy collection of *vermin*!' The Ambassador struck his deathly-pale fist on the large wooden desk, and left an indentation in the wood. 'This is totally unacceptable! You signed a treaty granting us *exclusive* rights to that area, and your pitiful *Goq'Maqar* have breached it!'

Turan felt slightly sick at the sound of the creature speaking its native tongue. He had no idea what the word meant, but the sound of it made his ears want to crawl inside his head.

Ulestran stammered as he tried to match the awful gaze coming from under the shadow of the heavy hood, but his eyes were locked on the imprint of the Feragoth's fist in the old, wooden desk. 'Your Excellency, there are reports that your countryman had attacked a child... and there are still questions as to what exactly caused the child's death...'

The Ambassador leaned across the desk. 'Are you insinuating something about my brethren, Chancellor?' he said, dangerously.

'Not at all,' squeaked Ulestran, shaking his head emphatically. 'I am simply stating the facts – a child *is* dead, Your Excellency, and the locals have accused one of the Feragoths from the encampment. I am insinuating nothing, simply stating the allegations.'

'I have no concern about such things,' spat the alien. 'My concern is – and yours should be – the preservation of our treaty! Now, I want you to assure the safety of my countrymen by stationing Confederate troops to guard the encampment. I will not have my people being attacked!'

'I cannot spare the men!' protested Ulestran. 'We are fighting a war, Ambassador...'

'That is not my concern!' roared the emissary. 'Your petty squabbles with the Protectorate do not concern me. Or the Emperor.' He added the last sentence almost as an afterthought. 'You will provide security for the encampment,' he said, 'or I will be forced to recommend that the Emperor review the terms of our treaty. Is that clear?'

Ulestran gazed at the shadowy apparition, his eyes wide with fear. His bottom lip trembled, and Turan watched the exchange in total silence. Finally, the Chancellor dropped his gaze. 'Yes, Your Excellency,' he murmured, and without another word, the Ambassador swept out of the room, his black cloak trailing behind him.

Ulestran sat down hurriedly, his legs turning to jelly, his face pale, and a cold sweat standing out on his brow. He glanced to the side, and saw Turan and Tellanor standing there, looking almost as shocked as him at what they had just witnessed.

'Get out,' he snarled, regaining some of his composure, and both of them left without a word.

-#-

'Killed?'

Allanor sat back in shock as Turan relayed the news of the attack in Dacia. They were in a quiet bar in a back street of the Capital. The place was dimly lit, with a large, grimy mirror behind the bar, and smelled vaguely of feet. Turan sipped his beer – it had been watered down.

'About twenty witnesses – including the boy's father – say they saw one of the Feragoths carrying him,' said Turan. 'From the town, back up into the mountains. They confronted and attacked it, but it fought them off.'

'One Feragoth fought off twenty people?'

'These things are strong, Governor, if the Ambassador is anything to go by.'

'Don't call me that,' she murmured, glancing around, and pulling up the collar of her coat, as if shielding herself against people who might recognise her.

Turan smiled. 'My apologies, Allanor,' he said. Allanor couldn't help but smile back.

'I suppose all of this has been censored?' she said.

Turan nodded. 'Tellanor sent the order to the media channels straightaway. As far as the government is concerned, it never happened.'

Allanor looked at Turan seriously. 'You do realise that, by telling me this, you are breaking several Confederate laws, and violating your oath as a policeman?'

Turan nodded slowly. 'Yes,' he said. 'But people need to know what's going on. These Feragoths are dangerous. *Very* dangerous. And the Chancellor is becoming a pawn of a foreign regime.'

Allanor nodded. 'Thank you, Turan,' she said, honestly, reaching across and resting her hand on his. 'You have no idea how much it means to me to know that someone else in this world cares about democracy.'

Turan felt a wonderful thrill as her fingers touched his, and found himself staring into her eyes. Despite herself, Allanor blushed slightly, and broke her gaze. Turan smiled. 'What are you going to do?' he said.

'Go public with it,' said Allanor. 'Distribute the news via word of mouth.'

'People won't believe it,' he said.

'Not at first,' conceded Allanor. 'But if you can keep feeding me these stories...' she trailed off, knowing full well the danger to Turan that she was implying. If he was caught, he would be executed. 'Will you do it?'

'Yes,' said Turan, unhesitatingly, and she squeezed his hand again, making him feel oddly giddy, in a way he had not felt in years.

-#-

Tellanor lay back on her bed, a glass of expensive red wine lolling between her fingers. Her hair, still wet from the shower, stained her pillow with dark streaks. She sat up, sighing contentedly and drank deeply from the glass, the wine's sweet taste coating her tongue, and feeling warm as it slipped down her throat.

She always felt this way after a session with the Chancellor. After allowing him to paw her for half an hour – *he couldn't last longer than that*, she thought to herself disgustedly – the only thing she could think about was having a shower and enjoying the wine, simply to get the taste of him out of her mouth and the feel of him off her skin.

She shuddered at the thought of Ulestran's cold, clammy hands caressing her. He had his uses, but they were few – and they came at a price. But like many men, the price was easily affordable, and Tellanor had what they wanted in abundance.

She had been sleeping with Ulestran since she had first entered the Palace staff as an intern four years ago, and consequently, had quickly moved up the ranks. Last year, he had appointed her Secretary, much to the consternation of the Opposition, who knew that she only received the promotion because she was prepared to bend over for Ulestran.

Tellanor smiled. Although it was the reason she had been promoted, she found it ironic that she was better at the job than anyone else. Of course she wouldn't have been promoted solely on the basis of merit – this was politics. You got promoted on the basis of what you had, not what you were capable of. Tellanor had sex, and it was better than hard currency.

She laughed at the thought of her sister, Allanor – so prim and proper, so cold and frigid. She had just the same intelligence and skills as Tellanor, but she refused to exploit every gift she had been given. *And that is why I am Secretary, and she is simply Opposition Leader, with no real prospect of attaining office*, thought Tellanor to herself. *She'll never win the support of the Governors, and no Chancellor will ever appoint her to the Cabinet.*

Her thoughts turned back to Ulestran. Today had been a difficult day – in their lovemaking session, he had been urgent and selfish, even more so than usual. No doubt trying to make up for the humiliation he had suffered that morning at the hands of the Feragothic Ambassador.

Tellanor marvelled to herself at the power of the emissary. He was truly inspiring, able to beget terror in people with such ease. For all his flaws, Ulestran was a very capable politician, and not easily intimidated, but the Ambassador had frightened him almost senseless.

She had been sleeping with Ulestran in order to further her position, but now she knew it would go no further. This treaty with the Empire of Feragoth was just the beginning – it was quite clear from the Ambassador's behaviour that they intended *much* closer relations with the Confederacy.

Tellanor, too, was an astute politician, and she could read the signs very well. *The Empire intends to annex the Confederacy*, she thought to herself. Where many people would feel horror at the idea of their homeland being absorbed by a foreign power, Tellanor felt nothing. She had no sense of patriotism; no attachment to the corrupt vestiges of democracy that the Confederacy had. She saw only the opportunity to advance herself.

There was no doubt in her mind that, if that were to happen, the Feragothic Ambassador would effectively become a Viceroy of the Confederacy, reporting directly to the Emperor. For all they knew, he was probably related to the Emperor – he certainly seemed to carry a large amount of influence.

If the Confederacy is to become part of the Empire, she mused, *then I'm fucking the wrong man.*

She smiled to herself and drained her glass of red wine. 'Time to go to work,' she giggled, and quickly set about blow-drying her hair. She dressed into a suitably provocative business suit with a low-cut blouse, a high, narrow pencil skirt, black leggings and high heels, before heading out.

Her private quarters were also located in the Palace, on the floor above the State Apartments, where the Ambassador resided. She quickly made her way down the corridor to the staircase, not meeting any of the Palace staff. The ancient building seemed empty and silent.

Her high heels clicked on the marble-and-gold-laid steps, before she reached the top of one of the Grand Staircases which led to the Ground Floor, then walked into the hallway. Turning left, she headed down towards her own office, but stopped outside the gold-inlaid double-doors leading to the State Apartments, which she walked past every day. *Not tonight*, she thought to herself, her body trembling with excitement at the thought of the power she would grasp if she succeeded.

A sudden thought occurred to her. She had no idea what the Feragoths looked like. From their hands and shape, they seemed humanoid, but she had no idea of their general appearance. Although she wasn't particularly bothered by it, it was a concern if they were not attracted to humans.

Yet some ancient instinct, some quiet part of her brain, told her that they were. For some reason, that instinct also commanded that she should be afraid... *very* afraid, of this creature that lurked in the darkness beyond those doors...

She dismissed it, and knocked on the door.

'Who is it?' came a cold voice from inside.

'Secretary Tellanor,' she said, her excitement at the possibility of advancement quenching the fear that the voice elicited.

The door opened, yawning blackly, the darkness surprising Tellanor. Then he was there, the Ambassador, towering over her, cloaked in black, his face hidden.

'What do you want?' he snapped contemptuously.

'I just wanted to apologise,' she said, turning on her charms and stepping closer to the emissary, 'for the way Ulestran behaved earlier. He didn't mean to upset or offend you, or the Emperor. Some of the locals in Dacia can be very... superstitious.' She gave him her most flattering smile.

The alien was completely silent, the eyeless gaze under the pitch shadow of the hood fixed on her.

Tellanor continued. 'I have personally censored the news reports of the unfortunate accident,' she said, leaning forward slightly, so that the emissary could see down her low-cut blouse, 'so I can assure you, the wider population will not become aware of the matter. There need not be any damage to... relations... between our people.'

She emphasised the word deliberately, a clear and intended euphemism.

The alien nodded slowly. 'Thank you, Secretary,' he said. 'Your efforts are appreciated.'

'Please...' she said, laughing, 'call me Tellanor.'

'Tellanor.' The syllables slammed like stone doors, but she continued, unperturbed.

'It has occurred to me, Ambassador,' she said, lightly touching the hem of one of his sleeves, 'that I have not yet demonstrated the full... courtesy... of diplomatic relations with you. At your convenience, I would be happy to.' She gave the apparition a slow wink.

Again, the alien nodded slowly. 'Unfortunately, Tellanor, I am otherwise engaged this evening. However, perhaps we can arrange something... mutually convenient?'

Tellanor smiled, an expression of delight on her face, at odds with the instinctive fear she felt. 'It would be my pleasure, Ambassador,' she said. 'And yours. Shall I call you tomorrow night?'

'I look forward to it,' replied the creature, and for the first time, Tellanor sensed genuine desire. She was succeeding.

'Again, please accept my apologies for this morning – and for interrupting you tonight,' she said, easily.

'Not at all,' said the Ambassador.

'It occurs to me, Ambassador,' she said lightly, 'that you have me at a disadvantage. You know my name, but I do not know yours.'

Silence fell between them, as the emissary seemed to consider what she was saying, weighing up some balance in his mind.

'Corin,' he answered. 'My name is Corin.'

'Corin,' said Tellanor, rolling the word around her mouth. 'Until tomorrow night, then. Good night.'

'Good night.' The door closed slowly, and Tellanor smiled to herself, trying to convince herself not to listen to that inner instinct, which was now screaming in horror.

Chapter Twenty-Four

Amon, Master of the Guardian Order, awoke with a start.

The old man sat up suddenly in his bed, his heart racing, cold sweat dripping from his brow. He forced himself to breathe slowly, practising an age-old technique to calm his mind, pausing for a few minutes in contemplation.

Amon's hair was a shock of tangled white wire. Blue eyes glittered with ancient wisdom in his wrinkled face. A small, neatly kept beard covered his chin, a moustache over his lips, the same colour as his hair. His skin was wrinkled like old paper, but there was strength in the bunched muscles on his arms. His barrel-chested figure conveyed power, authority and sagacity, with no hint of weakness.

He looked around his chambers, taking in the surroundings, and reminding himself of where he was. The walls were a bare, brown stone, the floor paved with cold, grey slabs. The room was about twelve feet square, with Amon's bed in the centre. Carefully embroidered carpets lay either side, mysterious patterns woven into the fabric in gold, silver and black. The bed itself was simple, carved roughly out of a black wood. A large oval window dominated the wall on Amon's left, commanding a spectacular view across a massive lake, spread out to the far distance, where blue mountains could be seen in the shadows on the horizon. A strange, green light glowed on the lake's rippling surface, from the glare of a planet in the night sky. It was Szotas, waning slightly from full, but still unbelievably bright in the sky, not through its luminosity, but its sheer size. It appeared over eight times bigger than Kaathar.

Amon breathed deeply and swung his feet off the bed, feeling the carpets beneath his feet.

'A dream,' he said to himself. 'I am on Beltrus.' He stood up and walked to the glassless window, relishing the cool breeze and the cold feeling of the flagstones beneath his bare feet. He was dressed in a simple black gown, open at the neck, hanging loose below his knees.

The dream still hung in his memory, vivid and clear. He saw, in his mind's eye, a dark, cold planet, orbiting a small, red sun. He saw a prison, a place of terrible violence, of horrors and injustice, and in that haven of filth, he saw a flame erupt, burning with a deadly heat, a fierce inferno lighting the entire galaxy – the entire Universe – with its flickering light. He sensed a broiling fume of black soot, the choking scent of smoke, a roar of dull thunder.

'The time has come,' he murmured to himself as he gazed up at the stars, and with a whisper of fear, 'the Destroyer is Risen.'

He suddenly burst into life, grabbing a sash from a table next to the window and cinching it around his waist. He pulled on loose-fitting trousers, black boots, and a hooded cloak that fastened around his throat with a silver chain. He walked to the far end of the room, where a mural was carved into the stone of the wall, forming a shrine. The mural was of a man, robed in black, holding a curved sword aloft, its blade flickering with fire. A heavy rapier-like sword rested on a stand on a low table, and beneath it, a circlet of silver.

Amon knelt in front of the shrine, closing his eyes briefly. Without needing to see, he reached out and lifted the sword in its scabbard from the stand, tucking it into the belt at his waist. He murmured a silent prayer, then lifted the silver crown, placing it on his brow, before standing and leaving the chamber.

The door opposite the great window led to a stairwell, and Amon quickly descended the steps. His chamber was in the Great Tower of the Guardian Monastery, which few people outside of the Order had ever laid eyes upon. At the bottom of the stairs, the tower door opened out onto the Inner Cloister – a quadrangle some fifty feet across, with covered arcades on each side. As he walked out onto the square lawn in the centre, two Guardians robed in black immediately approached from the other side.

'Master,' said one of them, bowing his head.

'We must leave for Astralas at once,' said Amon abruptly. 'There is no time to waste.'

-#-

Astralas, the gas giant planet which dominated the Lupus System, spun in the endless void, briefly eclipsing the light of Kraegan, the red dwarf at the utter edge of the system. The planet itself was huge, over sixty-four thousand kilometres in diameter, its atmosphere coloured in bands of light blue. The permanent aurorae around its poles were clearly visible, like those on Tarsus in the Vulpes System. However, the planet's most impressive feature was the collection of giant rings of dust and ice which extended for thousands of miles beyond its atmosphere. The dark side of the planet, even when not illuminated by either Kaathar or Kraegan, the two stars of the Lupus System, was lit by the reflective glow of those spectacular rings – bathed permanently in ringshine.

A starship accelerated out of high orbit of the planet, rotating steadily as its formation lights winked in the darkness. On its hull, the ship's name could be seen, painted on the stationary surface next to the rotating edge of the disc:

PSS VIGILANT

S-2193

Amon stood in the Command Centre of the ship, next to the Helm. He watched the Flight Display as the ship thrust forward into the darkness, its powerful Ion Drive propelling it away from the giant planet. The command crew were nervous in the presence of the Guardian Master, arguably the most influential person in the entire Protectorate, next to the Protector herself.

Amon was cloaked in black, his hood and cowl – symbolising his membership of the Guardian Conclave – around his shoulders. His hood was cast back, revealing his shock of white hair, and the silver crown upon his brow, in the same style as the gold one worn by the Protector. The Master of the Guardian Order was more than just a priest. He was the theocratic ruler of the Protectorate, representing the highest spiritual authority in their society, as well as the President of the Guardian Conclave, the Protectorate's Supreme Court.

The Captain, sat at the Helm, turned to the cloaked figure standing next to him. 'Master Amon,' he said, 'are you sure about this? Engaging the Wormhole Drive while we are still in the Lupus System...'

'I understand the risks, Captain,' said Amon evenly, 'but the circumstances call for it. Believe me, the alternatives do not bear contemplation.'

'As you wish, Master.' The Captain turned back to face the main Flight Display. 'Setting a course for the Vulpes Tunnel. Prepare to engage the Wormhole Drive.'

'Aye, sir,' replied the Chief Engineer, his voice cracking with nerves.

The Wormhole Drive was powered by the ship's Terculium Reactor to create a temporary tunnel in space-time. It allowed Protectorate starships to travel great distances very quickly, shortening journeys that would take thousands of years under the Ion Drive to a matter of months or weeks.

Between the major systems of the Protectorate, the Starforce had established permanent tunnels, which shortened the journeys even more. Each Protectorate system had two tunnels, one leading to each of the other systems. The openings to these tunnels were on the very edge of the systems, where the effect of gravity was minimal.

Gravity, being effectively the distortion of space-time caused by matter, caused problems for the tunnels – they distorted the entrances, making it very difficult for spacecraft to enter them without being torn apart by the gravitational shear. It was like tides of the sea crossing in two different directions. These tunnels could only be traversed by ships with Wormhole Drives, which served to let them enter the tunnels without being severely damaged or destroyed. However, the approach to a tunnel entrance was normally made using the Ion Drive, in order to minimise gravitational disruption.

Amon had ordered the *Vigilant's* captain to engage the Wormhole Drive whilst still inside the Lupus System, setting a course for the tunnel to the Vulpes System. This meant that the *Vigilant* would be creating a tunnel between its current location near Astralas to the Vulpes Tunnel entrance, and then entering the Vulpes Tunnel immediately. This would save nearly a week of travelling time, but require opening a wormhole whilst still in an area of space-time significantly curved by the gravitational effects of Astralas and Kaathar. It was extremely dangerous.

'All hands, this is the Captain. We are going to attempt Wormhole Drive whilst still in the Lupus System. Ready Stations, brace for impact!'

The Ready Stations siren sounded, and the Captain strapped himself into his chair, as did the rest of the command crew. 'You should take a seat, Master,' said the Captain.

Amon shook his head. 'If we make a mistake, the ship will be torn apart,' he said. 'If I'm to die, I prefer to meet Death standing.'

The Captain nodded. 'Engineering?'

'Ready, sir.'

'Engage Wormhole Drive.'

The *Vigilant's* Terculium Reactor, at the hub of the ship, lit suddenly in a brilliant bright light, as bright as a star, glaring with unrelenting power in the shadow of the freezing void. Ahead of the ship, the very fabric of space-time warped and distorted, as a giant translucent bubble seemed to form out of nothing, glowing faintly around the edges with a vague, metallic light. This was a vortex – the entrance to the wormhole tunnel, a dense globule of viscous liquid.

As the bubble ballooned outwards to the size of a small planet, the *Vigilant* lurched forward, pulled by the massive gravitational force of the vortex which had appeared out of nowhere. For a moment, as the ship was yanked deep into the gravity well of the vortex, the ship seemed to stretch, before disappearing into it.

Amon grabbed hold of the back of the Captain's chair as the *Vigilant* careened through the vortex. The sirens blared, and red strip lighting around the Command Centre flashed madly. The old man's heart pounded in his chest as the Flight Display flashed with swirling patterns of stars wheeling in weird patterns through the void. The ship was tossed around on the gravitational waves like a wooden sailing ship on the ocean.

'Full Ion Drive!' yelled the Captain. 'Full speed ahead!'

The *Vigilant* blasted ahead through the heaving waves of space-time, into the throat of the wormhole. The ship rattled and shook on the dangerous journey through to the other side. Finally, the Flight Display cleared, the shuddering stopped, and the ship blasted out at a hundred million kilometres per hour into normal space on the far edge of the Lupus System. Behind them, the vortex from which they had just emerged folded back in on itself, shrinking into nothingness as the star-like light in the *Vigilant's* hub dulled back to its pulsing, faint blue glow.

Amon breathed deeply, loosening his fingers from their claw-like grasp of the Captain's chair. The Captain turned to him and smiled in relief and astonishment at still being alive.

'I'm bringing us to all stop. Sensors, our position?'

'The outskirts of the Lupus System, sir,' said the Sensors Officer, his voice still shaking. 'Just outside the gravitational field of the Vulpes Tunnel.' He turned to the Captain, a broad smile on his face. 'We made it!'

The Captain nodded grimly. 'Well done, everyone,' he said. 'Damage report.'

'Minor damage only, Captain,' reported the Engineer.

The Captain breathed a sigh of relief. 'Well, Master Amon,' he said, turning to the Guardian Master, 'we've saved nearly a week's travelling time, and we're still alive. Where to?'

'Nowhere,' replied Amon, looking ahead at the Flight Display. He closed his eyes as he felt the presence that he had sensed in his dream, and that had dominated his waking moments since, grow suddenly closer. 'He's here,' he murmured.

'Captain, there's a ship coming through the Vulpes Tunnel vortex,' said the Science Officer. 'It's not a Protectorate vessel. Looks like a Confederate shuttlecraft!'

'All hands to Battle Stations!' ordered the Captain.

'Sir, the shuttle has changed course to intercept us,' shouted the Tactical Officer.

Amon opened his eyes and grasped the hilt of his *aelrak*, hidden beneath his cowl. 'Do not fire on the ship,' he said. 'Let it come.'

The shuttle rocketed out of the gravity well of the Vulpes Tunnel, slicing across the night sky like an arrow, rocketing towards the *Vigilant* at a mad speed.

'It's going to hit! All hands, brace for impact!'

The shuttle smashed into the hull of the *Vigilant*, the force of the impact knocking the ship in a semicircle. Consoles in the Command Centre exploded and the lights flickered erratically. The Flight Display flashed and burned out with a popping sound, going completely black, filling the

Command Centre with a sudden sense of claustrophobia, as the only window on the outside world was slammed shut.

Amon's mind was dominated by the powerful vision – a cloud of black smoke, an inferno burning within. He could feel the rage pouring from it, the visceral, animal energy, the will to destroy. *May all the Guardians help me*, he thought to himself.

'Stay here!' he barked at the command crew, and without another word, stalked out of the room.

Two hundred yards down the corridor, he met a sight of chaos and confusion. Entire walls and deck plates had been ripped away and crushed, and the blunt nose of the shuttle protruded up through the floor and part of the wall diagonally into the corridor. An emergency hatch had been blown open, partially embedded in the ceiling. The lights flashed, and exposed electrical cables flashed and danced wildly, swinging loose from the ceiling.

Amon inhaled sharply as he regarded the creature which had been calling to him. A young man was crouched on the floor just in front of the protruding shuttle nose. He wore nothing except a dirty shift made of rough sack-cloth. His arms and legs were bare. His head was shaved, only short stubble showing. He was filthy, covered in dirt, ash, and blood, but tear-tracks carved their way through the grime, running down his cheeks in angry white stripes. His arms were wrapped around his knees, and he rocked back and forth on his heels, sobbing, his eyes screwed shut.

Amon took a step forward, meaning to comfort him, but realised his error when the man's eyes opened suddenly. 'Tarsus,' muttered Amon, as he saw those eyes. They were lit with flame, burning *inside his head*. He could feel the awesome heat baking out of them, making sweat bead on his brow, a dry, furnace heat. The flames cast deadly, mocking shadows on the ruined walls of the corridor.

The creature's face twisted into a snarl, and it stood, throwing itself down the corridor, its arms spread wide. Amon watched in horror as the walls and floor were crushed outward by some invisible force with the passage of the demon, and stepped back, casting back his cloak and drawing his *aelrak*.

The blade was black, but shone with a strange lustre. As it moved swiftly in the flickering half-light, a bluish tinge crept along its length, a hint of the power that lay within the mysterious metal. The blade was terculium, the same which powered the Wormhole Drive of the *Vigilant*, the same which had driven the engines of the *Inominate* on its long journey from Therqa in the distant past.

'Halt!' commanded Amon, holding the sword overhead, its blade glittering dangerously. 'I am Amon, Master of the Order of Guardians, Keeper of the Secret Knowledge! You shall not defeat me!'

The creature roared, a harsh, guttural noise, and plunged onwards, tearing the corridor apart with the force which emanated from him, levitating off the floor. Amon stood his ground, his white hair blasting back by the searing wind coming from the approaching demon. At the last moment, when the creature was nearly on top of him, he stepped to the side, and brought his sword down in a diagonal slash, the tip of the sword cutting across his attacker's chest.

The creature howled in pain as it fell past Amon, landing on the floor with a thud that shook the entire ship. Amon sidestepped again to face the demon head-on. It stood, clutching its chest, and a thin rivulet of blood worked its way between its fingers. The heat from the creature abated, falling away, and the flames in its eyes receded, still burning, but without the same ferocity. It roared again in defiance, but also in fear.

'You cannot win!' shouted Amon, and raised his sword aloft with one hand. He extended the other hand to the creature, palm open. 'Let there be peace between us. I know the grief which torments your soul. I can help you.'

The creature burst into flame, the orange tongues of fire wreathing its very skin. With a new-found energy and rage, it leapt towards Amon, a brand of fire, a burning effigy of humanity. Amon pulled his hand back to prevent it being burned by the deadly flame, then struck again with his *aelrak*, this time the blade cutting deeper, slashing across the belly. The demon howled, the very air shaking with the torment of it, and doubled over. Without hesitation, Amon raised his sword overhead, and brought the heavy pommel crashing down onto the back of the creature's skull, knocking it senseless.

It slumped silently to the floor, and the heat and flame were extinguished as quickly as they had arrived, leaving the man's body unburned, only a thin film of ash where the hessian shift had been.

Amon exhaled slowly, his breath coming out in juddering gasps. His hands shook as he slid his *aelrak* back into its scabbard. He knelt beside the body of the man, pressing his fingers against the neck, feeling for a pulse. He wiped his brow and sighed with relief as he felt the strong beating of a healthy heart, and then turned over the body to get a clearer look at the face.

His eyes widened in shock as he recognised the figure, and he bit his lip in astonishment as he recalled an almost forgotten memory. He had seen this man before, or the boy he had been. He remembered performing the service of marriage for his parents in the Temple on Szotas, when he was a Peer of the Conclave. He remembered blessing the birth of the child. He remembered...

'By all the Guardians,' invoked Amon quietly. 'Welcome home – Psinaez Jamek.'

Chapter Twenty-Five

The days before had been clear, but a thick layer of grey cloud now obscured the skies. It was still warm; the heat of the previous days was trapped by the dark, brooding blanket.

Jamek sat silently on the bole of a collapsed tree, the bark long since stripped from the trunk, leaving only smooth-grained wood behind. Only a few steps away, the crystal clear lake caressed the salty rocks and sand with gentle waves. The shadows of corals and stones could be seen in the water. Across the bay, regal mountains stood stark against the grey sky, wearing evergreen forests like heavy cloaks, and crowned with circlets of rock. A few birds cried, circling the bay, but otherwise, the scene was silent and tranquil.

Jamek sat there, alone in his thoughts, wondering how he had come to be in this place. This place of calmness, of serenity.

Before...

There was very little before. What had happened? His memory was somehow... empty. He found it strangely disconcerting. He closed his eyes and tried to remember.

Before...

He remembered coming to this place. It had been dark and cold. There were others, but they were separated from him. His heart beat faster, and adrenaline surged as he remembered the anger, the pain, the constant, unending fury inside him, tearing him apart...

-#-

He prowled around the cage like a trapped animal, his mind on fire, a jumbled wreckage of seething flame. They watched him carefully, and he ran at them, hitting the bars, cracking his body against them, then sinking back, hissing malevolently. The bars would hold – it was what they were designed for – but still, he was testing them. His new-found strength was being put to good use.

Of course, this cage was no ordinary menagerie – its bars were wrought of terculium, the mysterious black metal which powered the heart of every Protectorate starship, and formed the blade of every Guardian's aelrak. *It had been built for precisely this purpose – to carry the Destroyer on his journey back home.*

They spoke to each other in quiet, soft voices, not to hide the conversation from the demon – he could hear it well enough – simply not to enrage him, not to provoke him into damaging himself any more. At least, this was the reason they gave themselves.

They feared him, and rightly so. He was dangerous. There had been none quite like him, none as strong, or fast, or brutal. They had been preparing for his arrival for nearly a thousand years, and now he was here. The thought curdled their blood.

There was much work to be done to turn him from the ravaged, senseless animal that he had become to the thing he must be, but he, and only he, was the only one who could do it. He had to realise his true worth, and his true abilities. He had to find himself amongst the chaos that now dominated him.

The darkness surrounded them, and the only sound that could be heard was the faint lapping of water against the boat's hull. The air was calm, but somehow detached, and cold. Soon this animal trapped inside the cage would be unleashed, and would have to calm himself. He would be alone...

-#-

Another memory, earlier...

-#-

He saw her, her naked form, lying in his arms. Her face was bruised and bleeding, and blood welled on her lips as she coughed, hacking sounds that shook her body. Grief, unimaginable and unexpected, leapt up his throat from his heart. He felt tears well up in his eyes, and stream down his face. He felt his mind wrench with the torment as she breathed her last breath, so sensitively, so delicately. But her eyes didn't close. She lay there in his arms, still and silent.

He screamed as a red cloud engulfed him, tormenting him with cruel malevolence, twisting his writhing body. Rage came unbidden, bright and furious, and flame exploded from him, a black cloud of death, and fire, and smoke. The red entity fled across the darkness of the void, and Jamek, empowered by the cloud which now surrounded and permeated him, followed. He knew that this was his destiny, driven by the grief and sorrow of his losses, to destroy this evil malevolence which threatened to destroy everything he had ever known...

-#-

'Jamek...'

The familiar voice brought Jamek out of his dreams with a start, and the memories came flooding back. He bit his lip to hold back the tears as the images of Adraea rushed into his conscious mind.

'Adraea...' he murmured, and tears tracked down his face. He turned and saw Amon sitting next to him.

Amon rested his hand on Jamek's shoulder. 'Do you remember?'

Jamek nodded. He remembered everything now. Being taken prisoner by the Confederacy, Adraea's murder, escaping from the prison, and the confrontation with Amon aboard the starship. It seemed an age ago.

'Memory dissociation is common after such deep meditation,' said Amon, and took both of Jamek's shoulders in his hands. 'When they come flooding back, it can be painful. Don't let them rule you, Jamek. You remember how?'

Jamek nodded, and instinctively closed his eyes, taking deep breaths, emptying his mind of thought in a technique only recently learned, but already mastered.

He had been training with Amon at the Guardian Monastery on Beltrus for nearly two months. The intensive regime of prayer, simple living and martial training had calmed his mind, driving the grief and misery deep down inside him, contained and controlled. Occasionally, these emotions tried to break free, manifesting themselves physically with frightening powers, but he could now hold them in check. This most recent meditation had been his final test – to see if he could deal with a sudden flood of emotion without regressing into the unrestrained animal he had been when Amon confronted him.

He had passed.

Amon released him gently. 'You are ready,' he said. 'Tomorrow, we will travel to Szotas. You will set upon the path of your destiny.'

'I'm afraid, Master.'

Amon smiled. 'Not as afraid as your enemies, Jamek,' he said.

'Adraea...'

'Adraea is dead,' said Amon softly. 'But that does not mean she is gone. She watches you. And you will be reunited with her. But you have much to do, now, Jamek.'

Jamek nodded. 'I am ready,' he said.

-#-

Laruak awoke suddenly, the alarm on his communicator ringing insistently. He groaned briefly, and then the reality of life quickly came flooding back into his tired brain. The Protectorate was at war, and he was head of state.

He snapped awake, sitting up in bed, grabbing his communicator and switching on his bedside lamp at the same time. The room flooded with an arc of light from the lamp, reflecting on the glass of the oval window opposite. The glare from the lamp slightly obscured the view from the window – to the north of the *Inominate,* across the top of the High Command building. Stars glimmered in the night sky, obscured by skyscrapers tapering down to the walled border of the Capitol. The city still spread as far as he could see.

He tapped the screen, turning on its loudspeaker. 'Laruak,' he muttered.

'I'm sorry to wake you, Proconsul,' came the voice of his secretary, 'but I've just received a transmission from the Guardian Monastery on Beltrus. Master Amon is on his way to Szotas.'

Laruak's eyes widened in surprise. Although the Guardian Order had oversight of the political process, they rarely took an active involvement. When they did, it was guaranteed to be of importance. News that the Guardian Master was on his way to Szotas was certainly indicative of importance. He was the head of the Order and the most powerful person in the Protectorate next to the Protector.

'I'm on my way,' replied Laruak, and hung up. He pulled himself out of bed, and stood by the window, looking out across the vast cityscape, stretching out into the distance. The stars twinkled in the night sky, and the city glowed with another thousand pinpricks of light, as if it were some great ocean reflecting the starlight. Despite the comforting glow of the city's lights, Laruak shivered as he regarded the black sky.

He hated the night, the real dark which was present when both Kaathar and Kraegan had set, and Szotas was plunged into the shadow, broken only by the distant glimmer of starlight. It seemed a fitting metaphor for these dark times, when the Protectorate was invaded, and Szotas itself was under threat of conquest.

And yet, something deep inside him stirred at the thought of the Guardian Master's arrival on Szotas. Was this another portent of doom, or was it, perhaps, a light at the end of the tunnel?

'The night is darkest before the dawn,' murmured Laruak, and hope was kindled in his heavy heart.

-#-

Master Amon walked through the silent halls and corridors of the *Inominate*, his black cloak swirling around him. His hood was thrown back, revealing his shock of wild white hair, his neatly kept beard, and the silver crown that stood on his brow. His hand rested on the silver hilt of his sword as he walked. Two other Guardians accompanied him, their faces hidden by shadowed hoods.

The Guardians turned a corner, and began walking down the corridor which led to the Office of the Protector. As ever, two Guardians stood guard at the entrance to the Office, and when they saw the head of their Order walking towards them, their eyes widened in surprise. As one, they dropped to one knee, their heads bowed in reverence.

Amon stopped outside the door, in front of the kneeling Guardians. 'Rise, Brothers,' he said, and they stood up, still keeping their heads bowed in respect and deference. 'I require an audience with the Protector,' he said. 'Tell Her Magnificence that Lord Amon, Master of the Order of Guardians, is desirous of speaking with her.'

'With respect, Master,' said one of the Guardians, 'the Protectorship is vacant, pending an election. The Proconsul holds the crown of office.'

Amon blinked in surprise. Such had been his focus on Jamek that he had not paid due attention to the political situation on Szotas. *An error,* he thought to himself determinedly. *One that will not be repeated.*

'Then inform His Grace of my arrival,' he said smoothly. The Guardian nodded, and they both opened the double-doors to the Office of the Protector, pulling them wide. They stepped in, and one of the Guardians spoke.

Lord Amon, Master of the Order of Guardians,' he said, and Amon stepped across the threshold, accompanied by his two hooded escorts.

Laruak stood behind the desk, in front of the window which commanded a view across the city, blanketed in night, the stars shining overhead. He wore his white robes, but the golden crown of the Protector lay on the desk in front of him, identical in gold to the silver one that rested on Amon's head. Daedra and Fedrus stood on either side of him.

Amon nodded as he regarded Laruak, and held out his hand as the doors were shut behind him. 'Proconsul,' he said, 'I don't believe I've yet had the pleasure of meeting you.'

Laruak reached forward and took the offered hand, shaking it. He was surprised at the strength of the old man.

'Master Amon,' he said. 'What brings you to Szotas at such a dark time?' He indicated for the Guardian Master to take a seat, and did so himself.

'Glad tidings, Proconsul,' said Amon, holding up his hand to refuse the seat, preferring to stand. 'From the sound of things, you are in need of them.'

'That is something of an understatement,' replied Laruak. 'I was going to contact you tomorrow, to ask you for assistance in the war with the Confederacy.' He sighed, looking at the Guardian Master's expressionless face. 'It does not go well. The Vulpes System is annexed, and we fear that an invasion of Lupus may be imminent. The Protectorate is in its darkest hour. I am afraid that we need the Guardians more than ever.'

Amon was taken aback. He hadn't realised the military situation was that bad. *I have been on Beltrus too long*, he thought to himself. *The Protectorate obviously needs more care than I thought. This* laissez-faire *approach of the Order will not do any longer.*

'Do you stand for election?' asked Amon, masking his concern effortlessly.

Laruak shook his head. 'No,' he replied, 'Karaea stands again, and Draelan contests her.'

Amon thought on this, his wrinkled brow furrowed even more. 'I have obviously not taken sufficient interest in the politics of the temporal government,' he said. 'That will change, I assure you.'

He took a deep breath. 'The glad tidings I bring are this, Proconsul – the Destroyer of Worlds has Risen. The enemies of the Protectorate will be vanquished. Hope has come at our darkest hour.'

Laruak sat back, dumbfounded, stunned into silence. Fedrus and Daedra looked sceptical, wondering just how much of the old prophecies were true. The religion of the Guardians was widespread – it had been a guiding influence throughout the history of the Protectorate. It had brought their ancestors comfort in the dark nights. The legend of Tarsus, the first Guardian, forging the sword of *Seyotaal* from the heart of the *Inominate*, was still told to children at bedtime.

And, of course, all knew of the greatest prophecy – that Tarsus bequeathed the sword to his disciples on his death, ordering them to guard it until his return. His return, it was said, would come at the Protectorate's darkest hour, and Tarsus would be reborn as a Destroyer of Worlds. He would take up the sword of *Seyotaal* and use it to defeat the Sorceror – a demon of ancient and terrible power.

This was indeed the Protectorate's darkest hour, but cynicism and doubt lay ever at the hearts of practical men.

'Master,' said Laruak, breaking the silence reluctantly, 'with all due respect...'

'I do not make these claims lightly, Proconsul,' interrupted Amon. 'The Destroyer is Risen. He has returned to us from the Confederacy itself. He is one of our own, one that has been known to me for some time. I officiated at his parents' wedding. You also attended, Fedrus.' He glared at the General, who lowered his gaze.

'His name is Psinaez Jamek.'

Fedrus gasped, and held his hand to his mouth, his eyes brimming with tears. Amon stood, and immediately went over to the grizzled General, laying his hand on his arm. Laruak sat in stunned silence. Anzaeus had been the first casualty of the war, and now his son had returned as the Destroyer. Could it possibly be true?

Fedrus sat down. 'Is it true?' he asked Amon.

'It is true,' Amon replied. 'He lives. He does honour to his father, and to you, Fedrus.'

Fedrus closed his eyes, and tears ran down his cheeks. His heart seemed to explode with relief, that his ward who he had sworn to protect after the death of his best friend had returned unharmed. And a mad, wild hope flashed deep inside him – that if Jamek were still alive, could Adraea be also? He almost couldn't dare to hope.

Amon stood upright, and turned to Laruak. 'It is true,' he said. 'He has powers beyond those of mortal men. He can move things with his mind. He can see the future, the past. He can perceive things across great distances. He can control fire.'

'Tomorrow, I will coronate him in the Temple, and he will wield *Seyotaal* – the first to do so since Tarsus entrusted it to us nearly a thousand years ago. And then this Confederacy will know the fury of Szotas.'

Chapter Twenty-Six

The Guardian Temple was one of the biggest and oldest buildings in the city. It stood at the southern end of Central Plaza, directly opposite the astonishing height of the *Inominate*. Where the *Inominate* was the centre of the temporal powers, so the Temple was the centre of the spiritual.

It stood at least five storeys high, a massive elliptical building, its major axis aligned directly north to south. It was made from Szotas's native brown stone, the very bones of the planet, each brick carved carefully by hand, fitting together seamlessly, with no need for mortar. Its walls were decorated with sweeping, graceful elliptical arches, and inset hollows where proud statues stood, gazing with unblinking eyes at the populace below. The Guardians of old were ever watchful.

A massive portico stood at the North Gate, opening onto Central Plaza. Five pillars rose up three storeys, before they reached a half-elliptic cross-stone at the top. At the top of this was the largest of the statues – Tarsus, the founder of the Guardian Order. He had been one of the survivors of the crash of the *Inominate* when it smashed onto the surface of Szotas nearly a thousand years ago, delivering the inhabitants to their new home from exile in space.

The statue stood upright and proud, his cloak caught in an intangible wind, staring defiantly across at the *Inominate.* A curved sword was in his hand, its tip pointing in the direction of his gaze, a constant reminder of the Order's oversight over the secular powers. The sword was *Seyotaal*, the first *aelrak*, forged by Tarsus himself from the heart of the *Inominate's* terculium core. The sword now rested on the High Altar in the Temple.

The roof of the portico connected with the main body of the building, where a circular tower rose up, its walls lined with pillars in a cylindrical colonnade. Its roof rose up in a great dome, topped with a rectangular housing at its apex. This was the North Tower, once the highest building on Szotas, until the *Inominate* was raised to its upright stance nearly four hundred years ago. It was still an impressive sight even in a city of towers and skyscrapers.

Above, the warm, yellow light of Kaathar, Szotas's larger star, cast the cityscape in a pleasant glow. Close to it, Kraegan, Kaathar's distant, red sister star, moved across the aquamarine sky, a small, faint, red dot compared to the glorious warmth of Kaathar. The golden sunlight filled the sky, Kaathar's disc nearly a full degree in diameter, as Szotas was close to its parent star. Tall, dark shadows fell from the towering skyscrapers, blotting the ground like stains of ink.

Central Plaza itself was filled with a great crowd of people, pressed into the great square, their backs turned to the *Inominate*, staring ahead at the mammoth Guardian Temple. The crowd spilled out onto the neighbouring streets and around the building, the people moving like tiny insects around a great hive. The North Gate yawned open behind its pillars of stone, revealing a hint of the majesty within.

The crowd talked in hushed voices in reverence of the Guardians that lined the steps leading up to the open doorway. They were cloaked and hooded in black, their faces hidden, gloved hands resting on the hilts of *aelraks* at their belts. Their hoods showed that they were Guardians of the Conclave – the high council of the Guardian Order – the supreme masters of law and order in the Protectorate. Warriors of great renown, they served as the Protectorate's Judges of Appeal. They were the most feared and respected men and women in society, and now, six of them stood guard – a duty normally delegated to common soldiers – at the entrance to the Guardian Temple.

Rumours had abounded across the planet for days. Amon, the Guardian Master himself, had returned to Szotas, to seek an audience with Proconsul Laruak. Starships had been monitored arriving and departing the Guardian Monastery on Beltrus, Szotas's sister planet, which was normally devoid of traffic except for a weekly shuttle service to Szotas. The Senate had assembled in the *Inominate.* The fact that the Protectorate was crippled by an election campaign, and had no formal Protector, made it even more unusual. The Guardian Master would normally only address himself to the Protector, and the Protector was the only one who could sign Acts of Senate into law.

And now, the Guardians of the Conclave guarded the steps to the Guardian Temple, one of the oldest and most revered places on Szotas. The Temple housed a treasure which had become an emblem for an exiled people – *Seyotaal*, the Sword of Unity, forged by Guardian Tarsus from the heart of the *Inominate.* The Sword which, before his death, he had placed on the very site where he had forged it, in an age gone by, where it rested still, the Temple having been built around it. The Sword which he had prophesied would be lifted only by a Destroyer of Worlds, who would destroy an empire, and bring his people home. Had the time, long awaited, and in the Protectorate's darkest hour, when they faced conquest again at the hands of their merciless enemies, come at last?

The tension and silence was broken temporarily when a car drove up one of the side streets and into Central Plaza itself. The crowd parted for it silently, closing the gap after the car had passed. The vehicle stopped outside the North Gate, and a figure stepped out.

He was dressed entirely in black, and wore the hood and cowl of a member of the Guardian Conclave, but the hood was pulled back, revealing his face. He was tall, and powerfully-built, but his hair was white and wild, his beard neat and trim. His skin was brown and wrinkled, but blue eyes glinted like flecks of steel. On his head, he wore a simple circlet of silver, engraved with ancient letters. On his hip was an ancient *aelrak*, a straight blade, styled like a rapier, but heavier-set. The crowd gasped as they saw him, and many immediately dropped to their knees, placing their foreheads on the marble stones of Central Plaza.

Amon, Guardian Master, stepped purposefully towards the North Gate. As he approached, the Conclave Guardians standing guard dropped to one knee, and offered their *aelraks* to him in a sign of total submission to his authority. He stopped just in front of the pillars, and turned to face the crowd.

'I am Amon,' he said, 'Master of the Guardians, and I hereby summon the Proconsul, as the Office of Protector is vacant, to attend me in the Temple of Tarsus with his Senators.' Though he was not shouting, his voice echoed around Central Plaza over the silent crowd.

The crowd turned to face the *Inominate*, on the opposite side of Central Plaza. They stood agape as they saw a figure in plain white robes, but wearing the golden circlet of the Protector upon his brow, step forth from the massive rockets clustered at the base of the ancient starship. Proconsul Laruak walked to the top of the steps leading down to Central Plaza, and glanced behind him.

The grey-robed Senators stepped out of the shadows. Draelan could be seen clearly among them, standing a full head taller than the others, his pale, hairless skin and gleaming blue eyes seeming out of place in the warm sunlight of Central Plaza. Karaea was also there – both she and Draelan wore white robes like Laruak, but without the golden trim. During the election, they were granted the ceremonial office of Praetor – ranked higher than Senators, but below the Proconsul, who was effectively Acting Protector.

Laruak immediately set off down the steps, heading towards the crowd, followed by the Senators and the Praetor, as sheep follow a shepherd. The crowd parted for them, the leaders of the Protectorate, answering the call of the Guardians.

Laruak walked across the cool, white marble of Central Plaza, his eyes fixed on the figure of Master Amon standing before the North Gate of the Temple. Amon's face was expressionless as he awaited the arrival of the politicians, each of them approved by the Conclave which he commanded, and which now stood guard for him.

When they all stood at the foot of the steps leading up to the North Gate, Amon turned and began walking slowly into the shadow of the great cathedral, accompanied by the hooded Conclave Guardians on either side of him. The stately procession of Guardians and Senators moved into the Temple. The Conclave Guardians, upon entering the building, threw back their hoods, revealing old and weathered faces, lined with hard experience.

The interior of the Temple was stunning – the warm golden sunlight shone through intricate stained glass windows, casting specular shadows on the stone floor. Great stone pillars ran the length of the magnificent hall on either side, their path following the contours of the curved walls. Great archways swept upwards to a vaulted ceiling, decorated with ornate frescos of frowning

Guardians and laughing children, staring down implacably on the congregation below. Just inside the North Gate, the great atrium of the North Tower stretched upwards, the ceiling of the dome some ten storeys above the floor. It was painted with silver, and a great oval window on the south side of the tower allowed the blazing light of Kaathar to shine through. The golden light reflected onto the floor below, so that a brilliant circle of light was emblazoned on the floor at the entrance to the Temple.

Laruak inhaled sharply as he stepped into the circle of light underneath the North Tower, his eyes half-closed as he squinted into the darkness. He looked to his left, and saw Karaea walking alongside him, wearing her plain white robes. He smiled to her briefly, and she smiled back. He wanted desperately to reach out and hold her hand. His stomach knotted as he watched her move. She was so beautiful he felt his heart might burst.

He stepped out of the light, and his gaze wandered to the walls, which were carved with stunning tableaux, depicting the history of the Protectorate. The Great War on Therqa, the defeat in battle, and the exile to the dark recesses of space. Planetfall – the crash-landing of the *Inominate* onto Szotas – the forging of *Seyotaal* and the founding of the Guardian Order. The death of Tarsus and the construction of the Temple. The raising of the *Inominate*, the Civil War and the Guardian Order's intervention to end it, and finally the colonisation of Beltrus and the establishment of the Monastery there. The great tapestry of the Protectorate's life was laid out on those walls. Laruak felt his skin break out into goosebumps as he thought that another chapter in that great history was being written right now, and that he was a part of it. Could they truly be about to witness the Rise of the Destroyer?

The procession moved silently down the nave, between the pews which filled the floor. Laruak looked behind him, and through the rank and file of grey-robed Senators following him, he could make out blue military uniforms as the High Command Staff made their way into the Temple. He caught a glimpse of Daedra and Fedrus, walking silently with their heads bowed. Behind them, members of the public pressed into the building, waiting silently until the procession had passed before grabbing what seats they could.

Laruak again looked forward, to the south end of the Temple. Where the great curved walls met, a giant oval stained glass window let the sunlight pour in, filling the solemn church with fantastic colours – reds, greens, yellows and oranges, blues and purples, a rainbow of wonder that reflected intricate patterns on the stone floor. Below this window, the High Altar stood upon a dais, a huge table wrought of brown stone and silver. It was nearly fifteen feet wide, its base bearing a sculptured tableau of Guardian Tarsus forging *Seyotaal* from the *Inominate's* terculium core. Behind it, on the stone wall below the Southern Window, was the most magnificent work of art on Szotas – a sculptured fresco, in full colour, of the Destroyer, robed in black, holding *Seyotaal* aloft, its blade wreathed in flame and lightning.

On the High Altar, *Seyotaal* itself rested on a cradle, its sheathed blade arching upwards and away from the Altar.

Its scabbard was as black as night, the pommel bright silver. The hilt was not a cross-bar, but an oval encircling the tang, the predatory bird of the Protectorate in the centre, the blade running through its chest. Its eyes glimmered with precious rubies. The handle itself was wrapped in tightly wound strips of leather, shining a lustrous black.

Amon reached the High Altar and turned to face the congregation. His black cowl hung from his back, his hood cast back, the sunlight from the stained glass windows glinting on his silver coronet. The Conclave Guardians took up positions on either side of the High Altar, unsheathing their own *aelraks* and holding them outwards as they took up ceremonial guard of the ancient sword which rested there.

Laruak and Karaea, accompanied by several Senators, filed into one of the pews at the front of the nave before the High Altar. The other Senators followed suit, accompanied by the Staff Officers, resplendent in their military dress uniforms. Fedrus sat down with Daedra, behind the Senators. The other pews in the Temple began to quickly fill up as civilians moved silently but swiftly to grab a seat, in order to bear witness to this episode in their history.

After what seemed like an age, the last whisper of shuffling footsteps fell silent, and Amon spoke.

'Proconsul, Praetors,' he said, 'Senators, Officers, Guardians and Citizens. A time of great sorrow is upon us. Our enemies of old stand at our threshold, once more threatening everything we hold dear. Szotas is in grave danger, for the Confederacy plan to seize it, to deny us our freedom, our right to exist. Many of our brave soldiers have given their lives in defence of the Protectorate, and their blood stains the earth of a dozen worlds, yet their sacrifice has not stemmed the evil tide of war.' He paused. 'This is the darkest chapter in our history.'

A brief murmur echoed around the Temple, and Amon held up his hand. The crowd fell silent again. 'Yet even in this hour of darkness, hope is kindled,' he said. 'A light shines in the darkness, for God has sent us an agent. He has sent us a warrior, he has sent us a king. He has sent us a saviour, a messiah. He has sent us... a Destroyer.'

'Jamek, of the Psinaez family,' said Amon, 'Corporal of the Protectorate Starforce, and Cleric of the Guardian Order, step forward.'

The congregation, many standing in the curved aisles either side of the nave, turned their heads. At the opposite end of the Temple, standing in the circle of light underneath the North Tower atrium, Jamek was waiting. He wore black from head to foot – black boots, loose black trousers and a loose, black, open-necked robe, cinched at his waist by a belt of the same material – the uniform of a Guardian. He walked down the central aisle, his boots clicking on the marble floor of the Temple, echoing around the cavernous hall.

Jamek kept his head down as he moved slowly up the nave, aware of the thousands of pairs of eyes watching his every move. The fire in his heart burned furiously, but he breathed deeply, keeping it constrained and controlled, chained inside him, lest it burst out and the flame manifest itself.

He could feel every pair of eyes, hear every thought, sense every emotion. The sheer marvel of it was enough to bring him to the verge of tears, such was the breadth and depth of human emotion in that hall. As he neared the front, he felt something familiar to him, a presence that resonated in his heart, and looked up, not daring to hope that he might see her, that what he had witnessed was after all just a terrible nightmare...

He found himself looking into the eyes of Fedrus. Jamek stopped for a moment, staring at Adraea's father, and he saw the old man looking for something in his own eyes, some sign of hope, some signal that his daughter was still alive. When the General closed his eyes, and a single tear rolled down his cheek, Jamek's heart broke a little more, but the emotion did not process properly in his grief-stricken mind, manifesting as confusion. He looked forward again, to his Master waiting before the High Altar, and carried on walking.

Every step he took seemed leaden and heavy. He missed her – his soul ached for her. Her absence was like a great, ragged hole in the world, as if some great piece of reality had simply been wrenched away by a callous force. 'Adraea,' he whispered to himself.

He slowly mounted the steps to the High Altar, and finally stood before his Master, who had taught him how to quell the fire that burned within him. He looked into his Master's eyes, and saw compassion and understanding, but also a determination, strength and faith which filled him with some semblance of hope. Although he doubted himself, his Master did not. And, in turn, that helped to assuage his doubt.

'Kneel,' commanded Amon, and Jamek sank to his knees, bowing his head before the Guardian Master. Amon placed his hand on the top of Jamek's head, murmuring an ancient prayer. Behind him, the crowd murmured as two Conclave Guardians lifted the ancient sword from its cradle on the High Altar.

Amon, having finished his prayer, turned behind him, and took hold of the sheathed sword. The other Guardians released it and bowed, stepping back to their positions. Amon drew the sword to another gasp from the audience, and its curved blade glinted, a crescent eye of night, reflecting the spectral colours from the stained glass window.

'In the words of the Prophecy,' intoned Amon, holding the sword, 'He will Destroy an Empire, and bring his people home. He is the End, He is the Fire. He is the Destroyer.'

Jamek, without looking up, held up both his hands, palms upward. Amon rested the blade on his opened hands. Some people in the crowd shouted in astonishment and wonder, for the terculium sword should have seared Jamek's skin from his flesh, and yet he knelt holding the most ancient of *aelraks* in his bare hands, showing no discomfort. He lifted his head, and to further shouts of amazement, stood up holding the blade of *Seyotaal,* before turning it and taking hold of the hilt. He turned to the crowd, and their shouts grew to roars of fear and approval.

Breathing heavily, Jamek held the sword over his head, lifting the blade to the sky, and a new fire seemed to seethe through his body – not the burning inferno of his manifest rage, but a pure, stunning white light, a pale silver glow that cleansed and washed away some of the grief that consumed him. He felt new born.

Amon roared to the crowd, 'Cower now, enemies of the sceptred Protectorate, for the Destroyer of Worlds is Risen!'

The blade of *Seyotaal* erupted in flame as it absorbed energy from Jamek's body, and blue lightning flickered and crackled along its length. Jamek felt a power he had never felt before course through his body, and his doubts fell away as he felt a certainty that he had never felt before. He felt a purpose, a meaning had come into his life, one unfettered by the morality of mere men. He opened his eyes, roared a terrible scream of fury and power, and embraced his destiny. In that pure white light that blazed from his *aelrak*, he saw a face, familiar to him as his own, and he smiled as Adraea watched him.

Chapter Twenty-Seven

Jamek stood in the hallway of the house, breathing in deeply. Memories washed over him like a river, its current carrying him away, his strongest strokes powerless against the might of the water. The smells of a thousand summer days and winter nights, the sights and shapes, familiar as his own reflection, evoked emotions that lay deep within him.

Sheets covered the furniture which stood like solemn ghosts watching him, the curtains were taken down, the walls were empty and bare. There were faint marks of discolour where pictures had once hung. The dust lay thick on the floor now, his boots leaving footprints of colour in the grey ether that suffused the place. Light, pale and cold, flooded in through the windows.

It was Fedrus's house – where he had lived with Adraea before the war. Out of all the barracks, apartments and houses he had lived in when he was a child, this house was the one he regarded as his home. Here, he had been content. Here, for a time, he had been happy.

He walked down he hall, his steps echoing hollowly in the empty house, and walked into the kitchen. Here was where he had breakfast with Adraea for the first time, where he had joked and celebrated with Mavrak about his relationship with her. Where Fedrus had given them his blessing.

Jamek squeezed his eyes shut against the bite of sudden tears, and grief welled unbidden in his throat. He looked out of the kitchen window to the garden beyond, and remembered her – lying in the grass. The contours of her body. The touch of her skin. The taste of her, the smell of her. Her brown hair. Her lips. Her eyes.

Gone.

This house was no home any more – it was a grave, a mausoleum, a tomb for a lost youth and a lost love. Stark and cold in grey twilight, it stood as a testament to everything that Jamek had lost, and that which could not be brought back.

Tears ran down Jamek's cheeks, and he wiped them away with the sleeve of his black robe. He wondered if his father could see him now, as a Guardian, and the Destroyer. The expectations of an entire nation – billions of people – rested on his shoulders. He wondered if Adraea could see him, and he remembered her face in the white light when he had held *Seyotaal* for the first time. His hand rested on the hilt of the sword at his waist unconsciously, and he secretly willed to be granted that vision again.

'Jamek,' came a voice from behind him, and he turned, seeing Fedrus standing in the hallway. The old soldier was dressed in his uniform, three gold twelve-pointed stars glittering on his high collar and sleeves. He looked exactly the same as when Jamek had last spoken to him, when he had left to join the Starforce, but his eyes betrayed grief and hard experience.

'Sir,' he said, standing to attention. Fedrus's insignia showed the rank of General, and Jamek, despite having been coronated as the Destroyer, still only held the rank of Corporal.

Fedrus smiled, the old soldier's face relaxing in a rare moment of gentleness. 'At ease, Corporal,' he said. 'Neither of us are on duty.' He walked up to Jamek, and rested his hand on his shoulder. 'It's good to see you again,' he said. 'I thought you were dead.'

Jamek nodded dumbly, unsure of how to proceed. An awkward silence grew between them.

'Do you want a coffee?' said Fedrus. 'Not much works in this place, but the kettle does.'

'Yes, please,' said Jamek, relaxing slightly, but still feeling numb despite Fedrus's attempt to introduce some sense of normality. Fedrus walked into the kitchen, and went about the business of making some coffee. Jamek followed him, feeling ill at ease in the empty house, filled with so many memories. He felt almost ashamed to be in Fedrus's presence, when it was his hubris and Adraea's love for him which had led her to join the Starforce with him. He felt ashamed that he should be standing here alive, while Adraea was dead, her charred bones lying in the freezing snow of some unknown Confederate prison planet.

He closed his eyes in pain at the terrible thought, squeezing them shut to block out the pain of the world. He almost jumped out of his skin when Fedrus gripped his shoulder. He opened his eyes, and saw the older man offering him a cup. He took it, savouring the aroma, and sipped it slowly.

'You know what I want to ask you,' said Fedrus, leaving his own cup unattended, his hands trembling, his voice shaking. 'I can see the answer in your eyes, but I have to ask. Is Adraea...?'

Tears welled in Jamek's eyes. 'I'm so sorry, Fedrus,' he said, his own voice breaking with the emotion. 'I'm so sorry.'

Fedrus's face crumpled in grief and agony as the dreaded confirmation was delivered. His daughter, his only child, his only source of happiness, was dead.

'How did she die?' he asked.

The terrible scene replayed itself in Jamek's mind. He watched in wordless horror as the thugs in the prison ravished her, beating her skull, breaking her arms and legs. He looked into Fedrus's eyes, and knew in that instant that he could never know the truth. No one could ever know, for it served only amplify the pain. The grief was his, and to spare those who cared for Adraea, he would keep that terrible secret to himself.

He reached out to Fedrus and gripped the older man's arm. 'She was avenged,' he said, and Fedrus looked into the younger man's eyes, and the hellish flame that flickered there.

'I don't doubt it,' murmured Fedrus. 'And somehow... that does comfort me.'

Jamek's eyes dimmed slightly, and he drank his coffee, savouring its smooth, rich taste. 'You're a General now?' he said, trying to change the subject.

Fedrus smiled. 'Yes, Proconsul Laruak saw fit to promote me. I'm charged with the defence of the Lupus System. But I have a feeling that my job is about to get easier, now that the Destroyer of Worlds has come.'

Jamek shifted uncomfortably. 'I'll do my best,' he said. 'But I don't feel like the Destroyer, Fedrus. I just hope that I can rise to the occasion.'

'You held *Seyotaal* with your bare hands, Jamek,' said Fedrus, his voice resonant with awe and wonder. 'I saw the fire and lightning burst from it, from your very *body*. You truly are the Destroyer. Sent by God... to save us all.'

'I couldn't save Adraea,' replied Jamek, bluntly. 'How can I save the Protectorate?'

Fedrus smiled. 'Because people believe in you,' he said. 'I fought in the defence of Vulpes, and I knew as soon as we engaged the enemy for the first time that we would lose. The soldiers didn't believe that we could win, and so we didn't.'

'I don't understand,' said Jamek, confused.

'Think of it this way, Jamek,' said Fedrus. 'Why do people get up in the morning? Why do they go to work? Why do they obey the law? Why do they vote in elections, why do they accept the supremacy of the Guardian Order? Because they *believe*. They believe in the system. They believe that their endeavours are for the common good, and that the laws of the Protectorate ensure that. They believe that they elect governments to marshal the resources of our society to reclaim Therqa. They believe that the Guardian Order keeps the peace. But of course, the great secret is that it is their belief that actually makes everything work. They believe that the Protectorate works, and so it does. If they did not believe, then it wouldn't.'

'They *believe* in you, Jamek. Regardless of whether or not you think you are the Destroyer, the people *believe* you are. And that makes you the Destroyer, as sure as if Tarsus himself had risen from the grave to take back the sword that hangs at your side.'

Fedrus grasped Jamek's shoulders. 'They *believe* in you, Jamek. They believe you can deliver them. And so do I.'

'Fedrus...'

'The way I see it, Jamek,' continued Fedrus, smiling, 'fate has thrown us together. This war has already deprived us both of what we care about the most. Your father, my friend. My daughter, your love. I made a promise to your father a long time ago, and him to me, that if anything happened to either of us, the other would look after both you and Adraea.'

Fedrus took a deep breath. 'I intend to honour that promise. I will not try to replace Anzaeus, but I will try to honour him by calling you my son. Will you honour my daughter by calling me your father?'

Jamek took Fedrus's arm, grasping it near the elbow, and Fedrus returned the gesture. 'The honour is mine, Fedrus.'

The two men stood together, united by their loss, by their patriotism, and by their need for vengeance.

Chapter Twenty-Eight

Jamek awoke.

For a moment, he didn't know where he was, and he wondered vaguely as he stared at the ceiling of brown, mottled stone. Then the events of the last few months came flooding back to him, and he sat up.

He was in a Cleric's quarters in the Guardian Temple – a simple square room, with a paved floor, low ceiling, and grated window. The air was rich with the smell of incense, and Jamek could hear Acolytes singing plainsong for their daily dedication. The melody was one he remembered from his boyhood, but he felt a shiver run down his spine as he realised the lyrics were different. The song had always been one of prayer and hope – prayer to *Seyotaal*, and hope for the resurrection of Tarsus, its creator. For the Rise of the Destroyer.

Now, the lyrics were thanking God, and all the Guardians past, for delivering them their saviour. Jamek bowed his head as he realised that they were singing about him – the prophesied Destroyer, made flesh once more, to destroy an empire, and bring his people home.

Jamek swung himself out of the small bed, kicking back the white, crumpled sheets. On a roughly-made wooden dresser nearby, *Seyotaal* rested in a stand, its sheathed blade curved upwards towards the ceiling. Black robes were laid out on a chair next to him – the uniform of a Guardian Cleric.

Normally, it took several years of dedicated service as an Acolyte of the Guardian Order before one was ordained into the Clergy. However, given Jamek's special significance, he had been somewhat fast-tracked. Somehow, Jamek felt almost fraudulent when he wore the black robes of the Order – he didn't feel that he had earned the right to wear them.

He pulled off his white linen bed smock, and quickly dressed, pulling on his cassock and black boots. He finally stood, running his fingers through his short hair. Having been several months since his incarceration, it was now re-growing, but slowly.

He stood at the end of his bed and looked at the mural engraved on the opposite wall. In keeping with Guardian tradition, all private quarters included an engraved shrine to the Destroyer. The depiction stood holding *Seyotaal* aloft, his black robes caught in the breeze, the power of heaven blasting forth from the deadly blade, and the enemies of the Protectorate lay smote in ruin about him.

Jamek gazed at the shrine, knowing that it was he who was depicted there, or at least, knowing the expectation that he would fulfil the prophecy told in that single image. He closed his eyes, and for a brief moment, recalled the sensation when he had held *Seyotaal* for the first time, in the Temple, and a power like he had never known had shone through him.

Adraea.

Watching him.

Smiling.

He opened his eyes again. The mural looked back at him with sightless, unblinking eyes.

'I only want to be with Adraea again,' he whispered, his heart aching with her awful absence. 'Grant me that, and I will do whatever it is you ask of me.'

He was met only with silence.

A knock on the door made him jump. 'Come in,' he said, and the heavy wooden door opened inwards, revealing Amon standing in the doorway. The old man smiled to see Jamek dressed in his robes – Jamek had initially refused to wear anything except an Acolyte's brown shift, and coaxing him into the Cleric's uniform had become something of a morning ritual.

'Destroyer,' said the Guardian Master, and nodded briefly. Jamek returned the motion, and Amon smiled again. He absently tapped the silver crown on his brow, a sharp contrast to his wrinkled, brown skin and white hair. He stepped into the room and closed the door behind him. 'I take it you slept well?'

Jamek nodded, silently. He always felt humbled in the presence of Amon. Despite his terrible powers, Amon had bested him, and taught him to control them. Over the last few months, he had become Jamek's mentor and guide, a calming voice in a tumultuous world.

'No dreams?'

Jamek shook his head.

'Good,' said Amon, satisfied. Jamek sat down on the bed, becoming almost sullen. He knew what was coming.

'I see you're wearing your robes,' said Amon.

Jamek rolled his eyes, exasperated. 'Given that you won't let me leave my quarters until I do, it seemed the best course of action,' he said.

'Ha!' laughed Amon. 'I'll hazard you put them on without even thinking about it.'

Jamek fell silent, half-smiling to himself, and silently wondering how the old man could manage to second-guess him so effectively.

'So!' the old man said, clapping his hands once and rubbing them together, as if staving off the cold. 'Your plans for today?'

'Service in the Temple,' muttered Jamek.

'Service in the...' Amon shook his head in disbelief. 'Is that really an appropriate task for the Destroyer of Worlds?'

'I am a Cleric, am I not?' demanded Jamek. 'You have made me thus, despite my insistence that I pass the Acolyte's training. Why can I not serve in the Temple?'

'Jamek,' said Amon patiently, 'you are not *just* a Cleric. You are the Destroyer. You have a higher purpose. There are others who can serve in the Temple.'

'Then what am I supposed to do, Master?' said Jamek, standing up again. He paced the room angrily. 'Raise an army? Assume a seat in the Senate? Elevate myself to the Conclave? Am I to be a Lord, a General, or a King? I have no idea of what I am supposed to do!'

'And what of the Sorceror – my supposed great enemy? Don't the prophecies say that he is moving against the Protectorate *before* the Destroyer's ascension? Where is he?'

Amon shifted uncomfortably as he saw a fire glimmer in Jamek's eyes, and the temperature in the cell moved up a few degrees. 'Calm yourself, Jamek,' he said sternly, and Jamek immediately closed his eyes, mouthing a silent prayer, and the room cooled once more. When Jamek opened his eyes, no flame flickered in the dark pools there.

Amon breathed deeply. The rage was never far from the surface, always threatening to boil out of control. That awesome power, beyond anything which had been seen for nearly a thousand years, and perhaps even before that.

'I'm sorry, Master,' said Jamek, and he sat down again. 'I just feel useless. People keep telling me that I'm the Destroyer, and there is this weight of expectation on me. But all I seem to do is spend time in solitude, praying for some message from God. He's not very talkative, you know.'

Amon smiled. 'I know you doubt yourself,' he said. 'But consider this, Jamek – no man can do what you can. No one has been able to do these things since Tarsus. What other answer is there? I cannot answer all of your questions.'

'But some answers may yet have presented themselves,' he said. 'Proconsul Laruak is here. He has requested an audience with you.'

Jamek nodded. 'Yes,' he said. 'Well, I appear to have plenty of time.' He stood up and lifted the ancient sword of *Seyotaal* from its resting place, tucking it into his belt. He found its weight reassuring, and absently caressed the hilt, hoping once more for a taste of that wonderful vision. In his hand, it seemed to thrum with promise.

'Let us meet the Proconsul,' he said, and Amon smiled.

-#-

Laruak sat in the front pew of the almost-empty Temple, listening to the Acolytes singing in plainsong. The air was heavy with the smell of rich incense, and the morning light of Kaathar flooded in from the windows, slanting down in golden shafts. In front of him, the High Altar, the resting place of *Seyotaal*, was now bare and empty, the sword now in the hands of the Destroyer. He felt his skin break out into gooseflesh at the thought. He looked across the dimly lit cathedral, where a new mural was being carved into the ancient stone by three Guardian Clerics. It would depict the coronation they had borne witness to scant days ago – the Rise of the Destroyer. History in the making.

Laruak scratched his head uncomfortably where the golden crown of office rested on his brow, and a tinge of guilt ran through him. He had no idea if what he was about to do was legal, but it certainly was inspired. He only hoped that it would work.

He heard footsteps and looked up. He saw Master Amon walking towards him, and next to him, the young man he had seen only a few days ago – his short hair growing out, his eyes dark pools of mystery. He was dressed entirely in black, and *Seyotaal* hung at his side.

Laruak bowed as the two approached, out of courtesy to the Master of the Guardian Order, but out of humility and reverence at the sight of the Destroyer. Any lingering doubts that existed in Laruak's mind were banished at the sight of him standing there. He could feel it in his very bones. He was in the presence of a terrible, awesome power.

'Rise, Proconsul, rise,' came Amon's voice, with a hint of laughter. 'The Destroyer has little patience with such displays, I am afraid.'

Laruak rose uncomfortably and found himself looking into Jamek's eyes. He could not match the gaze – it was like staring into an abyss. 'Master,' he said to Amon, and then turned back to Jamek.

'Destroyer,' he said.

Jamek shifted uncomfortably. 'You asked to see me, Proconsul,' he said.

'I did,' said Laruak. 'Without seeming to appear rude, I think it would be best if we talked in private?' He looked pointedly at Amon.

Jamek was surprised. What could the Proconsul want to talk to him about out of earshot of the Guardian Master?

'Of course,' said Jamek. 'Master, if I may use the Telsor Chapel?'

Amon nodded, obviously curious as to what the matter was that warranted such secrecy. 'I will ensure you are not disturbed,' he said, and subconsciously felt his relationship with Jamek change in that instant. The young man was no longer an apprentice, bound to his Master and looking to him for guidance, but an independent force in his own right, for better or worse. He rested his hand on Jamek's shoulder, almost as if reinforcing some of his lost authority. 'Let me know if you require assistance,' he said.

Jamek looked at him and smiled. 'I will,' he said. The smile reassured Amon slightly, reminding him of the vulnerability inherent to the powerful being that stood before him. Amon returned the smile and walked away, leaving the Destroyer and Proconsul together.

Jamek indicated for Laruak to follow him, and led him past the High Altar, through the choir stalls. The Acolytes' plainsong paused briefly, the brown-robed boys and girls bowing their heads in fear and reverence to allow the silent passage of their living saviour. Jamek then turned left into a quiet, secluded Chapel attached to the main nave of the Temple. He bid Laruak enter, and then closed a heavy wooden door behind them.

The Chapel was a simple affair – an oval window on the eastern wall, spilling Kaathar's warm light into the room. A small altar stood at the south end, with a mural of the Guardian Telsor above it. Four pews stood in front of it, and a single tapestry hung from the back wall, displaying the standard of the Protectorate – a giant predatory bird, the sword of *Seyotaal* clutched in its talons.

Laruak looked around him. 'I've never been in this part of the Temple,' he said.

Jamek smiled. 'It is reserved for the Guardians,' he said. 'Every morning, a dedication is made to Telsor, with the rising sun. It was Telsor that reinstituted the Protectorate after the Civil War, and established the Order's dominance in society. He was the guarantor of our freedoms and liberties.'

Laruak smiled mirthlessly. 'Didn't he also oversee the Order's intervention in the Civil War, when nearly two million people were put to death without trial?'

Jamek shrugged and lit a few candles on the altar. 'Isn't it always the same?' he said. 'One man's liberator is another man's terrorist. One man's guardian is another's oppressor.'

Laruak sat down in one of the pews, and Jamek did the same. 'So what is it you wish to discuss with me, Proconsul?' asked Jamek.

'The Protectorate is at a cross-roads, My Lord,' said Laruak, using the formal address for a Conclave

Guardian. Jamek looked mildly irked at the honorific, but said nothing. 'For the last five months, I have been Proconsul-in-State of the Protectorate – the office of Protector is vacant. Tomorrow, elections will be held across the Protectorate to determine the new holder of that office.'

'I fail to see how this concerns me,' said Jamek. 'I am a mere Cleric. Politics is the preserve of the Conclave in the Order – they approve candidacies.'

'It directly concerns you, My Lord,' said the Proconsul. 'Karaea... was removed from office by the Senate. She stands again, but Senator Draelan stands against her. Without a significant change in fortunes, Draelan will win the election tomorrow, and become Protector. He proposes to negotiate a peace with the Confederacy.'

Jamek's eyes narrowed. 'Then he is a fool,' he said. 'There will be no peace with them. They are merciless, cowardly bastards, Proconsul – and I speak from hard experience. There is nothing in that society that warrants saving – they are as cruel and as evil as the old stories made them to be.'

Laruak nodded. 'I feel that this is the wrong time for negotiations,' he said. 'The Confederacy occupied the Vulpes System five months ago. Since then, I have been marshalling the resources of the Protectorate to defend against a potential invasion of the Lupus System, but it has not happened. Some spy reports have come in from the Vulpes System – they show no Confederate plans to attack. I doubt the Confederacy will invade Lupus – they appear to have lost the will for it. But we should not be negotiating while they are in possession of the Vulpes System. It is key to the entire campaign – it has wormholes to both Lupus and Canis, but now also to Panthera...' he paused, 'and Felis.'

Jamek looked at the Proconsul in surprise. Laruak nodded. 'It is not public knowledge,' he said. 'I assume you knew about the Panthera wormhole – your father constructed it upon his arrival there in the *Provident*.'

Jamek nodded, ignoring the brief stab of grief at the mention of his father.

'The Confederacy constructed a wormhole from the Felis System,' continued Laruak. 'They used it to reinforce their invasion and shorten their supply lines. Our intelligence sources indicate that the majority of their military signals are directed there. It is a single-star system, and has several terrestrial planets.' He paused again. 'It's their home system, My Lord. If we can re-take Vulpes...'

'We have a short-cut to Therqa,' finished Jamek.

Laruak nodded. 'Five months ago, this would have been considered impossible,' he said. 'But the Confederacy have not pressed their advantage. It gives us a chance to regain the initiative. But if Draelan wins the Protectorship, that chance will be lost.'

Jamek's brow furrowed. 'I still fail to see why this concerns me,' he said.

'As Proconsul-in-State, I cannot be seen to favour one candidate over another,' replied Laruak. 'And neither can the Guardian Conclave. But you are a Cleric. There is nothing to stop you from speaking out in favour of a particular candidate.'

Jamek frowned. 'Clerics can vote in elections,' he said, 'but it is frowned upon for them to speak out in public about their decision. We are responsible for enforcing and interpreting the law. On top of that, as people do not tire of reminding me, I am not *just* a Cleric. I am the Destroyer. If I speak out in favour of a candidate, it may produce a substantial increase in support for them.'

'Precisely,' said Laruak earnestly. 'You have the power to change the outcome of this election – to keep Draelan from office, and ensure that the Protectorate does not become a mere vassal of the Confederacy – something which our ancestors fought to prevent, and accepted exile instead of it!'

'You would have me support Karaea?' asked Jamek.

'I would,' said Laruak honestly.

'Surely, what you are doing is illegal, in soliciting my support like this?'

'I do not use the weight of my office to do this,' said Laruak. 'I do not order you to do it. I ask you, as one man to another.'

Jamek thought to himself, his brow furrowed. 'I will meet with Praetor Karaea,' he said, at last. 'I will make no promises, though.'

-#-

Jamek sat alone in the Telsor Chapel. The sun was now higher in the sky, and beginning to pass from the sight of the Chapel's eastern window, golden light giving way to shadowed twilight. Jamek lit another candle on the altar and waited patiently.

Laruak had been gone an hour, and had promised to return with Karaea. Jamek fought hard to deal with the surge of emotions within him. He had known Karaea since he was a child. He closed his eyes against the sudden memory...

-#-

Standing in some forgotten hallway, a child of four, his finger bleeding. He could remember the pain – it had felt like hot needles. He remembered his own piercing wail, and the horror at the sight of the crimson stain slowly trickling down onto his palm, and then she was there – Karaea. She gathered him up in her arms and kissed his forehead, murmuring some comfort to him. He remembered being carried into the kitchen, the brief sting as the cut was cleaned, a plaster to cover the wound, and smiling as his tears were wiped away...

-#-

Jamek jolted himself out of the memory, and fire briefly flickered in his eyes. And then she had gone, leaving behind the man who would have been her husband, and the child who would have been her son. And now, he waited on a strange reunion – the mother, the disgraced queen; the son, the ascendant warrior.

There was a knock at the Chapel door, and Jamek stood up. 'Come in,' he said, and the door swung open. Laruak stood in the doorway, accompanied by a hooded figure. She stepped into the room, and pulled back the hood as Laruak closed the door behind her, revealing short brown hair, and shining green eyes resting in a wise and beautiful face. Jamek's heart missed a beat as he saw the woman who was a mother to him for a time – and she had barely changed in the last fifteen years, despite the cares of office.

She smiled at him. 'Hello, Jamek,' she said. 'It's been a long time.'

Jamek nodded. 'Over fifteen years,' he answered.

Karaea smiled again, tears pricking in her eyes. 'Has it really been that long?' she asked, half to herself. Her eyes turned once more to the tall dark man in front of her. Could this really be the boy she remembered? There was so much of his father in him – the same brooding stare, the same fierce determination, and yet the same secret vulnerability. He was Anzaeus amplified – every quality that Anzaeus had possessed was Jamek's in triplicate.

She became suddenly aware that she was staring at the mysterious young man nearly twenty years her junior, and managed to stop herself from blushing. She cleared her throat. 'I'm so sorry about your father, Jamek,' she said, and stepped a little closer to him. 'He was a good man.'

'He died doing his duty,' said Jamek, stiffly. 'It's what he would have wanted.'

Silence fell, and Laruak shifted his feet uncomfortably. Jamek stepped back, sitting down on one of the pews, and invited both Karaea and Laruak to do so.

'So,' said the Destroyer, 'you want me to speak out in support of you in this election.'

Karaea seemed a little taken aback by his directness, but recovered well. 'Yes,' she said. 'It would not be in the best interests of the Protectorate to allow Draelan to attain the Protectorship.'

'So the Proconsul has been telling me,' said Jamek. 'I understand that Draelan is the one responsible for calling this election in the first place?'

Karaea nodded, her dislike of Draelan plain to see. 'He forced a vote of confidence in the Senate,' she said, disgustedly, 'and his supporters helped vote me out.'

'Why?'

The question shocked Karaea. 'I beg your pardon?'

'Why did he call a vote of confidence?' asked Jamek. 'I may be a novice to the area of politics, but it seems to me that he must have had a reason.' His black eyes gazed searchingly at Karaea, and she found that she could not meet them. She dropped her eyes in shame.

'I... contrived to keep the Confederacy's invasion of Vulpes a secret,' she said. 'I refused to mobilise the

Starforce against them.' She took a deep breath. 'The fall of Vulpes is my fault.' Tears rolled down her cheeks, and she bowed her head.

Jamek looked at her. 'I was there,' he said, quietly. 'I was there when the Confederacy attacked Vulpes.'

Karaea looked up, her face smeared with tears, her eyes red with crying.

Jamek's closed his eyes as he recalled the memory. 'They tore through the system,' he murmured, 'destroying everything in their path. I've never seen such savagery. They attacked the Fleetyards where I was stationed. My girlfriend and I – we were both soldiers – we stood and fought, but we were both captured. Adraea...' he shook his head. 'She was killed in prison.'

'I'm so sorry,' said Karaea. 'You blame me for her death,' she said quietly.

'No,' said Jamek, and turned to face the Praetor. 'No. Any reinforcements would not have prevented that initial attack. You couldn't have prevented that.' His expression hardened. 'But now the Protectorate is in a most desperate situation. And if it weren't for your inaction, billions of Protectorate citizens would be free of the yoke of Confederate tyranny.'

Karaea nodded dumbly. 'You will not support me?'

'I will,' said Jamek, surprisingly. 'Because you are contrite. Because you have seen your faults, and have the courage to admit them. You must admit them to the people as well, Karaea. You must tell them the truth. You owe them that.'

Karaea nodded earnestly. 'I will,' she said. 'If you speak out in support of me, I will do anything you ask.'

Jamek's expression hardened further. 'I want you to govern the Protectorate in the best way possible,' he said. 'It is not for me to decide that. I am no politician.' He looked around the Chapel, and for the first time since his coronation, he realised the source of his frustration. 'And I am no priest, either,' he said, almost to himself.

He looked directly at Karaea. 'I am a soldier,' he said. 'If I support you, and you are made Protector again, I want command of the Starforce. I will lead this Crusade against the Confederacy. I will drive them from Vulpes, to right the wrong that has been done there, and I will chase them to Therqa. And there,' he said, his eyes narrowing, 'I shall avenge myself, and all the Protectorate, upon them.'

-#-

Jamek paced up and down at the far end of the Temple nave, close to the North Gate, which opened onto Central Plaza. The heavy doors were bolted shut, but Jamek could hear the crowd outside, chanting in prayer.

The crowd had been there ever since his coronation a week earlier, many camping out in Central Plaza in tents. Jamek had not left the Temple since his coronation, and every day at dawn, high noon and dusk the crowd held a mass, praying and calling for their Destroyer to come forth, to deliver them. Every day, the crowd had grown in number, until it now filled Central Plaza, spilling onto the side streets and even up the steps leading to the *Inominate* and High Command.

Jamek stopped pacing for a moment, standing before the great wooden doors, studded with bolts of metal. Around him, the light from the North Tower atrium flooded down, bathing the floor in front of the huge doors in a warm, golden light. Jamek closed his eyes for a brief moment, and his hand rested on the hilt of *Seyotaal*, feeling its weight. A warmth spread across his palm, and his vision was filled for an instant with the pure, white light that he had seen at his coronation.

His heart welled with joy for the briefest of instants. 'Adraea...' he murmured, and then the moment was gone, like a half-remembered dream. For one moment, he had once more touched destiny.

'Jamek,' came a voice behind him, and he turned to see Amon standing there.

'Master,' he answered, and bowed his head.

Amon stepped forward and grasped Jamek by the shoulders, a stern expression on his face. 'Jamek,' he said, 'tell me what is going on.'

'I am going to address the crowd outside,' said Jamek, feeling uncomfortable under Amon's gaze.

'What are you going to tell them?'

'Why does it matter?' answered Jamek, evasively.

'It matters,' said Amon, his grip momentarily tightening on Jamek's shoulders, 'because you are a member of my

Order, sworn to obey me and the Conclave I lead, and I have a constitutional duty to the Protectorate.' He paused for a moment, before releasing his grip. 'I gave you the privacy you asked for,' he said. 'I have not monitored your conversations in the Telsor Chapel. But I am at liberty to see who enters my own Temple. And I know you received a visit from Praetor Karaea.'

Jamek said nothing, but cast his eyes downward.

Amon sighed. 'You are not a Peer of the Conclave,' he said, 'and as such, I cannot command you not to involve yourself in the affairs of the Temporal Government. Many Clerics speak their minds as to how they will vote, and they are free to do so. But as I do not tire of reminding you, you are no ordinary Cleric, Jamek. You are the Destroyer, and that crowd out there, and thousands of others across the Protectorate, on other worlds than this, will hang on your every word, and follow your lead.' The old Guardian paused. 'I have helped you to control yourself. I have rehabilitated you, trained you, yoked and harnessed your powers for you. I cannot order you to tell me what you plan to do, but as one man to another, I think you owe it to me to let me know.'

Jamek nodded and felt suddenly ashamed of himself. For all his planning and skill, he had not for a minute presumed to tell Amon his plans. 'I plan to lend my support to Karaea in the election tomorrow,' he said.

Amon nodded slowly. 'I suspected as much,' he said. 'May I ask why?'

'This Draelan that stands against her,' answered Jamek, 'plans to negotiate with the Confederacy. In our current predicament, that will result in the Protectorate accepting Confederate control of the Vulpes System, which is an awful strategic position to be in. The Protectorate would become a slave to the Confederacy's whim, which is the one thing that we have always fought to oppose.'

'And?' asked Amon, knowing there was more to it than that.

'Karaea has promised me command of the Starforce if she becomes Protector,' said Jamek. 'I am not a priest, Master, nor a politician. I am a soldier. You urged me to make a decision of how I can fulfil my purpose. This is it – I feel it in my bones, and in my blood. I was not given the Sword of Unity to become a peacemaker – I was given it to destroy an empire, and to bring my people home. I will strike down this Confederacy, and take back Therqa – from those who stole it from us!' His voice rose in a crescendo, and the hellish flame burned brightly in his eyes. Amon stood back involuntarily from the sudden blazing heat, his skin breaking out into sweat.

My God, he thought, as he regarded the demon incarnate before him – a revenant of terrible power. *What have I unleashed?*

Jamek calmed himself, but the fire still glowered there in his eyes. Amon stepped close to him again, and held out his hand. Jamek took it in a firm grip.

'Go, then,' said Amon. 'Go, Destroyer, and fulfil your destiny.'

Jamek nodded, and released his hold on Amon's hand. He turned and faced the doors. He lifted his hands up, arms outstretched, palms facing the doors, and closed his eyes. He saw the doors still in his mind's eye, and reached out with his mind. He *touched* them, and invisible fingers sunk into the wood. Jamek smiled. It felt warm and soft, almost alive. His mind *pulled...*

And the doors slowly opened. Amon stood in astonishment as the Destroyer of Worlds exercised his powers, moving the heavy doors with the power of his thoughts. The doors normally took two fully grown men each to swing open, and yet Jamek pulled them open with nothing save the force of his mind, as if they were made of paper. Light from Kaathar flooded in as the doors opened. Jamek stood as a silhouette, a shadow of fear, a spectre of night, his arms upraised, the Sword of Unity at his side. He stepped forth onto Central Plaza.

Jamek stepped forward out of the shadow of the pillars in front of the North Gate, and to the top of the steps leading down to Central Plaza. Ahead of him, the towering form of the Inominate dominated the skyline, the grey, semicircular building of the High Command surrounding it. On his left and right, great skyscrapers of glass and metal reared their heads, glistening in the afternoon sun.

The cool marble of Central Plaza could not be seen, obscured by thousands of people, standing in prayer, looking forward to the Guardian Temple. As they saw Jamek step forward out of the shadows, their hypnotic chanting stopped, and hushed whispers echoed through the crowd.

Jamek's heart pounded in his chest, his throat felt dry, and his head thudded as blood thrummed through his temples, making him giddy. His rubbed his sweating palms on his black robes, but they found solace resting on the hilt of his sword. Seyotaal seemed to speak to him, to calm him – and whenever he held it, there was the hope and promise of that heavenly light, and the glimpse of his lost love.

'People of Szotas,' shouted Jamek, his voice carrying over the crowd, 'I am Psinaez Jamek, Destroyer of Worlds.' The last whispers of the crowd at last fell silent, and it fell thick and palpable over the great square.

'I have come to you,' said Jamek, 'in the Protectorate's darkest hour. We are a nation besieged – billions of our citizens lie under the yoke of conquest, our most hated enemy stands at our gates and our leadership has been thrown into chaos. The Crusade for Therqa – indeed, the existence of our very nation – stands upon the edge of a knife.'

'It is my task to deliver us from this doom. To bring us back from the brink, to destroy the vicious empire of the Confederacy, to free us once and for all from its evil tyranny and bring my people home. To take back what is ours, what was taken from us. To complete the most holy quest – the Crusade for Therqa!'

The crowd cheered and roared in approval, and Jamek held up his hand for silence. 'Yet even now, in this darkest of times, there are some who would extinguish the guttering flame of hope. There are those who would negotiate *peace*' – he spat the word like an insult – 'with the Confederacy – who would have us be servile, begging on our knees for whatever scraps they deign to give us. I say we do not beg them – I say we take back what is ours by force!'

'The crowd cheered again. 'Karaea, the former Protector,' said Jamek, 'has spoken with me. She has madc mistakes in the past, but I believe that her heart is true, that her intentions are good. She has told me that, if she is made Protector, she will not barter for an uneven truce with the Confederacy, and she will not tolerate their illegal conquest of Vulpes! She has told me that, if she is made Protector, she will call upon me to command the forces of the Protectorate in battle, to do bloody vengeance on those who have murdered our sons and daughters, our brothers and sisters, our fathers and mothers! Those who have made slaves of our citizens! Those who exiled our ancestors! Those who stole our homeworld from us!'

The crowd were now cheering in approval, in something close to ecstasy. 'I will vote for Karaea tomorrow,' shouted Jamek, as he reached his peroration, 'and take our vengeance on the Confederacy with her blessing!'

He stood back, his hands held high as the crowd screamed their approval. They took up his name, chanting it as it echoed throughout the city. The tide had turned, and in the Inominate far above, Praetor Karaea stood next to Laruak, smiling.

Chapter Twenty-Nine

The Senate Chamber, which had been quiet for weeks pending the outcome of the election, once more bustled with noise and activity as grey-robed men and women jostled for their seats. Laruak sat in the Proconsul's Chair at the front of the Chamber, looking out at the tiered semicircular rows of seats in front of him. At the back of the Chamber, wide oval windows commanded the view across Central Plaza, to the brown stone edifice of the Guardian Temple opposite. The Senate Chamber was at exactly the same height as the statue of Tarsus on the Temple's North Tower, gazing across through the Senate windows. It was no architectural accident – it served as another reminder of the Guardian Order's supervision of the political system.

Laruak sat in the Proconsul's Chair, waiting patiently for the Senators to settle in their seats. He wore his white robes of state and the golden crown of office on his head, which glinted in the warm morning sunlight streaming in from the windows opposite.

It was always like this on the first day after an election. But there was a lot to be done today.

Laruak stood up, and took one step forward towards the lectern. He ran his hands along its smooth, polished surface and smiled. He had served in the Senate for over twenty years, first as a Clerk, then as a Senator, and for five years as Proconsul, and he never ceased to relish the moment when the Senators fell silent as their Proconsul stood to address them.

The noise of four hundred voices died away, and Laruak looked out at the Chamber as the last few Senators took their seats. Four hundred pairs of eyes watched and waited expectantly. He looked across to his left, and noticed with some distaste that Draelan was present – he sat in his usual place on the front row on the left hand side, his eyes glowering with jealousy. His bid to become Protector had failed, but he had retained his Senate seat.

'Senators of the Protectorate,' said Laruak, 'you have been sworn into your offices by the Clerks sitting before me. I stand before you as Proconsul, but cannot assume those duties until you have confirmed me in office. I therefore humbly submit my candidacy. Is there any other who wishes to stand for election to this office?'

Laruak held his breath for a moment, half-expecting Draelan to stand up, but not one of the Senators rose to his feet. Draelan refused to meet Laruak's gaze, but instead fixed his eyes on the floor. Laruak half-smiled to himself. Draelan may be licking his political wounds for the moment, but he was not out of the race. Somehow, Laruak felt that Draelan had another part to play in the fate of the Protectorate, for good or ill.

'Then I assert the office of Proconsul,' said Laruak, 'supported by this Senate, and unopposed.'

The Senators murmured in agreement, the supporters of Laruak and Karaea smiling happily at the maintenance of the *status quo*, Draelan and his supporters grumbling quietly to themselves, but offering no challenge.

'This Senate does summon Praetor Karaea to appear here,' declared Laruak. A Clerk left one of the stalls below, walked down the aisle in the centre of the room before turning right to open the double-doors in the far-right corner of the room. He pulled both of them open, and Laruak again smiled as he saw Karaea standing there, waiting patiently. This time, she was dressed in her white robes trimmed with gold, indicating that she was Praetor, elected as Protector by the people. Of course, she had no crown on her head, for that was currently borne by Laruak.

She walked purposefully into the Senate Chamber, before reaching the central aisle. She turned and walked straight down the aisle towards the Proconsul's Chair, stopping in front of the dais on the Chamber Floor.

'Praetor Karaea,' said Laruak, 'you may ascend the Chair.'

Karaea smiled and walked around to the side of the dais, climbing the three steps up to Laruak's seat. She stood before him, smiling happily and nervously, resplendent in her robes of state. Laruak's heart beat giddily as he regarded her, and couldn't help smiling back.

'Praetor Karaea,' he said, 'you have been duly elected to serve as the Protector of this nation, to uphold its laws, to serve its people, and to protect it from enemies. Do you accept this charge?'

'I do,' replied Karaea.

Laruak lifted the crown of office from his own head, and placed it on Karaea's. 'Then I pronounce you, in the name of the People and the Senate of Szotas, Protector!'

The Senators cheered and applauded, and Laruak grinned, inviting Karaea to take the lectern to address the Senate. He stepped down and sat in one of the lower stalls, and Karaea stepped forward to the lectern, holding up her hand to silence the applause of the Senators, which gradually faded.

'Senators,' she said, 'the new session of this ancient body begins at a time of crisis. The Protectorate is embroiled in a war with our oldest and most hated enemy – the Confederacy of Nations, the vile ilk that sentenced our ancestors to exile to the dark recesses of space aboard this very starship. They were banished from the planet of their origin – the only place they had ever called home.

'Today, this same enemy has destroyed our starships, conquered our colonies, subjugated our citizens and murdered our soldiers. Even now, the forces of the Confederacy stand poised to attack Szotas itself, and put an end to the freedom we have enjoyed for centuries, despite our exile.' She paused. 'They propose to deny us our liberty for the second time in our history.'

'Some have said that we should sue for peace with our enemy – to settle our differences with negotiation, to prevent further loss of life and to make as best terms as we can. But it is only right to remind those people of who started this war. This war started when a Confederate battleship destroyed the *PSS Provident*, a Protectorate starship on a peaceful exploratory mission! This war started when they again attacked an Expeditionary Force sent to search for survivors! Has our enemy not proven, in the present as well as in the past, that they cannot be trusted?'

Some of the Senators cheered, and Karaea again held up her hand for silence. 'We cannot tolerate their continued attacks on our soldiers. We cannot tolerate the continued occupation of our colonies. And we cannot tolerate our continued exile from our homeworld, our birthright – Therqa!'

'Was it not the first stated aim of our ancestors to reclaim that which was taken from us? Is it not the most basic tenet of our society to seek vengeance on those that meted out our unjust sentence? Is it not our sacred duty to make war upon these tyrants, until they are utterly destroyed, and our race is united at last?'

Some Senators rose to their feet, shouting in appreciation. 'In my first act as Protector,' declared Karaea, 'I appoint Daedra, former Chief of Staff for the Starforce High Command, to the position of Minister of Defence, to take charge of our economy and gear it fully to total war. We are in a life-and-death struggle with the Confederacy – a fight for our very survival. We will throw everything we have at them!'

'I hereby promote General Fedrus, the hero of the defence of Vulpes, to the rank of Marshal, and to the position of Chief of Staff for the Starforce High Command,' said Karaea. 'We need a mind of audacious courage and resolute action to win the strategic battle against an enemy who has taken the initiative from us.'

'And finally,' she said, 'I appoint Psinaez Jamek, Destroyer of Worlds, to the position of Knight-Captain of the Protectorate – field commander of the Starforce! Let our enemies tremble before our Anointed Saviour! Let him fulfil his destiny! Let him destroy an empire, and bring his people home!'

The roar of approval, the thunderous applause and the stamping of feet was deafening, shaking the ancient Chamber to its rafters, and Karaea banged her fist on the lectern as she gritted her teeth. She had become the people's Warrior-Queen, and the Protectorate would follow her, and Jamek, into the jaws of Hell. 'Let there be war,' she murmured to herself quietly.

Chapter Thirty

Jamek sat in the shuttle passenger seat, looking out of the front window. The cockpit was darkened, but the panels were lit up, glowing eerily in the shadowed darkness of space. The command crew murmured quietly amongst themselves as they carried out their work, in awe of the terrifying figure they carried aboard their ship.

Below the ship, the curved horizon of Szotas was spread out, a tapestry of stunning white and green, with the occasional flash of blue where one of its great lakes shone through the clouds. Jamek sighed to himself. The sight of his homeworld, this close, and yet so far from its surface, was always spectacular. He had never forgotten his first journey into space, looking down on the planet of his birth, and Adraea holding his hand.

Adraea.

He bit back tears as he fought the rising grief, but it still felt as keen as a knife. Much of the anger was now gone, leaving only a deep emptiness inside him, which he had no knowledge of how to fill. Only sometimes, the rage would return, burning through his very skin, crackling from his fingertips, and then he would remember Amon's lessons to calm himself.

Above the horizon of Szotas was the sheer blackness of space, but lit with a million pinpricks of light. Stars of all different shapes, sizes and colours glinted in the darkness, not twinkling merrily as they did on the surface of Szotas, but glaring implacably across the vast emptiness. In the far distance, where the endless night met the surface of Szotas, a tiny object hung above the skyline, shining like a mirror.

Jamek shifted in his seat slightly, feeling the double-strapped seatbelt pull down on his shoulders. He dismissed the queasy feeling in his stomach caused by the zero-gravity. All the same, he would be happier once he was aboard a starship.

'Shuttle *Independent* to Szotas Fleetyard,' said the pilot, talking to his computer console. 'We now have visual contact. Knight-Captain Jamek is aboard – requesting permission to approach, over.'

The pilot's screen lit up with a man's face and a voice could be heard over the console's speakers. 'Roger that, Shuttle *Independent* – permission to approach granted. Please set thrusters to station-keeping, and proceed to Drydock One, over.'

'Roger, Fleetyard,' said the pilot. 'Thrusters at station-keeping.' He turned to Jamek. 'We'll have you there, momentarily, sir. What's the ship?'

'I don't know,' replied Jamek. 'Marshal Fedrus didn't tell me – he said that it'd be appropriate, however.'

The pilot smiled. 'I'm sure it'll be just that, sir.'

Jamek watched in silence as the tiny silver speck above the distant horizon gradually grew larger and larger. After a few moments, its structure became clear – it was a giant spinning disc, similar in design to the Protectorate starships, but this had a large superstructure attached to its underbelly. Cranes and scaffolds stretched out below it in a massive spiderweb of steel. Resting in the hollows between the silver strands were smaller discs – starships themselves. The enormous structure was nearly two miles in diameter, although the central disc that capped it in the centre was smaller at about four hundred metres across. Even so, the hub was still nearly twice the size of the largest starship. This was the Szotas Fleetyard – the primary construction facility for the Protectorate Starforce, and the current berth of Jamek's new flagship.

The pilot whistled as they grew closer, and the true scale of the enormous orbital scaffold became apparent. 'Never ceases to amaze me,' he said. 'That thing was created by the hands of men. It's almost impossible to believe, isn't it?'

Jamek nodded, watching the giant wheel rotating slowly above the gantry against the darkness of space, flecks of light glancing off its white, glassy surface. Up close, the whole structure now completely filled the cockpit window. Other shuttles could be seen running to the starships resting in their berths, or plunging back down to the surface of the planet, flashing brightly like shooting stars as they flared on re-entry.

The pilot pushed the steering array forward and turned it to the right. The shuttle's nose dipped and swung obligingly to starboard in response, and Jamek saw his first command for the first time.

The starship was resting in its drydock, which consisted of a hexagonal scaffold encircling the wheel of the ship. A bridge arm connected the hub of the starship to the gantry of the Fleetyard. The scaffolds and Command Centre arm were about four metres wide and high. The ship itself was about two hundred metres in diameter, and about fifty metres thick. The outer rim rotated steadily, a sign that the vessel was inhabited. Its formation lights cast illuminated arcs onto its surface, which was silver and white, studded with grey domes housing the ship's sensor arrays. Two cannons, streamlined into the hull, were mounted on its dorsal and ventral aspects, their black apertures opening out and staring eyelessly into the void. At the hub of the disc, the blue Terculium Reactor pulsed steadily. In a curved text, emblazoned on the hull just at the edge of the rotating rim of the ship, were the words:

PSS ASCENDANT

S-3204

Jamek smiled. The *Ascendant*. Fedrus was right – it was a very apt name for the flagship of the Destroyer. He regarded his first command. The ship was smooth and streamlined, but aggressive. Its aesthetic appealed to him.

The pilot whistled again. 'Would you look at that,' he said. 'That's a thing of beauty.'

'She certainly is,' said Jamek, smiling. 'My war horse. My chariot.'

The pilot swung the shuttle around and matched its speed to the rotation of the *Ascendant's* outer rim. As the shuttle did so, Jamek felt the bite of gravity begin to take hold of him, and the shuttle began to back up to the side of the rotating rim, preparing to latch on at the rear and dock with the ship. After a few moments, the shuttle gave a satisfying clunk.

'Docking clamps engaged,' said the pilot, 'and thrusters deactivated. Gravity reading as normal. You may unbuckle your seatbelt, sir.'

Jamek pressed a button on the side of his chair to release the double-strapped belt, and stood up, stretching his legs. He could feel the thrum of the *Ascendant's* Terculium Reactor through the deck plates of the shuttle. He walked into the rear cabin of the shuttle and turned to the luggage rack, where his only bag was strapped in. He quickly pulled it free, slinging it over his back, and tucking his *aelrak* into the black sash at his waist.

He then tapped a console to open the back door, which slid open with a hiss, flooding the darkened cabin with light from the corridor beyond. He shielded his eyes against the light, squinting, and addressed himself to a silhouetted figure standing in the *Ascendant's* corridor.

'Knight-Captain Psinaez Jamek,' he said. 'Permission to come aboard.'

'Permission granted, Captain,' said a familiar voice. Jamek gasped as his eyes became used to the light, and he saw Mavrak standing in front of him. Without saying a word, he rushed off the shuttle, dropping his bag, and embraced his lifelong friend in a fierce hug.

'Mavrak...' he said, his voice choking with emotion. Mavrak, taken a little aback, patted Jamek on the shoulder and hugged him back.

'I wasn't expecting that,' he said, mildly, and Jamek laughed for the first time in months. Mavrak was shocked to see tears in his friend's eyes. 'Are you okay?' he asked.

Jamek grinned and wiped away the tears. 'Much better now,' he said. 'I've not seen you since...' his voice trailed off. The last time he had seen Mavrak was in the Confederate prison, before Adraea's murder. He had not been sure that his friend had survived the devastation that followed.

'I know,' said Mavrak, and grasped his friend's forearm. 'It's okay, Jamek.'

'I thought you were dead,' said Jamek, and hugged his friend again. He pulled back, smiling, and Mavrak saw genuine happiness in his eyes, something he had not seen in a long time. 'How did you get out? What are you doing here?'

'I got out the same way you did,' said Mavrak. 'A few us managed to get hold of a Confederate shuttle, and followed the one you were in. We were right behind you when you came out into the Lupus System. The Guardians didn't bother to tell us what had happened to you, though.'

'I've been rested up on Szotas for a while. Saw my parents.' Mavrak paused for a moment. 'But it's all changed. Or I have. Either way, when I found out exactly what had happened to you, I knew my place was here.'

'Fedrus gave me a heads-up that this was your new command. I thought I'd offer my services. I don't know whether a lowly Private will be of any use to you...'

'A Private who can command a starship?' demanded Jamek. 'You told me about what happened aboard the *Constant*.'

'You'll be no enlisted man on my ship,' declared Jamek. 'I have no need of a Private, but I could do with a good Lieutenant. Consider yourself promoted.'

Mavrak stood agape. 'Can you really do that?'

'I'm the Destroyer – I'll do as I please,' replied Jamek. 'You are now Lieutenant, and CO of the *PSS Ascendant's* Contingent Infantry. Fedrus indicated to me that I might need such an officer – I didn't understand him at first, but I do now.'

Mavrak grinned. 'He's a wily old man, that's for sure.'

Jamek smiled and put his arm around his friend's shoulder. 'Today is a great day,' he said. 'Together, we will crush this Confederacy. Our people will have their homeworld, we shall have our freedom, and I...' – his lips tightened into half a snarl – 'I will have my vengeance.'

-#-

Jamek stalked into the Command Centre of the *Ascendant*. The room was large and well-lit, with consoles lining the walls. The Helm and Primary Support consoles were at the front of the room, just in front of the Flight Display which dominated the forward wall, curving outwards to cover part of the port and starboard walls, as well as part of the ceiling and even some of the floor. The view of the space surrounding the ship was even wider and clearer. It depicted an external view of the starship, showing the scaffold of the Fleetyard.

'Captain on deck!' shouted an officer as Jamek strode into the centre of the room, and all the officers stood to attention.

Jamek cleared his throat and pulled an electronic pad from his pocket. He tapped the screen and then read the text displayed.

PROTECTORATE STARFORCE

SECURE COMMUNICATION SYSTEM

FROM: Marshal Fedrus, High Command

TO: Knight-Captain Jamek

TIME: 1800, 32/05/944 (Capitol Time)

You are hereby requested and required to take command of the Protectorate Starship *Ascendant*, Serial No. 3204, with immediate effect. You are furthermore requested and required, by order of the Protector, to assemble a Task Force to liberate the Vulpes System from illegal Confederate occupation, with specific permission to use whatever means necessary to accomplish this order.

We will endeavour to provide any resources you require upon your request.

Long live the Protectorate! Long live Szotas! Hail, Destroyer!

Signed,

Marshal Fedrus

Chief of Staff, High Command

Jamek cleared his throat again. 'By order of the Chief of Staff, I hereby take command of this vessel.' He sat down at the Helm, and ran his fingers along the unspoiled black leather. It brought back memories of his father, when he had taken him aboard his own ship only a few years before. His father's first command. In his mind's eye, Jamek saw his father aboard the *Provident*, his hands gripping the steering column as the hull of his ship smashed into another in a deadly embrace...

He was a martyr, a hero of the Protectorate.

'Lieutenant,' said Jamek, addressing himself to the Communications Officer sat on the port side of the Command Centre. 'Signal all spaceworthy ships in the Lupus System that Knight-Captain Jamek, on the authority of the Protector, hereby assumes direct field command of the Starforce.' He leaned back and handed the officer his electronic pad. 'Order the following ships to assemble in high orbit of Astralas as soon as possible.'

'Aye, Captain.'

'Primary Support,' said Jamek, 'set course for Astralas, full Ion Drive.'

'Aye, sir.' Jamek's First Officer swiped his panel, transferring Helm control to his station.

'Signal the Fleetyards,' ordered Jamek.

'Communications open, sir,' said the Communications Officer.

'*PSS Ascendant* to Szotas Fleetyards,' said Jamek. 'Requesting permission to launch, over.'

A voice sounded over the speakers. 'Roger that, *Ascendant* – permission granted. Hail, Destroyer!'

A cheer rang through the command crew, and Jamek smiled. 'Thank you, Fleetyard.'

'Release docking clamps. Thrusters at station-keeping until we have cleared the Fleetyard,' ordered Jamek, 'then full Ion Drive to Astralas. To war!'

The silver disc of the *Ascendant* disconnected from the Fleetyard, and dropped out of its encircling Drydock. It turned, its outer rim rotating steadily, but inclined always on its side, to present a low profile and a smaller target. It carefully manoeuvred away from the spiderweb Fleetyard, before finally speeding away into the silent emptiness of space. It headed towards the distant gas giant on the edge of the Lupus System, where it would assemble with its allies, and then bloody war would be made upon its enemies.

-#-

Jamek dreamed.

He found himself floating, disconnected and alone, in the void, the vast, silent, emptiness of space. But no stars gazed unflinchingly across the shadow, no nebulae hung in spectral clouds in the darkness, and no planets moved gracefully in their celestial dance. This void was simply that – silent, empty, and black as the throat of Hell. It was the abyss – the nothingness that haunted his dreams.

In his mind's eye, he saw Adraea, her body broken and bleeding on the cold prison floor, and his heart thundered in his chest, his hands clawing madly at the indifferent night, his voice screaming soundlessly until his throat was numb. Terror slid into his heart, and he spun wordlessly in the dark, slowly crushed by the gathered night.

He had thought these dreams – these nightmares – banished. To feel them return, even with all his powers and abilities, struck a deep and ancestral fear into him, that despite all his might, he was still a child at heart, floundering in his dreaded fear of the dark.

With his strength gone, Jamek ceased, his breathing ragged and heavy, waiting for the inevitable.

He did not have long to wait.

In the far distance, he saw it. Merely a faint gleam in the shadow at first, but steadily growing larger and larger – a noxious fume of scarlet, a screech of banshees, the stink of old, dried blood, the taste of tin and iron, and the crawl of locusts. He shuddered in revulsion as the entity approached him, a malevolent apparition, tormenting him. A wisp of crimson cloud licked his skin, and he cried out noiselessly – the agony was exquisite, like an old rusty blade scraping his skin.

The monstrosity reacted to his pain in a way which horrified Jamek – he could not quite tell how he knew, but this creature was laughing at him. It was pleased that he was in pain. Another flash in his mind, and he saw Adraea again, her eyeballs blackened and bleeding. Another flash, and he saw his father, at the Helm of the Provident, *the ship collapsing around him, his body burning in a hellish tongue of flame, before exploding in a searing flash of light...*

Rage surged in Jamek, and with a sudden rush of fury, he felt himself expand. In previous dreams, the red cloud's combatant was always a black cloud, and Jamek had always been watching the battle from the outside. Now, his perspective changed. He became *the black cloud – a seething, burning vapour of fury, choking soot, roaring flame, stinging smoke.*

The red cloud this time recoiled in horror, as its victim became its enemy incarnate. It fled back across the void, across the empty silence from whence it came. Jamek stared after it, dark fire burning deep inside him, and for the first time, he saw inside *the red cloud, to its very heart, to its core. He was filled with a deathly horror and revulsion, but also a desperate compulsion to pursue it, to destroy it utterly...*

-#-

Jamek awoke screaming, clawing his bedsheets back and grabbing *Seyotaal* from the side of his bed. He unsheathed it in a single fluid movement, sitting up in bed, his eyes burning coals, his heart thudding wildly in his chest, his breath harsh and quick.

He gazed out into the darkness, and upon seeing his empty Quarters aboard the *Ascendant*, he relaxed his stiffened muscles, forcing himself to take deep breaths. He closed his eyes, and imagined the fire burning in his heart slowly diminishing, until it was simply the light of a candle.

The fire ebbed in his eyes and he re-sheathed his *aelrak*. His bedsheets were soaked in sweat, and he peeled them off his slick skin. He stood up and pulled them from his bed, throwing them into a corner of the room, before stumbling in the darkness to the bathroom. His hand found a panel on the inside of the room and the light came on. He found himself looking at his own reflection in the mirror.

Exhaling slowly, he put his hands under the tap and cold water streamed over them. He splashed his face and then stood again, staring at his own unblinking eyes in the bathroom mirror.

The cloud.

An image struck in the centre of his mind, an echo from his dream, where he had stared into the red cloud, and saw what lay at its heart.

He had seen a bleak, frozen world, devoid of light and life, plagued by a demon race. He saw planets burning and people screaming. He saw the stars turn dark, the light of life extinguished. He saw Therqa, a blue planet of oceans and green continents, wreathed in wispy clouds, and he knew he was seeing what this red cloud, this creature, was thinking. He was seeing into its thoughts, and he was filled with a single purpose – that this entity must be destroyed, for the sake of all things, even if it meant the destruction of the Protectorate. The fate of his entire species depended on it, perhaps even the fate of the universe itself.

Jamek closed his eyes, and fixed the image in his mind forever into his memory as he looked into the cloud and saw the creature at its heart, the fell being which he was destined to battle. The creature which, even as he sped through the dark recesses of space, was already on Therqa, close to completing its hellish mission which would see the entire galaxy crushed to ash...

A dark, cloaked figure, with a black blade.

TO BE CONTINUED...

ACKNOWLEDGEMENTS

As always, my first acknowledgement must go to Stephanie Lax, whose invaluable critique of this work has enabled me to do justice to the story.

Special thanks to all of my proof-readers who have taken the time to read this in its formative stages – Matt Lax, Lesley Prytherch (who both nag me every week to pull my finger out and get on with the sequel), Lewis Blackburn, Carl Ramplin, George Ramplin, Sarah Measures and probably more!

Destroyer has been part of my life for as long as I can remember. Some of my earliest nightmares were of the visceral figures that became Jamek and his demonic counterpart, the creature Corin. I have been writing this story for the better part of 15 years, and throughout all of that time, my family have been supportive and encouraging throughout. I owe more to them than they can possibly imagine.

Above all else, I dedicate this book to my children, William and Hannah. In the darkest of times, you gave me hope and purpose. You are a shining light in my life, and I would not have been able to write this book without you. I love you both with all my heart.

James Dennis

Nottingham, November 2014

ALSO BY THE AUTHOR

COMING SOON

ALSO BY THE AUTHOR

AVAILABLE NOW

ABOUT THE AUTHOR

James Dennis was born in Nottingham in the last millennium, which sounds longer ago than it actually is. He studied Computer Science at university, but ended up working in financial services. Writing isn't his only hobby – he also plays cornet and piano, and is even known to sing on occasion. He lives in Nottingham with his two children, and one day hopes to make enough money from his hobbies so that he can give up real work!

facebook.com/jamesdennisauthor

twitter.com/jdennis_author

james-dennis.blogspot.co.uk

Icons made by Elegant Themes

COPYRIGHT

8196386R00257

Printed in Great Britain
by Amazon.co.uk, Ltd.,
Marston Gate.